THE DROWNING POOL

Syd Moore is the author of *The Drowning Pool*, a novel inspired by the legend of a 19th Century Essex woman – the Sea Witch Sarah Moore.

She is also co-creator of Super Strumps, the game that reclaims female stereotypes through the medium of Top Trumps, and was founding editor of *Level 4*, an arts and culture magazine based in South Essex.

Syd has worked extensively in publishing and the book trade and presented Channel 4's late night book programme, *Pulp*.

The Drowning Pool is Syd's debut novel and her next book will be published by Avon in 2012.

D0892148

SYD MOORE

The Drowning Pool

AVON

AVON

A division of HarperCollins*Publishers*
1 London Bridge Street
London SE1 9GF

www.harpercollins.co.uk

A Paperback Original 2011

Copyright © Syd Moore 2011

Syd Moore asserts the moral right to
be identified as the author of this work

A catalogue record for this book is
available from the British Library

ISBN-13: 978-1-84756-266-1

Set in Minion by Palimpsest Book Production Limited,
Falkirk, Stirlingshire

Printed and bound in Great Britain by
CPI Group (UK) Ltd, Croydon CR0 4YY

MIX
Paper from
responsible sources
FSC FSC® C007454

For my boys Sean and Riley. And for Liz, undoubtedly causing havoc in the heavens.

I am hugely indebted to Kate Bradley, without whom *The Drowning Pool* would have never seen the light of day. I would also like to add to the long list of people I owe thank yous: Keshini Naidoo and the incredible team at Avon; Father Kenneth Havey, for his advice on the Robert Eden extracts; Cherry Sandover, for her introduction; Ian Platts for his; Clair Johnston for her research into Sarah Moore; Simon Fowler for his excellent photography; Harriett Gilbert, Jonathan Myerson and my tutors on the Masters in Creative Writing at City University, and the esteemed writing group that developed from it; Steph Roche for her unstinting support and late night chats; my friends and family, especially my dad for ensuring I always strive to do better and my mum, for keeping the faith.

Extract from
White's Directory of Essex 1848

LEIGH, a small ancient town, port, and fishing station, with a custom house and coast-guard, is mostly situated at the foot of a woody acclivity, on the north shore of Hadleigh Bay, or Leigh Roads, opposite the east point of Canvey Island, in the estuary of the busy Thames, 4 miles West of Southend, 5 miles South West of Rochford, and 39 miles East of London. The houses extended along the beach are generally small, but there are several neat mansions, with sylvan pleasure grounds, on the acclivity, which rises to considerable height, and affords, from various stations, extensive prospects of the Thames, and the numerous vessels constantly flitting to and fro upon its expansive bosom. The trade consists chiefly in the shrimp, oyster, and winkle fishery . . . Besides great quantities of oysters in the season, nearly a thousand gallons of shrimps are sent weekly to London. The boundary stone, marking the extent of the jurisdiction of the Lord Mayor of London, as a conservator of the Thames, is about 1½ mile east of Leigh, on a stone bank, a little below high water mark, and it is annually visited in form by the Corporation.

Lady Olivia Bernard Sparrow is lady of the manor of Leigh, or Lee, which was held by Ralph Peverall at the Domesday Survey, and afterwards by the Rochford, Bohon, Boteler, Bullen, Rich, and Bernard families. Three copious springs supply the inhabitants with pure water, and the parish contains 1271 inhabitants, and 2331 acres of land, including a long narrow island, called Leigh Marsh, between which and Canvey Island, are the oyster layings. A fair for pedlery etc., is held in the town on the second Tuesday in May.

The Church (St. Clement) is a large ancient structure, near the crown of the hill, and has a lofty ivy-mantled tower, containing five bells. It has a nave, aisles, and chancel, in the perpendicular style, and the latter is embellished with two painted windows, carved oak stalls etc., and contains several handsome monuments. The nave is neatly fitted up, and has a good organ, given by the present incumbent. The rectory . . . is in the patronage of the Bishop of London, and incumbency of the Rev. Robert Eden, who is also rural dean, and has erected a handsome Rectory House in the Elizabethan style. The tithes were commuted in 1847. The Wesleyans have a chapel here, and in the town is a large Free School, attended by about 170 children, and supported by Lady O.B. Sparrow, who established it about 16 years ago, for the gratuitous education of children of this parish and Hadleigh, in accordance with the principles of the Church of England.

George Gifford,
A Dialogue Concerning Witches and Witchcraftes 1593

'Truly we dwell in a bad countrey, I think even the worst in England . . . These witches, these evill favoured old witches doe trouble me . . . they lame men and kill their cattle, yea they destroy both men and children. They say there is scarce any towne or village in all this shire, but there is one or two witches at the least in it.'

Chapter One

The night it happened Rob, a friend of Sharon's, was down by the railway tracks walking his dog. He said the lights and the shrieking freaked the terrier and started it barking. I don't remember hearing it. But he heard us. 'You were making enough noise,' Rob said, 'to wake the dead.'

Which is kind of funny as that was exactly what we were doing.

Though, to be honest, we were so hammered none of us noticed the mist or a slip of shadow darting between us. We just wanted to carry on boozing. I used to think if they ever made a film of my life, that's what they'd call it. Though obviously now it'd have a very different title. *Drag Me to Hell* could be a contender.

Just shows you how much has changed.

Sitting here by the window, the chill kiss of autumn is on my cheek. Watching the dried lemon sunlight slanting across the room, summer feels like another world away. It's pretty difficult to get my head round what happened. But that's where this comes in: getting it out of my brain and onto paper, where it can be nicely controlled, explained and edited. To make sense of it before it dissipates and I forget it altogether. That's what they told me would happen.

Yet the making sense of it irks me so. Can one actually make sense of the senseless? Certain things happened because of bad luck, plain and simple: wrong person, wrong time, wrong confidence, misplaced trust. Call it chaos theory, the butterfly effect, or my personal favourite the *shit happens* model. You can't explain it because, from time to time, bad things happen just because they do.

I guess quite a lot of it comes under that heading.

But then there are those other experiences that can't be categorized or rationalized either. Yes, shit happens but weird stuff does too. Good weird stuff. Coincidences or what Jung called synchronicities – two or more events seemingly unrelated that happen together in a meaningful manner. I know that happens. Doesn't mean it's easy to make sense of though. You'll see what I mean.

'You'll forget'. That's what they said. Makes me laugh. As if I'd ever forget this. Sure, there's a massive part I want to blot out as quickly as possible. Believe me, I've got stuff up here that would scare the crap out of the general population. But there's another part I want to keep. A part that's so jaw-droppingly amazing that it blows your mind if you think it through.

Not that I can yet. Not being so close to it. I have to protect what's left of my sanity (and many would say that was debatable before all this happened). So I'll be getting through it bit by bit. Jotting it down. Before it goes.

I'm rambling.

Come on, Sarah. Get straight. Start at the beginning.

Put it all in. Who was there?

I think there were four of us:

First there's Martha. She's lovely. A highly skilled landscape gardener. Mum of two, partial to Spanish reds and the odd recreational drug. Big house, nice husband. Fairly content but misses the rave scene.

Then Corinne, who I met in the park – my Alfie was playing with her Ewan. We started chatting and that was the beginning of some serious binge drinking that commenced with the chilli vodka she'd brought back from Moscow, went on to red wine and never really stopped.

Corinne is some kind of hot-shot in local government. The Grace Kelly of our circle. She brings to parochial politics what the American movie star conferred on pug-faced Prince Rainier: glamour, darling. Corinne is blessed with unspeakably good taste in clothes, a sleek platinum bob, supermodel looks and the drinking capacity of a Millwall fan. Lucky cow. That evening she had managed to palm off her boys, Ewan and Jack, on her renegade husband and was well up for enjoying a rare moment of liberty. I think it was she who suggested the castle. She was desperate for a session.

So was the only childfree one of us, Ms Sharon Casey. She and Corinne had been friends for decades. Sharon did something that earned her a lot of dough in the city though I was never sure what. Corinne hinted it was to do with telecommunications but was hazy on the details. I think it involved deals, hospitality and a great deal of stress. That night Sharon had become newly single. I think she'd been dumped though she never said specifically; you could tell something was up. She was on a mission.

And that was it, I think. Oh, apart from me. My name is Sarah Grey, and that is a very important part of the puzzle.

It had started with a quiet drink in the local pub. Third

round down and we were getting lairy. Sharon, drunk as a skunk when she turned up, waltzed past our table wearing a massive 'birthday girl' medallion. It wasn't her birthday. Corinne reckoned the staff were giving our table some filthy looks, but for a while we just carried on. We were enjoying ourselves.

Back then, I got so much pleasure from the fuzzy softening that inebriation brought. We all did. It really bugged me when people started going off about it being a prop or insinuating you were running away from things. Of course we were. Life was hard. Being a mother was hard. Being a widow was harder. In the constant juggle of life, work and family, was it too much to ask for a couple of hours of solace and fun? That's what the wine fairy was bringing that night and to be honest, none of us gave a toss about what the bar staff thought. It was a pub for God's sake.

It was only when Sharon knocked into a couple of regulars and smashed a glass that we finally did the sensible thing – slurred out some abuse loudly, hit the toilets, grabbed aforesaid sloshed mate and left.

Outside the air felt balmy and there was a buzz on the Broadway. Groups of women were roaming the street in short dresses and sandals. A lot of the older guys were wearing light-coloured linens. A bunch of EMO kids hanging out by the library gardens had thrown off their black hoodies and were larking about on the benches. It was one of those early summer evenings that nobody wanted to end.

So we're standing there and one of us, I can't remember who (oh God, has it started?). It was probably Corinne, she's the organized one. Yes, Corinne suggested we get some bottles from the offy and walk up to the castle. It's not the kind of thing we would usually do, but like I said, there was something in the air. The sun hadn't yet sunk beyond Hadleigh Downs so there was still enough natural light to navigate the footpath.

I made a slight detour to my house, which was on the way, and grabbed a blanket while the others bought wine and plastic cups. Within forty-five minutes we were sat on the bushy grass in the shadow of Hadleigh Castle. Well, I use the term 'castle' but that's an exaggeration. It's been around since the thirteenth century but it's little more than a ruin: one and a half towers and an assortment of old stones.

As dusk ebbed into night I could just make out, to my left, the tiny white specks of boarded fishermen's cottages that speckled the dark slopes of Leigh, from the jagged tooth tower of St Clements church at the crest of the hill down to the cockle sheds on the waterfront. Scores of miniature boats nestled in the cradle of the bay.

Around us the hawthorns of Hadleigh whispered in the breeze, like softly crashing waves.

Corinne suggested we build a fire. Her husband, Pat, is into that survival rubbish and she gets dragged out to wooded places in the rain. Pat thinks it's character building for the boys but he can't deal with them on his own, so he bribes Corinne to accompany them with vouchers for The Sanctuary. Consequently, she has deliciously smooth skin and a talent for coaxing fire out of the most stubborn wood fragments and twigs.

As the last of twilight disappeared she did herself proud, which was perfect timing because the moon was on the rise now and the air had chilled. There were no clouds and, away from the fug of orange streetlights, out there on the hunchbacked hill, the icy light of the summer constellations was clear and bright. Moon-shadows were everywhere.

The tide had come in around the marsh of Two Tree Island and the gentle 'ting ting' of moored boats drifted up to us from Benfleet Creek. Across the estuary the pinprick lights of North Kent villages blinked like hundreds of tiny nervous eyes.

I remember Sharon saying how much she loved the view. Apart from the industrial plant on Canvey Island. 'That's a bloody eyesore,' she said.

Martha threw a fag butt into the fire and said, 'I like it. It's a contrast. Industry versus Romance.'

'It's ugly,' Sharon answered. 'This place is a Constable painting. Then you see that. It's horrid.'

People always got this wrong. True, Constable captured the castle in oils. I saw a sketch of it at the Tate. But it wasn't one of his romantic idylls. Painted after his wife's death, he had picked out browns the colour of crumbling leaves, livid raven blacks, dismal ash greys. The castle, a skeletal ruin, was desolate and alone. And the sky was strange. If you looked at it closely you could see Constable's brushstrokes were all over the place. The air was turbulent, full of dark storm clouds pregnant with terrible power.

Like something was in them. Waiting to come through.

I sensed that when I first saw the picture and I just know Constable felt it too.

Back then, in the 1820s, *she* would have been young and beautiful. She used to wander there often to escape the town. Maybe they met. Perhaps her story moved, horrified him?

So Sharon blah blahs about the rural prettiness being scarred and Martha's on about nature versus

10

industrialization, then I say something about how the biggest chimney, which has a ball of gas burning above it, reminds me of Mordor. The Eye of Sauron, to be precise. 'I kind of like its otherworldliness,' I said.

And Sharon went, 'Ooh. Hark at you, Mrs Spooky.' And everybody laughed. I don't know why. I never do generally. 'I don't mean it frightens me.' I knew I sounded like a petulant teen – the wine had fired my blood. 'There's plenty of other things round here that do.'

Sharon must have heard my indignant tone cos she got straight in and pacified me with platitudes. 'Yeah. Yeah,' she said. 'I know. Not all the local history's quaint.' She shot a look at Corinne. 'Isn't this place meant to have something to do with some old Earl's murder?'

We all looked at Corinne, who shrugged. Though not related, Sharon and Corinne's families were inextricably intertwined in the way that happens when generations are content to live in the same place for a good length of time. Corinne came from a very old Leigh family so we automatically deferred to her on local matters.

'Probably,' she said. 'I know a mysterious lead coffin was set down on Leigh beach around that time. Some locals had it that it was a murdered nobleman. My dad always said inside it was the body of Thomas, Duke of Gloucester, who had been killed by Richard II's men in Calais. He was strangled with a sheet so violently that his head was severed. The coffin was whisked up to the castle. The next day it had vanished.'

'How awfully sinister,' said Martha, and took a long swig of her wine.

Sharon coughed on her fag and told everyone the St Clements steps creeped her out. This was the steep pathway that connected the Old Town on the seafront to the newer part of town higher up. 'I always feel like I'm going to have a heart attack when I get to the top. And people have done: they used to try to bring the coffins up by a different route, which wasn't at such a sharp angle. But then some posh bloke built a new house and closed that road off as he wanted a bigger garden.'

'The Reverend Robert Eden actually,' said Corinne. 'And it wasn't exactly a house. He built a new rectory as the old one was falling down. It houses the library now.'

'Right,' said Sharon, completely disinterested. 'Anyway, everyone in the Old Town had to start using the steps to get the bodies to the church but it was so steep a few of the pallbearers started popping their clogs at their mates' funerals. Imagine that! My neighbour swears blind Church Hill is haunted.' She spoke the last words in a Vincent Price style and punctuated the sentence with a wicked cackle.

We all looked at Corinne again. This time she smiled. 'Perhaps it is. For such a small place, the town has lots of stories. There was Princess Beatrice way back in the thirteenth century. Daughter of Henry III. Obviously she was meant to marry well. Henry had arranged for her to marry a Spanish count but she fell in love with a young man, Ralph de Binley, and ran away to Leigh to elope. Someone found out about it and they caught the couple on Strand Wharf. Ralph was sent to Colchester, accused of murder, but managed to escape back here where he was banished from England never to return. Some say, on clear nights, you can see Beatrice out on the wharf, waiting for her lover, pacing up and down, crying her eyes out.'

I didn't want melancholy tales on a drinking night and

was about to make some kind of glib comment to lighten the tone, but Sharon got in before me. She must have still been raw from being dumped.

'Pass me the bucket. That's not spooky. I thought we were doing scary.'

Corinne looked put out again so I grabbed the wine and refilled her. She fixed her grey eyes on me like a cat noticing a wounded pigeon for the first time. Her eyes widened and she paused theatrically, then said, 'Aha, well if you want a scary story,' her fingers made a kind of flourishing gesture in my direction, 'look no further than our namesake here, Sarah Grey.'

I groaned and rolled my eyes. I shared my name with a local character and the pub named after her. There was lots of mileage in this one.

'The other Sarah Grey,' Corinne grinned and poked me in the ribs, 'was a right old witch. Have you heard the tale, Sarah?'

Of course I had. I couldn't move around the town without someone making a lewd comment about me doing favours for sailors.

But Sharon piped up that she didn't know the *whole* story and Martha wanted the gory details, so Corinne drew us closer to the fire and asked if we were sitting comfortably.

'Then I'll begin,' she whispered in a proper storyteller's voice. 'What we know is this – Sarah Grey was a nineteenth-century sea-witch who made her living from the pennies sailors threw her for a good wind. She would sit on the edge of Bell Wharf conjuring blessings for those that would pay. Until the captain of *The Smack* came along. Now he was a zealous man.'

'What's zealous?' asked Sharon and hiccupped. Everyone ignored her.

'A fervent Christian, he would have nothing to do with witchcraft so he forbade his crew to give her money.' Corinne licked her lips and lowered her voice further. 'It was a calm and sunny day when they set sail from the wharf.

'But as they steered into the estuary, a strong wind came out of nowhere and lashed the boat. The sailors tried desperately to bring the sails down but the wind had entangled them and *The Smack* was tossed about the waves like a . . .' she paused to find a simile.

'Plastic duck?' Sharon offered unhelpfully.

'They didn't have plastic back then,' said Martha, opening another bottle of wine. 'Like a cork perhaps?'

Corinne was irritated. We had broken her rhythm. 'OK, OK. *The Smack* was tossed around like a cork.'

'A cork's quite small though,' I said mildly. 'And a ship's quite big . . .'

'Do you want to hear this or not?' she snapped.

We muttered apologies and tried to focus.

Corinne cleared her throat and continued. 'So they're in this massive storm. One of the crew started shouting, "It's the witch! It's the witch!" Suddenly the captain picked up an axe and hit the mast. The sailors watched him thinking he had gone completely mad but when, on the third stroke the mast fell, the wind immediately dropped. When the boat eventually managed to limp home to Bell Wharf, do you know what they found? There, on the side, was the body of Sarah Grey, three axe wounds to her head.'

We made approving noises and raised our eyebrows.

'That made me shiver,' said Sharon.

'Well,' said Martha. 'It is a bit cold. You know, Corinne, I've heard another ending. Deano's cousin told me that, yes, the captain had forbidden his men to give her money, so Sarah Grey put a curse on them. The wind came up when they went out to sea and they couldn't get the mast down but, then he says, *every* member of the crew *but* the captain perished. When the captain finally made it back to the shore he swore vengeance on Sarah Grey. The next day her headless body was found floating in Doom Pond, the ducking pond.'

I sniffed. 'The ducking pond?'

'Where they used to dunk scolds. Most old villages used to have one: if a woman argued or quarrelled with her husband or neighbours, she'd be strapped into the "ducking stool" and dunked in the water.'

A small piece of wood exploded in the fire, sending sparks over Martha. We all jumped.

Martha brushed them off her jeans and laughed. 'Is that someone telling me I'm right or that I'm wrong?'

'I suppose that's quite likely to be true,' Corinne said. 'Who knows? It's a shame about Doom Pond.'

A relative newcomer to the town I'd failed to notice the pond and asked her where it was.

Corinne's voice became doleful. 'Underneath those horrid mock-Tudor flats in Leigh Road.'

We all went 'Ah!' and nodded.

I said that I had looked at a flat there.

'What was it like?' asked Sharon. 'Never been inside one of them.'

I thought back. God, it had been horrible. Not the interior or the layout but the atmosphere. There was a sharp sense

15

of misery lurking in the corners. It had hit me as soon as I'd walked through the door. But I was still raw then. I reckoned it was just the similarity to my flat back in London and the emotional wreckage that had surrounded me there. But I simply said, 'It was too small. Smart enough, good finish.'

Anyway, Corinne was off again so we returned to her pretty face flickering in the firelight. 'Before the flats there was a supermarket on the site. My friend's mum used to work there. She said the shelves were wonky. You used to put the tins on one end and they'd slide down the other and onto the floor. Then one day she went to work and it had gone. The whole place had slid into the pond.'

Martha shifted her weight from the left buttock to the right. 'So, is that why they call it Doom Pond?'

Corinne shook her head. 'Nah. It used to be referred to locally as the Drowning Pool.'

A flurry of unseen wings took off somewhere in the darkness.

'Really?' Goose bumps appeared across the bare flesh of my arms. The name sent a shudder right through me. 'Why the Drowning Pool? What else happened there, apart from dunking scolds? Blimey, did they actually drown people?'

Corinne shrugged. 'I guess it must have had something to do with local witches.'

'Local witches?' The casual comment intrigued me. 'You say that as if they were commonplace.'

Corinne's eyes flitted across Martha and Sharon then back to me. 'Sarah, this part of the country is riddled with folklore. I know you wouldn't think it now but Essex was once known as "Witch County". The village of Canewdon

16

is meant to be the most haunted place in England. And there was the wise-man and sorcerer Cunning Murrell in Hadleigh.'

Sharon straightened herself. 'So did he get done then? For being a witch?'

'No,' said Corinne. 'He was actually quite well-respected by the community, although he obviously still had a fearsome reputation.'

Martha leant forward and threw a couple of twigs on the fire. 'So witches got subjected to all sorts of ill treatment yet Mr Murrell's skills were, er, more appreciated?'

Corinne opened her mouth to reply but Sharon was in there immediately. 'Because, my dear Martha, he was in possession of a cock.'

I sniggered. Martha laughed and poked the fire. 'You're about right there.'

'So,' I said, steering the conversation back to the pond topic. 'Why the "Drowning Pool"? You said because of the witches. What have they got to do with the pond?'

'Oh right,' Corinne nodded and took a sip of her wine. You could see she was enjoying the limelight. 'They used to "swim" them there: the witches would get tied up, sometimes right thumb to left toe, other times they were bound to a chair, then they would be thrown in the pond. If they sank and drowned they were innocent, if they floated, they were a witch, and would be dragged off to the gallows to be hanged.'

Martha said, 'Talk about a no-win situation. Poor women.'

I sent up a silent prayer of thanks that I hadn't bought that flat.

'So,' said Corinne, anxious to go easy on the tragedy and

high on spooky. 'That's why locals say it was haunted. By the restless souls of the witches and innocents drowned there.'

'And Sarah Grey,' said Sharon sadly.

I went, 'Wooo.'

But nobody laughed this time.

Martha started talking about a ghost in the cemetery and we all crowded in. The stories picked up and whirled on and on into the midnight hour, with wine flowing, the girls howling and the fire roaring.

I now understand, as I'm writing it down, that what we were doing, without realizing it, was creating some kind of séance. We stirred things up, opening a rift. Things got channelled down.

But that's all come with the benefit of hindsight. If only I'd had a clue at the time. Things were, of course, happening but nothing really registered until the girl on fire.

But I need a drink before I start that one.

Chapter Two

That June was one of the hottest we'd had for years, which, on the plus side, meant that Alfie and I were able to spend a good deal of time down in the Old Town, a cobbled strip of nostalgia severed from the rest of the town by the Shoebury to Fenchurch Street train line. We liked it down there, crabbing, paddling and building sandcastles on the beach. Although Alfie was too young to miss his father, back then Josh's absence still stung like a fresh wound, so I tended to overcompensate with painstakingly organized 'constructed play' and serious quality time. But it was fun. Alfie was now four, a lovely boy with his dad's well-humoured outlook and a steady stream of gobbledegook that made me smile even on bad days.

On the down side, the heat-frayed tempers amongst students and staff at the private school where I taught Music and Media Studies. A few miles into the hinterland, surrounded by acres of carefully landscaped gardens, St John's had been one of the county's few remaining stately homes. It was converted from a family residence into a hospital during the First World War. In 1947 it became a private secondary school. Since then its buildings had encroached onto the lawns in a steady but haphazard and entirely unsympathetic manner. The block in which I worked was a 1980s concrete square that, rather surprisingly, managed to churn out excellent academic results and was in the process of expanding over the chrysanthemum gardens with another inappropriate modern glass structure.

Despite the new build however, the recession was eating into the public consciousness and the economy's jaws were contracting. As a consequence our day students were being pulled out left, right and centre.

My boss was Andrew McWhittard. A forty-year-old unmarried, bitter Scot with a malevolent mouth. Tall and lean with a smother of thick black hair, he caused quite a stir amongst the female support staff when he arrived to head up the team. The honeymoon lasted two weeks, by which point he had revealed himself to be an HR robot – built without a humour chip and programmed only to repeat St John's corporate policy. Personally, I found him arrogant in the extreme. When we were first introduced he gave me this look like he couldn't believe someone with my accent could possibly work in a *private* school.

You live and learn.

McWhittard was a bully at the best of times and of late had started reminding us that pupils meant jobs, and the loss of them did not bode well for our employment prospects. He loved the fear that generated amongst us, you could tell.

A couple of administrators had gone on maternity leave and had not been replaced. The unspoken suggestion was that we absorb the admin ourselves. I only taught three days a week but my paperwork increased substantially and what with the marking, exams, reports, open days and parents' evenings, June is the cruellest month of all.

Plus I had this other thing; one of my eyelids had started to droop. It wasn't immediately obvious to anyone else and, at first, even I assumed it was down to tiredness. But after a week without wine and five nights of unbroken sleep, it was still there, so I booked an appointment with the doctor. The receptionist told me the earliest they could see me was Friday morning before school so I took that slot.

So you see, I had a lot on my mind. Which is why it took me a while to tune into Alfie's strange mutterings.

Like I said, he was a born chatterbox – even before he formed words he'd sit in the living room with his Action men, soldiers, firemen and teddies and act out stories, giving them different voices and roles. The ground floor of our 1930s villa was open plan with large French doors leading out onto the garden. The design meant I could potter around with the vacuum cleaner or do the washing up with one ear on the radio and the other on my son. Though recently Alfie had taken to setting his toys out in the garden instead of staying indoors.

It was the Monday before my visit to the doctor's that it first occurred to me to question why. My initial thought was that Alfie wanted to enjoy the sunshine. But then that was such an adult custom: I remembered the bleaching hot summer Saturdays of my childhood, sat on the sofa with my sister, Charlotte, or Lottie as she preferred, watching children's TV, oblivious to the gloom of the room. How many times had Mum flung back the curtains and berated us for staying in on such a beautiful day? How many times had we shrugged and carried on regardless?

All kids love playing outside but they don't make the connection when the sunshine appears. It takes many more years to wise up to the fickle nature of our very British weather. You certainly don't get it when you're four.

So, I peeled off my Marigolds and went to stand by the French doors. Alfie was sitting on the grass by our old iron garden furniture. He had lined up his puppets to face the chairs, and was engrossed in 'doing a show'. It was a few minutes before he became aware of my presence, then, when he did, I was formally instructed to take a seat and join the audience.

There were four chairs, two either side of the table. I fetched my mug of coffee and was about to sit on the chair to the left when he shouted, 'No, no, no. Mummy, no!'

It's not unusual for kids to fuss over little things, they all have their own idiosyncrasies, so I let Alfie grab my skirt and guide me to the farther chair.

'Sorry, Alfie.' I grinned and leant over to put my mug on the table, but he was up again.

'No, Mummy. Not there!' A little toss of his golden locks told me he was cross now. He frowned, took my free hand and led me to the other side of the table. 'You sit there.'

'You sure, sir?' I said gravely.

'Not that one,' he said, indicating the chair which I had so rudely stretched across. 'The burning girl is there.'

He rubbed his nose and went back to the puppets.

'Sorry.' I laughed, indulging him. I had wondered if he'd develop any imaginary friends and secretly had hoped that he would. Lottie once befriended an imaginary giant called Hoggy who ate cars and ended up emigrating to Australia. As a kid I was absolutely enthralled by her Hoggy stories. Later they proved hugely amusing to an array of boyfriends.

'What's her name?' I asked Alfie. He was concentrating hard on pulling Mr Punch over his right hand and ignored me.

I reached over and tapped playfully on his head. 'Hello? Hello? Is there anyone there?'

Alfie wriggled away.

'What's your friend's name, Alfie?'

He turned his back on the irritation. 'Dunno.'

I was getting nowhere so contented myself with observing him. He was funny and sweet and growing up so quickly. It was in these quiet moments that I missed Josh. The reminder that there was no one else to share my fond smile was painful.

Widowhood is a lonely place.

After a few more tries Alfie mastered the puppet and spun round. 'That's the way to do it!' he squeaked in a pretty good imitation. Then, glancing at the empty chair, his face puffed out and his shoulders fell. He snatched the puppet off his hand and threw it on the floor. 'Look what you done!' Alfie jabbed his podgy index finger at the iron seat. 'You made her go! Mummy!'

He looked so cute when he was angry, with his fluffy blond hair and dimples, it was all I could do not to sweep him up in my arms and kiss him all over his beautiful scowling face. Instead I stuck out my bottom lip and apologized profusely, promising a special chocolate ice cream by way of recompense. This seemed to do the trick and I thought no more of the incident till later on Thursday night.

I'd cleared away the remnants of our pizza and was finishing up the last glass of a mellow rioja when I turned my attention to coaxing Alfie upstairs. He was resisting going to bed, unable to see the sense in sleeping when the sun was still up. No amount of explaining could persuade him that it was, in fact, bedtime.

So far he'd tried all the usual techniques: the protestations ('Not fair'), the distraction method ('Do robots go to heaven?'), the bare-faced lying ('But it's my birthday') and the outright imperative ('Story first!'). But he was pale and tired so brute force was necessary.

He was by the French doors, and as I lifted him, he stuck out his hand and caught one of the handles. As I tried to step away he hung on to them, preventing me from going any further.

'No, Mummy. Not yet. Girl's sick. See.' With his free hand he pointed into the garden. It was empty but for a spiral of mosquitoes above the rusting barbecue.

I was getting annoyed now – it had been a hard day at school. My neck hurt and I wanted to slip into the bath and soothe my aching muscles. 'There's no one there, honey. Come on, it really is time for bed.'

'But the girl.' His grip tightened. 'The girl is on fire.'

There was something plaintive in his voice and when I looked into his face, two little creases stitched across his forehead. I prised his fingers off the handle one by one and opened the doors. 'Look.'

In the garden a faint smell of wood smoke lingered and I wondered briefly if it had been the whiff of the neighbour's barbecue that had sparked his fantasy. 'There's no one out here, Alf.'

He wasn't convinced. 'Will you call the fire brigade, Mummy?'

The penny dropped. All kids love fire engines and Alfie was no exception.

'Oh yes, of course, darling. I'll call them right after you've had your bath.'

He shook his head. 'No, now.'

'OK. I'll call them now. Then will you come upstairs?'

He put his fingers on my chin and looked into my eyes. I poked my tongue out. He smiled. 'Yes. But now.'

After a quick call to 'Fireman Sam' (no one) at the Leigh fire station, he submitted and within an hour was tucked up in bed and dozing peacefully, leaving me exhausted. In fact an intense weariness came over me as I looked in the mirror and stripped my face of make-up and suddenly it was all I could manage to crawl into bed with my book.

I remember it well. I remember everything about that evening – the dappled sunshine that caught the shadows of the eucalyptus in the front garden, the aroma of lavender oil on my pillow, the fresh linen smell of my sheets and the pale amber glow in the room.

It was the night that I had my first dream.

It opened in the usual way that dreams do, with familiar places and people: Alfie and me on the sand. Corinne, Ewan and Jack were there too. And John, a rare breed of colleague *and* friend. We were at a picnic or something. Then I was on Strand Wharf, just along from the beach, my feet caked in clay the colour of charcoal. There was a scream and a young girl ran from one of the fishermen's cottages. She was making a strange noise, like the hungry cry of a seagull or the wail of a dying cat. When I looked at her again, flames were leaping up her pinafore. They licked onto her ringletted tresses and about her face. Filled with horror, I ran to her. I had a canvas bag in my hand, which I used to beat at the flames. But the fire wouldn't go out. It got worse, blustering up against me, enveloping the girl. Searing pain crept over my fingers but her dreadful cries forced me on quicker.

Then abruptly I was awake, covered in sweat, panting in the lemon sunlight that seeped through the blinds.

It took me a few seconds to work out where I was. I could have sworn the smell of burnt flesh lingered in my nostrils.

The nightmare had unsettled me but you didn't have to be a genius to work out what had inspired it.

I sank back into my pillow and steadied my breathing.

The clock showed that it was early morning, but the nightmare had been vivid and I realized that it would soon be time to get up. I wouldn't be able to go back to sleep anyway. Having missed my bath the previous night, I ran a tub full of water, laced it with lavender salts and gratefully sank in.

Fifteen minutes into the soak, as I reached for the soap, something caught my attention on the fleshy mound of skin beneath my right thumb and above my wrist: a crescent-shaped welt.

My fingertips traced it lightly. It was raw. A burn.

I paused, disorientated. I couldn't remember hurting myself. But then again I had polished off that bottle of red. Bad Sarah.

Relinquishing the warmth of the water, I stepped out of the tub and rummaged under the sink for some antiseptic ointment.

A squirt of Savlon softened the pain.

Alfie toddled into the bathroom and had a wee as I was bandaging it.

'Watcha done?' He had an acute interest in injuries.

'Mummy hurt her hand last night.'

He closed the toilet seat with a loud crack. 'How?'

'I think I burnt it while I was cooking the pizzas.'

Alfie stuck the tips of his fingers under the cold tap. 'Like the girl in the garden.'

That stopped me in my tracks. Something bitter in the pit of my stomach uncoiled. 'Now listen, Alf, I want you to stop talking about that. It's not very nice, you know.' I shivered.

He looked at me with wide eyes. 'But . . .'

I held up a finger. 'No buts. Now come on. Let's go and have a nice big breakfast. Then I've got to get you to nursery early – I've got to go to see the doctor today.'

Alfie reached out and stroked my bandage. 'About your burn?'

'No,' I hesitated. 'Yes, about Mummy's burn.'

'Poor Mummy,' he said, and kissed me. He could be such a darling at times.

Doctor Cook's surgery, situated in the right wing of his grand Georgian home, lacked the cleanliness of most GP's but his reputation was one of kindness and benevolence. Plus he'd come with Corinne's recommendation, having been her family's doctor since time began. So I'd picked him over the more contemporary surgery up the road.

The family from which the doctor was descended was one of the oldest in Leigh, well-respected and valued, often spoken of in hushed tones: back in the day when the place was significant enough to have its own mayor quite a few of the family passed through that role apparently elevating their reputation and wealth. The family seat itself was now something of a tourist spot, shrouded by lines of cedar trees and set back in sprawling but well-kept gardens. Locals were

27

able to enter it and marvel at the baroque interiors and lush furnishings but only as patients.

In fact, Doctor Cook was a bit of a local celebrity – not only an excellent GP and an active and well-respected councillor whose name featured frequently in many of the local papers. There was also a tinge of gossip linked to his past: an absent wife or some domestic scandal. I couldn't remember which and was very curious to meet him. Thus far my experience had been limited to his junior partner, as the senior doctor was booked up for weeks in advance, so I was somewhat surprised to be ushered into the head honcho's consulting room.

Cook turned out to be older than I had imagined, in his late sixties. He had an old-school bedside manner and a taste for natty bow ties. However, he exuded gentleness and I was glad I'd got him for the appointment. I had assumed I'd be in and out like a shot with some reassuring platitudes about the thirty-something ageing process and instructions to come back if the droopy lid got worse. But Doctor Cook was thorough. After an extensive inspection of both eyes and ears, he had me up on the couch, examining my arms and legs and listening to my chest.

After I'd got dressed and sat down in the leather chair by his desk, he asked, 'So Ms Grey, have you noticed any changes in your character lately?'

It totally threw me.

'I, um, well . . .' Blood rushed to my face. 'Not really. I'm a bit stressed at work, but . . .'

The doctor took off his spectacles and relaxed into his chair. 'And what is that, my dear?' His voice was rich and low with a hint of a hard upper-class accent.

'I teach. At St John's.'

Under bushy grey eyebrows his eyes glittered, very blue and piercing. I had the strangest feeling that he was looking right into me. 'And that's,' he paused to find the right word, 'manageable?'

'Well, yes. My boss is a bit of a nightmare but, you know, that's education for you.'

'Is it?' he said, rhetorically, and picked up my bulging brown wad of medical notes. 'I see here that you've been on anti-depressants for a while.'

I gulped hard as if I'd been caught out. 'That's right. I lost my husband about three years ago.' Two years, ten months and four days, to be precise.

Usually I held back on details like this. It had a peculiar effect on people, often stopping conversations. Women floundered, not knowing whether to ask for more details, worried that they may upset me or appear morbid. Men coloured, the more predator-like practically licked their lips and stepped closer. A few people physically recoiled when I told them, as if my status was contagious. Once, the thought of telling them that Josh had run off did cross my mind. But that was such a disservice to his memory I could never get the words out.

'You're a widow?'

'Yes.' I held his gaze.

'I'm sorry to hear that. Children?'

An image of Alfie toddling into his nursery flew into my mind. 'One, a boy. He's four.'

'Mm.' Doctor Cook appeared to mull it over. He nodded. 'Difficult. Are you coping?'

I kept my voice steady. 'I have family locally who help out

a great deal and good friends. Sorry, Doctor, but is this relevant?'

He pushed his chair back and faced me. 'Well, my dear. In a way. I'd like you to consider coming off the tablets. Do you think you could?' His eyebrows twitched into his forehead.

This was a surprising turn of events.

My feet hadn't touched the ground since Josh's accident. Then there had been so much to organize with the move back to Essex, finding a house in Leigh, starting the teaching job, sorting out a nursery. I'd started taking the pills when my body had been on autopilot and my head became frazzled with grief. Things were calmer now, it was true.

'I don't know. Why?'

'Well, it might help us get a clearer picture.'

I cleared my throat. 'A clearer picture of what?'

Cook leant towards me and assumed a kindly smile as he spoke. 'I'd like to refer you to a neurologist. It's nothing to worry about.'

I laughed, shocked. 'In my book a neurologist *is* something to worry about.'

'Yes, I quite see. Well, you're on two tablets a day. Stop taking the 10mg. I think the 20mg tablet alone will work just as well.' He tapped his desk. 'It's probably nothing, but I'm not sure that your eyelid has drooped as you've suggested.'

A small rush of heat spread over my palms. 'Really? What is it?'

'I'm not too sure, and that's why I'd like to refer you. You have a weakness in your left side and I'm wondering if, perhaps, it's your left eye that has swollen rather than the right lid that has drooped. I'd like to check, that's all.'

'Check? What would you be looking for?'

Cook looked away to his computer and jabbed at a couple of keys. 'It could be that there is something behind the eyeball that is pressing against it and pushing it out. I don't know.'

A wave of sweat broke out above my top lip. 'A tumour?' I blenched.

He continued to talk to his computer screen. 'Let's not leap to conclusions. This is why we have specialists and dotty old GPs like me aren't allowed to make such diagnoses.' He pushed his chair back and swung it to face me. 'But it would be helpful if you came off the tablets so that we might be able to monitor your progress, as it were, chemical free. Reduce your dose by 10mg please.'

Suddenly I wanted to get out of there as quickly as possible.

I got to my feet shakily and held out my hand. 'Thank you, Doctor. I shall. I guess I'll be hearing from you.'

I tried to calm myself by repeating his words – there was nothing to worry about – but already unwelcome images had begun to crowd my head: Alfie alone, Alfie crying, Alfie orphaned. My throat tightened.

'Do you want me to take a look at this while you're here?' He was examining my amateur attempt at a bandage. 'What have you done?'

My head was still reeling. 'Oh,' I said absently, as he came round the side of the desk and began unwinding the fabric, 'a burn.'

I mustn't die. Alfie could not lose two parents. To lose one was bad enough. It couldn't happen.

Doctor Cook was looking at me. '. . . perfectly well,' he was saying, finishing his sentence with a grin.

I got a grip and spoke. 'I'm sorry?'

31

'I said, whatever it was, it's healed perfectly now.' He released my hand.

I looked down: the skin was smooth and pink. There was no sign of the burn.

I picked up my bag and staggered out without saying goodbye.

Later, after Alfie had gone to bed, I phoned Corinne. She couldn't come over, as it was her au pair's night off, so we opened our own bottles of wine and sat in separate houses, chewing the fat.

She was a down-to-earth woman. She had to be. Her son Jack was precocious, astonishingly so. Learning his alphabet at three and reading Enid Blyton on his own by five. Now, at eight years old, he was studying GCSE text books.

At the other end of the scale Ewan was a hyperactive four-year-old. Pat worked in sales and was often away for several weeks at a time, while Corinne managed the house, the bulk of the childcare and a full-time senior job in local government. Help was supplied by a network of relations and a stream of au pairs that trudged in and then promptly out of her home when they discovered the bright lights of London, too close to Leigh to resist for long. The girls (Ilana, Tia, Cesca, Vilette, Sofia, Anna and most recently Giselle, in the twenty-six months since I'd moved here) seemed like they were on a constant rotation from Europe to Leigh to London then back to Europe. Corinne coped with it all, remaining optimistic in the face of constant chaos and disruption. She was a good friend to have around in times of crisis.

So, first I told her about the doctor. She was concerned and then, when she detected hysteria in my voice, incredibly reassuring.

'That's what Doctor Cook is like,' she said. 'Why do you think he's got such a massive patient list? Because he's *really* good. Leaves no stone unturned. It's probably routine.' I noticed her pronounced Essex twang was softened by the drawn-out vowel sounds she used when she was calming Ewan. It worked on me too.

'Do you think so?' My voice sounded high and girlish compared to hers.

'Of course! Sarah, remember back when we were talking about your school's maypole dance being cancelled?'

'Yes?' I couldn't see where this was going.

'And you were banging on about what a litigious society we live in and doing your nut about health and safety?'

'Oh yes.' The incident had got under my skin for some reason. It had been a tradition at the school for as long as the place had stood but this year, my manager, McWhittard, or McBastard as we oh so wittily called him behind his back, had been appointed manager for Health and Safety. I don't know who had made that decision and hoped that they regretted it now as McBastard had embraced his additional responsibilities with the zeal of a new convert. So far this year, several events had succumbed to his stringent application of risk assessment; the maypole dance being the latest victim. McBastard insisted we would need to sink a concrete base into the sports field in order to conform to new European safety standards. He'd also confided in John that he didn't approve of the 'pagan connotations'. Gerry the caretaker had started running a book on McBastard's next reforms. I'd got

£20 riding on the Halloween party being cancelled but hoped secretly I wouldn't win.

Corinne coughed and continued. 'Well, imagine if your McBastard went to Doctor Cook and he didn't spot what was wrong with him. Do you think he'd sue?'

I nodded so vigorously I almost dropped the phone. 'Oh he'd sue all right, and screw the NHS for all he could get.'

'Right. Well, that's why the good doctor has to cover everything. He can't leave himself open for people like that to take advantage. Not that someone like you would, of course. But he doesn't know you, does he? He's making sure he's doing the right thing. I really don't think you should worry about it and he did tell you not to. Just forget it.'

Reassured, I said, 'Do you think so?'

'Yes, I do.'

'OK. I'll try not to think about it then. But there is another thing I wanted to talk to you about.' I swapped the phone into my left hand so that I could inspect the skin where the burn had been.

'What's that?'

There was an irritation behind Corinne's drawl that made me hesitate.

'I had this dream, last night . . .'

A distant wail started somewhere in the depths of her house.

'Hang on.' The phone muffled. 'Gi-selle? Oh bugger. I forgot: she's gone to the Billet. Fancies one of the fishermen.'

I smiled. A couple of previous au pairs had fallen for Londoners and moved up to be with them. The Crooked Billet was a popular pub in the Old Town. 'At least he's local.'

'Yeah, I suppose.' Corinne sounded as flustered as she ever got. 'Look, it's Ewan. I'll have to call you back.'

I hung up and went to replenish my glass.

In the kitchen it was quiet. The CD had finished playing and whilst we'd been drinking and talking darkness had crept in through the open French doors. I sat down at the table and lit a scented candle.

Something cracked on the window. A sting of adrenalin shot through me.

I put down my glass and crept towards the window. Despite the heat, by the door there was a pool of cool air just outside. Something little and white gleamed on the decking. I picked it up.

A cockleshell.

For a moment I was confused, then remembering Alfie's room was right above, I wondered if he'd left it on his windowsill. Or perhaps a seagull had dropped it.

I turned it over in my hand. Curious. It was wet.

Crack. Another sound came from behind me. This time in the living room, softer than before. I spun around and stared into the gloom. Nothing moved.

My heart was hammering.

I wished for Josh's reassuring presence but knowing he wasn't there I made an effort to bring myself under control. 'Don't be silly,' I whispered aloud. 'It's an old house with its own creaks and groans.'

I forced myself to walk to the centre of the room where the noise had come from. A gasp escaped me as I saw, there on the carpet, another shadowy shape. This was larger and darker. A pine cone.

The sound of my mobile ringing made me jump. When I

answered it, Corinne's gravelly voice brought me back to my senses. 'Sorry, Sarah. Another nightmare. He's fine now.' Then, hearing my breathy pants, 'You all right, chick?'

It was right on the tip of my tongue to tell her about my dream but in that instant I knew what she would say, and somehow right then, Corinne's dismissive but sensible advice was the last thing I wanted to hear. She'd done enough for one night and she had more than a handful in Ewan.

My voice was scratchy and dry but I managed a squeak. 'Yes, sorry. Hayfever.'

'Quite bad this year I've heard. Rachel's had it awful and she's even had these injection things that are meant to clear it up for years, poor thing . . .' And she was off and into the night, chatting about our mutual friends, oblivious to my silence.

When we'd said goodbye I went around the house and locked up carefully. I crept to my room and turned on the television, the radio and both of my night lights.

As I sank under the duvet and closed my eyes against the light, I couldn't shift the feeling that I was waiting for something.

It would take another seven nights for me to find out what that was.

Chapter Three

Looking back, all the signs were there. Human beings have a tendency to forget what they can't explain: the misplaced key, left on the sideboard but found in the lock; the lost treasured trinket, carefully tracked and then suddenly gone; the darkening shadow in the hot glare of day. But they're alarm bells.

Would it have all turned out differently if I had paid heed? I think not. The chain of events that would carry me across seas, to foreign shores and through time, had already been set in motion.

But I didn't know that then.

In fact, as I contemplated the past week from the end of my summer garden, things seemed so obvious and straight-forward. To my mind they were almost bordering on the mundane. But then I had cosseted myself in the flower-boat, one of my favourite places to be: a hammock strung between an apple tree and the fence post, beside an ancient pink rose bush. Alfie christened it the flower-boat as I'd fashioned it from a faded tarpaulin with a swirl of daffodils and gerbera printed upon it. In its saggy hug, when the sun sank and the jasmine that wound itself around the fence scented the air, it was impossible to feel anxious. I had even fixed a shelf into the lower branches of the apple tree so that we could reach toys, drinks and magazines as we gently rocked. The scent of floribunda and ripening apple fruit, the faint gurgle of traffic and life that wafted along on the breeze, couldn't help but soothe the nerves.

It *must* have been Alfie who had left the shell and the cone about the house; there were only two people who lived here, after all – me and him. And I hadn't done it. It *is* the kind of thing that kids do. My attention had been drawn to them as the house creaked that darkened Friday night. The seasonal heat had surely disorientated a winged insect, which had flown into the window, hence the cracking sound. The groan of a floorboard, contracting as it cooled in the night air, had alerted me to the cone.

The burn was more of a puzzle. But I'm scatty at the best of times and in the rush to get dressed, pop Alfie to nursery and scoop up my lesson plans, it was quite possible that I'd simply imagined the scar, a residual phantasm created by the dramatic dream.

I'd tell the neurologist.

I took my anti-depressant, minus 10mg.

All too soon the week's mundanities had me.

I don't like using the term 'roller coaster of a ride'. Whenever I see it on the back of books it makes my bottom tighten. So without using crappy marketing-speak, let me tell you the week that followed was so frenzied it was easy to forget about the cockleshell and pine cone incident.

St John's was busy. It was the last week of lessons and the students weren't interested in their work. Not that they had much at that point in the academic year. I was half inclined to let them do as they pleased, but the college executive herded us in to the Grand Hall at 8.30 a.m. Monday morning and instructed us that this was no time to let standards slip. According to the management, this week was the perfect time to introduce students to next year's curriculum.

McBastard suggested that if we wanted to relax a bit we could carry out summative assessments in the form of quizzes. 'Party on, dude,' said John, in a rare moment of rebellion. The management made him stay behind.

They were like that at St John's.

I'd come out of the music business, which doesn't have the reputation of a caring profession, and thought that perhaps teaching might be a less stressful, more wholesome career. Ha ha ha.

On the Tuesday I sneaked Twister in to my Textual Analysis lesson. The kids were enjoying it until McBastard caught us and hauled me into his office. If that sort of thing continued, he growled at the floor, I could end up on the Sex Offenders Register.

I laughed.

He fixed his strange brown eyes on me. Ambers and reds swirled within them like fiery lava.

'This is serious,' he said. 'You should be careful.'

I frowned and shifted on the stool where I was sitting in front of his desk. 'What do you mean?'

McBastard leant back and clasped his bony hands in a prayer-like fashion.

Malevolence glittered beyond his volcanic eyes, anger preparing to erupt.

'You need to keep your job.' He stayed motionless, hard, like a statue.

I wasn't absolutely sure what he was trying to say and told him so.

Finally he spat out, 'A woman in your position.'

It took me off guard.

'Yes? What exactly *is* that?' My eyebrows had raised and I'd assumed an expression of confusion.

Thin white lips pushed themselves into an arrangement that almost resembled a smile. 'A single mother, after all.'

Reading my puzzlement he seemed about to say more but stopped. 'You'd better toddle along to your class.' Then he dismissed me by spinning his chair round and staring out of the window.

Gawping at the back of his head, I was shocked into silence, as his meaning dawned.

It was true, I needed to earn money and I couldn't afford to lose my job. But I didn't need reminding that whether I stayed in it or not was largely up to him. The shit had used this opportunity to warn me: fall in line or fuck off.

I quivered at my impotence in the face of such barefaced blackmail but with great self-control I thanked him and 'toddled' back to my students.

The following day McBastard stalked me like a wolf. Thankfully there wasn't much I could screw up: end of year shows, graduation ceremonies, leaving lunches and then on Thursday, a trip to Wimbledon.

On Friday the school was shut to students and staff were subjected to what the management term a Development Day, but what we call Degenerate Day on account of the stupefaction factor – the programme comprised policy talks and lectures.

I took my place at the back of the staff room between John and Sue, who was pregnant and perpetually pissed off that she couldn't smoke or drink.

'Do we know how long this will be?' I squeezed into the cramped makeshift seating.

John grimaced. 'They confiscated my shoelaces on the way in.'

'I can't fucking believe it,' said Sue, sucking on a biro. 'There's so much else I could be doing. Don't they realize we have all this end of year admin to tie up?'

'Oh, they realize all right,' said John.

One of the management posse had positioned himself right in front of the coffee machine, cutting off our lifeline to the one thing that might keep us conscious. He clapped his hands to get our attention.

Not a good start.

His name was Harvey. Apparently he'd been doing this for three years now and had got a lot of positive feedback.

'Inadequate,' John whispered. 'Needs to self-reinforce.'

Harvey launched into a 'discussion' of why students should be called customers. He got some audience interaction going with a show of hands – who was for it? McBastard. Who was against it? The plebs voted unanimously. Then he did this sickly smile and said: 'Well, I'm afraid these days anyone with that way of thinking is completely out of sync with new models of educational theory. It may have been OK thirty years ago but now the terminology is inconsistent with new approaches to learning and changes in funding.'

Harvey continued to bellow: in order to survive in the new market place, every single one of us had to commit ourselves to 'rethink, reset and reframe'. Just then a ball of paper arced over from the back and got Harvey right on the chin.

McBastard leapt to his feet. 'Who did that? Come on now!'

Everyone looked at the floor.

Harvey ploughed on.

The room calmed down and we started settling in for a nap, when he repeated his point that we 'needed to change or become history'.

This was the last straw for the History 'facilitator', a quiet guy called Edwin with hair like a toilet brush. He leapt to his feet and shrieked something sarcastic about that not being so terrible as we could learn from history, if 'learn' was still a permissible verb, given current educational thinking.

If he'd been more popular there might have been a revolt at this point, but Edwin was a bit of a dick so no one joined in.

Harvey looked embarrassed and back-pedalled to qualify 'history'.

John bobbed his head in Edwin's direction, mouthed 'wanker' and supplied a pertinent hand gesture.

'Good point,' I sighed. 'I bet he's added at least another five minutes on.'

He had.

Time slowed.

John fell asleep. Sue's biro leaked over her chin and onto her polo neck.

I watched McBastard out of the corner of my eye.

For two hours and seven minutes he didn't once take those fireball eyes off me.

* * *

After lunch things worsened. But at 4.30 there was a serious breach of health and safety when the entire staff (plebs) of the Humanities and Arts Department stampeded to the Red Lion.

There was no way I was missing out on a much needed dose of medicine. Luckily I'd got the bus into work this morning so didn't have to worry about the car.

A quick call to Corinne resulted in Giselle agreeing to pick up Alfie and babysit. Thank God for the empathy of fellow mum friends. Adversity unites.

My pass for the night acquired, I joined the last of the stragglers beating a path to the local.

John was in fine form. The day had supplied him with plenty of ammunition. Especially Harvey's utterly absurd suggestion that, to help us memorize what we learnt from the session, we could make up our own raps. A natural mime with a wicked sense of humour, his impression of Harvey's twitches, stammers and idiosyncrasies was cruel, excruciating and magnificently funny.

A charismatic teacher with a background in media law, the students, I mean, customers, loved John. You could understand why when you saw him in this context, holding court; engrossed and animated. His curly brown hair tumbled down past his ears, lending him a naturally cheeky quality that was muted somewhat by serious blue eyes, a clean-shaven face and an insistence on wearing a suit. God knows why he accepted a fifth of what he could be earning, working harder than he would in a small law firm. I liked his intelligence and respected his mind. He'd almost become a good friend.

Later, as the conversation waterfalled into pockets of twos and threes, we found ourselves together.

'You all right then, Ms Grey?'

I paused and took a slug from my glass. 'D'you know what? It's not been the greatest of weeks.'

'It's always like this,' he said. 'End of term. Shit to do. Shit to teach.'

It wasn't work, I told him, and was about to relay my medical experience when I remembered that he was a colleague and much as I liked him, there was the possibility that, well-oiled and talkative, he might mention it to one of HR. That might kick-start a sequence of events that I couldn't afford right now. Not with McBastard on the prowl.

'What is it then?' He looked concerned and I felt a bit daft looking at him with my mouth open, so I told him about the cockleshell instead.

'Jesus,' he said. 'You sound like my sister. Marie's nuts, obsessed with crystals and weirdies and things that go bump in the night. She's on her own too. Out in California now. Do you know what I reckon?' He slurred the last part of the question so I had to ask him to repeat it.

'That,' he wagged an unsteady finger at me, 'women on their own tend to imagine stuff. I'm not being sexist here but when you're living with someone, you talk to them, you know, you share stuff. You talk things through. You don't let things run away with you. Do you know what I mean?'

As unwilling as I was to let the poke go unchallenged I *did* know exactly what he was getting at. Especially after that night. But I didn't think it was a gender thing so instead I said, 'Are you inferring that us independent ladies become hysterical without a rational male mind, Doctor Freud?'

'Yes of course, dear,' he said, and made a big thing of patting my hand. Then Nancy, one of the administrators, swung our way. 'What are you two talking about?' Her beady eyes strayed over John.

'Nothing,' we chimed together.

She looked at us sceptically but didn't move. 'Whatever.' Her voice always sounded thin and discordant.

John started doing his impressions thing again and having heard it all once, I got up and staggered over to Sue. The subject there was giving up fags so when, inevitably, everyone got up to go for a smoke, I went too.

Outside Edwin was hailing a cab for Leigh, and realizing I was more wrecked than anticipated and that it was only half ten, I joined him. Twenty minutes later I'd paid Giselle and had seen her off in a cab of her own.

Alfie was snoring lightly so I jumped into the shower, ran the water lukewarm and lathered one of my favourite exotic gels over my sticky body. It felt good. In fact, I felt good. Considering the day I'd had, this was something of a miracle.

I closed my eyes and let my mind drift. My hands took the lather and soaped my breasts. I turned the hot tap up and killed the cold, soaked my hair in the shower spray and let the shampoo's foam glide over my midriff and drip down my thighs.

The hot water ran out. I squealed as a prickly blast of cold hit my belly and reached out to turn it off, cursing the immersion heater. I stepped out of the cubicle and grabbed the nearest towel.

Wrapping it around my body, I felt the weight of the last week enveloping me. I dried myself then cleared the steam from the mirror to apply some face serum.

That's when I saw it.

As I looked in the mirror I saw my face, but hovering over

it there was another – the same shape, but with a firmer chin. Locks of hair blocked out my own wet brown wisps – hers was a darker shade and thicker. But it was the eyes that held me – vivid green, bright, almond shaped – that fixed onto mine. Compelling me to hold her gaze.

My mouth, reflected in the mirror, froze open in shock, and morphed into two thin pink closed lips.

The vision held, then blurred.

I blinked and it had gone.

The air was steaming up the mirror once more. I steadied my breath and rubbed the condensation away. My reflection stared back: pale, crumpled and very, very tired.

I was still tipsy. I had to get a grip; my imagination was running away with itself, playing tricks on me.

'Pull yourself together,' I instructed my reflection. 'You just need a good night's sleep.' I took my own advice and pushed the fear to the very back of my mind.

Flinging on my pyjamas I shuffled out of the bathroom as quickly as my tired legs could manage, dragged my body to my fluffy bed and pulled my duvet tight around me.

It wouldn't register consciously then, but just before I sank into oblivion, I saw a small cloud of my breath.

Despite the warmth outside, my bedroom was as cold as a crypt.

Chapter Four

When I woke I was moody and morose. Though I tried to perk myself up when I roused Alfie, I never really got rid of that shirty, melancholy the whole weekend. In fact it got worse.

I had a slight reprieve late Saturday morning (less of the melancholy, more of the shirtiness) when my sister, Lottie, and nephew, Thomas, turned up for a picnic at Leigh beach. Thomas was eight months older than Alfie and the boys got on very well together.

The sun was nearing its noon zenith when they arrived. My hangover had slowed me so I was still half dressed. Lottie made it clear that she wanted to spend no time inside. A true sun-worshipper, she insisted we packed a picnic lunch and got down to the beach as soon as possible. I tried not to sulk but my older sister's assumed authority and unassailable competence always brought out the child in me. Lottie had always been more organized, more academic and wittier than anyone else. Leaving college with a first-class degree in English, and with an outstanding final term as an award-winning editor of the college mag, she dashed everyone's expectations by turning her back on a promising career in journalism and established her own theatre company, which she ran for several years before a BBC head-hunter netted her. She gave up working for the BBC when she was pregnant with Thomas and now worked as a freelance consultant. In her spare time she was writing a trilogy of children's books for a US publisher.

I examined her from beneath my mat of stringy uncombed fringe. In immaculate Capri pants and oversized black sunglasses, she resembled a sexy sixties siren.

'Come on, Sarah. I want to get down to the beach before one. Let's make the most of the sunshine.' She swished her curtain of shiny black hair and winked. 'Chop chop.'

I fingered my pyjama bottoms gingerly and told her to keep her hair on, then stomped upstairs while she made sandwiches for the four of us.

Outdoors the full impact of last night's two (or was it three?) bottles of wine kicked in. My tongue was so absurdly dry I downed a litre bottle of water in ten minutes.

We wandered down the Broadway keeping one eye on the boys and another on the windows of the boutique shops and bursting cafés, stopping at the greengrocer's that sold Alfie's favourite ice creams, a soft, local recipe introduced to the area by a family of Italian ice-cream makers. We fetched the two 99's and two colas and then went across the road into The Library Gardens.

Situated by St Clements church, off the main street, and right at the top of the hill the library gardens weren't the geographical centre of town yet the small park felt like the heart of Leigh. A place where the different communities that existed in the town converged and relaxed: the lower gardens provided a meeting place for teenage gangs and novice smokers. The upper ground, with its compact playground area, had fostered many a friendship amongst young families. The actual gardens were the perfect place for old timers to take in the views across the estuary and down into the Old Town. There were lots of benches dotted around to do just that.

I told Lottie I could do with a rest so we took a seat between the herb garden and the red-brick walls of the Victorian rectory, now the library.

The sun was so strong now it scorched the skin on the crown of my head. The others had sun hats but I, of course, had forgotten mine so wrapped my scarf around my head.

'You look like a bag lady,' said Lottie. I made a face and stretched across her to adjust Alfie's ice-cream-stained shirt.

This corner of the park had an aromatic garden for the blind. The air was thick with the citrus tang of catnip and meaty wafts of purple sage and rosemary. On other days I'd sit here with pleasure, but now the pungent earthy reek made me feel like I was roasting.

I suggested we move on so Lottie led the way through the park down into the Old Town.

It was almost high tide and the modest scrap of Leigh beach was crammed. Day-trippers and locals filled every square metre of sand with towels, blankets, buckets, spades, sandcastles, lilos and rapidly reddening flesh.

We made the decision to walk east along the towpath to the larger and less crowded beach at Chalkwell and saw off a mutiny from Thomas and Alfie with the shameless promise of more ice cream. I know you're not meant to bribe kids but honestly, sometimes, it's the only way. Plus Lottie was making sounds that she wanted to talk. Proper grown-up talk.

Her husband, David, had piled up some ludicrous debt and, although it was a dead cert their marriage would survive, Lottie was livid and bandying around words like 'divorce' and 'separation'.

They say usually the thing that attracts you to your lover is what irritates the hell out of you in the end. I remembered how Lottie loved David's easy generosity when she met him. Now look at the pair of them.

I'd never know if it would have gone that way with Josh for two reasons. Firstly, I've realized I'm not like other people so I'm not sure any of those generalizations really apply to me. Granted, physically, I look fairly human: two arms, two legs, average build, height, weight. Mousy hair, which I dye, sometimes auburn, occasionally red, currently brown. But psychologically and sociologically I really have no idea what makes other people tick. I don't follow *The X-Factor* or *Strictly Come Dancing*. In fact, I don't watch TV. I didn't get excited about my son's first tooth, first word, first wet bed or bad dream. I don't drink modestly and I don't wear widow's weeds. I achieved ten GCSE's, five 'A' Levels, and have a good degree in music and education yet the majority of people think I'm thick on account of my estuarine accent. My IQ plunges with each dropped consonant.

Secondly, when the number 73 lost control at Newington Green and mangled Josh and his bike into its back left wheel, it robbed me of the chance to find all that stuff out.

I was so warped with shock at the time I never really got that it was game over. I kept wanting to turn around and ask him, 'Can you believe this is happening? I mean, can you?'

So when they told us later that he didn't feel anything, I just stared at them with my mouth open. They wanted a reaction but I couldn't get it going so the policeman added, 'It would have been too quick. He wouldn't have had time to realize what was happening. He wouldn't have felt a thing.'

And I did this weird thing, apparently, so his mum, Margaret, said. I don't think she's ever forgiven me for it. I said, 'Easy come, easy go.'

That's when Margaret started hitting me and, by all accounts, the police had to intervene.

I don't remember it, and I know it must have seemed heartless, but I can understand what I meant. Josh was easy: persistently mild and laid back. I have this enduring image of him, hunched over his laptop with headphones on. His straw-like gingery hair jutting out at odd angles, Paul Newman blue eyes closed, head nodding, mouth creeping into a dopey grin. Not stoned. Just happy. He loved his tunes, the pitches, chords, non-sequential effects, banging rhythms. Most of it bored me, but I used to make the right noises as if I totally loved his creations. He didn't care anyway. If we'd been on the *Titanic* he would have packed me and Alfie off in a lifeboat and happily joined the orchestra. Nothing fazed Josh. And *that*'s what I liked about him when I first met him. Everyone at Stealth Records, where I used to work, used to flap like seals on speed if a taxi didn't arrive on time or if a press release missed its deadline. But it was impossible to get a rise out of Josh.

He'd just shrug and come out with some kind of *non sequitur*, giving the impression of confusion and/or low IQ, so the executives mostly left him alone.

He never said much. Even when we were married he wasn't verbally expressive. But he'd write messages on Post-it notes and leave them around the flat and sometimes in my desk at work for me to find.

I loved it that he hadn't got sucked into the utterly manic culture of Stealth, especially as, when I started, I got landed with a massive campaign and spent my first year spinning in a PR tiz. But on Friday afternoons, after the marketing meeting, I'd sneak off down to the studio and watch Josh work, not listening or paying much attention to the music but basking in the calm he radiated.

He was in constant demand for engineering even though, truth be told, he wasn't the best. Josh was simply cool. He was cool in life and he was cool at the end. I was glad he felt nothing.

I didn't either for the first week.

Then the rage and frustration came.

The pain was my connection for a long time. He had given it to me. It was all that was left attaching me to him, along with his name, the care of our son and an insurance policy that eventually paid off the mortgage on our flat.

I tried to keep things normal for Alfie but it was hard to live there with the constant expectation Josh would wheel his bike through the front door.

One day I found a Post-it in my jumper drawer. He must have hidden it months before. It read 'I don't tell you enough that I love you'.

It killed me.

I mean, it really, truly finished me off. The old Sarah died that day.

After the sobbing and puking and screaming I knew I couldn't remain in the husk of my old life.

Josh had moved on and so must I.

So that was that.

I left the flat that night and returned to Essex to stay with my mum. The next day I put the flat on the market. Three months later Alfie and I moved into the house in Leigh-on-Sea.

For the most part it pleased me to live in Leigh. There was a sense of community, tradition. People knew each other and soon started to recognize me and Alfie. It was nice, different to London, although sometimes, I've got to say, I missed the cynicism, the illegal twenty-four-hour off-licences and the anonymity. Down here you couldn't mention someone's name without being overheard by their wife/husband/cousin/sister/brother-in-law/mum/best friend (delete as appropriate).

But the up side was that the grocer called you by your first name when he handed over your change, on Thursdays the Rag and Bone man drove down the street, the butcher saved you lardons on a Saturday, and the library would phone you to let you know that book you were discussing had arrived.

No, at that point in time, I didn't mind Leigh at all.

We reached the beach and as I came out of my thoughts I heard Lottie saying 'And then the credit card! Honestly, Sarah, I could have killed him.'

Remembering herself she apologized. 'I'm sorry. Metaphorical and all that.'

I was used to it. 'It's OK,' I said. But I was pleased when, once we'd set out the blanket and the picnic, Lottie took the boys off to get their sugary rewards.

Determined to enjoy a moment to myself I removed my sandals, rolled up my trousers and sauntered down to the sea.

The noise levels were more subdued here than at Leigh. The lazy rhythmic lap of the waves frothed about my ankles, warm and inviting. Out on the grey horizon a large transport tanker crept towards the North Sea.

I closed my eyes, lifted my head to the sun and breathed the salty air in deeply. The tension in my body started to dissipate.

'Sarah.'

It was a low whisper, close to my ear. I opened my eyes and turned around. A quick scan of the beach revealed no one that I knew. I stood alone in the surf. On the beach I saw our blanket was empty. Lottie and the boys were still on their ice-cream expedition.

'Sarah.'

A woman's voice.

This time it seemed to come from my left but there were only two children determinedly building a wall against the encroaching tide. The voice was much older.

'Sarah.'

Something drew my eyes down to look at the sand.

I froze.

Caught in the high beam of the one o'clock sun, my shadow barely stretched before me – a fat compact dwarf-like outline.

But beside it there was another shadow – the long blackened haze of a woman's shape.

As I stared transfixed, small strands of shadow hair wisped out of what looked like a bonnet and fluttered in the breeze.

And then it came to me, like a forgotten memory or a dream, swamping me, taking me down.

Running aimlessly through a garden: hurtling, staggering, losing my footing in the loose earth, sprawling, staggering, rushing towards . . . no, no, not going towards, but running from something or someone. My sobs choke me and I feel the desperate strangling claustrophobia of misery, of utter desolation, entrapment. There is no hope. Then out of the garden up to the road. Slowing to an unsteady walk. Vision blurred. Panting. Wet face.

Clouds roll in over the heavens. Grey sky. Buildings the colour of slate give way to reveal the water surrounded by rushes. It is waiting for me, the Drowning Pool, my saviour, my haven. Take me.

Through the reeds, I descend deeper into the water's embrace. Then from behind, a shout. 'Sarah!' A middle-aged man in an ochre jacket. Father. Panic, thrashing into the pool. No! I step backwards. Away. Wading further into the centre.

Take me.

The heavy drag of wet fabric makes me stumble. Water-drenched, my skirt billows out beneath me in the shallows.

My doom.

A foot catches the floating cloth and I am under, gulping the pond into my lungs, filling them, losing myself in the pool's murky depths.

Take me to him.

Down, deeper into the blackness of death, swirling, searching for welcoming numbness.

Then suddenly fingers around the back of my neck, gripping my dress. Hands about my waist, heaving, lifting, bearing me through the water. Staggering, falling, up again. On the grass. The hardness of the road, mud under my head. Coughing water, air. Two faces above, father and another, a woman full of tears: Mother. Oh, Mother. Look what has become of me.

Beyond them, a crowd.

A woman in a black bonnet has stopped to stare. She nudges her gentleman companion. 'Who is it there?'

A voice loud and booming. ''Tis the Sutton girl in the Drowning Pool.'

The woman clucks. 'It wouldn't take her, see. She floats.'

'No, the water will not take her sort.' A large man now, white beard, shabby frock coat. Fierce. 'She cannot drown herself.' He makes the sign of the cross.

Spittle on my feet.

'Witch.'

'Sarah!' The voice cut through the scene like a blast of cold air. Familiar, shrill – Lottie.

'Deaf as a bloody post. What are you doing? Standing there like a zombie? Your jeans are soaked.' She was holding an ice cream to me. 'I thought I may as well get one for us too.'

The sun was burning my back. The cheerful sound of beach pandemonium hit me again.

I was back.

The sea lapped at my knees.

The children to my left had retreated, their sea wall long defeated by the tide.

'What's up?' Lottie grimaced at my stricken expression. 'Did the tide creep up on you? Have you got a cossie underneath that? If not I think I've got a spare pair of shorts somewhere. Come on.' Her sturdy ankles sank into the sand as she returned to the blanket.

I tumbled forwards out of the sea and sat down. My shadow mimicked me but it was alone.

What had just happened?

I touched the centre of my chest, lightly. It rose and fell in a super-quick rhythm. There was some pain but not of a physical kind. I had known this misery when I first lost Josh: I was cloaked in gloom, the feeling had followed me back from the dream.

What on earth was I doing to myself?

It must have been brought on by my earlier musings about Josh. I cursed and kicked up the sand with my foot.

I'd heard a phrase used once to describe this sort of thing. What was it called? Oh yes – a waking dream.

That must have been it.

Perhaps I still had a lot of alcohol in my system. I had certainly been knocking it back last night. The natural balance of my brain must be off. A sudden surge of the wrong chemical had churned up some morbid hallucination.

'It's the booze,' I thought.

'It's the tumour,' an inner demon said.

Or perhaps it was a side effect of cutting back the medication?

I'd seen a woman at Stealth Records come straight off lithium and go completely hat stand. One day she was striding through the atrium in a neat Chanel two-piece,

57

barking orders at her p.a., the next she was barefoot and wandering the corridors. She went on sick leave and never came back.

I wasn't going to go that way.

My hands were trembling so I clenched them tightly and took a deep breath in, held it, then blew out slowly. After several repetitions the shakes started to subside.

With some effort I took a step forwards. Plastering a bright smile onto my face, I returned to Lottie and the boys.

Alfie and Thomas were a way away. They had built a sandcastle and were using it as a backdrop to some as yet unwritten Spiderman episode featuring lots of explosions.

I sat down next to Lottie and licked my ice cream, trying to settle my nerves and ignore the aftershocks of the incident.

'Sorry, Sarah. Couldn't find the shorts. Must have left them at home.' Lottie dabbed her hands with a wet wipe and offered me the pack.

'No thanks.' My cone trembled. 'In a minute.'

'What's up, Sarah?' Lottie's smile was encouraging.

I contemplated her open, oval face, the dark glossy locks that curved around it, the slightly Roman line of her nose and her big loud mouth. A sensible and rather noble older sister, Charlotte Rose was a good woman. Strong too. Her broad shoulders had taken much of the burden when our dad died.

I took a breath. Now was the time. 'I might have a brain tumour.'

The smile melted down her face.

'But then again, I might not.' I told her why.

She didn't take it very well, so after I recounted most of what Doctor Cook had said, I omitted the hallucinations bit. 'So what's next? When do you get the hospital appointment?' Lottie's eyebrows knitted together. There she went – organizing, reorganizing, taking charge, planning, trying to contain her alarm.

I couldn't remember. 'I guess it'll come in the post.'

'Yes, but when?'

'Soon.'

My big sister sighed and gazed out into the estuary. The tide had turned and some of the children were picking over the rock pools with buckets and fishing nets. Alfie and Thomas had abandoned their Spiderman game and were crouching over a dead crab. 'Well, will you let me know?'

I nodded.

'Have you told Mum?'

I shook my head. 'No. There's no point worrying her at this stage.'

'OK.' Lottie leant over, grabbed my free hand and rubbed it. 'You know it's probably nothing. Like the doctor said. But I'm glad you're taking it seriously. I understand that you don't want to tell Mum now but if something does . . .' she trailed off and sent me this small, mournful smile. 'You'll be fine, I'm sure.'

I stuffed the remnants of the cone into my mouth and tried hard not to cry.

Lottie and Thomas came back to the house to clean up. After tea I opened a bottle of Spanish wine. I shared half of it with Lottie before David arrived to pick up his clan. He had a sheepish air about him, perhaps guessing that Lottie had confided in me. I did my best to be bright and jolly. Then Alfie chucked a hissy fit about Thomas packing up, and demanded his cousin stay for a sleepover. But it was gone seven so once Lottie and co. had beaten a hasty exit I plopped him briefly in the bath then sang him to sleep.

It was still early evening for me, and after the day I'd had, I didn't want to be alone. I composed a message requesting company then texted Martha, Sharon and Corinne. I added John as an afterthought though the chances of him being allowed out were remote.

Downstairs I threw back the French doors and breathed in jasmine-soaked air. Though the dusky shadow of the house covered most of the back garden, the furthermost part was alight with the amber pink luminosity of high summer. The flower-boat swayed seductively in the soft evening breeze, lifting my spirits a little, which was just as well as at that moment my phone beeped several times: Martha was feeling the same as me but was also stranded in her home with kids and no babysitter. Corinne was in London and Sharon was on an internet date. Nothing from John, but then he didn't monitor his phone religiously like the rest of us.

I grabbed the wine off the kitchen table and optimistically took two glasses to the hammock. There was something so comforting about its gentle rock that I soon let my eyes close. The worries of the day slipped far away.

About half-past ten I was woken into a moonlit garden by the bleep of the mobile in the pocket of my jeans. One text from a private gym offering me a membership trial. And one missed call: private number.

I dialled my voicemail. 'You have one new message. Last message left at 12.01 a.m.'

Strange that it had only just notified me of the call almost twenty-two hours later. Although with the cliffs and the beach, the signal in these parts was quite often intermittent.

As I listened, I could hear hissing interference like choppy waves lurching high and low, similar to when someone has accidentally misdialled you and you can hear the sound of the phone jogging around in a jacket or handbag. Then there was a crashing sound and a bang. The roaring sound rose abruptly and then just before it cut out I heard a woman's voice, muffled against the sibilant white noise.

'Help me,' she pleaded.

The tone was desperate, the texture of her voice rough and rasping. I mentally filed through a list of people who could have dialled my number at midnight last night. All my Leigh chicks were accounted for. Who had I left in the pub? Nancy? No, the voice was older. Sue? Pregnant Sue! But why would she phone me?

A thought flashed. Of course – check the call log. And that's when I saw it. The last missed call at 12.01 yesterday night had been dialled from 01702 785471 – my own landline.

It didn't make sense. I was home then. I'd got the cab around ten thirty, got rid of Giselle and had passed out by 11.15.

I played it again.

This time the voice was clearer, more disturbing.

'Help me.'

I shivered.

The garden was in complete darkness now but I must have left a light on in the kitchen because I could see the phone sitting on the wall.

An uncomfortable thought was starting to form at the back of my mind but I managed to contain it and dropped out of the hammock.

I walked up the garden path towards the phone.

A crack on the windowpane stopped me rock still.

I eased my breathing and strained my ears.

Somewhere in the distance a dog barked in warning.

A flutter of panic hit.

I didn't want to look at the decking by the window. And yet I couldn't help myself. Something was drawing me to the French doors.

Even though I kind of knew it would be there my eyes widened with shock as they absorbed the small, white, gleaming cockleshell.

I hugged myself, too frightened now to move closer. A strangled whistle sound wheezed in my throat.

The temperature had dropped to cold, almost frosty.

About the French doors the air began to crackle.

Draughts stirred, lifting and billowing the curtains at their sides.

A darkness beside them was thickening and warping. Something was coming, swirling into being – a shape, a dark mass.

Then I saw it clearly – the murky shade of a woman in a long gown, discarnate, shadowed with blacks and greys. I had the impression of dark curls snaking around the palest of faces like seaweed clinging to a corpse, a marbled neck and stained cotton dress. But it was just that – a notion. I didn't see them with my eyes but with my mind, like my imagination was filling the contours within the depth of blackness.

There was the acrid smell of muddy sulphur and an unbearable feeling of loss.

For a long second it hovered there like a storm cloud.

Then a heartbeat later it was gone.

Chapter Five

My computer screen flicked on. I fingered the scrap of paper in my hand. It read 'Marie143' in John's looping handwriting.

When I drove into St John's on Monday morning, he had been leaning against the wall, waiting for me. As soon as he spotted my red VW Beetle he nipped over and held the door open for me.

I watched his face wrinkle with concern. 'I left my phone at the pub. Nancy brought it in this morning. I just got your messages. You sounded weird. What's going on? You OK?'

Good question. What was going on? Was I OK? Were things happening because of something going wrong in my brain? Or was this stuff external?

I hadn't been able to come to a conclusion on Sunday. Which was an improvement on Saturday when I had been simply 'weird' as John had correctly suggested. The seeming physical nature of whatever had manifested seemed very real and I was certain that something supernatural had turned its gaze on me.

*   *   *

Martha was alarmed, of course. It was all over her face when she arrived late on Saturday night. She came over as soon as her husband, Deano, got home, on the off chance that I was still up for company.

I had left a rather hysterical message on John's phone and was just calming myself down, trying to get a grip on what I'd just seen, so her timing was perfect.

Martha could be counted on for good solid comfort. Her green fingers tended our social circle's gardens and house-plants when we went away, while her gentle manner and nurturing aura had us all calling on her for a shoulder to cry on whenever things got tough. There was something indescribably soft about her, without any drippy overtone, that made you feel safe in her company.

Ever practical she sat me down around the large pine kitchen table and made us a cup of tea while I gasped and spluttered through what had happened in the garden, climaxing with the revelation of the phone message.

I know I sounded quite crazy as when I looked up Martha's face was crossed by heavy lines of strain. Her honey-sweet voice told me that in her opinion I was probably just overdoing things.

'You know, darling,' she soothed, 'you have really been through the wringer these past few years. Life's not easy and I know being a widow with a young child must seem an awful lot to cope with. Do you not think that perhaps your brain is creating an outlet for you?'

She was being rational and I would have loved to believe her, but there was no denying something peculiar was happening. Something that went beyond psychological stress, even perhaps beyond mental illness or the possibility that my brain was rewiring itself around a blockage.

The quiet lull of her voice, the reason in her argument, the relief of her physical presence served to pacify me a bit. Even her suggestion that I might want to see a counsellor was acceptable although wide of the mark, but then she added, almost as an afterthought: 'Of course you want to keep the memory of Josh alive, it's a completely natural impulse, but this way,' she shrugged limply, 'just seems so negative, Sarah.'

'What are you talking about?' The words exploded out of my mouth without thought or care. 'How dare you?'

Martha took in my expression and started to backtrack. 'God, I'm sorry, Sarah. I know it's a touchy subject.'

But I was on my feet, walking up and down the kitchen, hands gesturing to the ceiling with outrage and exasperation. 'You think this thing is my *husband*?'

'Well, I . . .' Martha's eyebrows knitted together. She shrank into her chair.

'That's bloody ridiculous.'

Martha relaxed a little. 'I'm glad to hear it, Sarah, really I am. I know you've not been yourself lately.'

I stopped pacing, rested my knuckles on the table and took a deep breath. 'This has nothing to do with Josh. Nothing.' I tried to speak in a controlled voice. 'This thing, Martha, is female.'

She had her mouth open as if she was going to speak but then closed it. A small sigh escaped her. 'Really?'

I knew she was trying to help but she sounded so insincere, I realized that it was pointless talking to her, and rather than offend her again with another exasperated tut or sigh I answered her with a small shrug.

She cocked her head to one side and held my gaze. 'Have you ever read Stephen King?'

OK, I thought, now she's getting it and replied, 'Maybe. Yes, when I was a teenager. I'm not reading anything like that now and before you suggest it, Martha, no I'm not letting my imagination run away with me.'

She smiled and stretched her hand to me across the table. 'Honey, I wouldn't dream of patronizing you like that. What I was going to say is I once remember reading an interview with him, where he said something that had quite an impact on me.'

'Go on.'

'We make up horrors to help us cope with the real ones.'

Exhaustion fell across me.

She must have seen it because she asked if I wanted to go to bed.

I nodded.

Martha got to her feet pretty damn quickly.

At the front door, she paused and held out a little green pill. 'Valium. Get some sleep, Sarah. Call me in the morning if you need to talk. You're not alone.'

'I know. That's the problem,' I said and closed the door.

The next morning I woke up with a sentence going round my head. It was a phrase Sharon had used to describe coming off the anti-depressants she'd taken once when she was younger. It was a hard time and she said she weirded out a bit. 'Until you get balanced again . . .' she told me, '. . . it can be just like a bad trip.'

Having had a few early forays into recreational drugs during my twenties this made sense. Once, in the bath, coming down from something or other, I was convinced I could hear voices in the water pipes begging me to release them from their watery prison. By the time Josh found me I'd scratched the paintwork off the u-bend and was searching for a hammer.

I entertained the idea of a flashback. The incident by the French doors had been, it was fair to say, rather trippy. And with regard to the mobile, there was a possibility that I could have sent the message to myself while I was half asleep or sleepwalking. Though it seemed unlikely.

In the afternoon I summoned the courage to listen to the message again and tried dialling into it but it was gone. I wasn't sure if I had failed to save it or perhaps Martha may have deleted it in a well-meaning attempt to help. That would be just like her. The possibility rather put me out – I hadn't given her permission to tamper with my phone. I would certainly speak to her about it when I next saw her. It was frustrating. Now I only had my memory of it to go from and it was becoming hazier the more I tried to concentrate on its recall.

By evening I had a heavy feeling in the pit of my stomach and by nightfall I was edgy as hell. I didn't want to admit it at the time, but I was getting scared. I think part of me knew what was going to happen.

The dreary sameness of Monday morning felt like something of a reprieve. In fact I'd go as far as to say that I was almost pleased to be going into St John's. The students were gone and we had a week of administrative duties to sort before we were allowed to bugger off on summer leave.

As I turned into the drive and clocked the grey steel girders of the new music block extension with its vaulted see-through roof, the absolute soulnessness of the place suddenly heartened me. There's a first time for everything. Nothing organic stirred here. Thank God.

A break from restless spirits was required.

I needed to get in and get my head down. Work would absorb me and for a while I could feel almost normal.

The last thing I wanted to do was talk it over again. So when John fired up I told him just that. But the silly sod wouldn't leave me alone.

'Sarah? ARE YOU OK?'

I locked the door of the car and picked up my bag and started marching to the entrance. It had rained the previous night and the air was damp and verdant.

'I'm not really sure if I am OK, to be honest. If I told you what happened, you'd just think I'm mad and to be honest, I'm starting to wonder about that myself.'

He nipped ahead and turned to face me, blocking my path. 'Hey, slow down. Do you want to talk about it? I'm going to go into the research room and do some marking, if you want somewhere private to chat.'

'Actually, I don't, John. I'm sorry about calling you on Saturday night. I had a bit of a fright – a missed call from some woman asking for help. I thought it might be Sue? What with the pregnancy and everything. Is she OK?'

John nodded. 'I just saw her in the staff room. She's fine. Everyone's fine. Are you fine?'

'Please forget it.'

He was scuttling alongside me. 'Was it another cockleshell?'

I shook my head and scowled knowing that I would appear either rude or irritable or probably both.

'Thank God for that. Solitary female hysteria.' My eyes met his, which crinkled warmly. 'Joke,' he added.

But I wasn't in the mood. 'I'm going to the staff room.'

'Well, come and find me if you're bored. You sure you're OK? Don't worry about drinking too much, if that's what you're thinking. An early death might save you from the horrors of new education models.' And he bounced off.

I turned into the staff room and made for the coffee machine. I was being too hard on him I ruminated, now regretful, as I set my load down on the side. He was just trying to help.

I fumbled in my bag for my purse, finally scooping out a handful of coins, which promptly scattered across the ledge that the machine perched on.

I cursed and picked up a twenty-pence piece. It went into the coin slot and straight out of the return. 'Fuck.'

'Having one of those days are we?'

McBastard stood beside me. A half smile curled his lips, suggestive of glee at my blinding incompetence.

As there were no students present in school that week, we were permitted to wear jeans. McBastard's grey chinos had been swapped for dark denim that caught across the hips and tailored down over his long legs, fleshing him out for a change. To my surprise I saw he was wearing a t-shirt with a logo of a cool band that I had once publicized. Was the robot becoming human?

'Let's say I've had better mornings.' Struggling with the coin slot, I glanced at him in time to see his volcano eyes fix on me. He looked away immediately, embarrassed to be caught staring. Could he tell something strange was happening to me? Was I dragging around an aura of weirdness?

The coins returned once more. I was starting to feel self-conscious.

McBastard coughed. 'Here, let me.' He retrieved the money and this time, his efforts produced a coffee. His fingertips brushed against my palm as he handed over my change.

Without thanking him I scrambled my stuff together hastily and made towards the desks at the far side of the room.

'Sarah!' he called after me. I turned and met his stare. The openness of his face had melted away. 'I need your course review. Tomorrow at the latest, please.'

I answered him with a grunt and sat down, spreading my papers over the wooden top, noting with bewilderment that my hand was tingling where he had touched me.

At lunch John found me in the canteen mauling a stale beef sandwich and trying to put the horrors of the weekend out of my mind.

He wedged his butt along the pine bench next to mine. 'Have you seen Sue?' He was trying to make conversation.

I informed him she had an ante-natal appointment at the hospital but didn't expand. I wasn't in the mood for conversation.

John poked a dried-up triangle of something pizza-like on his plate. The food, which was below average at the best of times, was virtually inedible once the students, sorry customers, had departed.

He forced himself to bite the cheesy triangle and winced.

'Good night on Friday, wasn't it?' he said, through a mouthful of dried bread.

My mind went straight to the phone call, the haunting watery words, the strangulated tone of the woman. With some effort, I focused on the Red Lion hours.

'I was quite drunk. Any gossip?' I did my best to engage.

'One of Finance got chucked out for doing coke in the loo.'

'Oh, who?'

'Tina Worten.'

John took another bite and we munched in silence until he put down his crust and said, 'You're a bit pissed off with me, aren't you? What is it? The hysterical woman reference? I was being silly. I thought we had that kind of relationship. I'm sorry. Is that why you phoned me Saturday night? To be hysterical? I was only concerned because I didn't realize you were joking.'

I stared at him blankly. I had phoned him when I was upset Saturday night, hoping he might be up. But when the call went to his voicemail I left some garbled message for him to call me. It hadn't occurred to me that he would assume the call was a prank, although part of me was mighty relieved that he might.

'Now you're pissed off with me for not getting it. I understand. But can we just go back to being normal? I won't mention it again.'

I wondered briefly if I should go with the prank call idea. It certainly made me feel better. Better than him thinking I was mad.

'Sorry, John. Something happened on Saturday night but I don't want to go into it.'

'Something else? I'm here if you need to talk.'

'I have to try and work a few things out in my head first.'

'And you think I'll think you're hysterical.'

'Perhaps.'

'Shit, don't punish me for something stupid I said when I was pissed.'

'I'm not. Honestly. I'm just not sure what's going on and . . .' I faltered.

'You're under a lot of stress, Sarah. We all are. It's the end of term and we all need a good rest. I'm sure you'll be back on form by September. Give yourself a break. Go away. Have some fun.'

I balked at the mention of September. The idea that this might escalate, that I might return to school with the current situation unresolved was terrifying.

'Oh God.' I hadn't meant to say it aloud.

John's eyes narrowed. 'Is it something else? I'm getting the sense that you don't want to talk to me.'

'You got it, Columbo.'

He ignored my barb and continued. 'OK, you may not want to talk to me, but how do you feel about talking to my sister? I spoke to her over the weekend. She's a little left of centre but I mentioned your cockleshell thing and she said she'd heard of that kind of thing happening.'

His sister. 'Oh yes, the one into "weirdies" and stuff.' The thought was appealing however. 'But you said she was in California?'

'She is. You know the wonders of technology can reach out across the miles. Do you have Skype on your trendy new internet?'

I nodded.

73

He wrote her handle on a piece of paper. 'I'll send her an email this afternoon and let her know you may call. Do it. She won't think you're nutsville, which everyone knows you are anyway. Give her a try. Seriously, it might just be worth talking to someone. If not to put the whole thing to rest, at least to let off steam at someone who's odder than your good self.'

That night I settled Alfie early. It took a while as he was agitated and didn't want to be on his own but eventually his tired little body won over his restless mind and he fell asleep. and I was able to go downstairs and have a little me-time.

The living room was dark, the windows onto the street were still open and yet hardly any noise drifted in. There was no hum of traffic or doors slamming, only the calm of Monday evening hibernation.

I dug into my pocket and pulled out John's sister's details. 'Put it to rest,' he had said.

He was right. I wasn't passive by nature. Well, there was no time like the present.

In the kitchen I set up my laptop, pressed the on button and poured myself a glass of red as the Skype loaded onto my home page.

I took a sip and entered Marie's details into the contact box.

The woman who popped up seconds later on the video stream had John's easy eyes, his pronounced chin, which suited him more than her, and his heavily textured voice softened by a slight East Coast twang. She was lean, with a healthy tan, and in her mid- to late thirties.

74

'Hi,' I said.

She grinned at me, her image pixellating slightly as the information whizzed through the modem. 'Sarah?'

In the smaller video screen to the bottom right of the monitor I could see an image of myself disintegrating into little blocks and reintegrating again.

'Yes, hi. You're Marie?'

She nodded, a big, shaggy mane of mahogany hair tumbling about her shoulders as she did so. 'John said you might phone sometime. I didn't think it would be so soon. You OK?'

'You look like John,' I said, changing the subject. It was odd having a face-to-face conversation with someone you would probably never meet in the flesh.

'Yes, we're related.' She tossed her head back as she laughed. Same gesture as John. I wondered briefly what their parents were like.

I raised my eyebrows and shook my head. 'Of course. Sorry. This is a bit weird isn't it?'

She leant closer to the screen as if scrutinizing my image. 'You mean Skyping or your situation?'

I hadn't expected her to bring it up so soon. 'Well, er, both really.'

She grinned again showing good, strong teeth. 'Not in California, honey, believe me!' I think she winked but it could have been a time delay on the screen. 'Do you fancy a cup of chamomile?' she asked.

'I think I might have a glass of red if it's not too early for you?' I raised my glass to the screen and laughed. She saw it and nodded. 'Normally I'd join you but it's not yet noon here, honey. The neighbours would talk.'

There was a lot of John's comfortable easiness about her, which made me relax more than I'd anticipated.

'Gimme forty seconds,' she said, 'and I'll be all yours.'

'OK.'

Marie had a pleasant living room. Behind the empty wicker chair on screen there was a white stucco arch that led out onto what looked to be a wooden deck furnished with tropical plants. The room was full of bright late morning sunlight and crammed with bookshelves and more plants. Pictures on either side of the walls spoke of a love of contemporary art and esoteric objects. I was trying to place one of the paintings when Marie's torso filled the screen. A porcelain mug bearing a picture of a cat came into view followed by her shoulders and head.

'Right,' she took a sip of tea. 'Fire away. It started with a cockleshell? Am I right?'

I bit my lip, unsure of whether to mention my appointment with Doctor Cook. Marie read the slight pause as hesitation. 'Hey, honestly you don't need to tell me everything. I'm just assuming that as you called you needed some advice.'

'No. It's not that. It's just— Oh, never mind . . .' and I started at the beginning.

Several minutes later I reached the Saturday night climax. 'I can't describe it. I'm pretty sure it was female and human, or had been once upon a time. Long gown, black hair . . .' I was speaking quickly, gabbling. 'But I got this awful feeling of tragedy. You know I've felt that before. I've been through loss. But this was kind of saturating. Overwhelming. Like drowning. Like the feeling I came back with from the Drowning Pool. That's what this is about.'

At this point I realized I must have sounded insane as Marie's eyes widened and her eyebrows rose virtually up into her hairline. She shuddered and moved back momentarily from the webcam.

I stopped. My shoulders were aching with tension so I too sat back into my chair with a small sigh. My breath vaporized in front of me. Instinctively I thought of smoke and reached for my cigarette packet. 'Oh God. Sorry. This sounds so nuts, I know.'

Marie looked sort of frozen and for a second I thought I'd lost the connection, and then I saw her breathe in. 'It's OK,' she said, with a tremor to her voice that had been absent before. I guessed she wanted to stop and get away from her brother's mental mate as soon as possible. I cursed myself and took a cigarette from the pack.

'Marie. I can't believe I'm telling you all this.' I paused and pulled on the fag. 'Perhaps I am ill?'

'Sarah, it's OK . . .' Marie had leant forward and was looking intently into the screen. Her voice was purposefully gentle but I could make out worry lines streaking across a forehead that had had clearly lost some of its ruddiness.

'I can tell from your face that you must think I'm crazy. I don't blame you. I shouldn't have . . .' I shivered involuntarily. The room had grown cold. Very cold.

She broke in. 'Sarah, listen – I believe you.'

But I wasn't listening. '. . . Skyped you. Perhaps I am nuts. Saturday night just felt *real*.' And then her words sank in.

On the computer her head nodded.

'You believe me?'

Her face was filling the screen now so it was easy to see her swallow and hesitate.

'Why?' I said, fixing onto the whites of her eyes.

She paused and then in a very slow voice she said, 'Because I can see her. She's standing behind you.'

Chapter Six

It's difficult in retrospect to try and describe how I felt at that moment. You always imagine you're going to behave in a certain way then when bad things happen, you can surprise yourself. I had thought I'd be one to run screaming from the house. Maybe stopping to get Alfie first.

But I didn't.

My body seemed to react to what Marie was saying before my brain processed the words. I had been about to light the cigarette but as realization dawned, my right hand froze mid-air, gripping the lighter tightly. My left, which had been idling on my lap, clutched the arm of the chair. Across my back and down my arms, goose bumps crawled. I stared back at Marie, utterly petrified.

She was easing herself back into her chair. 'I'm not getting any sense of antagonism from her, Sarah.' Her movements were controlled and tense but she smiled. 'I can see her outline. It's like she's wearing an old dress. Victorian? I can't tell. She keeps fading out. Now she's like a shadow.'

I kept my eyes firmly on her face and avoided the smaller rectangular image in the lower right-hand corner, the one that showed me in situ. This was weird and getting weirder by the second.

When my voice came it was high. 'How can you tell all this?'

Marie said carefully, 'I don't know. I just do. Can't you see her?'

Fuck, no. 'I'm not looking.'

'I think she wants you to. She's coming towards you, Sarah.'

My breath was coming quick and fast.

'I really think you should turn and face her. Be quick. I'm not sure she's going to hold together much longer.'

I was burning up with fear. 'I don't think I can do that.'

'I think it's important to try, Sarah,' she said. 'This is happening for a reason, right? Please.'

I let out a small sob, took a deep breath, and then slowly forced my eyes down to the screen, only to see the vague black shadow at my shoulder dissolve.

The air came out of me and I turned around. There was nothing in the kitchen but a fly beating its wings against the window. My nose tingled as if thawing out after an icy blast. I sniffed, the room temperature was back to normal, and faced the screen.

Marie had moved closer. 'She's gone, right?'

I nodded, unable to speak.

'Geez. That was . . . well, that was freaky.' Marie sat back into her chair and took a sip from her mug. 'I suggest you have a good glug of that red wine you've got there. You look pale.'

'It's a shock,' I said, finding my voice. The wine tasted bitter, of hawthorns and mud, but I drank it down anyway.

'OK?'

'Better.'

Marie cradled her tea. After a few moments she spoke. 'Has anything like this happened to you before?'

I shook my head. 'Never. There was a time after my husband's death when I really wanted something to happen, but it never did.' I took another gulp as a thought hit me. 'Oh God. Do you think that's where this has come from? Have I conjured this up because I want Josh back?'

But Marie spoke firmly. 'No, no way. I think this has more to do with your present circumstances.' Her eyes held my gaze. 'Do you ever sense your husband around you?'

I thought for a moment then replied sadly. 'No.' I was going to say more but it seemed pointless. The question could be answered with a simple word. Wherever Josh was, he wasn't here in Leigh with me and Alfie. This I knew with a painful certainty.

Marie nodded then frowned. 'Any idea why a cockleshell? Or a pine cone?'

I hadn't thought about it. 'We're by the sea. Have you been to Leigh?'

'Many moons ago. Is there a cockle industry?'

'It's a working fishing town. Down in the Old Town there's a lane full of cockle sheds. Part of the beach outside of the Crooked Billet pub is completely made from the shells.'

'So our visitor may be trying to let us know there's a connection with that area. And the pine cone? Are there pine trees anywhere down there?'

The main part of the Old Town comprised small fishermen's cottages, cobbled streets, pubs, cafés and boatyards. There was scarcely any vegetation down there at all. 'No. I don't think so.'

'Hmm. Pine cones. The cedar is the tree of life. Did you know that? It's bound to be a symbolic gesture. We just have to work out what it represents,' Marie ruminated. I took another sip of wine. She cleared her voice. 'Do you want to know what I think?'

I wasn't sure I did at that point but I answered her yes.

She looked up away from the screen, gathering her thoughts. 'She's disturbed, this being.' She took a moment then continued. 'I think that she's here because of you.'

At this I balked. 'Hey, I haven't invited her in. I didn't do anything to wish this on myself or my child! Don't say that.'

Marie held a hand up. 'Not knowingly you haven't, but sometimes when manifestations occur it can be the slightest thing that activates them: a change in hormone levels, puberty in adolescents, arguments. Have you had any work done on the house recently? Held a séance?'

I shook my head vigorously. 'No, no. None of those things. And I wouldn't meddle with the occult. That's not my bag.'

Marie finished her tea and put her mug on the desk. 'Well, she's after something, Sarah, and whatever it is, it's connected to you.'

I poured myself another glass of wine and considered it. 'Is it possible that I'm imagining this? That maybe there is something going on with my brain and you're picking it up? Like a shared delusion? Could I be projecting this?'

Her eyes softened and despite the distance her sympathy touched me. 'Anything is possible, honey. I think you should go back to the doc and tell him what's been going on. Carefully, though. Even if this thing is a symptom, it's symbolizing something. You need to find out what and understand it. You know, I have friends who come to me when they're sick. They want me to tell them not to heed the recommendations of their doctors and to give them herbs and chants that can cure them instead. My advice to them is the same to you – do everything – mix the conventional with the unconventional. It's all there for a reason. And whatever's going on with you, it's there for a reason too.'

'OK, I'll make an appointment. But what do you suggest I do about . . .' I tried to find the right word, '. . . the manifestation?'

Marie cocked her head. 'Well, if you want, we could try it again? See if she comes through? Then you could ask her what she wants.'

I shuddered violently and took another gulp of wine. It wasn't what I wanted. But nor did the alternative appeal – waiting around for something else to happen.

Marie coughed. 'I've got to work tomorrow and Wednesday but I could dial in on Thursday?'

That sounded far enough away for me to acquire a backbone so I agreed.

'But email me if you need to before.'

I told her I would.

'Oh yes, one more thing,' she said, reaching for her mouse to terminate the session. 'Imagine yourself and your son in brilliant and vivid spheres of blue – once in the morning and once in the evening. That'll protect you. Not that I think she's harmful. But it might make you feel more secure, yeah?'

I nodded then sat there for twenty minutes after she signed off doing just that. Then, when I could not concentrate any more, I took my wine and sat outside on the deck. I hadn't been out there since Saturday night and I was jumpy. But the night was balmy and the wine was calming my pulse.

Things were happening.

I couldn't escape that.

Although my instinct was to bury my head in Leigh sand and pretend things were OK, I knew that soon I would have to face my fears. Once you acknowledge that something is going to happen you take away much of its dreadful power. As I sat there on the hot June night I experienced something akin to relief.

I didn't know it then but I was taking my first step of the journey.

I had no idea just how much it would change everything.

Chapter Seven

As it was, on the Thursday, nothing happened. I psyched myself up, visualizing blue spheres at every conscious moment, but after an hour of talking and waiting and even a couple of jokes, Marie called it a day. Under her eyes were puffy bags. Her job obviously wore her out. I hadn't asked her what it was she did. It seemed to be an intrusion – our relationship wasn't conventional. It was another layer in this weird surreal world in which I'd found myself and in which she now found herself, too. Sure, she'd explained how she'd got into this stuff (a chance meeting with some kind of East Coast guru, followed up by workshops, crystals and then a channelling group), but I didn't probe further. I had told her what I believed were the necessary details from my life. Nothing more, nothing less. Not because I didn't like her or trust her. I did. But because it seemed irrelevant to my present situation. And at the back of my mind I had a strong sense that we were being watched.

Nevertheless on Thursday Marie appeared relieved the 'entity', as she called it, hadn't materialized.

Cradling the same cat mug she'd drunk from on Monday she shrugged. 'Most mediums I've talked to say time operates entirely differently on the spirit plane. You can't force these things and I would strongly advise that you don't. In my somewhat limited experience invocations, séances, Ouija boards and such tend to attract rather the wrong type of entity. I'm presuming here that you don't want more turning up at your house.'

'Or garden,' I added. 'No thanks. So what now?'

She shrugged. 'Play it by ear. See how you go. Tune in over the weekend. I'm around most of the time. You never know, this might be the extent of it. Could be a blip in the space-time continuum, or something.' She laughed.

'Could just be my brain,' I said, without mirth.

'Oh yeah.' Her face grew larger on the screen. 'You seen your doc yet?'

'Tomorrow, before work' I told her. 'Way things are going though, I might not mention it.'

'Do what you need to,' she said, and waved goodbye.

I did end up telling Doctor Cook some of the incidents. It was hard not to. He had such an accomplished bedside manner and for a doctor's surgery his was one of the nicest I'd been in. Once upon a time it must have been the formal dining room of the house. It was dominated, on its northerly wall, by an impressive marble fireplace adorned with grapevines and pheasants. A bit more rural than you'd connect with Leigh but nevertheless, it had charm.

Behind Doctor Cook's desk, double windows opened onto a large, rambling back garden. Flowerbeds to each side of the lawn burst with roses, hollyhocks, sweet peas and other plants I couldn't name. Their cheerful scent mercifully over-powered the more clinical smell of the room.

Further back, behind a rickety glasshouse, stood a

magnificent cedar so aged and heavy that its lower limbs were supported by wooden posts. Belted around its trunk was a large wooden bench. It must have been the perfect place to sit in summer evenings, which I mentioned to Doctor Cook, in a futile attempt to evade the reason for my appointment.

'Yes,' he smiled, crinkling his eyes. Today he had on a red bow tie with pale pink stripes and a white waistcoat that made him look like he'd be quite at home in a barber shop quartet. 'I built the seat myself, many years ago when I was far younger and far more confident with my DIY skills than I really should have been.'

I glanced at it again. It was sagging on its left side. 'Looks all right to me.'

'The tree needs constant attention but it's worth it.' He tilted his chin up signalling a change of subject. 'Now, how are you coming along, Ms Grey?'

I had decided to couch my worries as a question about medicinal dosage and told him that since I'd reduced my anti-depressants I had seen a few weird things. He tried to get me to elaborate but I managed to make the events sound fairly innocuous. I didn't want him locking me up.

'My temperature has been fluctuating quite wildly and sometimes I'm seeing shadows or I think I'm seeing shadows.'

'Hm.' He frowned. 'Have you been sleeping well?'

Several times over the past ten days I had woken up throughout the night in a knot of sheets, covered in perspiration. 'Not really.'

'That may have more to do with it than the medication but these things tend to be interrelated. I can write you a prescription for sleeping pills if you think that might help? We all need sleep. Very good for one's mental health.'

I hesitated then shook my head. Lately Alfie hadn't been going through the night either. I needed to sleep lightly enough to respond to his cries.

'Well, why don't you see how it goes and come back to me in a couple of weeks if things haven't improved?'

His lack of insistence was comforting.

'Have you had your referral from the hospital yet, my dear?'

'It would be a letter, wouldn't it? No, I've not had it.'

He tutted. 'I think that needs to be our priority at the moment. Let me just check with Janice to make sure she sent the request through, although I imagine it's more likely to be a delay at the other end.' He was nimble on his feet and out of the door within seconds, leaving me on my own.

I sat back into the chair and studied the heavy framed painting hanging over the fireplace. It was a landscape of the Old Town looking up over the fishermen's sheds to Belton Hills. In the distance you could see the crumbling tower of Hadleigh Castle pointing its bony finger up at the sky. Beyond it, to the west, the artist had depicted a glorious sunset full of ambers and lilacs. It was a delightful pastoral verging on the saccharine. There was a signature in the corner. I got up, about to inspect it more closely. As I passed the French doors something cracked on the lower pane. I stopped for a moment then turned my face to the sound.

The doors had been wedged open by ruddy clay bricks. Rolling away from them on the patio was a small brown pine cone.

I did a double take and drew my breath in sharply. It was identical to the cone I'd found in my living room; same length, identical pattern.

For a moment the world stilled.

Then the door between the consultation room and the hallway flew open.

If Doctor Cook was surprised by my position he didn't let on. His tone was concerned. 'Is everything all right, my dear?'

I pointed to the pine cone. We both noticed the tremble to my hand. 'That cone. It just dropped against the window.'

Doctor Cook stepped behind the desk. 'It's from the cedar tree,' he said, and sat down expectantly.

But I couldn't move. 'From the cedar?' I repeated uncertainly. 'But the tree is all the way down there, at the bottom of the garden.'

Clouds passed over the sun throwing the garden into gloom. An intense feeling of unease flooded me.

Doctor Cook's brow creased. 'There's a pair of mischievous magpies who call it home. They're constantly stealing things and dropping them en route back to the tree.'

I took a last look at the pine cone and shivered.

He spoke gently. 'Sit down. Are you sure you won't take a prescription? If you don't mind me saying, you look like you could do with a rest.'

'No. No, thank you.' I went to the chair and picked up my jacket.

'The referral is well under way. You should be contacted very shortly. Now do take some time to relax.' He stood to see me out.

'Yes. I will.' I turned at the door to send him a quick smile of thanks but he was looking away from me out of the window.

* * *

89

I kept my head down at work, reluctant to interact with anyone. I'm not good at small talk at the best of times and today I needed some solitude so I could bury myself in the course review – an analysis of the previous year's strengths, weaknesses, retention, achievement and success rates. It wasn't my favourite part of the job but within an hour the statistical overload had blocked out the morning's incident and by the time Sue popped in to see if I fancied coffee I had more or less convinced myself that sometimes coincidences were just that.

It was Sue's last day before she went on maternity leave and she was determined to have a single glass of wine to celebrate. So after work a bunch of us headed down to the Red Lion to toast her. I was irritated by the appearance of McBastard, nearly an hour later, and even more alarmed when he sauntered over to the table where John and I sat.

John, of course, was an impeccable host but McBastard jittered uncomfortably as he socialized with the plebs. You could tell he was uncomfortable and veered from slightly too informal with John and Edwin, who had also joined us, to rigid and closed off in his exchanges with me. To be honest, I didn't encourage much dialogue and I probably would have left earlier if it hadn't been for the fact that Alfie had gone for a sleepover with Martha's two and I had the evening to myself.

After another hour the vast consumption of alcohol meant everyone loosened up. Sue was looking at everyone's drinks jealously and someone suggested it would be a good time to do the presentation. McBastard said a few words about what an impact she'd made, how she'd be sorely missed and that he wanted all the details about the birth (yeah right) and pictures of the baby.

Everybody clapped. Someone bought another couple of bottles of plonk. I gave Sue a big hug and she unwrapped her present of nappies, baby grows, chocolates and Mothercare vouchers, and promptly burst into tears. John, well-oiled now, started singing 'For she's a jolly good fellow' and everyone, the regulars, the bar staff and even our po-faced manager, joined in.

At some point Sue left and our numbers dwindled. It was only when I found myself outside having a fag with Edwin that I noticed the sun had gone down. Above us clouds the colour of burnt amber sealed in the day's heat. Edwin commented that he could feel a storm coming and I agreed.

'I have a twinge above my eyebrows. That's usually a sign of imminent meteorological disturbance.' McBastard had slithered up behind us. He shot a glance at me. 'A storm.'

I knew it was a conversational inroad, but it was late and we were all slaughtered so I just couldn't help myself. 'I watch the weather reports, thank you.'

He shifted uncomfortably for a second then seemed to square up to me.

Sensing another imminent disturbance, Edwin excused himself and escaped to the bar. I was desperate to follow suit but I was only halfway through my cigarette. It would have been rude, and although McBastard's company set my teeth on edge, he was still my boss.

'It's so hot in there,' he commented, trying to fill the conversational vacuum Edwin had left behind.

I would have disagreed for the sake of it but even on the street, sweat was creeping down my hairline. 'In summer too,' I rejoined, content to offer sarcasm.

McBastard breathed out wearily and looked at me. He

was holding a pint and had pushed his hair back so that I got the full benefit of those brown eyes, and their swirling iris lava. 'You seem tense lately, Sarah. Is everything OK?'

A snort escaped me – the number of people who enquired after my health was increasing by the day – and I raised my glass. 'Nothing that a few bevvies can't cure.'

To my astonishment he clinked his pint to mine. 'I'll drink to that.' He took another sip. 'I don't know about you, but I can't wait for the holidays.'

His candour took me off guard: he'd never said anything negative about work. 'I suppose so,' I replied, more glumly than I intended.

'Oh? Aren't you doing anything nice over the break?' He shook his head quickly and sighed. 'God. I sound like a hairdresser. Sorry, I mean – are you going on holiday?'

He was wobbling slightly on the pavement, his tight, work persona diluted by beer, so I cut him some slack. 'That could be another vocation for you perhaps?'

McBastard creased his eyebrows together and grunted. 'It'd be the third.' I watched as he leant his angular frame against the wall and rubbed his eye. He had a shattered look about him. 'After the clergy and education.'

A bunch of drinkers swept through the doors and bundled into me. I took a step towards him. 'What? Really? You were a vicar?' My eyes were wide.

'Rector, actually. It's a bit of a family tradition.'

'Wow.'

He smiled enigmatically at my expression.

'That kind of explains a lot,' I said, externalizing thoughts that should have remained unspoken.

'Explains what?' He was still smiling.

'Well,' I gestured my fag hand at him. 'The brimstone and fire. Health and Safety and all that crap.'

The corners of his mouth fell slightly but the smile hung on in there. 'Go on.' Threat lingered in the undertone.

I was slurring now, oblivious to any boundaries I might be bulldozing over. 'Rector = Rectitude, Properness = Health and Safety = McBastard.'

Now his mouth dropped right open and his eyes clamped on me. They were large and wild. 'What?'

I'd always thought that he didn't care for the opinions of others. True, I was drunk and had little empathy, but for a moment there, I felt his shock. I guess I'd imagined that somewhere in that heart, if he had one, he wasn't swayed by what inferiors thought of him. But his expression spoke volumes. McBastard cared.

I had to stop calling him that.

Startled by this revelation, I pulled on my fag and recovered enough to smooth it over. 'McWhittard = Health and Safety. You know, it's your thing isn't it? Quality. Course Review. Discipline.'

He glanced away at the smokers beside us and I saw him sag a little. An index finger crept to his lips. He bit the nail. 'Are you comparing those to the duties of a man of God?'

It had me floundering, not entirely sure where to go with the conversation. There was a challenge in his words that I couldn't meet. Give me a staff meeting and I'd have nailed him. But here, outside the pub with a sackful of vino under my belt my resources escaped me.

McBastard, sorry, McWhittard fixed me with a strange half-gaze – eyes down, mouth closed, contemplative, then he pointed to the cigarette packet half tucked into the arm of my dress. 'Give me one of those.'

'A fag?'

He took a long slug of beer. 'Old habits . . .'

'Which reminds me of monks,' I said, but this time, thankfully, he laughed. I returned his gaze and for a moment we watched each other. He was the first to look away. 'Indeed,' he said. There was a blush to his cheek.

The lighter sparked, went out, sparked again, spluttered and died. McWhittard stepped up to the group of smokers beside us – younger and far more boisterous – and asked them, very politely, for a light. One of them, the tallest, took out a Zippo and lit the cigarette eagerly. McWhittard returned and drew hard, really hard, on the cigarette. He so wanted it.

'So, how long has it been? Since you stopped?' It was obvious he'd been a smoker. Some people fake it but you could see he was famished.

He exhaled a long plume of smoke out of his mouth and both nostrils. 'Since I started this job. Eight months and two weeks.'

My own fag was out now. I flicked it to the floor and ground it with my heel. 'That sounds like you've been counting the days,' I chuckled.

He blew out again, slumped an inch and gazed over my shoulder into the middle distance. 'There are some things we just have to do. Might not like them. But have to do them.' For a moment it looked as if a cloud was passing over him: his eyes fell and his face darkened. Then he tossed back his hair and straightened up. 'Know what I mean?'

'What kind of things?' I asked, almost starting to enjoy the exchange.

He looked up the street, took another long drag, then turned and faced me. It was dark, and his eyes were filled with black shadows. 'You left this area, but you've been drawn back, right? What for? Do you ever wonder?' His voice was low but he spoke quickly with intensity to his voice that I had never heard before.

For a moment I wondered if John had passed on anything that I'd told him in confidence. Surely not? He was reliable.

'I'm not sure what you mean,' I told him.

He paused, then stepped out of the shadows towards me. I could see his eyes now and they were wide, focused on my own.

He opened his mouth to speak then something behind me caught his eye. A sharp nip to my left buttock had me spinning round to find John standing behind us, dribbling. He winked. His hair was messed up and clammy, his face greasy, and he had tied his jumper around his waist. Somehow he had lost several shirt buttons.

'What was that for, you cheeky git?'

He was swaying and leant an arm on me to steady himself. My bag was draped over his shoulder.

'Called a cab. I'll take you home.' I glanced at McWhittard, who had stood back from me, dragging hard on his cigarette, and told John I wasn't sure that I wanted to go home right now. But as I did a white taxi pulled up by the kerb.

McWhittard leant over and touched my arm. 'I think someone needs to get him back, don't you?' I caught a whiff of hops, smoke and superior attitude. But for once it wasn't unpleasant. In fact it was very human and more than slightly intriguing.

I glared at John, but McWhittard was opening the taxi door and helping him into the back of the cab. 'Sarah, there are some things we just have to do, right?' And then he laughed.

I smiled back, took my place beside my drunken friend and pulled the seatbelt across my body with reluctance. McWhittard closed the door and popped his head through the open window. 'Night, John. Sleep well.' He faced me. 'Sarah, course review on Monday.' Then he grinned and banged on the roof of the cab.

'Fucking hell,' John said, as soon as we pulled away. 'That bloke never stops, does he?'

'Oh, I dunno,' I said quietly. 'I think he just did.'

Once home I made the most of what me-time I had left. I showered then rubbed myself down with a silky eucalyptus body cream.

As I lay on my bed I let my mind wander over the day. It ignored Doctor Cook and went straight to McBastard. No, McWhittard. He'd been chilled and borderline human and, after the initial slip with his nickname, I'd found myself almost enjoying his company. And I knew that he wanted to talk more.

His eyes came to me. That strong vivid gaze. The constant swirling of reds and ambers in the pool of dense brown. The wrinkles around them and across his forehead now spoke to me more of character, the strength of his stature.

There was something alluring, it had to be said, in his

build, in his power. Now I knew that he was a man of conviction, too. I liked that.

I should ease up on him. I *would* ease up on him as long as he eased up on me.

A waft of laughter from the bar down the road blew in on the breeze.

It was still early but I was done in and soon I'd drifted off.

The dream when it came started calmly enough.

I was at once in the scene and yet not part of it. I was an observer, a drifting consciousness. The panelled room in which I floated was quiet. Deathly quiet. Its silence was broken only by the thrumming tick tock of the grandfather clock. The day outside was bright but grey. By the window stood a man I vaguely recognized from my episode on the beach, the man who had waded into Drowning Pool to try to pull me out. *Father.* He wore the same buttoned down coat and trousers. As he stared out of the window, his hand flitted over his brow. His kindly face was grim.

On a wooden chair opposite him sat a woman, roughly the same age, sitting stiff-backed and upright. *Mother.* On her lead-grey face she wore a pained expression and wrung her hands unconsciously in her lap.

The next sound that drew my attention came from a chair opposite. There sat a young woman, in her early twenties. Her dark hair was drawn up into a straw bonnet that tied under her chin with a pink ribbon. I recognized her pale blue and white striped cotton dress that tapered in under the bust and spread down to the floor. I had worn it in my vision. It had pulled me under the water in the Drowning Pool. There was

97

something strange about the way she looked. She was breathing fast but her eyes were empty and uncomprehending like someone who was disorientated, or in shock.

The silence was intense.

Nobody spoke.

The door opened and a blue-eyed man with gingery, blond hair entered. He was lean and well groomed but a few years older than the girl. He was dressed smartly, like the man by the window, but you could see his suit was of a better cut. He wore an intricately embroidered waistcoat with a chain that reached up into his breast pocket. This was a wealthy man, handsome. And yet as he turned his eyes on the girl they filled with malice. It made his face look dark.

'Miss Sutton,' he said to the girl in the bonnet. 'Come into the parlour now please.'

She didn't move so he repeated his request again. The man by the window had turned into the room now. He stood still, watching the scene, looking from one woman to the other, unsure, it seemed, of whether he was required to do something.

The older woman stood and went to the girl.

'Sarah,' she said to her soothingly as one might speak to a patient or a very young child. Then she lifted her arm, pulled her up and gently pushed her towards the door.

The girl, in all her terrible misery, moved like a somnambulist. Her walk was aimless, stumbling slightly, but she made it to the man, who took her arm, signalled to her parents they should not follow, and guided her across a large hallway into a room with floor-length French doors.

I knew this place.

I had seen this view of the garden and the cedar tree. But

now there was nothing but farmland beyond. On the furthest wall, over the mantelpiece, hung a painting of Hadleigh Castle.

In the room sat a heavy-set man with a fat belly, perhaps forty or older, in a dark jacket. Holding his hat in his hands he got to his feet.

The other man, still holding Sarah by the arm, led her to him. 'There, Billing. What do you think? Satisfactory?' he asked.

The man in the dark jacket took a step forward and inspected the girl. His eyes licked over her face and down her body. The calculating edge to his gaze chilled me. Even as I watched I could sense danger in the room. I wanted to scream at her to run away, but I was numb, unable to do anything but watch the scene play out before me.

At length the man spoke. His voice was rough, born of years on the sea. 'Open your mouth.'

Sarah didn't move so he said it again, louder. She didn't flinch though for a second confusion seemed to cloud over her eyes, then she complied. The heavy-set man poked a finger around her teeth, then he nodded. 'All right. But with the payment too.'

The man who had brought her in nodded his assent. 'We shall call it a dowry and leave it at that. It is more generous than a man in your position could otherwise expect.'

The heavy man snorted. 'And you say she will recover? I want a woman who will perform *all* wifely duties.'

The other man nodded.

My stomach was churning. Something bad was happening here. The girl was being traded. I found my voice: 'Sarah! Leave.'

Sarah remained mute and unmoving, so I shouted again, 'For God's sake get out of there.'

For a moment her eyes flitted over to where I stood. Coming out of her trance she seemed to take in her surroundings for the first time.

The rich man snorted. 'You have my promise. She will be ready to wed next week.'

Sarah had wakened fully now and looked up at him, her eyes widening as the sense of his words hit her.

The large man, satisfied, set his hat upon his head. 'Well, I'll take your leave and await instructions.' Then he got to his feet and hurriedly left the room.

Sarah seemed to have some sense of what had just occurred. Her eyes skated from the closing door to the man who remained. 'I will not marry him,' was all she said simply. 'My heart will not let me.'

Without turning to face her, the well-dressed man raised his hand and in one short movement slapped Sarah across the face. She staggered back, her hand going to her cheek.

The man took a step towards her and pushed her once, twice, until her back was against the wall. He brought his face so close to hers that only a couple of inches separated them. His pale blue eyes tightened into sharp arrows, then snarling, he hissed, 'Stupid girl. Of course you will. Or perhaps . . . I am a widower.' Tentacle-like fingers curled over her body and moved down to her belly. 'I could remove it and then no one would know and you could come into my service. I could put you to good use.'

With some effort Sarah pushed him away and headed for the open French doors. 'I will not.'

The man, who had toppled slightly in the struggle, called after her. 'A woman in your position has no choice.'

But Sarah was out now, hitching her skirts and running past the cedar tree, through the garden, across the lane down towards the cliffs, to the Drowning Pool.

The scream of a fox in the street woke me abruptly. The night was still and muggy. The digital clock on my bedside table blinked its red eyes: 2.13 a.m.

I sighed and sank onto my pillows full of anxiety. The dream had been vivid and clear.

And it had been terrifying.

That poor girl. What had happened to her?

I shook my head trying to shake out more of the dream. None came.

Who was that?

Sarah.

My name.

Was the dream an echo of the day mixed up with messages from my subconscious?

Despite my racing mind I was full of fatigue and soon my thoughts dissolved and sleep came for me.

At 3.30 a.m. a huge clap of thunder crashed. I awoke once more with a start. Lightning flashed, followed by a roar of thunder so voluminous I could feel it resonate inside me. The mirror on my dressing table trembled. I crawled from the bed and pulled back the curtain. In the street it was dark and empty. The fox shrieked again.

The air was charged with tension.

Rain was waiting to break.

A purple fork of lightning darted across the sky. There was an explosion as it hit something on the cliff which echoed across the rooftops. Another clap of thunder followed.

The storm was getting closer.

I drew back the curtain and started back to the bed when lightning flashed once more, illuminating the room. The ruffled duvet I had just thrown off had slipped onto the floor and there, beyond it, the figure of a woman stood by the door.

It was her.

Frozen in light, I made out smooth alabaster skin, a bonnet keeping back unruly dark hair, young piercing green eyes, the line of the plain white dress that disappeared into nothing below the knee.

Her outstretched arm pointed at me.

No one will ever know what I felt at that moment. Terror is not agony. It is not a slow drawn-out thing. It is quick and instantly enveloping, like a stab in the stomach, as sudden as a viper's bite, bringing with it creeping paralysis.

I stood there unblinking, unable to move, half reaching for the bed, watching the terrible thing float soundlessly towards me.

My heart was thumping hard. I heard my gasps and saw my breath turning to mist.

A deathly stillness had crept into the room. No, it was more than stillness, it was stagnation penetrating everything. The sickening stench of decay and rotting flesh warped and thickened then hung in the air like invisible lengths of smoke.

The thing hovered now over the middle of the bed. I tried to tear my gaze away, but her eyes, glowing green in the gloom, held me in their terrible thrall. Then there was the most chilling of sounds – halfway between a cry of pain and a strangled sob, broken and faulting, entwined with a shrill blast of static.

'*Please.*'

It was as if the word had battered me physically. A wave of nausea flooded over me. I staggered back a step and hit my thigh against the dressing table, causing the bottles and hair products to spill across its surface with a clatter. The bruising sting of its wooden corner had, however, roused me, bringing me back to my senses. I was still as frightened as hell but some part of me had recovered. I stood up to it. 'What do you want?' My voice was shrill.

The temperature was icy yet sweat streaked my body. I held my breath.

The wraith flickered and buzzed in the dimness like a faulty fluorescent tube.

Another clap of thunder roared above us.

She stared at me.

'Why are you doing this to me?' I clenched my fists for strength, my nails digging into my palms.

The voice spoke again, this time in a hoarse whisper right beside my ear. '*Help me. Sarah Grey, you must.*'

'How?'

Another flash of lightning filled the room.

I watched in mortification, unable to look away, as her white gown started to darken. Thick, globular black liquid seeped from a gaping wound on the spectre's head: layers of skin had been pulled roughly away from the flesh underneath. The thing raised its skeletal hands either side of it.

If I could have moved, I think I would have jumped out

of the window to escape it but my feet felt leaden. The awful sight of her bleeding wound made me feel dizzy, almost winded and I struggled for breath.

The storm broke in a sheet of heavy drops. The tree outside lashed against the windows, scratching against the panes like fingernails.

Lightning tore into the room once more, illuminating the creature's grotesque crucifixion-like pose.

It brought its head up, fixing bulging eyes on me, drifting closer, closer till I could feel its breath on my cheeks: 'He came back.'

And then it sucked me in.

I am back in the Old Town, shuffling over the cobbles by Strand Wharf. Icy wind biting my face and lashing my hair from my bonnet. My body crunches in on itself, stiff, aching with familiar pain. My fingers gnarled and curled with arthritis. The pail that I carry in them is heavy and cold. I rest the bucket for a moment and straighten my back as best I can. A young man has come alongside. He catches my gaze, tips his cap then, with a neatly aimed kick, sends the bucket flying. The water spills out over the cobbles.

'Oh dear,' *he sneers.* 'Ye have bad luck with water don't ye, Mother Grey? But then witches do, so they say . . .'

'Get out of it, Thomas Tulley.' *A voice shrieks from behind. Liza steps in front of me protectively.* 'Clear off. You should be ashamed of yourself. Let Mother be.'

I put my hand on her arm. 'Leave it, Liza.' *She is a good girl but she has a sharp temper that invites trouble.*

Whenever I see a Tulley my heart shrinks. It isn't our place to scold him so. Not after his sister . . .

I try to pull Liza back yet she wrests herself from my weak grip and makes some sign at the lad that I can't see. Whatever it is he scarpers down the street as quickly as he can. I chuckle. Spirited and proud my Liza is.

'You shouldn't let them get away with it, Mother.' She turns to me. 'Jane Tulley's death was not your fault. The Tulleys know it too. Tommy's a bully boy who should know better.' Her face is red from the bitter wind but her dress, as always, is neat and pretty.

'Liza, Tommy still feels the pain of it. Leave him be.'

My daughter tut-tuts but says no more. Smoothing her hands over her apron her words are a reprimand. 'I told you I'd get the water. You shouldn't have gone to the well.'

My protestations take as much time as she does to fetch the pail. 'No, Mother, I'm taking you home. I'll get the water. It's too cold to be out today.'

She links her arm through mine and slowly we make our way back. At the black panelled door of the cottage I pause. Though not yet up, the moon is fast pulling in the tide. Beyond the wharf, waves are getting up. Their frothy heads rise and fall further out into the sea, flipping and pitching the several fishing boats that have braved the wind. Alongside the wharf a foreign ship is rocked back and forth.

I smell blood in the air.

Gulls circle up and down on the breeze, crying warnings. Does no one hear them but me? On the horizon thick, muddy clouds of violet grey are gathering for a fight. My wrist aches at the sight of it all: a storm is on its way. The foul smell the sea has tossed up tells me what I already know: this one will be a beast.

There is an evil coming through that I will not be able to counter.

*   *   *

My eyes snapped open with a click that seemed to reverberate through the house. My whole body was stiff with tension.

Sunlight streamed into the bedroom. It was late morning.

I sat up and looked at the dressing table. All the bottles stood there upright.

Gingerly I lifted the duvet and felt my right leg for a bruise. Nothing.

Rationally one might have concluded this was a bad dream. But I was beyond logic.

Though now I knew who she was.

Chapter Eight

The storm was on everyone's lips that day. When I went to pick up Alfie Martha was full of it.

'We all woke up at once, didn't we, Alfie?' She was making sandwiches for the boys. Alfie nodded disinterestedly and continued 'brumming' his truck over the tiled floor. 'I thought they'd be scared but it was all quite exciting.'

I took a sip of the freshly ground coffee Martha had forced on me when I arrived. 'I think I heard it.'

'You think you heard it! You must have been out for the count.'

'Yes, I was.' The lie came easily. I had prepared for this. The night before had left me so completely shaken that I had rehearsed what to say. I'd been unable to move for what seemed like hours. When I finally threw the duvet off the bed I wrapped it round me tightly and rocked myself back and forth. I had seen something significant, that I knew. But I had brought from the dream a misery that racked me.

In the warm light of Martha's kitchen it would have been easy to put the whole thing down to a nightmare. But I knew better. I had stuff to do.

'All right, Sarah?' Martha asked without looking up. She was cutting the sandwiches diagonally into quarters. She wiped her eyebrow with the back of her hand and then placed the small white triangles on a plate shaped like a cow.

'Oh yes,' I said. 'Just tired.'

'Helen next door said lightning struck one of the old oaks along Marine Parade. Shame really. If it had to hit anything you'd hope it would go for one of those hideous new apartment complexes they're building down there. Still, can't have everything can we? Boys! Lunch is ready.'

She produced a jug of squash and filled the three plastic cups on the table. Then she opened the back door and beckoned me out. 'Come and sit on the deck. It's glorious today.' To the kids she said, 'You lot sit down and eat while I talk to Auntie Sarah.'

I followed her out and took a seat on one of the sunloungers.

Martha brought another one alongside me and sat down. We sat in silence for a moment, enjoying the calm of the garden. It had been landscaped to resemble a modern Spanish courtyard: white concrete planters full of tropical plants and cacti ran up each side. Beyond the decking the lawn was covered with smart grey shingle and dotted with solar-powered uplighters that gave the garden a chic ultramarine glow in the evenings. Halfway down several palm trees clustered before stone steps that led onto an alfresco dining area. A swarm of mosquitoes chased each other in the shade.

'I expect you're looking forward to the break, aren't you?' Martha said, after a pause.

It was hard to follow the conversation. The shock hadn't

dissipated altogether yet. My head was still foggy, like it had been packed with cotton wool. I couldn't stop thinking about the dream. It was like an obsession: every second thought returned to Sarah. I could feel her – I had absorbed her sorrow and I could feel it growing. I still felt the despair that had emanated from her in the first vision last night. The terrible sense of entrapment; the loss of all hope. And then, the suffocating sense of menace in the air.

Every so often an image of her floating above my bed, blood seeping from the yawning gash on her head, would flash like last night's lightning across my brain, making me queasy and anxious.

Martha coughed. 'You all right? You seem a bit vacant.'

I forced a grin. 'Hangover.'

She gave me a nod of empathy. 'You're not having any more of those cockleshell episodes then?'

'No,' I replied truthfully. Pine cones, terrifying spooks, desperate dreams, but hey, the shell problem seemed to have sorted itself out. One must be grateful for small mercies.

'Good, good. Well, I'm here if you ever need to chat.' She patted my arm. She was lovely, Martha: thoroughly whole-some and brimming with generosity of spirit.

Spirit.

She was in my head again.

I knew who she was.

It was astonishing. But it had to be her. In the visions she was called Sarah. She had failed to kill herself in the Drowning Pool and thus been branded a witch. Then Thomas Tulley had called her by her name: 'Mother Grey'.

109

There it was.

Sarah Grey.

Her name.

My name.

Was that why she'd come to me? Because we shared a name? Could it be that tenuous? Surely not. There must be something else, logically. But then nothing about any of this seemed logical.

But I was sure it was her.

Though I hadn't had time to work out what to do about it yet.

'I said – are you bringing anyone?' I had zoned out. Martha prodded me. 'Blimey, it must have been a good one last night. You're barely here.' She stretched her legs out and put on a pair of huge tortoiseshell sunglasses and turned her face to the sun. 'To my party. It's in three weeks' time. I just wondered if you had anyone that you might want to bring? Man-wise.'

My heavy head felt the lounger and I closed my eyes. The storm had cleared the air and the temperature wasn't yet unbearable. 'No. Not really.'

'Not really?' I registered the interest in her voice. 'Is that a maybe?'

My friend would have liked me to be with someone. Not because she saw it as the natural order of things, Martha had a thoroughly post-feminist outlook in that respect, but because she sensed it would make me more comfortable – happy, even. 'I'm sorry to report that it's a "no".'

'Well, Deano's invited a few of his friends from work and two of them are single.'

I let out a sigh, which Martha either didn't hear or chose not to acknowledge.

A nearby neighbour powered up a hedge-trimmer. The buzz reinforced the atmosphere of cosy suburbia.

'I'm not saying you should come and get off with them or anything. But I'd like to introduce you. One of them, Ben, I've met before. He's really nice. Cool. He's in a band.' She sent me a sidelong glance. 'I think you'd get on well.'

I took a sip of coffee. 'You know I'm not looking for anyone, right?'

'But it'd do you good to have a bit of male company from time to time.'

'I do keep male company at work. And I have Alfie.'

Martha playfully slapped my arm. 'You know what I mean. You're still an attractive woman. I just think that sometimes you need to remind yourself of that.' She angled her body towards me. 'There's more to life than work and home, you know.'

I kept my eyes closed but my lips curled as I spoke. 'Don't I just know it.'

'Do you?' I was sure that behind those huge shades her eyes had narrowed.

'I . . .'

A loud crash from the kitchen cut me off. It was followed swiftly by a shriek.

'Bugger. You all right, boys?' Martha got to her feet but kept my gaze. 'Let me sort them out. Just hold that thought.' And she dashed into the house.

But the moment had gone. When she returned we made small talk until Alfie had finished lunch. Then we left.

* * *

The atmosphere at home was lighter than it had been first thing. Alfie and I sat in the garden for some of the afternoon. He didn't seem to want to go into the house either. It was as though he could sense something wasn't right.

Later we made pizzas and then ate them in the flower-boat.

'Are zombies real?' he asked, brushing away some crumbs from his lap. The question seemed to come out of nowhere.

'Why do you ask, honey?' I kept my tone even.

'Oliver, at nursery, says they are.'

I smiled. 'No, they're not real. They're just stories people make up to frighten themselves.'

He took this on board with a nod. 'I know ghosts are real.'

My heartbeat went up a notch. 'Oh yeah?' I accompanied it with a smile and a sniff. Keep it light, Sarah, I urged myself.

'Grandma says there's the God and the Jesus and the Holy Ghost. But I've never seen him.'

'You've never seen who?' I was tense but intrigued.

'I saw Jesus at Christmas. He was a doll. In a cot. Kirsty was his mum, Mary. She did a wee wee in her pants.'

Ah yes, the nursery nativity. Mary had appeared in an appropriate headdress on top, yet cords and t-shirt below. 'Poor Kirsty.'

He ignored me and continued. 'God came down at Easter and told us not to eat all our eggs at once.'

That rang a bell with something Mum had said. An appearance of the bishop at her local church. There'd been an Easter service for kids and she'd insisted on taking Alfie along.

He giggled. 'He was wearing a dress!'

'Oh yes. That was a bishop, Alfs. That wasn't God.'

'He was God. He had a beard. He said "by the word of God,

the Lord." My son raised his hands up to the heavens. It was a gesture I could see a clergyman making at the summing up of prayers. 'Like a Jedi. And the Dark Lord. Shwoom, shwoom.' Then he swished an imaginary lightsaber at me. 'But I ain't seen the ghost.'

I could have cut in here and had a conversation but he was off, tumbling out of the hammock and making like Lord Vader in pantomime: 'Don't eat your eggs. We will. Oh no you won't.' Swish.

The rose bush quivered.

Later, after I had put him down I took my place in front of the computer and Skyped Marie.

'What's happened?' Her face was expectant. Today she had on a tight white t-shirt which emphasized her well-toned shoulders and arms. Her skin was taut and golden. If I didn't know better I would have said she was Californian born and bred.

It took me ten minutes to fill her in on the latest developments. She sat there quietly, nodding from time to time. Finally she sat back and looked me squarely in the face, or as squarely as one can when talking through a computer monitor.

'Shit,' she said slowly, drawing out the vowel, in that lazy way Americans do. 'That's grim. Sounds like some night. So you had a dream of an older woman, then you had a manifestation then another dream? Is that right?'

I shook my head. 'The first was a dream. Definitely. It was the same woman but older. Sad. Resigned. There was a sense of something else. Like she was trying to send me a message. Something to do with someone coming back. A man.'

113

'Any ideas who he is?'

'No.'

'Or who she is?'

'Actually yes. I'm not sure whether it was a manifestation. It might have been another dream.' I rubbed my brow. I was finding it all quite hard to explain in solid terms. 'I can't really tell. It was vivid like it was really happening but when I woke up there was no sign that I had been moving around the room. I thought I had spilt some bottles on the dressing table when the, the . . .' I was struggling to find words to describe it, 'horrible thing scared me, but when I saw them this morning they hadn't been touched. But the ghost kind of pulled me into a dream, and a scene. They weren't nice. But, at least now I think that I know who she is.' I clicked my tongue and looked out over the garden thinking – I was stupid for not seeing it before.

'So, who is she?' An overtone of excitement sent her voice whistling over the line.

'Sarah Grey, the sea-witch.' There, I'd said it.

Marie shifted visibly. 'A sea-witch?'

I relayed the legend as I knew it, with both of the possible endings – first the three axe wounds then the headless body in the ducking pond.

'That's when I first heard them. The night that we went up across the fields to Hadleigh Castle. I was with my friends. We started telling ghost stories then Sarah Grey came up. We talked about her for a bit then moved on to other stuff.'

'Aha!' Marie sounded pleased with herself. 'Sounds like you created some kind of séance. And before you say it, you don't have to do it on purpose. Castles, rocks, mountains, sacred sites all have a very different kind of energy. These

114

are places where time shifts, creating portals almost. Every so often time folds back on itself. Words, rhythms, stories echo through them across the centuries. If you start going down certain paths you start waking ghosts. Sometimes you set in motion things you have no idea about. I think perhaps the stories that you told each other by the fire combined with where you were must have stirred up something. And though you didn't realize it, one of you, or you yourself, Sarah, brought her through.'

'We didn't – *I* didn't – do it on purpose.'

'No, of course not.' Marie frowned. 'But you have her name. You live in the area she did. People take different paths all the time but the thing with paths is that they converge. When you retrace some of those paths you evoke the ghosts of the people that have walked them before. That night at the castle, *you*, her namesake, must have walked the same path; you talked about her, there in the shadow of the ancient place, your coven of friends evoked her by name, feeding her energy, sending her strength. And now she's here and you've got to deal with her.'

'Hang on,' I held up my hand to the screen. 'We're not a coven.'

'The point is you know who she is now. She's obviously not at rest and she's chosen you to help her resolve whatever it is that's keeping her here. Something is still tying her to the living.'

I looked out of the French doors. A couple of rose petals had blown across the decking.

'When she appeared in the second dream or manifestation, it was really frightening.'

Marie bit her cheek and thought a moment before

115

replying. 'I doubt if she's aware of what she looks like to your eyes. The way she has shown herself to you means something. You have to work out what it is. Hey, you OK?'

I was thinking about the blood oozing from the apparition's head wound. It occurred to me that her knees looked like they might have been tied together too. I shuddered.

'I wasn't good this morning but I'm holding it together now. As the day has moved on I've calmed down a bit. For Alfie.'

'Well, that's great,' she nodded. 'You're doing really well, Sarah. Honestly. Hang on in there.' Safe in California Marie smiled and crossed her legs.

'So now you know,' I said slowly, coming to my point. 'Can you get rid of her?'

Marie looked surprised. 'Get rid of her?'

'Perform an exorcism or something like that.'

Marie was taken aback. 'That's like an eviction or banishment. Do you really want to do that? Have you no empathy for the poor soul?'

'No,' I said, banging the table with my fist, suddenly angry. 'This poor soul is haunting me! Do you know what that's like? It's terrifying, Marie. I can't bear it.'

Marie sat back and bit her tongue. 'I can appreciate the way you feel, Sarah . . .'

'Can you really? Sometimes I think I'm going mad. I can't sit in my own home without jumping. Now I can't even go to sleep without freaking out either. I don't want this, Marie. I want it to go away.'

I felt like crying but I didn't. Instead I sniffed and wiped my nose on the sleeve of the cotton cardigan I was wearing.

'I think it's more about you helping her move on, Sarah,' Marie spoke slowly as if measuring each word before she chose to articulate it. 'I don't think an exorcism would be very easy. Or even work. It's used a lot in films, that's true. But it's a Roman Catholic tradition that requires faith in the Roman Catholic catechism. Don't be offended, but you don't strike me as the overtly religious type.'

I was still glowering. 'I don't?'

'I imagine that if you were, you might have consulted with your local priest rather than me.'

I snorted, which sounded dismissive. That wasn't how I felt. I guess I was more dumbfounded then. I knew what she meant. I just didn't like it. I wanted her to sort me out and get rid of all this insanity.

For a few seconds we sat in our own distant pools of silence.

Eventually Marie spoke. 'Look, Sarah, I think you know this deep inside you, but for the moment you're freaked out and in denial – but there is undoubtedly a connection between you and Sarah Grey.'

'We share a surname, that's it.'

'You've told me that you're both widows. And you both live or lived in Leigh. Maybe it doesn't actually matter what the connection is, but if you want to make this go away you're going to have to work out why she's focusing on you and what she wants.'

I leant on my elbow and scratched my nose slowly. She was right. I did know it. When I spoke my voice cracked. 'What do you think I need to do then? I mean, how can I possibly find that out? Please don't ask me to speak to her again.'

'You know,' Marie said in a softer voice now, 'I know the "witch" tag sounds alarming but most of the women accused of witchcraft or labelled as witches were either ugly, or poor and scary looking. Their poverty meant that they existed outside of society. They were the ones that had the label "witch" projected onto them. Very few of them chose it themselves. Of course there were some who meddled with herbs, but that's hardly dark and sinister is it? You said this woman, Sarah Grey, lived in the nineteenth century? Well, that century saw orthodox medicine rise in popular regard while using herbs to heal became suspect and went into a decline.'

'No,' I shook my head sadly. 'It wasn't just that she worked with herbal cures. I've dreamt about her when she was young and when she was old. People thought she was a witch. It had something to do with the Drowning Pool. I saw the scene. She was running away from that awful man. He wanted to take something from her. I don't know what it was. But he was nasty. He slapped her. That's why she went into the Drowning Pool. But she didn't drown. She was rescued. I think, by her father. But anyway it didn't matter to the crowd that looked on. The water wouldn't take her so she was seen as a witch. The townspeople turned on her after that. Everyone did.'

It seemed too much for Marie to take in. But she said, 'OK.'

After a long minute, during which Marie stared at a spot behind my head and squinted, she said softly, 'Let me tune in now and try to pick something up. There's a vibe I've been getting but it's just not clear. Can you sit back and relax while I try?'

'OK. But how can you do that over there? Don't you need something to hold on to? Something from the person?'

Marie sort of clucked. 'You've been watching too much TV. It's a matter of what you believe. If you think you need a personal possession to tune in, then you won't be able to do it without one. Personally, I think you and I have developed a relationship of sorts so that's what I'm going to concentrate

118

on – our communication. Then I'll focus on you and your dealings with Sarah Grey. OK?'

I assented and waited for several moments while Marie sat there, eyes closed, arms outstretched, in what I guessed was some kind of meditative trance. She was curious to watch, her brow creasing slightly and her nose wrinkling. As the minutes passed anxiety started to creep across me.

Suddenly Marie clapped her hands together, threading her fingers into a knot.

'It seems to me,' she said at last, 'that Sarah Grey probably wants you to solve the mystery of her death. She's sending you clues by appearing with a gash in her head, through you dreaming of her life,' she was speaking quickly, her eyes alert and urgent. 'It's got to be about the legend. You've got two endings and neither of them works out well for her. There's violence in both stories. Violence always leaves a rupture, like ripples in time. You need to help her rest in peace by finding out what happened to her. In reality. You need to get beyond the myth.'

Marie watched my face, waiting for a reaction.

Electronic static filtered through the computer speakers. In the distance seagulls cried. Outside the clouds had turned from pink to lilac to grey.

I think I knew this was what I'd have to do even before Marie said it. But I wasn't ready to hear it, and suddenly I found that I was angry. Angry with Marie for suggesting it, with Sarah for haunting me and with myself for not being someone else. 'Well, how the hell do I do that?'

Marie smiled. 'Simple. If you can't find out any more on the internet, you need a local historian.'

Chapter Nine

The conversation with Marie had been pretty sobering. Inside it was obvious to me that this thing wasn't going to go away without some serious investigation of Sarah's story. That's not to say I wanted things that way.

I spent a lot of time thinking – why me? Was it really just my name that connected us so strongly? Or something else. The place where I lived? All of it? Or none of it?

I wasn't the kind of person who got off on weird stuff like this. I'd moved to Leigh to get away from all the excitement.

As the summer holidays drew closer I thought of planning an escape somewhere to shrug off this cloak of supernatural doom. But on Thursday morning my appointment with the neurologist arrived. It was scheduled for ten days hence. I realized that Alfie and I shouldn't plan to go away. Just in case.

On the Friday I finally handed my course review in to the boss. Taking the sheaf of papers from me he scanned them and tutted. He'd slunk back inside his granite persona. Straight off he spotted a spelling mistake. No 'Thanks, Sarah, well done.' Just 'Tsk, tsk. There's only two e's in ProAchieve.'

'Really?' I tried to camouflage my irritation by yawning. It got him going.

'Come on, Sarah. The course reviews are important. You mustn't be slapdash.' He was sitting behind his desk looking flustered and angry and upset and disappointed and worried. All at the same time.

I didn't get it and frowned, then decided on a neutral smile instead. He sighed and shuffled through the pages then he gave me another look with those killer eyes. They must have made a whole gaggle of girls swoon when he was younger. But I couldn't read what he was trying to infer.

I broke through the silence that was creeping between us and making me feel a tad jittery. 'So, can I go? It's my last day and I'd like to get off early, if there's nothing else?'

His eyebrows rose. He opened his mouth to say something but thought better of it and asked if I was going for a drink after work. I said no and scuttled out of his office, wishing him a happy holiday as I closed the door.

A swift half wouldn't have gone amiss but Margaret and Keith, Josh's parents, were due to visit on Saturday and the house was in need of some industrial cleaning. What with everything, I'd let things slip a bit.

It had been a while since we'd seen them. Alfie adored them both. Margaret spoilt him rotten and Keith, his only granddad and a former naval officer, loved to get down and play rough and tumble. Alfie wouldn't shut up about Granddad coming and was very excited at the prospect of presents. Although he needed a good night's sleep he resisted my efforts for an age. I finally got online that evening about ten o'clock. Fatigue was clawing at my resolve by then but

I knew I should have a stab at finding something out about Sarah Grey, having put it off all week.

I shouldn't have worried. The Google results were inconclusive, churning up the address of the pub named after her with beer ratings, a TV presenter, a number of Facebook sites and a caterer. With time to spare I tried a new search and entered 'Witches of Essex' into the subject bar. This yielded a legion of websites.

A salsa CD played softly in the background. The fast-paced beats and joyful trumpet accompaniment couldn't have been more inappropriate as I surfed through the first website. It was my intention to look for Sarah, or failing that, locate where Leigh witches had been hanged. I thought it might be a good starting point.

There were three Leigh witches listed: Joan Allen in 1547, Alice Soles in 1622 and Joan Rowle in 1645. No mention of Sarah Grey but the list of other poor souls who had been sacrificed because people thought they were witches was both deeply disturbing and distracting.

Witchcraft, it seemed, had been commonplace and treated without severity. Often the punishments came in the form of a fine or a mild telling off. That was until the mid-sixteenth century, when just in Essex, hundreds of names of women (and some men and children) started appearing. As the accusations increased the punishments grew increasingly inhumane, climaxing in 1645 with the emergence of the notorious Mathew Hopkins, the self-styled Witchfinder General. I flicked through to his pages and read with increasing horror the methods he used to extract his confessions. Torture, being illegal at that time, meant Hopkins had to be lateral in his approach. The witch pricker was a small dagger with a retractable blade.

This was thrust into the accused. With the blade full out it would stab into their flesh so they would bleed. However, Hopkins asserted that witches concealed on their bodies a 'Devil's Mark' where Satan and his imps sucked the witch's blood. The Devil's Mark was diabolical and therefore insensitive to pain. It could be as insignificant as a birthmark or even a flea bite. If the accused didn't bleed or cry out in pain when stabbed in that area it would be deemed the 'Devil's Mark', and therefore evidence of their guilt. Hopkins' witch prickers had secret compartments in the handle into which the blade would retract at the flick of a switch, when the witch hunters believed they had found the mark. Onlookers and witnesses would marvel as the blade, which had appeared to penetrate the flesh, elicited no reaction from the victim and then no blood. This awful one-sided trickery, I went on to read, was all the more despicable as these 'marks' were often located in the 'privvy parts'. In August 1646, John Stearne, Hopkins' second in command, sent eighteen witches to the scaffold at Bury St Edmunds. His only comment on their execution was that they all were found to have 'teats or dugs which their imps used to suck'. These were located in the *labia majora* and were no more than a bruised or inflamed clitoris.

If the poor women still maintained their innocence after this ordeal, they would then be 'walked', that is, sleep-deprived, and marched up and down by two men until they broke. At this point they seemed to have made up lurid, fantastical confessions, which often implicated others.

But Hopkins didn't act alone. He was borne along by a society afflicted by failed crops, a mini-ice age, poverty and civil war. Folk needed someone to blame and, let's face it, the Devil has never shown up at his trials. Instead women old, young, hook-nosed or attractive, disabled, mostly poor or those who existed without the protection of men or status, took the fall.

It was a numbing discovery. I have to admit, my notions of witchcraft had been firmly forged from Meg and Mog, Halloween fun, fairy tales and soft toys on broomsticks. The realization of what this camouflaged forced me to take a breather. I went into the garden to smoke a cigarette, feeling guilty and repulsed by what I had discovered.

Hadn't I read a report in the paper recently that said people were still at a loss to explain the hysteria of the witch hunts? Hadn't they researched it? Being forced to strip in front of 'a dozen of the ablest men in the parish' who would bear witness as you were pricked all over by a blade, then sleep-deprived for two or three days after must surely have had the toughest of women admitting to anything just to end the ordeal.

It was a no-brainer. The witch hunts weren't about hysteria. They were about sex and death and control and power. Again.

At least these days we were more alert.

The salsa tune stopped. I went inside and put on the radio in time to catch a chat show host introducing the subject of the evening: Can women ever be responsible for rape?

I turned it off and suppressed an urge to vomit. That was enough for now.

With a feeling of dread growing in my stomach I retired.

'What do I do now, Josh?' I asked silently.

There was no reply.

Chapter Ten

I'd forgotten that this weekend was the annual Leigh folk festival. Margaret and Keith hadn't. They were keen to get out into the library gardens, where a number of bands were due to perform.

I wasn't fussed about folk music but it was nice to sit on a blanket under a tree with a picnic. Margaret had packed some champagne in her basket so we toasted the summer. Alfie suckered Granddad Keith into pushing him endlessly on the swings in the playground, leaving Margaret and I to settle down and watch a young woman singing a ballad about her dead love, a sailor lost at sea. This, it seemed, was the perfect cue for Margaret to ask me how I was doing.

She was a kind woman, in her late sixties, with peppery blonde hair. When the breeze fluttered the leaves and the dappled sunshine shone across her face, Josh's eyes twinkled back, surrounded by deep laughter lines. Sometimes it disconcerted me. That day it was reassuring.

Margaret had taken her son's death very hard. Although his elder sister, Elaine, and her three kids lived close to the family home in Suffolk, I gathered from Josh when we first got together, that she was a bit of a daddy's girl. Fate had cruelly inflicted Keith's small eyes, stiff manner and portly build on his daughter whilst Josh inherited his mother's nimble figure, innate grace and huge bright eyes the colour of forget-me-nots. Like most parents Margaret and Keith did as much as they could to hide their preferences but Josh told me that both he and Elaine always knew. And like most children to whom this happens he unconsciously navigated towards Margaret's passion for music and books while Elaine followed Keith into the navy.

She meant well but there was something cloying, almost desperate, in Margaret's enquiring tone when she addressed me. At times I wondered if she wanted me to throw myself at her feet and weep so that she could feel she was still needed. Though I suspect she just wanted to keep the connection between us – there was much of Josh in Alfie – we could all see that. Margaret could never have countenanced a separation from him. It would be like losing her son all over again. But I had no wish to do this and she knew that.

We'd spent a lot of time together after Josh's death. Margaret was a huge support, especially with Alfie: he was a year and four months, restless and disturbed by Daddy's sudden absence. When Grandma came to stay she cooked and cleaned and played and talked and wept and for a while, as I was barely capable of speech let alone running a household, made herself utterly indispensable. Keith used to pop in from time to time but he had his own private way of dealing with grief and I think seeing us made it too raw.

I knew all this and yet, whenever the 'How are you?' question popped up the impulse to scoot a zillion miles away faster than the speed of light was virtually irresistible. I didn't want to be the sum total of my tragedy. It had been difficult, but I was getting over it and both Alfie and I needed to move on. I didn't want to talk grief and I didn't want to talk healing. And the last thing I wanted to tell Margaret about was all the weird things that were happening to me. Despite the eyelid thing and the paranormal intervention I was still a fit parent. I just wouldn't sound like one if I told her.

No, I didn't want to talk about how I was.

'I'm fine thanks, Margaret.' It sounded sincere.

She returned with her customary rejoinder. 'I mean, how are you *really*?'

I shot her what I hoped was a bright open smile. 'Really, I'm fine. We're both fine.'

It seemed to work. 'I can't believe how big Alfie's got.' She clasped her hands under her knee and rocked to the music. 'It seems absurd that he's going to start school in September.'

I agreed: he seemed to have just suddenly grown up.

'Another milestone,' she said, and looked at me. I smiled but we were both thinking 'Without Josh'.

God I missed him. I let myself have a micro-second of panic then shut it down.

Above us the tree swayed and a dazzling shard of sunlight caught Margaret in the eyes. Her pale-blue eyes glittered with energy and compassion. 'It'll be all right,' she said, her voice suddenly rich and low. And for a moment I could have sworn it was Josh.

The girl finished singing and Margaret swivelled her eyes to the stage. 'Beautiful voice,' she said, her voice modulating back into her light jaunty pitch.

We both applauded loudly.

I was proud of the way the park looked. The trees were full of ripe green leaves, criss-crossed with bunting. Handfuls

127

of craft stalls were dotted towards the playground. Between us and the stage the lawns were strewn with picnic blankets and festival chairs, populated by a very broad range of people: semi-clad crusties sporting long, dark dreadlocks and cans of lager sat alongside old ladies in sun hats.

'Sarah!' A voice rang out across the lawn. Sharon waved furiously and beckoned me over to her uproarious group who were sitting about fifteen feet away. It was great to see her though the last thing I could do was desert the in-laws. I called out a greeting, jerked my head at Margaret and mouthed 'No, you come here.'

You could tell from the sluggish reaction that she'd had a few beers. The way she stumbled over bodies to reach us and the pewter tankard in her hand was totally at odds with the smart white jeans and tasselled designer top she had on.

'What's with the folksy drinking equipment?' I nodded at her tankard.

She giggled. 'When in Rome . . .' and burped. 'Ooops, sorry,' she said, looking in my mother-in-law's direction.

I introduced Margaret as Alfie's Grandma. Sharon had met my mum before so I hoped she'd infer the relationship without me having to go into details. That always put a real downer on things. She did and immediately sat down beside Margaret and bombarded her with a barrage of questions about where she lived, what she did and what she thought of Leigh, which continued long after Keith and Alfie had returned.

Whatever people said about Sharon, and she did have a few detractors, you had to admit the girl was damn gregarious. Blessed with a directness of speech that some found confrontational, her good friends appreciated her honesty, which was like a breath of fresh air. You always knew where you were with Sharon and usually it was a very fun place to be. Sure, she drank a lot and smoked too much but there was an infectious mischief beyond her eyes that reached out to people. Her long reddish hair always looked like it hadn't been brushed for a week but in a sexy way that most could never achieve.

Martha, Corinne and I could never understand why she hadn't been netted by some besotted broker. The girl was a charmer and sure enough, after a quarter of an hour Keith had taken his eyes off his grandson long enough to linger slyly on Sharon's grin. He even cracked a few jokes, which had her slapping the blanket with glee, a gesture that in turn tickled Alfie. And Alfie was like Bagpuss: when he laughed, everyone laughed along too.

When she made to return to her own blanket, we felt a little deflated. 'But,' she said, as she got to her feet unsteadily, 'we're going to the Sarah Grey for a couple of beers after this, if you fancy it? It's child-friendly till 6 p.m.'

My in-laws weren't pub people so I quickly declined, but Margaret interrupted: 'Go for a bit, Sarah. Keith and I can take Alfie back. Please. It'd do you good to spend a bit of time with your friends.'

I wasn't sure where that had come from but I wasn't about to look a gift horse in the mouth. 'Really? You don't mind?'

Margaret nodded.

I turned to my son. His cheeks were plastered with dried ice cream. 'What do you think, Alfie? Will you be all right if Grandma Margaret and Granddad put you to bed?' He ignored me, too absorbed in motoring a toy car over Margaret's shoulder and up her hair.

I shrugged and looked to Keith. He nodded and smiled up at Sharon. 'Now, you look after her, young lady. I've got the measure of you.'

The cheeky minx sent him a wink and gave Margaret the thumbs up.

'What an extraordinary young woman,' remarked Keith, as we watched her stagger back.

'Delightful,' Margaret concurred. 'Now run along, Sarah. Go and have a bit of fun.'

The festival mood extended to the pub where Sharon introduced me to her friends. They were friendly albeit slurring. I'd met one or two of them before: Jim, who commuted up to town with Sharon in the mornings. Rob propped up Leigh bars most evenings and knew everyone; a couple, Clare and Phil, were the drunkest of the lot.

Sharon was a great host: throwing out conversational inroads for subjects about which she knew I'd have an opinion, asking my advice, pointing out things I had in common with her friends. I'd taken a liking to her as soon I'd met her at Martha's barbecue two years ago. She turned up late with a very young and frightened-looking posh guy from Surrey, who only lasted a couple of months. The party was dwindling and running dry, much to Sharon's alarm, who whipped out her phone and in a fit of what I was to learn was her customary generosity, ordered a crate of champagne from a local off-licence with whom she had a long-standing arrangement.

Needless to say when it arrived the remains of the crowd were injected with fizz and energy. We ended up putting the kids to sleep in Martha's boys' bedrooms and dancing into the small hours.

At some point I found myself sitting between Martha and Sharon, hovering between awe and trepidation, an emotional cocktail that left me tongue-tied and self-conscious. Martha introduced us, and Sharon, remarking that she'd heard a lot about me, threw her arms around me and gave me a kiss and a bear hug. I suspected that Martha had informed her of the circumstances of my arrival in Leigh and later I was to learn that Sharon, who had lost her mother when she was fifteen, was especially empathetic when it came to bereavement. But at that moment, what with the champers and the warmth of the greeting, I fell in love with the girl. She had this incredible ability to make everyone believe they were the centre of her world for as long as she was with them. There are not many people I can say that about.

Even that night, in the Sarah Grey, as we sat within the throng of drinkers we all felt privileged to be in her circle, you could tell. She didn't hold court, just your attention, whenever Rob, Jim, Clare or Phil told a story their eyes would rest on Sharon longest, seeking out her laughter, approval and entertaining ripostes.

When it was my turn to get a round in I took the opportunity to ask the barman if he knew anything about the woman after whom the pub was named. He replied that she'd been a sea-witch and cursed sailors but said he didn't have any more information. However he did promise to ask his boss. I hung around the bar but his boss told me he had nothing else to add. Although he did suggest I visit the Leigh Heritage Centre down in the Old Town, where, he had it on good authority, there was lots of information about 'history and stuff'. I thanked him and returned to the table.

Sharon practically leapt on me. 'What was that all about? Credit card declined?'

I squeezed in beside her. 'I'm not that skint. Yet.'

'If you ever need some, just let me know.'

I thanked her and said that wasn't necessary but that I was trying to find out about Sarah Grey. That the story had sparked my interest.

'Oh,' she said. 'The witch. Why? I thought Grey was your married name?'

It hadn't occurred to me that I might need an answer as to why I was making enquiries. 'Just interested,' I said, though this sounded flimsy. It seemed to do the trick though; Sharon was too smashed to query anything right now. 'But I'm not making much headway. I don't even know when she lived.'

Sharon agreed. 'Yes, that's difficult. Parish records are your best bet. But you'll need a rough idea of when. Even if you find a christening date that won't necessarily help you to pin-point her age. People used to save up for years to pay the church's fee and they weren't that bothered about recording births. Most used to estimate and few people could read. They didn't keep track of time like we do.'

My eyebrows soared into my forehead. 'How come you're suddenly the world's authority on this?'

She necked the rest of her pint and exchanged her empty for the one I'd just bought. 'Family tree. My granddad started looking into it. When he died, my mum asked me to carry it on. I wasn't bothered at first but it's got really interesting.'

The warmth of the wine made me wrinkle my nose in disgust. 'Found any famous ancestors then?'

Sharon pulled a face and crossed her legs. 'Common as

muck. Tillers, farmers and a couple of tradesmen. Nothing glamorous. But I'm still working on it. You never know – might stumble across a long-lost rich aunt. What have you got to go on?'

I recounted my limited research online and at the bar. She nodded and took another slurp of beer. 'I reckon he's right. The Heritage Centre would be a good place. Tell you what – get me a rough date and I'll see what I can dig up.'

It was a kind offer but I didn't want to put her out.

'Sod off,' she said, cheerfully, and told me she had unlimited access to ancestry.co.uk and was happy to get online and have a scout. 'It'll be no trouble at all,' she told me. 'Might even keep me out of the pub for a bit. Talking of which, Rob's out and it's my round. Fancy another?'

The alcohol was thrumming in my blood so I stayed for another and another.

Around ten o'clock, when we were very sloshed, Sharon started getting weepy. I was talking to Rob at the time so couldn't really work out what had happened. A few minutes later Corinne appeared and took her home. After that I finished up my drink and left.

When I got home the lights were out. Margaret and Keith had my bed for the night so I threw myself on the sofa and covered myself in a sheet.

I've always wondered what would have happened if Sharon hadn't spotted me or if the in-laws hadn't warmed to her so, or if we'd never had that conversation.

Maybe I wouldn't have killed her, as I did.

Chapter Eleven

The Old Town was packed. Sunday was the less traditional day of the festival. Bands varied in style from your generic folk to indie and rock as well. Stages had been erected at the seafront pubs, the Peter Boat, the Crooked Billet, outside the Smack and in a car park that had once been the old foundry. The tiny streets thronged with thousands of out-of-towners rubbing shoulders with locals and a great number of shaven-headed bare-chested Southenders who had come over for the day.

Alfie kicked off his sandals as soon as we got there, expecting to head for the beach, then chucked a wobbler when Margaret told him we were going to look at the bands. Music, apparently, was stupid and nothing could pacify him for the good five minutes it took Keith to queue for an ice cream. This, as per usual, did the trick but we knew it wouldn't last long and that our time at the festival was limited. He was mildly distracted by the parade, which waltzed down the cobbled main street. Men playing bagpipes headed it up, followed by several groups of morris dancers: some wore traditional outfits of black, white and red, others were black-faced and gothic. A kind of new neo-morris.

Keith blew a wolf-whistle as a troupe of antique belly dancers wobbled by and was silenced by a blistering look from Margaret. Alfie got scared by a mummer dressed in black, wearing a bird-shaped headdress and carrying a cane with a skull on the top. But he liked the man dressed as a baby girl and giggled for ages after she/he danced by.

Once the Spanish dancers had brought up the rear, we crossed over the cobbles and walked in the shade, past the expensive modern restaurant to the Peter Boat pub. I pointed out the Heritage Centre on the way and mentioned I'd like to pop in later. No one objected so I took it that we'd go there on our way back.

The Peter Boat was teeming. Unable to find a bench we perched ourselves on the sea wall and watched Alfie run up and down the pavement while Keith queued up again, this time for drinks. While he did I made a quick phone call to Corinne. I wanted to check on Sharon. I was used to seeing her over-confident and loud, not fragile like last night.

She was, according to her best friend, fine. 'She usually gets like that at this time of year. It's coming up to a couple of anniversaries, one of which is her mum's death.'

'Oh,' I said. The hangover had dulled my diplomatic tendencies. 'Was it sudden then? Sorry. That doesn't sound very sensitive, it's just that if it's still upsetting her . . . it was a while ago wasn't it?'

Corinne sighed. 'Well yeah. About twenty odd years. It's all quite mixed up in my head. There was a lot of other stuff going on at the time. Sharon went a bit off the rails and started making accusations against Doctor Cook.'

'Doctor Cook? Why?'

'Oh, well,' she sounded uneasy. 'At the inquest, it was

revealed that Cook's notes indicated Cheryl, Sharon's mum, had developed a terminal condition and not told anyone about it. Sharon took it very badly. But obviously Cook couldn't tell the family. Not if Cheryl didn't want to herself. Doctor–patient confidentiality. Sharon reckoned there was more to it than that, but she was in denial. Even Brian, her dad, could see it was an open and shut case, as tragic and unfair as it was. But Sharon, well, you know how it is when something like that happens. People want a reason. Someone to blame. And like I said, she'd started drinking and staying out. Her dad thought she was experimenting with drugs.'

'Oh, I see. What was the other stuff that was going on?'

Corinne let out a mirthless laugh. 'Isn't that bad enough, Sarah?'

'Sorry,' I said. 'You said there was other stuff going on at the time.'

Corinne paused for a second then said, 'Things were going on in their circle of friends. But that's another conversation. Look, I've got to dash. We're off to the Old Town for the festival.'

'We're here. It's packed.'

She ruminated for a minute then said she might catch us later. I let her go, feeling rather heavy and sad. Poor Sharon.

Keith emerged from the bar after twenty minutes extremely flustered.

'It's bloody packed in there.' It was unusual for him to swear so I got the message – we weren't staying for another. He undid his top button and flapped his arms. After last

136

night I couldn't face alcohol so when Margaret suggested we move on to the Crooked Billet I hopped off the wall and took the lead.

Out on the estuary a couple of jet-skiers showed off, trying to out-do the displays from the glorious thirty-foot yachts that sailed the high tide. The fishermen's cottages that backed onto the pavement gleamed in the mid-afternoon sun and reflected the heat back onto the growing horde of festival-goers.

We wove our way down the lane. Someone called my name. It was Ronnie, my grocer, as famous for his chirpy banter and eye for the ladies as he was for his generosity. I stopped for a few minutes but didn't bother introducing Margaret and Keith. As we talked Ronnie ruffled Alfie's hair. He squirmed away so I said goodbye and ran to catch up with him.

When we reached the Crooked Billet Margaret asked me how I knew Ronnie. I explained and caught her glance at Keith. She said nothing, though her expression spoke volumes – 'Won't be long now before she's off with another one'.

How could they make such sweeping judgements? 'He's just the bloody grocer!' I repeated, with perhaps unnecessary sharpness.

Last night I had dreamt of Josh. It was one of those frustrating chase dreams: I searched for him in roads and alleys and the offices of Stealth Records with no joy. I went up to the castle and was about to give up when I turned around and realized he'd been following me all the time.

I was so happy to see him. I said, 'They told me you were dead. I knew you'd come back.'

137

'Don't be silly,' he said. 'I've been here all the time.' He smiled and took my hands in his. I glanced down at them and saw our wedding bands glow. When I looked up at him again, his skin had darkened and his hair had turned white. It was not Josh at all. It was another man. But I was safe. He said, 'I never meant to leave you.'

I said, 'But you did.'

And he said he was sorry and then he was Josh again. I stepped towards him and pulled down his face. Then we kissed.

When I woke up the sweet aftertaste of happiness lingered on my lips for a split second, before the customary dread of reality kicked in. Then, in a rare moment of self-pity, I cried till my nose was wet.

The thought had crossed my mind that my visions of the other Sarah might be a delayed reaction to everything that happened back then. After all, it had been so sudden – one minute Josh was there, the next gone. Vanished. It was so difficult to accept that not only would he not be coming back, but that he had ceased to exist. In fact I was never sure that I had.

Cue Sarah Grey.

If anything, she was proof of an afterlife of sorts, wasn't she? And didn't I want Josh to be there too? It was somewhere for him to exist outside of my memory, which was human and flawed and could fade. There is so much pressure to keep the memory alive.

Sarah had the same name as me. She was of a similar height and build, and during the storm, when I had seen her quite clearly for the first time, I put her age about ten years younger than mine.

Perhaps she *was* a younger me? A creation of my dreams?

But why would I do that? If indeed I was creating her, as Marie suggested. Grey was allegedly a sea-witch. Think witch, think bent old crone. The woman pushing herself through to my world was none of those.

In fact, get beyond the pale skin and seaweed-like coils of hair, oh yeah, and the deadness, and there was something almost beautiful in the curve of her face, the intensity of her eyes.

If I was doing this to myself what message was my subconscious trying to send?

I had no answer.

But then I didn't really think this was being generated by me.

Not any more.

The night Martha came round her words sounded empty. Superficial almost. Rather than allay my fears of ghosts and hauntings and things that were going bump, dropping pine cones and phoning me in the night, the simplicity of her rational explanation moved me to resist her and dig in my heels: No way was the thing happening here solely down to stress. Her theory was too reductive.

Plus Marie had seen Sarah too.

Marie the 'nutter' was how John had described his sister.

Then the night of the storm, I *saw* her. She had spoken to me and I had *heard* her.

Or perhaps I was simply going mad, losing my mind? And didn't the insane utterly believe in their delusions?

There was really only one way to find out and that was to dig deeper into the life and death of Sarah Grey.

And attend the neurologist's appointment.

But first things first: the Heritage Centre.

It was a discreet building, painted dark green and situated on the south side of the High Street. To be honest, if you didn't know it was there you would probably walk past it. Displayed in one of its windows stood a model of a Thames barge, the only thing that encouraged Alfie to step across the threshold. I had expected more of museum but it was essentially an information centre with books and postcards for sale. There were a couple of local history books, pricey hardbacks. The woman at the counter was pleased to help me and produced a slim paperback. There was lots of local information within its pages so I paid for it and asked her if she knew anything about the sea-witch.

'No. That's funny. I had another enquiry about her the other day.' She straightened the neckline of her lace blouse and shot me a furtive look from under thick rimmed glasses. 'No one seems to know much about her. There is a pub named after her. One of the Leigh Society was trying to do some research but didn't get anywhere. We suspect she may be a myth, an amalgam of several local legends.'

'Oh, really?' The disappointment was overwhelming. I tried not to show it and bit my lip hard. Inside I felt no small measure of loss.

It was quite astonishing that she had come to mean so much to me in such a short space of time. My acute reaction to this piece of news revealed that I had built some kind of emotional connection with her, though until that point it had lain in my subconscious.

But if Sarah Grey didn't exist, I had to wonder who was haunting me and why?

The woman was looking at me expectantly.

'That's a shame. I was trying to do some research too.'

She smiled in recognition of my interest. 'Well, Sarah Grey is a mystery.'

Margaret bounded up beside me having listened in to the tail end of our conversation. 'We're Greys too,' she told the cashier, brightly. The latter pushed her spectacles up her nose to inspect my mother-in-law, and extended her hand in greeting. 'Sheila. It's a pleasure. It's the name that intrigues you is it? Though it's very common.' Then, without waiting for an answer, she grabbed a small brown paper bag and started to write something down on it. 'There is one place you could look,' she told us. 'The local library.' She scribbled down the name of an author. 'Stephen Brightling. He collected local legends. Not completely accurate, you understand. He's more of an oral historian. Lots of self-published books. Try him. You may find something useful.'

As we left Margaret touched my arm. Her eyes were more animated than they'd been all weekend. 'I don't think there's a link but it's jolly sweet of you. Josh would be so pleased to know you're still taking an interest in the family.'

I gathered Alfie into my arms and blew a raspberry on his tummy, hoping his little body would obscure my flaming cheeks. It wasn't the first time I'd felt like a charlatan, though it was the first time I felt I'd used Josh.

Chapter Twelve

The holidays stretched before me like a lazy cat. Although we had enjoyed our time with them, Margaret and Keith's visit had not been without its tensions and when they left a palpable relief overcame me.

I had got the dates wrong about my leave and discovered I had paid for an additional week's nursery for Alfie. This would have been a good time to carry on with my research into Sarah Grey but instead I threw myself into intensive cleaning rituals: scrubbing the windows and throwing them wide open to give the house a thorough airing and bring in the sunshine. The decking received a sweep and a bleach, the carpets got a shampoo. I washed down all the bed frames. The washing machine barely stopped for the first few days. By mid-week the weather had turned bad and along with the heavy rain brought a feeling of claustrophobia.

Alfie was in a bad mood when I picked him up from nursery on the Wednesday. They had been meaning to go for a walk down to the seaside but the rain had forced them to cancel. As a result all the kids who could actually talk were complaining like a bunch of teachers.

He took a long time to settle that night. But when he did, he turned to the wall and went off quickly.

I took my book to bed and read by lamplight.

It must have been about two when I first heard him moaning lightly. I had fallen asleep with the light on and my book across my lap. Alert to his cries I sat up and leant slightly to the open door, listening out – hoping that he might go back to sleep. He often did. For two minutes I heard only the quiet creak of the house and the slam of a car door somewhere up the road. Then suddenly, splitting the silence like the crash of a cymbal, Alfie's voice rose into a terrible scream. 'No. No. Get him off.'

I jumped up in bed at once, threw off the bedclothes, and burst into his room. It was a small box room with only one window. I'd left it open as I was putting him down and for some reason had forgotten to close it.

In the pale blue glow of the nightlight I could see him standing on the bed thrashing his arms wildly in front of him, his back dangerously edging towards the open window.

I wanted to gasp but I knew I shouldn't – in case he was sleepwalking. It was hard to tell: his lips were contorted, his hair plastered down on his head, eyes wide open. But though he struck out, as if hitting something or someone just in front of him, there was nothing there.

'Alfie, sweetheart. Sit down.' I kept my voice even.

There was no way of telling if he had registered my presence. 'Alfie.' He paused for a moment, then took a small step backwards and I leapt, catching his wrists in one hand, pulling him to me. With the other hand I slammed the window shut.

Alfie screamed and pushed me away. 'Too much blood, Mummy.'

I picked him up in my arms and carried him into the centre of the room. 'It's OK, darling. You've had a bad dream.'

He sobbed and buried his head in my chest. 'But he cut her.'

'Shh.' I stroked his hair back off his forehead. 'Don't upset yourself, Alfie. It's just a nightmare, honey.' He was burning up so I blew on his skin.

After a couple of minutes of hushing, he seemed to come to and looked at me as if surprised to find himself where he was. He was still crying but soon he sank his head on my shoulder and the sobs became little hics.

'Shh. There you go.' I was jigging him up and down gently in my arms. 'It was just a nightmare.'

I carried him back to the bed and plopped him on the mattress.

He lay down, calmer now, and looked up to me. 'There was a bad man. He did a bad thing to the burning girl's friend.'

It was like a blow to the stomach. I felt winded but kept my voice as steady as possible. 'Oh Alfie, not the burning girl again? I don't want you to think about her any more. That's what gives you these nightmares.'

He frowned and squirmed, pulling down hard on his Superman pyjamas. 'Ouch.'

I pulled the sheet up over his short twisting body and tucked it in at his shoulders.

'Ouch. Stop!' He was really wriggling now.

As I leant over to kiss him on the forehead, my chin

brushed against something hard. I jerked back. He had pulled something sharp from underneath the bedclothes.

'I said "Ouch"; he muttered, and waved it in his hand. 'Take it away.' He held it out for me.

For a terrible moment before I saw it I knew what would be there. Things had been quiet lately. Far too quiet. Though I hadn't thought Sarah was targeting Alfie instead.

But there it was, in his hand, its leaves poking out from the central spine, half of them broken and stuck out at odd angles.

A short, stubby pine cone.

When my voice finally found itself it was tremulous and low. 'Where did you get that?'

Alfie was seemingly calm now, his nightmare forgotten, the irritating object removed. He rubbed his eyes and yawned. 'From the burning girl's friend, Sarah. They are friends now. It wasn't her fault. She knows now. After she died.'

I tried to keep my face clear of the terrible feeling creeping over me. 'Sarah gave this to you?'

He didn't speak but pulled the sheet up to his chin and nodded gradually, starting to get sleepy and bored now. 'Yes,' it came out with mild disdain. 'She said you don't listen to her, so she has to tell me.' He yawned and turned to the wall again, his back to me. It was a gesture of dismissal.

I sat there for a few minutes. My head ached and I was sweating. Then I gently kissed him goodnight.

Without thinking about what I was doing, I strode downstairs and threw back the French doors. 'Listen, Sarah. Listen to me. You do not go to my son again, do you hear me?' I tried to keep my volume to a whisper but I was shaking with fear and anger and potent maternal outrage.

In the garden the air was tense and alert.

'I will do what you want but you leave him alone. You hear me? Or you get nothing. Do you hear?'

A bat swooped down low over the flower-boat and arced off into the night.

There was no answer. I stepped inside the doors and closed them, double-locking them to be sure. Then I turned into the house and leant against the windows. The whole thing collapsed on me like a hundredweight.

I don't know how long I spent down there on the floorboards but at some early hour, when the sky had started turning grey, I got up and went into the living room. I was on autopilot, not conscious of my movements, until I found myself at the sideboard opening the bottom drawer where I kept my favourite photo. Our wedding day, outside Finsbury Registry Office. It was a snapshot taken by my mum. I had my head turned to Josh, lips puckered up, squashed against his cheek, short white veil at ninety degrees to my head. Confetti showers had been captured by the lens so it looked like we were caught in a pastel-coloured snow storm. My husband faced the camera, looking for all the world like he couldn't believe his luck. His mouth stretched into a proper cartoon smile – a capital D on its side – curved and wide. His eyes were crinkled with laughter yet open wide and sparkling. You could just see his grey topcoat and the rim of his white collar, absurdly smart. But his hair was a mess, as always: rusty gold spokes that no amount of gel could induce to slick down.

The camera had captured his essence. And the total unswerving adoration I felt on that day.

'Josh,' I whispered, my face wet with tears. 'Come back. I need you. I can't do this on my own.'

I took the photograph and lay on the sofa, curling my body round the frame.

Somewhere in my head I heard a voice saying softly, 'You can. You know you can.'

Alfie found me there at seven o'clock, still holding on to the picture frame. As I surfaced into consciousness I realized he was forcing my eyes open. Even though the lounge was light, I jumped up, worried that he'd had another bad dream.

'Alfie, how are you?'

I need not have worried. 'Fine,' he said. 'Hungry.'

I thought about letting him stay off nursery but he insisted he should go in case they went to the seaside, so in the end I dropped him off with extra kisses and a promise from the nursery manager that she'd phone me if he started to look peaky or behave strangely. Then I raced back home and got straight onto Skype.

Marie didn't answer straight away. After a few minutes an instant message popped up on the screen: 'Just on a call. Can I call you in the morning?'

It would have been about 12.30 at night but I needed her now.

I responded in caps: 'NO. NEED TO TALK NOW. PLEASE. URGENT.'

There was a four-minute pause then I got: 'OK. Give me 5.' I made a strong mug of coffee and settled back in front of the screen.

When she came on she looked a bit peeved. I didn't care.

Her hair was falling about her face and she looked flushed. There was a half-filled wine glass by the side of her desk. Perhaps I'd caught her entertaining? 'Chick, how you doing?' I could see she was forcing a smile.

My words came thick and fast. 'Not good. She's coming to Alfie, Marie . . .' I told her what had happened in the night.

To give her some credit, she did understand the urgency immediately. There was a noticeable change in her demeanour when I mentioned the cone in his bed. Not alarm but her eyebrows went up and I saw her top teeth creep out to bite her lip.

'Why Alfie? Why's she targeting my son?' I slammed my fist onto the table, without even realizing it until I heard the thud. 'And who's the burning girl?'

'I don't know. She might not be connected at all. It does happen sometimes. A kind of sub-haunting. Don't get too het up about Alfie's visions. After all, if you think he's not that bothered by it, that's great. You'd know if he was, right?' She'd moved closer to the screen now and was giving it her full attention. 'That's the thing with kids. You must have heard all the tales about children seeing things that adults don't?'

I shook my head. 'Why would I have heard that?'

'OK, calm down, Sarah. I'm here. I'm with you. I understand that this must be upsetting for you. It's taken you out of your comfort zone . . .'

My noisy exhalation forced the screen to pixellate. It echoed from Leigh to California then back again. 'My fucking comfort zone! Are you joking? I'm shit scared, Marie. This is my son. My son. I'm a single parent. I'm responsible for this. I can't do this. I can't . . .' And before I could stop, tears had welled up in my eyes. I put my hands over my face to cover them and stopped speaking, concentrating on pacing my heavy breathing. All of last night's emotions came flooding back.

Marie said nothing. When I peeled my fingers away from my face and heaved a big enough sigh to slow up the fitful breaths, she was full of sympathy. 'If I were there with you, I'd give you a hug,' she said simply.

I wiped my nose, swallowed and apologized.

'The thing with children,' she said, modulating her voice, speaking softly now, 'is that they *want* to believe. They love magic and fairy tales and Santa. And they don't see anything funny about visions like these. They're just learning about the world and these things are part of it. They haven't been told that they don't exist. They've only been told that they do: in books, films, cartoons. It's as natural for them to talk to an entity as it is for you to talk to,' she looked around her room for inspiration, 'a milkman, or someone you meet in the park or me. *They* haven't been told otherwise. Alfie's what, five?'

I sniffed and corrected her. 'Four.'

She nodded. 'OK he's four. That's even more pertinent. He's not even in the school system yet, right?' She looked up hesitantly, as if worried I might blow up again.

My anger subsided. She was the wrong target. 'Yes. You're quite right. I'm starting to get it. But, I went outside and shouted at her. I told her to leave him alone. That I'd do it, that I'd help her.'

'OK, OK,' Marie nodded. 'That's good. You're speaking to her. That's what she wants. Be strong now. Carry on talking

149

to her. Just because you can't see her or hear her doesn't mean she can't hear you.'

The thought made me shudder. I didn't like the idea of some disembodied entity tuning into me. Though better me than my son. 'Listen, Marie, I don't want her coming to Alfie again. I don't care if he can see things. I'll do what she wants. Not him.'

'And you told her this?'

'Yes. I whispered it aloud on the spot where she first appeared.'

'That might do the trick. And you've started the research. How far have you got?'

'I, well, I've been busy.'

Marie's face hardened. 'Listen, Sarah, you want this to stop, you play the game. No wonder she's focused on your son. She might think you're a dead end, so to speak. You're not responding. You've got to let her know that you're helping.'

It was my turn to feel embarrassed now. 'I will. I'll start this afternoon.'

To be fair to her, Marie didn't linger on this. She knew I was frantic. 'There are other things that you can do, too. I've got a book. Hang on.'

She left the screen though I saw her flit across it, presumably going to her bookshelves. She was back in moments.

'Here,' she thumbed through a couple of leaves of a blue hardback book. 'To prevent spirits from entering a dwelling drive iron nails into the corners of the abode.'

'Where do I get them?'

She smiled a little. 'Local hardware store?'

I shrugged, aware of my silly petulance. It wasn't her fault. The phrase evoked a memory from last night: it wasn't

Sarah's fault. That's what Alfie had said about the burning girl. They had made their peace, after Sarah died.

I shivered and muttered involuntarily, 'Christ.'

Marie looked up from the book sharply. 'It's what it says here. Do you want this advice or not?'

I was quick to backtrack. 'Sorry. I was thinking about something that Alfie said. That it wasn't Sarah's fault – the burning girl. They'd made their peace.'

Marie cocked her head to one side. 'That's good. Now listen, I've got another call coming through and I've got to take this. Sorry. You can also sprinkle salt around the perimeter of your house. That'll keep her out. It's an old wives' tale but I know for a fact that works, OK?'

I nodded, and was about to thank her but the connection faltered. Her face lingered for a moment on the screen, then disintegrated.

'Right,' I said to myself. 'Let's get to the DIY shop.'

Suffice it to say that the morning was spent sourcing nails and hammering them into the four corners of the house. The plaster cracked when I banged two of them in, but by then I was well past house-proud. The neighbours must have thought I was a loon scattering three pounds of salt outside the house and up the alley on the south side. I was kind of with them on that one. Mrs Lucas from across the road gave me a 'weirdo' look when I was doing the front garden but I muttered something about slugs and got on my way.

By the afternoon I had screwed myself into a knot of determination and wasted no time in hitting the library.

It was a magnificent gabled construction with a warm atmosphere. High panelled windows let in the light from all sides and offered magnificent views of the park gardens in which it stood. But it smelt like most public buildings: of musty carpets, dust and the faint aroma of urine.

The local history section was located between Parenting and information on Southend Council and was similarly uninspiring. I browsed through a couple of the hardbacks that I had glimpsed at the Heritage Centre and took time to speed-read a few.

Some were very dated, the language reminding me of childhood day trips – pointing out places of interest using words that seemed so old-fashioned: 'pleasure grounds', 'boating pool', 'paupers'. A couple of heavily pictorial tomes piqued my interest. I took them to the reading table and laid them out beside an old emphysemic man who was scanning the *Telegraph* page by page.

Mostly taken over the previous two centuries, the photographs and illustrations built a vivid picture of Leigh-on-Sea before progress came steaming along the train line in 1852: a pretty town with a main market square (later demolished for the railway) bordered by inns, shops and lopsided cottages. I recognized the Old Custom House, which still stood in the High Street and was now privately owned. A lot of the more picturesque buildings had been destroyed in the fifties. According to local tradition one particularly quaint shop, Juniper's, was where John Constable stayed when he painted Hadleigh Castle. I squirmed as I read it had made way for a car park.

Another text from the nineteenth century noted, with a prudery that brought a smile to my lips, that the place was notorious for 'its drunkenness and the coarseness of its fishermen' until its rehabilitation was overseen by Olivia

Sparrow, the Lady of the Manor, and the Reverend Robert Eden in the early to mid-1800s. Though the two had fallen out, for reasons not mentioned in any book, they were credited with rescuing Leigh from the 'degradation' into which it had fallen.

A large weather-boarded house on Strand Wharf, owned by a Richard Chester, dated back to the Tudor period. This was demolished after the Second World War.

The old King's Head was less interesting architecturally but a fascinating entry caught my eye: it had been the meeting place for a society called the Druids. Far from sinister in his description, the author of the book alleged that members attended the meetings, which were loud and very merry, in full regalia. He lamented the fact that the books, banners, staves and insignia were destroyed in a fire at the Peter Boat in 1892. Evidently popular, in 1850 the Druids had over 150 members. I paused to marvel at the commonplace acceptance of druids in this small waterfront town. It sounded rather dodgy, although the impression the author gave was of some sort of social club.

I skimmed through the remaining pages, and finding nothing more of interest, I returned the book to its shelf and browsed through the remaining volumes until I came to a thin paperback that had slipped down the back. It was one of the titles recommended by the lady at the Heritage Centre. On the back cover there was a photograph of the author: a benevolent-looking man of senior years, dressed in a boating blazer.

As I opened it my skin began to prickle. There were several legends of highwaymen and murderers, skeletons and skulls then, just about halfway through, I came to a chapter entitled 'The Sea-witch'.

Bingo.

It was all about Sarah.

She was, so the book described her, 'a toothless and crooked shrew with an ugly, wrinkled old face. This shrivelled witch was reputed to brew up satanic concoctions that would poison enemies or bring bad luck on those who touched them. Her manner and breath was foul and her fiendish looks were known to strike terror into the sturdiest of fishermen.

'Rumoured to have been descended from Romany people, Mother Grey was able to see into the future. She would do this by dripping sand into a silver cauldron and scrying, or reading, the shapes that it formed within.

'She was also said to live with an enormously fat cat called Harpinker who would eat whole birds, and was often spied fishing at the side of the wharf for his dinner. Many folk alleged that Harpinker was a demon who directed Mother Grey in her spells. For often he would be seen in the window as she went about her satanic business, brewing up her devilish cures which, despite their unholy origin, folk came from miles to buy.'

Brightling described her death just as Corinne had those few weeks back. The captain and his crew of *The Smack* sailed back to shore to find Mother Grey dead on the wharf, covered in blood, with three gashes in her head.

The bias in authorial interpretation was evident in the two tragic stories he chose to represent the evil witch. A cholera epidemic of 1849 was referred to. I noted the date. During this outbreak, two of Sarah's sons fell prey to the virulent disease and died within four days of each other. Poor woman, I thought. But Brightling seemed to relish the tragedy.

'Almost a year to the day of her last son's death, the Old Town was gripped by yet another outbreak of the pestilent disease. Old Grey took to the gin, some say to alleviate her grief. Others maintain the witch was scheming, devising a plan that would wreak vengeance on the unsuspecting town. When she had at last come to her senses, she returned to her cave-like shack, where she prayed to the Devil and, under Harpinker's watchful eye, cooked up an appalling potion. This she left on the steps of the cottages of families whose children and babies were afflicted. Of these families who took down the medicine, no babies survived. The sea-witch had poisoned them! Mother Grey would not have young children live while her sons lay rotting in the graveyard.'

Such casual infanticide was not worthy of more comment it seemed. The next story, however, was nastier. I could almost see Brightling licking his lips with glee.

'The Devil also bestowed on grim Grey the power to kindle sparks in her eyes and flash streams of fire from them. On one occasion, some townsfolk testified, Grey was actually able to kill people with her fireball spell. The parish registers substantiate this as does the honest testimony of one of her potential victims, Emily Langdon, who survived the wrath of Grey's evil eye.

'As the story goes, there were three children: Emily Langdon, Thomas and Jane Tulley, playing happily in inno-cence by Strand Wharf, where they lived. They watched Grey leave her cottage one gusty afternoon. The children were curious souls, as little children are, and spied the door of Grey's shack banging to and fro in the fierce south-easterly gale. Despite her careful trickery in all other things, the witch had not locked her own door.

'The children said they saw an unearthly red light coming out of her small, squalid cottage. The little ones ran over to it. Inside it was black and miserable. The children looked around: on the farthest wall a shelf was fixed. On this stood an oil lamp and a dozen strange bottles, with a foul smell oozing from them. The stench of damnation no less. As the witch liked to keep the place in darkness, one of the children lit a candle from the hearth fire, intent on examining the fiendish brews. They lifted the candle up to the shelf but just as they did they heard old Grey's footsteps coming up the passage.

'Realizing they were about to be caught the children rushed to the furthest corner and banged into the partition wall where the bottles were balanced. A couple of the potions fell over. The disgusting contents dripped down, covering the eldest girl, Jane. In her panic, as she clutched for her friend, seven-year-old Emily knocked over the candle.

'The door flew open with a howl and the sea-witch entered the room. Sparks flashed from her eerie green eyes and Jane burst at once into flames. The children shrieked and ran out the door. Grey snatched an old canvas sack from the wall and chased after them, trying to catch the burning girl in her witch's bag, but they had run down the alley to the creek.

'Alerted by the screams, the children's parents and neighbours came from their houses to see what was going on. The sight that greeted them was forged into their hearts for ever more. The eldest girl was covered in a cloak of flames, as Grey attacked her with an old sack. But the scene would not last long – there was a strong wind that day, which whipped the flames up, transforming the girl into her own terrible funeral pyre. And slowly her screams faded into silence.

'Although Emily maintained it was the witch who had done it, Thomas, who was eight years old, suggested that the liquid must have been paraffin, which had ignited on contact with the fallen candle flame. But no one listened to him. The people had seen it for themselves. In fury they turned to look for the witch but she had vanished in a cloud of smoke.'

I was cold now, my stomach churning as I recalled Alfie's reference to the girl on fire. The horror of it. Could that possibly be what he'd seen? Poor Alfie.

Next, my own dream came flooding back. The one in the Old Town. The burning girl. The acrid stench of smoking flesh. Could I have dreamt the scene described in the book so vividly that night? Had Sarah Grey and Jane Tulley connected telepathically with me and my child?

I had never read this before. I couldn't have made it up as accurately.

Though perhaps I had overheard the story somewhere and absorbed it, storing it subconsciously until Alfie's words triggered a response.

Nothing was certain but that the tale was appalling. I sighed and released from within a wave of pity for the child burnt and the woman blamed.

And then behind that I felt anger rising. Sarah had tried to put the flames out. Of course the children were terrified and saw it as the wicked act of a witch or a child-catcher. But surely not the adults around them?

Whenever there is horrendous suffering, I reminded myself, someone must always be found to blame. It's the only way humanity can make some sense of the chaos in which we exist.

If Sarah had a reputation as a witch by then, it would have been confirmed in the eyes of those who witnessed the dreadful scene.

Hideous. My heart grew heavy with grief for the parents robbed of their daughter so cruelly. I couldn't begin to imagine what they had gone through – the devastation, the helplessness, then the guilt and the rage. Would they have been angry enough to exact revenge on Grey? To take an old life for one so young?

The incident took place in 1852. After the cholera epidemic of 1849 and the 'poisoning' of 1850, the death of Jane Tulley would have confirmed Sarah's murderous malevolence.

You see, although I didn't realize it, I was assembling the fragments and dreams into a narrative of her life. The vision that night of the storm had left me in no doubt that some great misfortune had befallen Sarah.

In the room that was now part of Doctor Cook's surgery, I had watched as she was traded like an old pair of boots. Then on the beach I had become her as she fled from that terrible man and headed for the only thing that could help her escape her fate – the dismal embrace of the Drowning Pool.

But it had rejected her, so she had been branded a witch by those ignorant onlookers.

Perhaps that had been enough to start the gossip mill turning.

Whatever, Leigh had its new victim – every ship that went down, every child that died, each crop that failed, could have been, *would* have been, blamed on the witch. It had been that way all over England for hundreds and hundreds of years.

With every calamity her reputation would have grown. When Jane Tulley burst into flames, Sarah Grey became the hag of old Leigh: the sea-witch.

Poor Sarah. Her only crime was to have been a herbalist and a soothsayer in an age that respected 'cunning men' as the sanctioned experts in divination and healing. I remembered Corinne recounting the tale of Cunning Murrell. He was a sorcerer, and reportedly an intelligent man. The community treated him with deference as he also led crusades against witches. Whereas Sarah . . .

It was all so very tragic and unjust. I threw the book across the table with disgust. The old man shot me a warning glance. I brought my furious resentment under control. If I was to find what had happened to her, to see beneath the legends to the truth, I needed to think rationally. Like a policeman. I took out my notebook and scribbled 'suspects' in a column. Then I entered the names of the child cholera victims and made a note to find out who their parents were. Underneath I wrote the names of the children involved in the fire: Emily Langdon, Thomas Tulley and his poor sister, Jane Tulley. I jotted down their parents too.

Then there was the captain of legend. Hero or villain, in both versions the killing was laid at his feet. That was beyond dispute but I doubted now that all the myths were true. Brightling had noted that the Great Storm of 1870 was attributed to Grey's curse and invocation. Later, however, he admitted discovering her death registered in the church records in 1867 aged 80, three years before the storm. At least I had a date that I could pass on to Sharon. And I knew now that Sarah Grey had lived and wasn't just a legend.

I sat there for a few long minutes, while my neighbour

coughed and spluttered. I hadn't noticed the rain but now it lashed against the windows. A sharp south-east wind swayed the arms of the trees in the gardens back and forth like they were waving at me.

I gazed out of the window and was soon overcome by a feeling of gloom. Something was out there, waiting to happen. I could feel it throughout my body. Slowly I put the book to one side, intending to take it out, and then turned to the last volume on my pile, another illustrated tome on Leigh.

There was nothing more on Sarah, but flicking through the pages I came to a section on nineteenth-century Leigh characters. Lady Olivia Sparrow was in there. A photograph of a painting depicted a dignified woman sitting on an ornate carved chair, drenched in yards and yards of taffeta or silk, I don't know which, but it was shiny and fashioned into a crinoline, very much of the time. The portrait had been reproduced in black and white but I imagined the fabric to be a royal blue or emerald green. Her cap was so full of lace it could have been mistaken for a fluffy white beard. She looked off dreamily to the right of the artist, her eyes clear and warm, her mouth pursed into a neutral expression that gave nothing away. Her right hand rested on the Bible by her side. She pointed to a particular passage, but there were no clues as to what that could be. Beside her was a three-tiered tray, which contained an assortment of mysterious objects. I couldn't see what they might be as the reproduction was too blurred.

Lady Sparrow was described underneath as a benefactor of Leigh, and a frequent visitor, though not a resident. The benefactor of the spiritual evangelist, Ridley Herschell, a

Polish Jew, who converted to the faith, and with whom she set up a school. Her coat of arms was depicted in another photograph with that of the town's mayor, Doctor Festus Hunter. There was a familiarity about his very large, fussy portrait that I couldn't place. It showed an older man with pinched white lips and small ferret-like eyes. Dressed in fine velvets he was surrounded by the symbols of recently accrued wealth.

Beneath Hunter was a photograph of a bust of the Reverend Robert Eden. He had strong features: a high forehead, and aquiline nose. A man of resolve, he looked with purpose, off to his right. Eden came to Leigh in 1837 and spent much of his private income on establishing a school for local children, refurbishing the church and building a new rectory. The blurb stated he was respected by the people of Leigh. Perceived as a good pastor, he was said to have been influenced by the Tractarian movement, and in the cholera epidemic of 1849 he nursed victims and massaged them with his own hands.

The reverend was succeeded by Canon Walker King, who held the office for many years and as a consequence there were several pictures of him. All showed a middle-aged man with kindly eyes and a two-pronged beard, which I supposed was fashionable at the time. In one picture the family were posed formally outside the rectory, looking stern but as friendly as Victorians ever did. The canon, facing slightly away from the camera, eyes gazing thoughtfully seawards, was surrounded by his large family, four dogs and Bishop Edward King of Lincoln.

From the distinctive eyes and nose he was obviously the canon's brother. I paused to read the key, which identified

161

each member of the family, and was about to turn the page when I started at the rectory window on the right-hand side of the photograph. At first sight it looked like a reflection clouding the window to the right of the group. Though a reflection of what, I wasn't sure. Cloud-like swirls and smudges of something like window cleaner appeared to fill the glass of the bay window behind the family. To my eyes the window was barely bigger than a thumbnail but then I saw something that stilled my heart. For there, in one of the window panes, was Sarah Grey. Two tiny dark patches formed the distinctive almond-shape of her eyes, a diagonal smudge on the glass evoked her strong aquiline nose, dim smears gave the impression of ringlets. There she was, a disembodied face, suspended in the glass, mouth open as if calling out.

It was a small image but it was definitely there.

I must have gasped as the old man across the table glanced up from his paper again and grunted.

I held my hand over my mouth, and breathed heavily.

My brain had frozen, stilled by disbelief, but my eyes raced on, looking back to the page again. I was positive now – I would recognize those doleful eyes anywhere.

What did it mean? What was she trying to say?

As my wits slowly returned, I became aware of a strange sensation: a tiny voice, not quite a whisper, was emanating from the page, pleading softly. As I tuned into the noiseless voice it was as if something touched my soul. A strange lovely melancholy seemed to wrap itself about me and pull me down as though through water into the page. As seductive as it was, I felt sure I shouldn't sink into it and with some effort I shut the book with a loud crack.

The sound shocked me back to reality.

My neighbour raised an eyebrow. Uncomfortable under his gaze, I collected myself and went to the window, uncertain of what had just taken place.

I was standing over the spot the photographer had taken the portrait of the King family. Sarah's window was directly below. Perhaps she was there now? With a message?

I tore down the stairs and rushed into the park. The casement was still there on the south side of the rectory, in what had once been Eden's study.

But I was to be disappointed. I could make out an indefinite reflection of the park vegetation but there was nothing else in the windowpane. The gardens had no doubt changed since the picture was taken, though there was nothing in the grounds now that could have produced such an image in the rectory's glass.

A little deflated, I returned to the reading table and flicked through to the photograph again. The face was still there. In fact, I could perceive another two: two older women in bonnets, with faces too obscured to identify.

What did it mean? Were they souls trapped in the rectory? Other witches?

Or perhaps Sarah was indicating something significant happened here. What, I could not yet know.

I replaced the book on the shelf, unwilling to take it home, and questioned why no one else had commented on the photograph? Books on the supernatural were full of photos far less distinct.

Unsure of what to make of it I noted the name Canon Walker King in my notebook. Perhaps not a suspect, but the man was connected somehow. I could feel it. The picture was a sign.

The after effects of seeing the women in the window had utterly drained me so I decided to call it a day. I'd covered a lot of ground after all. I gathered my belongings together, shoved my mobile and purse in my bag, and headed for the stairs.

I couldn't have been paying any attention to my surroundings because in a matter of seconds I had collided with someone. A wet black leather jacket had me rebounding sharply. 'My fault,' I said, looking up with an apologetic smile, and found Andrew McWhittard standing there on the landing, glowering. I'd knocked his bag from his hands.

'Oh, hello,' it wasn't a very welcoming greeting. For a second I thought he looked angry, but then he said, 'What are you doing here?'

Typical bloody manager. I swooped down and caught his bag strap before he could grab it. Handing it back I went, 'It's my local library.'

'Oh right,' he said. 'Text books?'

I didn't want to go into details so I nodded and said goodbye. Then I went to the desk and booked out the Brightling title.

As I left the building I rubbed my arms until the goose bumps had subsided.

When I got home I read out the summary of my notes.

Then I added, raising my voice to the air, 'I do understand, Sarah. I know you weren't responsible for the girl's death. You were trying to put out the flames. I know that. I can read between the lines.' The words sounded strange, slightly sarcastic.

My body tensed as I waited for a reply.

In the silence that followed my eyes rested on the small stubby cone on my pine table.

I couldn't remember if I had left it there.

Chapter Thirteen

The Records Office was an odd-looking modernist structure set in a car park in the heart of Chelmsford, the county town of Essex. Previous connotations that the town held for me (slightly boring, allegedly posh, and parochial) were now overlaid by the morbid discovery last week that most of Matthew Hopkins' victims had spent their last days in the prison there before being tried at the Assizes and hanged.

It was another one of those tightly coiled mornings; under low heavy clouds the temperature headed for the mid-twenties. We needed a breeze that wouldn't come.

When I got there the weather, which had started quite brightly, had turned grey and sallow.

I had brought with me the full list of items necessary to secure a membership card, which I supplied to the man behind the desk. I was instructed to put my belongings in a locker and only take a pencil and notebook into the main reading room.

I wasn't sure what I was looking for but I thought I'd try to confirm when Sarah Grey died. This would perhaps give me some clues as to the circumstances of her death.

The stiff-faced man at the front desk suggested I scrutinized the microfiche of parish records. Once I had located St Clements in the main index I started scrolling through the records.

It was fascinating to see the handwriting in the registers. Despite different record-keepers, nineteenth-century writing was similar in style, all slanted loops. As the records neared the middle of the century the hand became more consistent and firm. Approaching the end of 1867 I saw her entry. 'Sarah Grey of Leigh, December 9th 80 years old. The signature seemed to resemble 'W. King'. Canon Walker King presumably. The man in the photograph in which I had seen Sarah's face suspended in glass.

I shivered, still unsure of what to make of it. I considered what to do next then decided to try and find her birth date.

At the chest in which the microfiche were stored I found the 1798 section had gone.

There were about twenty or so people, heads silently bent over machines, computers and books. One of them was interested in the same town, same church and same year as me.

Rather than waste time, I sauntered over to the book section and browsed through some local histories. One mentioned the 'Doom Pond' or 'Drowning Pool' of Leigh-on-Sea and described the method used to ascertain the guilt (or, more rarely, the innocence) of those accused of witch-craft. I'd heard Corinne describe it before but this passage had more detail and a pretty lurid illustration: the hands and feet of the 'so-called witch' would be bound tightly. A rope would be tied around the victim's waist. If she (the author referred to them all as female) sank and drowned, she was innocent. If she floated, she would be guilty and hanged. The accompanying picture depicted a woman, wide-eyed and naked, twisting and choking as she fell through the water.

There was more about the legendary witches of Canewdon, a nearby village further inland, that had a strong association with spooks and hauntings. Then there was a passage on the mighty 'Cunning Murrell', which segued into a section on Sarah Grey, who was of course depicted as ugly, fearsome and bad. In addition to this, she was allegedly able to out-swear most fishermen, and was made to sound like a thoroughly unpleasant person. The author outlined what I was coming to realize was the generally accepted version of the story, although in this version it was a foreign skipper who cut the mast (and Sarah) down.

I shut the book and went back to the fiche chest. 1798 had still not yet returned. A little mental arithmetic had me wondering if it was worth looking at fiche in the early 1820s for any relevant births or marriages.

1820–1823 were missing.

I frowned and looked up, scanning the reading area to see if there was anyone watching me. Although more researchers had arrived there was no one familiar. All I could see were heads bent; everyone was absorbed by their own studies.

The thought that someone here was preventing my investigation occurred to me.

'Don't be silly,' I told myself. I didn't want paranoia becoming my regular state of mind.

I wandered over to the archivist and told her of my discovery of Sarah's death. She was a little taken aback and suggested trying the computer to see if there was an entry on the 1851 census.

After a quick search I found Sarah living with Harriet, 16, Eliza, 17, Alfred, 24 and Ector, 22, on Strand Wharf. Sarah had given her age then as 53.

I returned to the fiche chest: 1798 had still not returned.

I selected the 1797 section and scrolled through to the end of the year. But there was a funny thing: half of the pages from the earlier months had been scanned in upside down, overlapping the latter months and rendering them illegible. It didn't look like it was a recent mistake. Perhaps the pages of the parish register had been forced back or stuck together-unpeeling them might have damaged the antique paper. Or was there something more sinister going on? Was someone deliberately obscuring Sarah's identity?

My imagination was going into overdrive and I needed to calm down. I returned the fiche to the chest, grabbed my bag from my locker and went downstairs to the small café.

Coffee probably wasn't a wise choice for calming the nerves but it seemed to work. I took some time to review what I had found and was deep in thought when I heard my name called. I say called but it was more of an exclamation. When I looked up Andrew McWhittard stood in front of me, face aghast.

I was just as shocked and, in a fluster, I offered him a seat.

He continued staring for a moment more, then wordlessly pulled out the chair opposite and slumped down.

I managed to recover myself and tried to form my mouth into a smile. 'Andrew. We meet again. Whatever are you doing here?'

He gazed at me, shifting uncomfortably in his seat. I stared

169

back. We were like two cats prowling about each other, unsure whether to fight or flee.

Those fiery eyes shifted away from me, glancing down at my notebook. He opened his mouth then closed it, like he wanted to say something but kept changing his mind.

I took control in an attempt to normalize the situation. 'I'm doing some family history.'

It didn't have the effect that I'd hoped for. McWhittard propped his elbows onto the table and sank his head into his hands. His dark hair covered his face for a moment so I couldn't see his expression. Then he jerked his head back to reveal a broad, albeit forced, smile. His eyes were still narrowed as he spoke. 'That's odd. So am I.'

I took a sip of my coffee, ignoring the slight tremor to the cup, and wiped my upper lip of the sweat which had broken out all over my body. The air between us crackled with tension. Had he been looking at the same fiche as me?

'But I thought your family were Scottish?'

He leant back and fixed me with a hard stare. 'There are connections down here.' It wasn't a statement as such, more of a challenge.

I decided not to speak. Silence, I found, was an effective but quite underused method of class control. Instead I nodded. It did the trick. He relinquished my gaze and shifted his eyes to my notebook.

'So who are you delving into?'

I tossed the book to him. 'Sarah Grey.'

His right hand, which had crept out to take the book, withdrew with a sharpness neither of us could ignore.

His eyes met mine again. For a long moment it felt like he was looking deep inside me, trying to find something or read a motive of sorts. Then, all of a sudden, he stood up. 'I think it's time you and I had a proper chat.'

With an energy that surprised and confused me, he strode round to my side of the table and thrust out his hand. Without thinking I took it and stood up.

'Have you had lunch yet?'

I shook my head, half conscious of the fact we were still holding hands. 'There's a nice little pub about ten minutes' drive from here. Have you got your car?'

I said that I hadn't and allowed him to lead me out of the Records Office and into his car.

The journey had been awkward and surreal with neither of us speaking. But once we had got into the pub, a seventeenth-century inn, and ensconced ourselves in a quiet corner beside a large unlit inglenook fireplace, I began to relax a little.

It was Andrew who spoke first and once he started he didn't stop. His tale was almost as bizarre as my own.

Born in a suburb of Glasgow to young parents he'd enjoyed a happy childhood, he said. His father was a communist, a form of rebellion against his mother's parents who were quite religious. They had some connection of which they were very proud, to a past bishop of the Episcopal Church, the Primus of Scotland.

McWhittard spoke fondly of the holidays he spent with his maternal grandparents and was even comical as he relayed his own teenage rebellion – finding God outside of a communist rally. A huge disappointment to his father, he wanted to study Theology at university but was persuaded by his mum to read Economics to avoid a family rift.

On graduation however, having fulfilled his filial duties,

he applied to a theology college and so started on a course that wound up with him making a living some years later in a small parish outside of Aberdeen. There was a tinge of regret in his eyes as he told me about the quiet happy life he had led there.

'I met my wife, Imogen. She wasn't a churchgoer but she did the flowers for us. She was lovely,' he said with a deep sigh. 'Our first child, Amelia, was born at home. Quite effortlessly.'

He looked up to find my eyebrows arched up high and smiled at me briefly. 'When I say "effortlessly" I mean it was as easy a childbirth as it could have been,' he explained.

But the shock he read in my face had more to do with the revelation of his fatherhood. Where is she now? I wondered, but he was off again.

'I was quite ambitious then. After we'd got over the shock of becoming parents and had settled down into a familiar routine I got itchy feet. Things were too comfortable there in the village. I wanted to find a bigger parish. Imogen was reluctant to leave the place she had grown up in and the extended family that supported us.'

He gripped his glass tightly now. 'She wanted stability. And of course, who could blame her?' Andrew leant forwards and propped his elbows on the table. He ran his fingers through his hair and took a long swig of beer. 'The schools were good where we were. I just wanted to move on in some way. But I understood why she wanted to stay. Anyway, when she told me she was pregnant again, I knew that was going to seal the deal. We were going to be staying for a good while.' His eyes searched my face for signs of consent or approval.

172

I was a bit stunned by it all so I simply nodded.

He went on to praise his wife's sensitivity. 'Imogen knew I would do the right thing. She always said I was noble.' He glanced at me again and laughed harshly. 'A lot of things have changed since then.'

I didn't know how to take this so I murmured somewhat sarcastically, 'I see.'

'She knew,' he went on steadily, 'that I would abandon the idea of relocation, so, as a kind of alternative or a distraction, she planted a new idea in my head. She suggested I should steer my ambitions towards more academic goals and write a biography of the man who had so influenced my grandparents, and my own path in life – the Primus of Scotland, Robert Eden.'

The name rang a bell. Yes, Eden had been rector of St Clements. He had overseen the building of the new rectory, now the library.

'Not much had been written about him so it was a bit of a challenge. She understood exactly what I was like. And of course I grasped the opportunity. She knew it meant days away for me while I visited various archives, but Imogen was happy that I was happy. And I was.' He blew out his cheeks and rubbed his right eye with his palm.

'So off I went on my research. It was fairly bog-standard academic trawling at first but I was tipped off by a librarian in Edinburgh, who directed me to the recent discovery found in a chest rescued from a derelict old house in the city. It contained the Primus's journals. There were about twenty books, chronologically arranged, with an assortment of catalogues, papers and letters. It was a treasure-trove.

'The library was happy to give me full access to the

records. But of course it meant more time away from Imogen and Amelia. But I was enthralled. I don't remember thinking I had a choice at the time but of course I did. Anyway, I started my investigations, focusing on the end of the Primus's life, purely because it was easier; he had published more documents and pamphlets than he had as a simple reverend.

'One day, when I was trawling through one of the journals that the Primus had written in his latter years, I found an entry that intrigued me. It was regarding a trip made by the Bishop to the small parish of Leigh-on-Sea in the south of England.'

I shifted in my chair and leant closer to him.

'He once spent time there as the rector of St Clements. It transpired that the Primus had received a letter from one of his old parishioners. Written by an old widow that he'd had some dealings with in the past, it begged him to help her find justice for an offence unmentioned but which, the letter inferred, the Primus had some secret knowledge of. It hooked me. Totally.'

At this point Andrew stopped, and I supposed he was going to fetch another glass or go for a fag. It was that kind of pause. But he didn't.

He breathed in deeply through his nostrils and bent his head. His face had paled in colour, from his usual pastiness to ashen.

His brow puckered in a deep line across his forehead indicating a real internal conflict within. Amidst my own bemusement I kind of felt sorry for him so didn't press, although, to be fair, the urge was coming on strong.

After yet another moment's consideration, in which he

bit his lip and nervously ran his fingers through his hair, he went on. 'The Primus constantly referred to letting the woman down. OK? You got that?' He leant forwards across the table and repeated 'Constantly?'

'Yeah, I've got it,' I replied, but I hadn't got a clue where he was going now.

'I was intrigued. Really fascinated. I felt for him. It was almost as if he was haunted by his failure for the rest of his life. So I looked into it further. In fact, I cancelled my afternoon ticket home and booked into a nearby hotel. I phoned Imogen but got the answer-phone so I left a message. Then I went back to the library and worked through the journals for hours until finally I found a passage that seemed to shed some light on the mystery.'

McWhittard had been talking for an hour, during which time we had paused to eat lunch. By now, however, I was on the edge of my seat, barely able to contain my excitement. 'Well, what did it say? Was the woman Sarah Grey?'

He took a deep breath and to my bewilderment his eyes filled with water. I marvelled briefly at the academic fervour of the man. Such passion for the dead; I had underestimated him. He glanced at the empty fireplace beside us. 'I have a copy of the passages in the notebook at home. You must read them yourself.' His voice was heavy with a tone I couldn't fathom.

Had he taken me to this point only to leave me dangling there? 'Oh come on, Andrew. What did it say?'

He sniffed, still looking at the hearth. 'I wasn't able to photocopy it in case the pages were damaged so spent some time writing it out. I was there longer than I ever should have been and my mobile was turned off. When I finally got back to the hotel late that night I switched on my phone. There was a message from the police: there had been an accident. Imogen's car had been hit by a young man who had just passed his test. She hadn't got my message and had been on the way to collect me from the station. I rushed back as soon as I could but by the time I got to the hospital, my daughter Amelia was already dead.'

I took in a deep breath and stared at him as he told me that for ten long days Imogen and their unborn baby fought for their lives, during which time McWhittard prayed. Then when that didn't work, he negotiated with his boss to save them. On the tenth day his wife succumbed to her injuries taking his unborn son to the grave with her.

The pub was filling up now. A couple had joined the table next to us and were busily chatting about their day. The waitress came over and cleared our table of cutlery and dirty plates, clearly disconcerted by the sight of two people sitting in their own still pool of absolute silence.

Eventually I spoke. 'Is that why you left the church?'

He didn't answer. He didn't have to.

Instead he said, 'Do you want a lift back?'

I struggled out of my stupor and glanced at the antique iron clock above the fireplace. It was nearly time to get Alfie. 'Yes please. Do you mind if we stop at the nursery . . .' I trailed off, acutely embarrassed by my lack of tact.

'It's fine,' he said.

We took another car journey in silence. It wasn't companionable. More like the surface of a sea rip: calm at first sight, concealing a host of dark currents that would toss you around and drag you down if you swam too close.

I stared out the window at the flat landscape, not seeing any of it.

It was something of a relief to install Alfie in the back seat. He immediately demanded to know who Andrew was, if he had any sweets, and whether or not he was coming to play at our house. I excused Alfie's demands but politely asked if Andrew would like to come in for a cup of tea.

As we pulled up outside our house he surprised me by saying, 'Why not?'

Once Alfie had been set up with his supper and *CBeebies* I took out one of my favourite teapots – pretty pink bone china, decorated with small yellow roses. I popped two floral cups and saucers onto the tray with it and joined my boss outside in the garden. I set the tray on the table and he poured the tea into both cups, sugared and added milk to his although, I noticed, he did not touch it until I had picked up mine.

'Cheers,' I said, for want of anything better, and clinked my cup to his.

He seemed more relaxed and smiled as he said, 'I'm sorry.'

I told him he had nothing to apologize for. 'In fact,' I continued, 'I would be very interested in reading your transcript. If that's OK with you? I realize that it has a difficult personal resonance and I really don't want to . . .'

He cut in. 'I'd like you to. I said you should earlier.'

I became aware that I hadn't reapplied my lipstick for hours and was thinking of nipping off to freshen up when he gave me a little half smile and said, 'You didn't like me, did you? Not at first. I could tell.' His right hand fluttered up to his hair and tugged on a small black lock by his ear.

This was awkward. We had just shared an intimate

exchange. That is, he had shared with me. He certainly wasn't the person I had assumed him to be a mere four weeks ago. 'I've always had a problem with authority.'

'I know,' he said glumly. 'That's why . . .' He paused, took a large gulp of tea and changed tack. 'Can you imagine?' he said at last. 'What a shock it was to meet you, Sarah Grey.'

It was dawning on me.

I recalled our first meeting: I'd assumed my common accent had been the thing to shock him so.

I was beginning to realize I'd assumed a lot about this man.

'And then when I learnt you too were a widow.' He replaced the cup in its saucer in a heavy, cack-handed way, spilling half the tea though he seemed not to notice, and began thumbing the rusty iron edges of the table as he went on. 'At first I thought it was a sign. Some kind of omen. It irritated the fuck out of me.'

I'd never heard him swear before. On his forehead small drops of perspiration wetted strands of fringe. It was hot but not *that* hot. He took another swig. 'I know I was perhaps a little harsh with you when I needn't have been, but I was alarmed.' His cup came down on the table with a crack. 'And protective.'

'Protective? That's an unusual word to use.'

He shrugged. 'The Primus had not been there for old Sarah Grey when she needed him. I wondered if you'd been sent to me for some reason, if there wasn't some kind of moral obligation or duty.' He uncrossed his legs and moved forward in his chair. He was articulating half-thoughts, his mind rushing over others spoken only inside his mind. 'It brought a great deal back and I . . .'

A plane flew across the sun, casting him into momentary darkness. The vein on the left of his neck pulsed and without thinking I reached out and put my hand out and covered his. 'I know what it's like. Don't go there now.'

He took my hand. 'I know you know,' he said, after a few moments then released me and clenched his fist. 'And *I* know,' he said as if to himself, 'that there is no rhyme nor rhythm nor reason to the universe. But to see you there today . . .'

He shook his head at some inner confusion. 'Ending up here as I had . . . I resolved to investigate what happened to Sarah Grey. Purely out of curiosity, you understand. I didn't get round to it, but when I had a spare couple of days I went to the Records Office and, well, it was a shock. There you were. Sitting there in the café like a . . .' He paused to take a long breath and steadied his voice. 'It was as if He was back again trying to get my attention.' He threw back his head and let out an icy laugh that chilled me. 'But you're just researching your family tree. More fool me. There's nothing divine or unusual in that. I'm sorry. It just threw me.'

He was looking away now, watching his foot dangle over the decking, thinking about events that had led him to this point.

It was fortunate for me that he couldn't see my cheeks burn. Of all the situations I could have imagined this was not one of them. I bowed my head and tried to think about the best thing to say. Should I tell him the truth and be labelled a nutter? He might have confided in me but he was still my boss, and what I had to say was insane. Yet he had opened his heart to me. Could I really return his honesty with a lie?

179

It would certainly protect me. And protect him. But would it be the right thing to do? Was there a right thing to do?

I didn't have to make a decision. He picked up the teapot and refilled his cup and my own. 'I've upset you.' He took in my ruddy complexion. 'I'm sorry. I realize I'm being quite unprofessional.'

'That's OK.' I smiled brightly, and forced my eyes as wide as possible. 'I like you better this way.'

He laughed and as the sun shifted through the leaves of the ivy it caught his eyes. They twinkled, swirling like dark brown pools in the depths of the ocean, and just as unknown. His lips settled into a genuine smile this time. A shot of adrenalin surged through me. I blushed yet again and tried to disguise it by topping up my teacup. This must have appeared silly after he had just filled them, and of course I ended up overfilling it. I don't know what he must have thought. But he only remarked, 'Careful, it's still hot.'

I blurt things out, I always have. It's a terrible trait. Mostly I manage to control it but over the past couple of weeks my control mechanisms had had a hell of a lot to cope with. 'Health and Safety,' I said, in a strange, funny voice.

Thank God, he smiled. 'McBastard. Yes, I remember our conversation outside the Red Lion.'

'Sorry. Old habits . . .'

But he didn't look annoyed.

'So.' I changed direction. 'Is that what brought you to Leigh? The connection? To the Primus?'

He shook his head and picked a small piece of lint off his pale blue t-shirt. It was clean and well-laundered today. 'No. I was already down South but in quite a tough school in London. People don't last long there. Two or three years at the most. I'd done four out of pride, but I was ready to move on. I'd obviously heard of Leigh before but I'd not visited. A colleague came back from a weekend trip raving about it. We both applied for the St John's job but in the end I got it. You know the rest.'

My stomach growled, audibly punctuating his sentence. How embarrassing. I dashed inside, fixed a plate of olives and grabbed a large bag of tortilla chips. I scooped a handful out for Alfie, with a dab of hummus, and added some chopped carrots on the side. Alfie yelped with glee when he saw the crisps and ignored the carrots. I asked him if he would like a juice or if he wanted to come outside and talk with the grown-ups. He pulled one of his 'you've-gotta-be-joking' faces and went back to the TV.

Andrew was delighted by the spread, which I laid across the table. We nibbled at it for a while before I picked up the conversation where we had left off. 'So do you like it down here?'

He propped himself up in his chair, back in command of the situation, formal almost. I wondered if he was regretting telling me his story.

'It's charming. Very pretty. Good community spirit. The kids are all right. There are some parochial attitudes amongst the staff that need challenging but generally I can't complain.'

I remarked that I was surprised that, given his previous vocation, he had chosen a private school.

'The money was good. You?' He popped an olive in his mouth and tossed his head back. Although I still didn't know him well, I saw instantly that it was an act of defiance. Beyond the glassy coat of his eyes there burnt a great rage against a

181

God who had deserted him. This cocky materialism was just one aspect to the rebellion.

I pulled my gaze from his. I knew that type of anger too, and if the conditions were right it could re-ignite from nothing, like a forest fire, spreading destruction. 'It was the first job I got after I moved here,' I told him.

He nodded but didn't look at me. He was staring down the garden, at the rose bushes near the hammock. A small tortoiseshell butterfly sunned its wings on one of the tall pink blooms.

'So how much do you know about your namesake?' he said slowly, eyes still on the bush.

An image of Sarah flashed into my mind. She stood on the sand near Bell Wharf, hair fluttering in the breeze.

He came back.

I frowned and pushed the image away. Then I told him what I had learnt from the books, from the fiche and from the library, omitting the small matter of why I had started my investigations.

He was attentive, and listened with interest. Occasionally he commented on my findings, at other points he raised his eyebrows to signify that some of what I had to tell was news to him. He sighed when I told him the story of the child who had burnt and shook his head. 'Life is tragic and cruel. The loss of a child . . .' He didn't finish the sentence.

I told him about the cholera epidemics and Sarah's own bereavements and finally wound up with the legend of her death, first relaying the axe-wound climax, then outlining the myth (if myth it was) of her headless body afloat in Doom Pond.

'You need to read the journals,' he said, when I'd done.

'There's a lot of information in them that you should know.'

'I'd love to,' I answered quickly.

'Then we can share theories,' he said with a smile.

'Of course,' I added. The man was proving a very useful ally.

If you can trust him.

The words popped into my head out of nowhere.

I looked about. We were alone in the garden. There was no one else there. I craned my ear: there was a faint growl of a car engine powering down the street, the soft whistle of a swift, a small child exclaiming in a nearby garden. But the voice had been as clear as if someone had been behind me, whispering in my ear.

Andrew searched my face. 'What's that? A wasp? So who is she?'

For a second I was unsure if he hadn't heard the voice too. 'Wh . . . who?'

He sat back and studied my face. 'Sarah Grey. I mean – who is she in relation to you? Who did you think I meant?'

I was stammering. 'I'm not sure.'

He frowned. 'You OK?'

Sweat was pouring down my body and between my legs. I shifted with discomfort. 'Yes. She's a relation.'

'I got that. Which one? Great, great, great grandmother?'

'Well, kind of. Add a couple of "greats" here or there.'

Andrew cocked his head to one side. 'How can you not know exactly? Surely you've traced the lineage?'

It seemed to me at that moment that there was a threat in his words, and for a second I felt his eyes fix on my face. I put a hand up to cover the prickling flesh of my cheeks.

It must have been a peculiar movement for he leant in. 'Are you sure you're OK? Is it the heat?'

There was a screech inside the house and Alfie tottered out complaining loudly that the TV had finished. I scooped him up in my arms and held him tight. Much to his dismay I kissed him.

Andrew took it as a cue to leave. 'Thanks. It's getting late I realize. Time for the little man to go to bed.'

The look of horror on my son's face made him laugh. He leant over and ruffled his hair. Unusually Alfie let him.

'I'll get that journal to you,' he said to me.

Despite my discomfort I didn't want to see him go. He collected his car keys from the table.

I stood and saw him into the kitchen. 'It sounds interesting. Any chance you could pop it by tomorrow?'

He turned with an amused expression on his lips. 'I'm afraid not. It's at home. Well, my parents' house in Glasgow. I'm going up there on Saturday for a week to see the folks. I'll have a good look for it.'

'Oh.' I was doubly disappointed.

Alfie stuck his hand out and caught the sleeve of Andrew's t-shirt. 'But Mummy wants you to come back soon.'

'Alfie, leave Andrew alone.' I counted to ten, trying not to blush for the umpteenth time.

'But you dooooo.' He squirmed in my arms: I squirmed internally.

I returned him to the floor and told him to go and find a biscuit, then I quickly led Andrew through the hall.

Just before he left he asked me what plans I had for the summer. I told him, truthfully, not much. He didn't follow it up but asked if I'd come across the name Tobias Fitch.

I ran it through my brain. 'Nope. Not heard of him. Who is he? A student?'

He smiled thoughtfully. 'I'll pop round once I'm back.'

That would be nice, I told him, and leant in to give him a kiss on the cheek but he had already started down the garden path.

I closed the door after him and leant against it.

My heart didn't stop hammering until I heard his car exit my road.

Chapter Fourteen

The other day I found the book I had been reading at that time. In the margin of one page there is a crude likeness of Andrew. I had spent time wrapping the tiny curls of his hair about his face but had concentrated mostly on the deep russet pools of his eyes. Even now they startle me as they peer up from the page, vivid and alive but not as astonishing as the real thing. I didn't realize it at the time, but it's clear to me as I flick through the doodles on the pages of the paperback, that I was rather taken with Mr McWhittard.

This was problematic on a couple of levels, not least because he was my boss. Nor did I want to get involved with another mess. That is, I didn't want another relationship. They were ridiculously untidy. And difficult and dangerous. People you love do things you can't control and make you feel awful even if they love you.

Especially if they love you.

Of course I yearned for certain aspects of the mess, but I was afraid too. Whether you liked to admit it or not, sex made you feel stuff. Not just physical pleasure. The hormones it whips up play havoc with the delicate chemical balance that constitutes your official stable personality and before you know it you start experiencing odd emotions, come over all starry-eyed and then you're opening yourself wide.

That's when the trouble starts.

Anyway, at the same time, I couldn't be bothered with it all. From memory, courtship was exhausting. It sapped energy you should be putting into other areas of your life and it took from other relationships. Now I had a son I couldn't be thinking of it. I was the only parent he had. Alfie was my priority.

Plus there had been that warning. Even if it had come from my own subconscious, there were good reasons for me to err on the side of caution when I dealt with this man. Trust had to be earned. I hadn't seen enough from him to confide the supernatural reasons for my research into Sarah Grey.

And yet how uncanny that he should have come across her years before I even heard her name. And for it too to have occurred in some convoluted and chaotic way, associated with a tragedy that in some ways mirrored mine.

His sense of duty towards old Sarah Grey had not been lost on me either. If indeed he was telling the truth. There was no reason why he shouldn't but the voice had been there for a purpose, even if I couldn't understand what it was.

None of this stopped me thinking about him.

How quickly revulsion had turned in on itself to become intrigue, then sympathy and finally, though unconsciously, desire.

I spent a lot of time that week going over our day together. More than was absolutely necessary. True, there was a lot to think about: the distressing circumstances of his widowing, so like mine. Though his had snatched away his children too. It made me shudder to contemplate how on earth I would have found the resources to continue living if Alfie had . . . I can't even bring myself to write it now. It was no surprise that all who crossed his path sensed, on some level, the desperate bitterness and sorrow deep inside him. To his credit, he masked it well enough for it to be mistaken for sullen officiousness couched in rigid bureaucracy.

And to think he had been a rector! I could see him in a dog collar but I could not picture him about his duties: opening fetes, comforting the bereaved, officiating at funerals, weddings, christenings. How could he have carried on after Imogen and Amelia's death, thanking God for the union of others, blessing their children?

It was unthinkable.

The harshness of his manner, I was now beginning to realize, spoke more of a willingness to alienate others. He had once been privy to all sorts of cares and woes and life-changing experiences. After your God had dealt you a hand so cruel, why on earth would you continue to worship him?

Why on earth?

And that was another thing going off in my head. I was not a believer myself and it was numbing to realize that I had been called by something that my grandmother would have termed 'unearthly'. I had never felt beholden to the traditions of the religion into which I had been born. Though my mother was still a God-fearing Christian, my father had languished on religion's outer circles. Dad had been more 'progressive' in his thinking, as I came to understand. In my childhood his scientific rationalism had me utterly perplexed, but as I matured I had come to comprehend the calm logic of his wisdom. He had been deprived of a mother when he was young and had found no comfort in the reasoning that the church espoused.

As I grew up, I began to tune in, to appreciate his way of thinking. By the time of Josh's accident I had more or less taken on board his cool approximation of existentialism.

Which made my husband's death all the harder to take. Of course Dad had been long gone by then. I often wondered what words he would have offered me by way of comfort. If any.

My father had been a pious man without a religion. He did not believe in the good of mankind, and having been a policeman, he had sought not to induct me into the dull, rather stupid belief that people were good or indeed innocent until proven otherwise. His years on the job had taught him that acts of evil were as random and as frequent as those of pure good. And that if there was a divine being above, it was as confused and complex as the rest of us.

Was this where Andrew was? He must have experienced some of it but, as a member of the cloth, his experience surely had led him into the abyss of spiritual misery. Why would God have taken the ones that His servant loved? Only an Old Testament deity could do that for no discernible reason. Though, knowing Andrew even as little as I did, I guessed it had been the compassionate son, Jesus Christ, that had fixed him so.

Andrew, I saw then, was a man knotted. So awry with the world and irate at its injustice.

Like me.

I understood his anger more than I could comprehend the man he had become. But that was OK. For now, we had become united under the same cause.

And that cause still sang.

That week Sarah lingered in the dark shadows of my house and stalked me in my dreams at night. I saw nothing specific, just vague resonances and feelings that surrounded me as I woke into the day.

I never felt alone.

She was there all the time.

On Sunday Mum, Lottie, David and Thomas came over. After lunch Mum and David volunteered to take the boys to the library gardens for a bit. Lottie and I cleared the plates, washed up then decided to saunter down the Broadway and join them in the park.

It was a pleasant day and we ambled along the south side of the road, staying in the shade. Lottie had calmed down about David and their debts, deciding instead to focus her irritation on Malcolm, her agent, with whom she was due to meet the following week.

'I don't even know what my royalties are in regard to e-books,' she was bleating. 'Can't find the contract so asked him. But he's just so evasive. I mean, it's ridiculous isn't it? . . .'

I made some sympathetic noises.

'I've got to really bring some force to bear on Malc. I've been letting him get away with doing very little for far too long. Wow!' She stopped in front of a boutique we were passing. 'They are perfect.' With one beautifully manicured finger Lottie pointed to the feet of a mannequin perched in the shop window. The shoes it was wearing were lush: aqua in colour, decorated with a velvet bow and pearls, and completed with a pair of sharp kitten heels. 'I could certainly kick some ass in them.'

The price tag, placed discreetly between the dummy's two

feet, indicated they were way out of my price range. I sighed lightly and looked up to the mannequin's head. 'Nice hat,' I said, commenting on the light straw boater. 'I could wear that, um, down the beach.'

Then it was as if the street emptied, and all noise was sucked from the air. Giddiness came over me and an intense feeling of doom, then, as I continued to stare in some kind of hypnotic state, the mannequin turned its head to me. Its painted eyes glowed an unearthly jade green.

Sarah!

I gasped, recoiled, and glanced at my sister. Lottie was stooped over the shoes. She had been looking down and not observed the movement.

Inside the shop the sales assistant was serving another woman, oblivious.

But I was sure it moved; it was still in its new position. I stared at it again, fighting back an incredible urge to flee, when suddenly, hideously, the awful thing blinked.

Sarah.

Dear God, no. It was her again.

Reeling with shock I sprang back. Lottie stood up. 'Hey, what's up? You OK?'

But I couldn't speak. My throat had become so dry that I could hardly breathe. My neck muscles were contracting, forcing out an insistent cough. I leant forwards, holding on to Lottie, spluttering as my stomach went into a spasm. I made it to the gutter just in time to throw up what looked like sallow, dirty water.

'Sarah, are you OK? Oh God,' Lottie placed a reassuring hand on my shoulder and started stroking and rubbing my back. 'Oh, Sarah. I'm sorry.'

I was far too shocked to speak and concentrated on my breathing. Lottie brought out a pack of tissues and began to dab my face. 'What can I get you, honey?'

I managed to indicate I wanted some water to take away the bitter taste in my mouth so she ran off to the newsagents.

The mannequin watched on.

When she had returned I had found a bench down the road a little and got myself into a more reasonable state.

She sat down beside me and handed over the bottle. 'What *was* that?'

I shrugged. 'I don't know. The heat? Dehydration?'

She bit her lip before she asked the next question. 'It's not the . . .? Is it?'

I avoided her question by getting to my feet. 'Look, Lottie, would you do me a favour? I feel like I need to lie down. Can you go on ahead and bring Alfie back later?'

'No problem.' She was glad to be of some use. 'You'll be all right?'

'Just tired,' I told her as I crossed the road.

I was still agitated on Sunday evening. My brain would not let the incident go and kept playing it over and over again. The same fears went round my head; the tumour, or another illness, the possibility of madness, followed by the notion of the haunting.

Which one was real? Perhaps they were all real?

Even as I think back now, in the comfort of my leather armchair enjoying the view from the window of the softened October landscape, heating on full blast, those thoughts chill me to the bone: the bewilderment I felt on an almost day to day basis; the feeling that I was nearing a precipice over which I would fall to my death. The absolute conviction that someone or something was coming for me. It was a time of tumult and perhaps I *was* half mad with stress. Sometimes I wonder how I managed to get through it all. I guess we are more resilient than we give ourselves credit for. We never know just how tough we are until circumstances conspire to draw it from us. I didn't know it then but my biggest battle would make the mannequin episode look like playtime.

That evening I was still fretful, so it was with some relief that I heard the doorbell go at about 9 o'clock. It was Sharon, with Corinne in tow. Their timing couldn't have been more perfect and their effect on me was grounding. My friends were my saviours back then. I don't know what I would have done without those small reprieves. Lost it altogether I imagine.

The girls had brought two bottles of white wine and a good measure of high spirits (they had obviously had a drink or two before they had arrived on my doorstep).

Their good humour was instantly contagious and soon lifted my mood.

I was grateful.

Alfie had gone down easily, for once, and been fast asleep for a good hour now so I was able to turn up the stereo and aim a speaker at the garden, though the night was cooler than it had been for weeks.

I had given Sharon the date of Sarah Grey's death after Andrew had gone to Scotland. She'd wasted no time in knuckling down to some serious investigation and when she phoned me, on Saturday morning, exclaimed that she had found out 'a shit load'.

As they wobbled through the kitchen, Sharon insisted that the music must change. She didn't want the 'foreign Latino crap' and demanded something more recent. I pointed her in the direction of the CD stack, took Corinne by the elbow and guided her down to the chairs in the garden.

'I'm not pissed,' she said. 'Not at all.' But there was a distinct slur to her voice that was ever so slightly gratifying: Corinne was usually able to drink a horse under the table. Well, Sharon anyway – quite a feat in itself. Indeed, my other, far drunker friend had sat herself in front of the stereo and was methodically going through my collection, tossing any CD that didn't appeal over her shoulder. The silver discs piled up behind her like a shiny two-dimensional beehive spread over the floorboards.

'So,' I said to Corinne, over a glass of warm fizz. 'Where have you been?'

'Family thing.'

The two had known each other since they were five. Their parents had been great friends and Sharon and Corinne, being roughly the same age, both attended the same infant, junior and senior school.

The stereo blared into action. For some reason that I'll never fathom Sharon put on a Christmas hit, *Sleigh Run*, and came bounding down the garden pretending to be a reindeer.

Corinne and I fell about in fits until the reindeer demanded a fire and I obligingly went into the shed and dragged out my makeshift fire pit – an old washing machine drum on a stand. It didn't look much but it did the trick. Within minutes the three of us had gathered enough twigs to start a small fire. Sharon complained it wasn't hot enough so I fetched a barbecue tin and emptied the contents into the pit. It immediately put the flame out, forcing us to spend another half hour resurrecting the glow. Finally we settled in around the fire like old timers making camp.

Sharon rummaged in her bag and brought out a notebook.

'Sarah Grey. My findings!' she said with a flourish, and unfolded a couple of neatly typed A4 sheets. 'I've put it all down here. It's complicated so I'm happy to go over it with you when I'm sober. But, man! That chick had a hard life.'

Corinne drew closer and warmed her hands. Her face flickered amber and brown. 'They often did, back then. It's easy to look at the Old Town and get nostalgic but life was terrible if you were poor, which most people were. There was a workhouse, you know. An old cottage on Billet Lane.'

I shuddered at the thought of it. 'How very Dickensian,' and turned to Sharon. 'Did she go into it? The workhouse?'

She put on a pair of reading spectacles and squinted at the sheets, moving them back and forth till the text came into focus. The glasses totally altered her look from woozy floozy to rather academic. I liked it. and had a brief insight into her highly paid work life: Sharon could do serious when she wanted to.

'No, she didn't.' My friend traced her index finger over the notes. 'She had descendants, who I assume cared for her as she aged. Well, one hopes. There were lots of them. In fact that was half the problem. She got saddled with a hell of a lot of kids during her life. Her husbands kept kicking the bucket.

'You know,' she looked up at Corinne and me, 'I've always thought that Sarah probably wasn't a witch at all but some

195

poor widow with a hump back and a stoop, that got picked on by the rest of the town because she looked like a witch, poor moo. She probably did mutter curses under her breath because everyone was so horrible to her. I would. Although I guess it's quite nice that she is now immortaliszed in her hometown.'

Corinne nodded sagely. 'There used to be that picture of her on the pub sign. Do you remember? She was all bent over in black, shuffling past a field with that great witch's bag.'

'That large bundle on her back,' Sharon glanced back at her notes. 'That was how laundresses carried laundry to and from the place where it was washed. I bet it was carrying all that laundry that gave her the stoop. She probably ended up gnarled and twisted. And skint, though she didn't start off like that, mind. I think she was born a Sutton, daughter of a linen draper. A wholesale cloth merchant. Her dad would have been regarded as a respectable tradesman. She wouldn't have been too educated but she might have been quite a good marriage proposition. But she ends up married to a Robert Billing in 1823. That is, I think she's married in that year. According to my calculations she would have been in her early twenties then. I think Robert Billing was older and already a widower with kids so it's quite surprising that she went for that. I mean, I wouldn't and actually, she was in a good situation. Perhaps a little old, but she would have been a fair prospect.'

My mind had gone back to the scene from that dream the night of the storm. The one in the doctor's room: that loathsome rich man and his stocky companion. 'Maybe she was forced to marry him,' I suggested.

Corinne turned to me and shrugged. 'Why would she be forced to marry someone? Arranged marriages were the realm of the wealthy. They were about property and dynasty. That wouldn't have been an issue for her.'

'Perhaps she was pregnant? Child born out of wedlock and all that,' I said slowly. I had seen the man place a hand on her stomach. 'I could remove it,' he'd told her. 'And then no one would know.'

Sharon was looking at me with a quizzical expression. 'Then she would have likely married the father. The upper-class Victorians were very proper but the lower classes let their hair down a little bit more. That sort of carry on wasn't completely unheard of.'

But there had been desperation in Sarah's face. I had seen it quite clearly. She had felt trapped. 'What if she couldn't marry the father?' My voice was rising. Corinne and Sharon exchanged a glance.

'Don't you think you're romanticizing this all a bit, Sarah?' It was Corinne in no-nonsense mode.

Sharon answered for me. 'I think it's fair to say that the choice was unusual for the daughter of a linen draper at that time. Unless she was really ugly!' She laughed.

It was on the tip of my tongue to counter that suggestion but I held it back and Sharon continued.

'I haven't found the marriage certificate yet but she certainly had a baby that year, William. He dies nine years later. Then in 1827 she has Alfred, then Sarah in 1832, but little Sarah junior doesn't make it into childhood, dying one year later. In 1834 she has Eliza who, thankfully, lives and goes on to marry one of the Deals. In 1836 she has Mary Anne.'

'Then in 1839 Robert Billing dies, leaving her with five kids, three of her own, two of his. That must have been hard. In 1845 she's married to John Grey, another widower. I found her living with some of the Greys in the 1841 census so I think she might have been cohabiting for a while out of wedlock – another reason she may have been ostracized. But then again, with no husband, no income and five children to support you have to wonder how she managed to get that far. Anyway, in 1841 you can see that Alfred has taken Grey's name, as has Sarah, probably an attempt at some form of propriety. I doubt they had much money to spare for a wedding. After all John's got George, John Junior, Harriet and Ector. Sarah takes them all on. That's nine children! Imagine that!'

Corinne sighed loudly. 'You just can't really, can you? It would have been like living in an orphanage!'

Sharon nodded in agreement. 'Anyhow, at some point over the next couple of years, John makes an honest woman of her and she becomes a Grey officially. Then things start to go downhill. In the 1849 cholera outbreak her husband dies. So do John junior and George and also Mary Anne, Sarah's real daughter. A couple of months after Mary Anne, Beattie and Freddie Billing, her step-children from her first marriage, also die. So, in just a couple of months she's widowed again, bereaved, her family's practically halved and she's left alone to provide for four kids, with only Alfred and Eliza of her own blood. You have to feel sorry for her.'

'I do,' I said quietly.

Sharon sniffed. 'Her burial date is 1867. I expect she was totally knackered by then.'

Something in the bushes stirred. The leaves of the rose bush fluttered. Out in the street a moped backfired.

I processed Sharon's findings for a moment then thanked her for her work.

'No worries,' she replied. 'It was fun. I enjoyed it and I'll carry on. See if I can root out any more info. The whole story though, as it unfolded, was gutting. I'm sure all the witch stuff has been exaggerated . . . her daughter, Eliza, goes on to marry well.'

'God, yeah,' chimed Corinne. 'If they really thought her mother was a witch, I'm sure Eliza would have been tarred with the same brush. And let's face it, Sarah herself appears to have married at least twice.'

'Not sure about that,' said Sharon. 'Robert Deal, who married Liza, was a newcomer to the town. He may have dismissed the myths about his mother-in-law as hearsay. Especially if he met her and thought that she was OK. Love can have that effect.' She sighed. 'Or so I'm told. And also, Robert Deal became a successful man. Money and success are a powerful tool when it comes to changing reputations: tongues become quietened and success tends to attract people who want to bask in some of the glory.'

'So,' I asked, 'do you think Sarah's story, the one that we know, that we talk about today is made up of myths? Loose connections with the Drowning Pool?'

Corinne was getting practical again. 'Perhaps. She may not have been a legend in her lifetime. Maybe mothers would tell their children that the ugly lady who used to live down the road was an old sea-witch, who would curse them from beyond the grave if they didn't behave themselves, and it just took off from there.'

'Not fair really, is it?' It was my turn now. 'She wasn't ugly at all.' The young Sarah, who had appeared twice, had not been buckled. On the contrary, there was a haunting loveliness to her pale features. It was only the elder Sarah who was weatherworn and bent.

Corinne jumped. 'Oh, have you found a portrait?'

Oops. A slip-up. How did I get out of this one?

Sharon and Corinne leant forwards in expectation.

I came up with this. 'An artist's impression.'

'Contemporary?' Corinne asked.

I shook my head. 'No, later. 1950s.'

Corinne sneered. 'As good as useless then.'

Happy she was letting it go, I sank back into my garden chair and poked the fire with a long stick. One of the twigs let out a hiss. 'Something bad did happen to her though, I'm sure.'

'You don't really think she had her head cut off, do you?' Sharon hugged herself to suppress a shudder.

'I don't know,' I said, and decided it was time to share the new information that Andrew had given me.

They listened with interest. Sharon took out her writing pad and jotted down some notes.

'So the Reverend Eden . . .' Corinne outlined the new information when I had finished.

'Who,' I added, 'at that time was the Primus of Scotland.'

'Yes,' she continued. 'Came down after the letter?'

I repeated what I had just told them, more slowly this time so they could follow me. 'It was strange though. Andrew wouldn't tell me any more. Said I had to see it for myself. But he did say Eden carried on referring to his guilt, throughout the rest of the journals, for his life.'

'But you haven't read it?' Corinne downed her fizz.

'Not yet. Hopefully he'll bring it at the end of the week.'

'Interesting.' She reached for the bottle and topped up Sharon's and then her own glass. 'Another?' She held it out to me.

'No. I'm fine thanks.' Both the light and the evening's jollity were fading.

Sharon had fallen silent over the past twenty minutes.

Corinne was still intrigued. 'I'm speculating here but do you think the legend might have some basis in fact? That she might have been murdered and her death covered up? But why?'

Sharon looked up and sighed. When she spoke her voice was taut.

'Why would anyone want to cover up any death? Because they had a hand in it, of course.'

Corinne darted a glance at her and shook her head lightly. 'But why would anyone want to kill Sarah Grey? A poor old woman with a tragic life. What would be the motive?'

I had this one nailed. 'You really want to know?'

They both nodded, so I nipped into the kitchen and returned with my own notebook. 'There are quite a few suspects,' I told them, and read out my list:

'OK, first up. The parents of the babies that were "poisoned" by her herbal cures. It's obvious that if the babies had cholera they weren't likely to survive. I don't imagine all the parents blamed Sarah for the death of their children but some of them may have. Five babies died in twenty days. But that was September 1850. Sarah's not dead and buried till 1867, seventeen years later. Would the parents wait that long for vengeance?'

'Mmm,' Corinne nodded. 'Death was all around them

back then. Infant mortality was so high it was almost commonplace. I think they would have just got on with things.'

'Well, I've put them down anyway,' I said. 'Then there's the parents of the child she was alleged to have set on fire with sparks from her eyes – Jane Tulley. That was 1852.'

'Ditto,' said Corinne. 'Too much water under the bridge for them to murder her in 1867.'

'But,' it was Sharon now, wobbling an angry finger at us, 'a lot of murder is opportunistic. People grab their chance when it presents itself. When they think they can cover their tracks.'

Corinne shot me a look I couldn't interpret and urged me on, in a sort of quick harsh voice. 'I can see more names on your list. Who else?'

I shrugged. 'Well, going back to the parents, I would say I'd agree with you, Corinne. One of the parents was the town crier. Not sure they'd want to get involved with anything untoward. They were too prominent.'

'Who else?' Corinne asked again.

'Of course there's the most obvious suspect – the captain of *The Smack*. He's totally fingered in the legend.'

'And that's it so far?' Corinne had counted them on her fingers. 'That's about fifteen, sixteen people if you go for two parents per dead child.' She was so matter-of-fact.

'Well, I wonder if I shouldn't add the Primus of Scotland, the Reverend Eden, or Canon Walker King? There's something going on there. I can feel it. St Clements is part of this. Or was part of it. I don't know. I guess I'll give them the benefit of the doubt for now. Until I read the journals.'

'You absolutely must let us know, Sarah,' Corinne was sincere now. 'You really think one of them might have murdered her?'

'I'm not sure. Something happened. Something which won't . . .' I stopped myself from saying *let her rest in peace*. 'I mean, something that still blackens her name. I need to find out what that was and who was responsible for it.'

In a garden somewhere up the street a young man and woman were arguing. The breeze tugged snatches of their heated exchange to us.

'So much anger. So much death,' Sharon said, although neither myself nor Corinne were too aware of her at that point. 'Always death,' she said, and stood up. 'Loo.' Then she stumbled into the house.

'Interesting project,' Corinne said. 'Not much to go on though.'

'Oh, I don't know. I'm getting further than I thought I would.'

'And what are you going to do with your findings?'

'Sleep easy once more' was on the tip of my tongue but I just told her I didn't know.

Corinne poked the fire and I went to get another bottle of wine. As I was coming back I heard a grunt from the sofa. Sharon had spread herself across it, and was now unconscious. She had found a blanket and pulled it up to her chin. Her head rested on a pile of silk cushions. Light snores punctuated the music. She looked as vulnerable and as untroubled as a baby and suddenly the memory of my phone conversation with Corinne came back to me and my heart went out to my sleeping friend.

I bent down and brushed a tangle of hair away from her

lips, then moved to her feet. She murmured faintly as I took off her shoes. I shushed her and turned the music down.

In the garden I informed Corinne that Sharon had retired. On my couch.

Corinne smiled with the affectionate sadness of a long-term friend. 'She's been drinking since three. We had cocktails at her cousin's place to celebrate her mum's birthday. They do it every year. Sometimes it's a real knees-up, other times she gets maudlin. Death and family have that effect, I find.'

'She's not unusual in that respect,' I said, and took my place on the chair beside Corinne. 'What were you saying the other day about the "other stuff" that was going on back then?' I was being nosey more than anything else.

Corinne looked a bit put out but was drunk enough to go with it. 'Did I?'

'Yes, I'm just curious. It's just it was a long time ago and if she hasn't got over it now . . .' I thought of Josh and wondered if I would still be grieving for him in twenty years. I guessed I probably would. Though perhaps not with Sharon's heartrending gusto.

'One of their friends upped and left a couple of days before Cheryl, Sharon's mum, died.'

'One of Sharon's friends?'

'No. One of my mum's and Cheryl's. It was all a bit scandalous at the time. You know how Leigh folk love to gossip.' A soft breeze lifted the hair from Corinne's face, revealing an expression that was a mixture of reflection and irritation.

'Who was it?'

Corinne started swinging her leg. 'Well, that was the thing that got Sharon going. But to be honest she was half nuts with grief. It was Doctor Cook's wife, Veronica. The three of them were virtually inseparable. I guess a bit like we are now. Always in each other's houses for tea and a chat. Regularly off to the cinema together. They never confided in us. We were too young for that kind of relationship but we picked up things from overheard conversations: Veronica wanted to leave her husband. I don't think Cheryl wanted her to. I can't be sure, but I remember there were some pretty heated discussions. Veronica obviously didn't listen because one day she just upped sticks.'

My eyes widened as I listened. 'She left him.'

'Yep. She wrote a letter, though. Said she needed to go and find herself. It was the eighties. A lot of people were going over and doing the spice trail and that. And there was that *Shirley Valentine* movie that got them all going.'

'And that upset Sharon?'

'Well, sort of. She swears that there was some kind of argument between Doctor Cook and her mum. He probably assumed Cheryl knew where Veronica had gone. Whatever, Cheryl died shortly after. Massive heart attack. Sharon blamed Doctor Cook for it. And you've got to admit, if he knew she had a weak heart, he really shouldn't have got her so wound up. But that's life.'

'And death,' I said.

Corinne shrugged. 'You get to this point of the year and it's fifty:fifty as to whether Sharon will start raking it up again. She tries to hide how she feels about it but sometimes it all spills over.'

I could understand the reason for Cheryl's concealment but I could also appreciate the depths of misery that the revelation incurred: the guilt and regrets.

'Poor Sharon,' I said. 'Is she still a patient there?'

She snorted. 'No way. She left the practice after that.'

'You didn't leave then? Out of solidarity?'

'He's the best doctor in Leigh. Nicest practice too.'

'Yes,' I agreed. 'It's a lovely house. Strange atmosphere though.'

Corinne took a sip from her glass and coughed. 'I did wonder at some point if she was having an affair with Sharon's Uncle Chris,' she said into the fire.

My ears pricked up. 'Who?'

'Veronica,' she said dreamily, as if she wasn't really talking to me. 'But it was strange because Chris was a warden at St Clements.'

'The church?'

'Uh-huh. He was very proper. Quite religious. Engaged at the time too. Of course I've got no real proof. I just remember Sharon and I going back to her place for tea one day back then – Cheryl made the best fairy cakes in Leigh. School had closed early. Leaky water pipe I think. When we got there Veronica and Chris were leaving the cottage. They were a little embarrassed and they had that look about them. You know, they couldn't stop smiling or looking at each other. And they were giggly. I thought it was kind of odd – two adults acting like that. We were meant to be the teenagers! Said they'd dropped something off for Cheryl. Sharon didn't bat an eyelid, but I remember thinking "Ooooh".'

'Did he hear from her? Chris?'

Corinne shook her head. 'I don't think so. I'm not sure I would have found out. The adults closed ranks. Anyway, I have no idea if it was serious or a flirtation or a friendship.

206

And I expect Veronica wanted a clean break. People do that sometimes, don't they?'

I didn't say anything.

The fire blew sparks over Corinne's side. She stamped them out and then stared into the flames. I followed her gaze. In the centre of the drum shapes were shifting, mirroring each other in a ghostly preternatural dance.

'Sharon though,' Corinne was speaking slowly now, in the hypnotic thrall of the fiery spectacle. 'Veronica had been fond of her, not having any children of her own. She liked me too but I think she saw something in Sharon that she admired. She was a quiet woman herself. After she left Leigh, and then when her mother died, I think Sharon felt it was a double bereavement. That's when she got involved with drugs.' She continued to stare into the heart of the fire. 'And when she started saying weird things, making accusations.'

'Like what?' I asked carefully.

But Corinne made no reply. And I could tell she wasn't going to.

Under the darkening sky we sat in silence, lost in our thoughts. If you had found us then you would have seen that both of us were frowning.

Chapter Fifteen

Sharon's untimely collapse that night proved fortunate, at least for me.

When I woke her in the morning she looked awful and phoned her work, professing a seasonal cold. Later, over coffee, when I told her I needed to go to the hospital, she insisted on driving us there and occupying Alfie whilst I saw the neurologist. I didn't protest. Really I should have organized childcare but what with one thing and another I hadn't got round to it. So while I was prodded, peered at, inspected and tested, Sharon took my son to McDonald's, a rare politically incorrect treat.

Mrs Falwahi was thorough, methodical but silent. A similarly mute nurse sat in the corner of the consulting room inputting comments on the computer. At the end of the examination I was asked how long the eyelid had been drooping, if I had noticed anything unusual and if I could return in a couple of weeks with some old photos? Despite fairly rigorous probing on my half the consultant calmly told me that she would write a report to my GP and that I should make an appointment with him to discuss it.

'But am I OK?' I asked as I stood up to leave.

'Yes, yes. Don't worry. There is some swelling but . . .' She made a gesture that indicated she was searching for a word she couldn't find. 'It is nothing much.' She stood up. The next patient was due. Mrs Falwahi wanted me to go. 'See you soon.'

The nurse confirmed my details and told me to expect an appointment through in another couple of weeks.

Back at home Sharon was rather more alarmed. I had figured, while I waited for them in the car park, that it couldn't be urgent or even life threatening if Mrs Falwahi thought it was 'nothing much' and was prepared to wait to look at old snapshots. After all, the government was trying to improve waiting lists and NHS care, weren't they? Surely if you had something serious you'd be whizzed through to the front of the queue.

But Sharon was aghast as I relayed the appointment details. Her reaction might have produced something stronger and more fearful in myself had not her pale, perspiring face and endless paracetamol-popping reminded me that she was extremely hungover. Now that Corinne had filled me in on the details I could see that my friend was also morose. Yet her concern was comforting and when she left, late that afternoon, I realized that I had enjoyed the remainder of my day with her.

On Tuesday I took Alfie to my mum's on the east side of Southend, Thorpe Bay, so he could be spoilt rotten again. I thought that Lottie may have mentioned my appointment but Mum didn't allude to anything in her general chit-chat and 'how are yous'. I knew she would have, if she'd had the faintest inkling that I might be ill. Instead we sat in the garden and had tea and then wine and discussed relatives and their doings then, when I had been brought fully up to date, I mentioned my research project. Though I neglected to state why I was doing it. Mum had always been interested in history. A wannabe grammar-school girl, she had been forced to give up dreams of becoming a teacher when her father died and financial hardship meant she needed to go out to work along with my gran to maintain the household income and support her younger siblings. The novels of Jean Plaidy and an attraction to the folk revival scene of the sixties sustained her intellectually for decades. Recently she had begun to sketch out ideas for a series of historical novels.

I guess I hadn't said anything to her before as, until that point, I hadn't been entirely convinced what I was doing was sane and hadn't been produced by pressure exerted on my frontal lobe. Things were coming together though: the appearance of Sarah, the stunning insights of Andrew McWhittard, the similarities in our positions, the emergence of themes – all combined to convince me that now I was being propelled forwards by things beyond my control.

Of course none of this was mentioned to Mum as we sat under her parasol that sunny summer day, basking in the scent of nearby lavender. The conversation went from a brief report of what I'd learnt of Sarah Grey, to a more generalized chat about Leigh.

Mum was delighted that I was taking an interest in the town. She leant forwards to brush crumbs from the tablecloth. Her eyes always sparkled when she got excited. 'It's a fascinating area, Leigh. I had a couple of ideas for stories there. Have you discovered Elizabeth Little?'

I shook my head. I'd have remembered that name.

'An interesting lady. Smuggler. Top of her game about the same time as your Sarah Grey. Her speciality was lace and silks. She had a shop by the Peter Boat. Actually, come to think of it, I did read somewhere that the Littles put about that there were witches in Leigh, especially in St Clements' graveyard. The stories frightened the locals and stopped them investigating the lights and strange sounds that people saw in the churchyard at night.'

'Really? Poor Sarah, she had everything stacked against her.' I sighed, picturing a woman shunned by peers, made a scapegoat by the smugglers, stifled by poverty, scarred by endless bereavement. What a wretched, joyless life.

'You know Pauline Dobinson? From the folk club? Used to make those awful macramé plant holders . . .'

I delved back into my childhood and came up with a thin woman in white jeans and orange lipstick.

'Her dad, when he was alive, used to have a cottage in the Old Town. Do you remember? I think we went there when you were young, though you couldn't have been more than eight at the time.'

Vague memories of an old man with a stick and a puppy dog came to mind but there was nothing concrete.

'Well, it doesn't matter. At the back of his garden he had a shed, and on the back wall of the shed there was a door that opened onto a dark passage. He reckoned it used to lead up to one of the graves in St Clements. The coastguard was just down the road patrolling the open roads up the hill, so the smugglers had to use other means to transport illegal goods. Old Mr Dobinson's tunnel must have been one of the smugglers' routes up. And what better way of stopping folks from poking their nose into your business than scaring them off with stories of foul witches and terrifying ghosts?'

'Wow,' I said. 'It's all very Scooby-Doo!'

'Yes, quite clever. I can't see them having anything to do with her death, though. The criminal element surely would want her alive to keep the rumours rife. A crooked, scary, old spell-casting shrew would have been a strong deterrent for busybodies.'

'She wasn't that bad,' I said, with irritation. 'Old yes, and worn out, but not dirty. Arthritic perhaps.' I stopped myself. These details had come from my dreams, not the books and records. I was giving myself away. Again.

Mum didn't challenge my sources. 'You know we've got connections in Leigh. Not your dad's side. His lot come from Walthamstow. No, on my side. We're Essex through and through. Aunty Brenda knows more about it than me. Apparently we go back to one of the fishing families. I did often wonder whether there was something in you deciding to relocate to Leigh and not Thorpe Bay. Almost like you were drawn there. I mean, Charlotte's over this side of town, and Thomas, and . . .'

I stopped her. 'You don't think we could possibly be related, do you?'

Mum laughed. 'That'd be funny, wouldn't it? It is a small world after all.'

But my interest was piqued. 'Seriously, Mum, is there any way you could find out?'

She sat back in her deck chair, folded her arms across her lap and tilted her face sunwards. 'I could ask Aunty Brenda. I've been meaning to call her. She'd know.'

Since Mum's sister had moved to Surrey their

communication had become erratic. Not because of any kind of rift but because absence does that sometimes. 'When are you going to phone?'

'Within the next week or so, I expect,' Mum said, noncommittally. 'But anyway, I always used to think that old women have been given bad PR by history. Young women, too. And those of middle-age.' She laughed bitterly. 'It still puzzles me how "bachelordom" conjures up visions of cheerful young men yet "spinsterhood" gives you sour rejects. Wizard – wise, witch – evil. Actually, now I'm not sure that wicked Sarah Grey might have been worth more dead than alive. What's more frightening – a witch or the ghost of a witch?'

I sat back and pondered. That night I thought about Sarah Grey and Aunty Brenda. Then I added Elizabeth Little to my list of suspects.

I was sitting down to some empty American cop show with a bag of toffee popcorn late on Friday night, when there was a knock at the door. As most childless friends tend to ring the bell I was surprised to find Andrew McWhittard on my doorstep. Of course, he hadn't always been childless, I remembered guiltily as he strode into the living room.

The week had done him good. He'd filled out a tad and there was a healthy colour to his cheeks. He was in good spirits too: I offered him a wine or cup of tea and he clapped his hands together and declared he'd love 'a proper English cuppa'.

While we waited for the kettle to boil he chatted about what he'd done in the week: caught up with friends in Glasgow, attended family barbecues and visited Aberdeen.

He didn't say why but I remembered Imogen had come from there and asked him gingerly, 'Did you see your wife's family?'

He looked at me rather indignantly. 'Why do you ask?'

I'd made a mistake. 'Oh, nothing. Just wondered.'

'Well don't,' he said, then he sort of straightened himself up and rephrased his answer. 'Don't worry yourself about me. I'm all right.'

'Sure thing,' I muttered as I filled the kettle, deciding this was my house and my rules. 'Go into the living room and make yourself comfortable.'

To my surprise he followed orders and disappeared.

When I brought the two mugs through we sat opposite each other and blew the steaming tea. I had my eye on the black record bag at his feet but didn't want to mention it.

Andrew spoke first. 'You got any further with your investigation?'

'Actually yes,' and I told him about Sharon's findings, adding the Elizabeth Little tale at the end. He didn't think the smuggler was a goer as a suspect but he was very interested in the fact that Sarah Grey had had a child in 1823 and that she was married to Robert Billing, a widower then.

'That bears out what she said,' he said, more to himself than me.

'What she said? What who said? Sarah?'

Andrew set down his mug carefully, pulled the bag onto his lap and produced three sketchbooks. 'You'll have to forgive the writing. It's a little all over the place. I can't stand working on lined paper.' He took a heavy brown book from the top of the pile and handed it to me. 'I didn't research chronologically so I've flagged up the order that would be

214

most logical for you, using these Post-it notes. Start with that,' he pointed to the one in my hands. 'You can get the gist of what's going on with one of the early letters.' He wasn't making much sense so I made a mental effort to commit these directions to memory.

'Then it's best to move on to this one.' He passed over a thicker journal. It weighed a tonne. 'It may seem a little fragmented but I don't want to overwhelm you. It's not what you're after really, as fascinating as I might have once found it myself.' He brought the last book over to my sofa and sat beside me. Not too close. Though several respectable inches lay between us, I could feel his body heat.

'Finish with this.' He held up a book bound in racing-green leather. It was thinner than the other two and had been well thumbed. 'Try to keep to the order specified. It'll make more sense.' A managerial tone was creeping into his voice again.

'Right.' He got to his feet and made for the door. 'I could really do with a lie-in tomorrow. The drive down was pretty horrendous so can you phone me after ten please?'

I laughed.

He didn't smile back. 'I'm not joking. You'll be on the phone as soon as you've finished. I'll make time for you tomorrow but I do need to rest. OK?'

A familiar indignation came over me. Arrogant fucker. Who did he think he was?

At the door McWhittard stopped and turned to me. 'Good luck,' he said, and kissed me on my cheek.

I didn't get myself together enough to say goodbye, and stood there dumbly as he walked off to his car.

Andrew McWhittard was revealing himself to be a host

of contradictions, I thought, shutting the door and returning inside. I turned over the books and took them into the kitchen.

It was a quarter past nine.

I shifted the first journal onto the table and began to read the Reverend Eden's words in McWhittard's stumpy calligraphy.

Chapter Sixteen

Letter to Thomas Gooden

18th of January, 1838

Dear Thomas,

I must apologise for the delay in my return correspondence. I promised to give you some account of my new position in Essex but have found little time to sit at my desk. As you know from my last missive much change has been afoot.

The seasonal tasks and responsibilities here have been manifold. In addition to the duties of the position, I have needed to assist the settling of the children and appointment of a new governess as Emma is with child. Although Mary, our eldest, has been a great support and Frederick has returned to his schooling, Caroline and little Alice have taken quite some time to adjust to their new home.

It is clear to see that the air agrees with Emma, she has been quite exhausted by her new duties as Rector's wife. Last week we acknowledged we both felt some relief as the old year came to pass.

The parish, which is sprawling, has been most receptive to the liberation of God's word in the services that I have vigorously delivered to them. And thankfully so. It appears my predecessor did not venture down towards the town, afraid it seems of the untoward character of the people thereabouts. The Lady of the Manor, Lady Olivia Bernard Sparrow, did at one time engage the services of one Ridley Herschell to preach to the congregations here. It seems the man, a convert from abroad, was much loved by the people of Leigh and, so my neighbours tell me, was presented with a Bible and Prayer Book when he left after but a year and a half.

Terrible poverty exists in the complex of dwellings belonging to the fishing folk by the water's edge. The residents are rough and boisterous. They work hard and long. Yet, not a year goes by without a tragedy and, as such, when ashore they take their pleasure in the numerous public houses.

The town is much diminished from that which it once was at the height of its wealth: a small port that housed a remarkable shipbuilding centre unrivalled outside of London. Its demise can, I am told on good authority, be attributed to the silting up of this part of the Thames.

There are several fine estates and furthermore, some admirable inhabitants that distinguish the town from its neighbouring villages. Some of the more prominent members of this society I have had the good fortune to meet at the St Stephen's Day ball given by the Lady of the Manor at her lodgings, Cliff Hall. The Lady of the Manor does not reside in Leigh permanently and rents Leigh Hall to a tenant farmer, preferring to keep lodgings when she visits the town. She is a keen huntress and has retained the right to shoot and fish on Leigh Hall land. She has built stables and keeps a gamekeeper there to manage it for her. By reputation she is a God-fearing woman of strong will and a benefactor to the people of Leigh.

Despite the outwardly impressive structure, the interior of Cliff Hall was surprisingly dour for the festive occasion. The good Lady Olivia does not approve of decorative fripperies. The large hall was possessed of some interesting Spanish panelling and a mantelpiece in the same oak. The only indication of the blessed day was a tree by the door. The room was tastefully furnished but chilly. There was, however, a largely agreeable gathering of persons who more than filled the room with festive cheer, one of these being our neighbour Mr John Snewin, a local land owner and fellow of exceeding good nature whose acquaintance I was fortunate to make prior to the party, and who since our first meeting has been a frequent dinner guest at our table.

In the service of good Mr Snewin we were introduced to several quite charming families of Leigh who offered dinner invitations, the promise of which enthused Emma (the location further south has necessitated a removal from society which she has not enjoyed).

A small group of guests, clustered sycophantically around the Lady of the Manor, were rather more cautious in their welcome: a sullen farmer, Henry Wilde, and a widowed physician by the name of Doctor Festus Hunter, being but two. Wilde's expressions were awkward and he seemed uncomfortable in society, for lack of manners more than anything else, barely answering Emma's mild enquiries into his farmlands. Like most agriculturalists I have encountered, he appears to find the company of women frivolous and cares not to conceal it. Hunter, however, does not.

The man was of middle-age and handsome for it. Eyes of the palest blue were set in watery pools as if he were constantly on the verge of weeping. It lent him a womanly aspect to his character that I found disagreeable. Snewin had warned me of the Doctor's acute ambition for the favours of Lady Sparrow. His political manoeuvring, indelicate and clumsy, soon became plain to see.

I was impressed by her Ladyship's dress, comportment and her presence, that left none unacquainted of her importance. Her face, however, attractive as it can be for a woman in her fifth or sixth decade, bears the bitter scars of bereavement and cares. There was compassion in her Ladyship's smile of greeting but an ice to her eyes that I was soon to experience.

After initial introductions, Hunter's would-be patroness enquired into plans for my incumbency. Prompted by Lady Olivia I eagerly outlined the first intended project: that day I had just approved architectural applications for the construction of a new rectory (our present accommodation is a crumbling wreck) and advised Lady Olivia of the design, which follows a fashionable Elizabethan style.

'I have a legacy, which I wish to put to good use,' I told her, with my customary passion. Though Snewin offered a 'bravo' the effect on the other members of my audience was quite the reverse. Wilde withdrew abruptly on the pretence of addressing a newcomer. Doctor Hunter withheld his expression, looking after the Lady of the Manor. Lady Olivia had remained expressionless throughout my short speech, the faint smile that had greeted us growing colder on her lips. After a moment of thought she ventured, 'But what of your new role, pastor?'

I was sure it was not a rebuff but a prompt to some verbal amusement and was about to respond with a smile when Doctor Hunter cut me off with the most obsequious of replies: 'It is not in works or glorifications that one finds salvation. It is in the heart and scripture.'

The impertinence of the man! I expected Lady Olivia to rebuke him instantly but to my horror I found her smile had returned to shine on the doctor. The remark had unequivocally endeared him to her and at once I saw what he was – one of the most dangerous types of men: a political creature. Hunter would injure those of his own standing to ingratiate himself to those above. His dress was ostentatious, garish even, and yet in his words he concurred with this plain Lady. And she, for all her outward austerity, clearly enjoyed his lavish attentions. I would have to watch my step, I rued.

The good Snewin commented that the words seemed not of Hunter's own mind but smacked of dissent, which the latter would not rejoin. Lady Sparrow, sensing the distasteful turn of atmosphere, took Emma by the arm and led her to a group of aged dowagers gathered round the furthest hearth who would 'delight' in her company.

Never before have I regretted the departure of my dear wife so directly.

For a moment it seemed that Hunter faced me with a look of triumph, which then disappeared with his protector. Left with two gentlemen superior in rank and intellect the doctor shrivelled and assumed the unease that farmer Wilde had previously displayed.

'Lady Sparrow will not tolerate popery, Rector.' This was said without malice of tone by Hunter, but the effect of his words was to anger me once more.

'Sir, nor would I. The church that I serve is the one true church,' I retorted.

Hunter smirked. 'You serve the church, not the Lord?'

At this point Snewin intervened. 'Goodness, Hunter! What a welcome is this for our new pastor? Never fear. The reverend has much to occupy himself with in the parish and will not usurp the dog on the lap of the Lady.'

Hunter apprehended the insult and turned on his heel, making first in the direction of his mistress, then came to a stop and instead left the room, darting one last look at us.

I remarked to Snewin what an extraordinary character the doctor had.

Snewin shook his head. 'He has much wealth and authority here and yet his hunger for more continues to grow. Rumours suggest that with Lady Olivia's assistance, he intends to become mayor.'

The thought was repugnant but I withheld additional comment on spying Emma return with two female companions. These, I was made aware, were two charming daughters of a local family, the Hiltons, and quite agreeable in their disposition. Soon they had delighted myself and Mr Snewin out of our previous ill temper and back into the life of the party.

The night passed without any further occurrence and Emma and I found ourselves at home just after midnight. And yet over my mind a sense of foreboding had crept. I believe I must take care with the Lady of the Manor and

222

her puppy dog. This would be a sensible course of action by any means.

I look forward to your next letter and hope you continue to excel in health and spirits and persist in the advancement of your career.

Believe me, sincerely your friend
Robert Eden

My head was beginning to ache as I put down the first book. Night had eased into the kitchen without me noticing. I stretched my arms and yawned. A glance at the clock told me bedtime was approaching but I was desperate to know where the journal would take me, and curious as to Andrew's reasons in starting me with the letter. Was it scene setting or something more?

I switched on the table lamp and put the kettle on for coffee. Then I opened the second sketchbook at the place indicated by the Post-it. Here was an extract from the reverend's personal journal.

The exact date had been smeared but I could make out the month: August, 1849. Eleven years had passed. I waded through a lot of extraneous detail about sermons and notes to visit parishioners. Then I came to this:

The events of the last week have depleted my resources so. I have been unable to sleep, nourish myself adequately or come to my writing desk, something of an extravagance at this time. I scoff at my vanity when my mind wanders back to the disputes of last year that induced such a wretchedness about my own self. Lady Olivia's irksome rebuttal of my teachings, her insistence and dissemination of such Low Church views, are factors as influential to the administration of my parish as the children's quarrels. The dreadful events of the past six days has hardened my resolve to carry on my work as I see fit. I will not be drawn away from the service of God by the interference and defamation of the Lady's agents, though now I believe my suspicions are confirmed as to the origin of that slanderous letter to my parish. While the men, women and children of Leigh lay dying, Doctor Hunter remains at Lady Olivia's Suffolk rest. The man is as a snake in the grass, duplicitous and able to weave through society, claiming favour and consolidating power. Indeed if things were not such as they were I would have a mind to pursue the doctor through the courts. But no, the distraction of anger will not take me. It is wasteful and no good will come of it I am sure. My Lord above has sent me to this place where more than ever my services are required to assist the sick of heart and body.

The cholera has worsened, claiming more innocents. It is of little surprise the disease has spread throughout the town: the fishermen's cottages by the riverside are little more than slums with only a conduit and two wells to afford them fresh water. The conduit is often contaminated by weeds and waste. The stench of disease reaches everywhere. As the populace has grown the sanitation has become inadequate.

The people of Leigh have shown their customary charity in the face of such dire circumstances and the parish has donated funds enough to employ two women to launder infected linen. Some of the men have taken charge of burning the bedding of the deceased.

My wife's Christian charity has been rousing. The children make enough demands on her, yet gentle Emma has not ceased in her efforts to relieve the suffering of the afflicted:

travelling to Southend to collect fresh linen and food relief for the poor.

Stimulated to action by my wife's example, I too resolved to go down to the sick to offer my hands in the comfort of God and administer to the dying.

On Saturday I attended a cramped dwelling on Strand Wharf to assist a local woman by the name of Sarah Grey. I had been warned by several upright and decent men to avoid Mother Grey on account of her 'cunning' cures. The citation of Deuteronomy did silence their tongues: 'Thou shalt not harden thine heart, nor shut thine from thy poor brother.' In the event she seemed no more than other wretches.

Her household was badly afflicted. The cottage was small and draughty and infected with the dreadful smell of death. In such conditions the disease had already claimed her husband. The woman had lived a tragic life, with not one but two of her husbands taken by the Lord: Robert Billing, the first, I heard tell, was lost at sea; John Grey, her second, to this dreadful cholera. Now two of her sons were stricken: George, but sixteen years and unlikely to reach his seventeenth, and John Grey, the elder of the two at nineteen. With seven other children to tend I ascertained on my arrival the woman was in dire need of assistance yet was in receipt of none from her neighbours.

I immediately made myself useful with the ailing men, bathing their heads and rubbing their flesh. They were both pale and confused. George was by far the worse of the two. Mrs Grey urged him to drink water and offered a salty concoction, but his heart was failing and as the hours passed his breathing came in short, fast gulps. It became plain to me there would be little I could do to avert God's will. George's soul was soon to go before Him. I urged his mother and the children to come together in a family prayer. Mrs Grey refused and persisted in the belief that both her sons would regain their health. I should state for my own memory that this repulsed not my sensibilities. The woman's rejection was born out of fear. She was not as I expected from the reports of gentle folk. Certainly she made potions from herbs; evidently these gave some relief to her sons. There was no evidence of witchery, only poverty and a bleakness of vision that had come from her recent loss.

She spoke in a quiet manner. Though the texture of her voice was as coarse as her hands, she enunciated her words like a gentle woman. If I had not been busied with nursing the sick I would have entertained the idea of knowing her story. I did not know I would hear it later.

As the sun faded beyond the castle we nursed the men through the night in silence that was broken only by the arrival of her daughter, Harriet, with a broth. By then John's condition had also deteriorated. Mrs Grey urged me to go home and rest. I assured her I was an instrument of God's will and He had directed me to her.

I lose track of time as I recall those nights but I think it was before dawn on Sunday morning that young George expired. He had lapsed into an unresponsive sleep, which was at least of some comfort to his mother, who was spared the unendurable cries of delirium that this illness provokes.

Mrs Grey could not be removed from the corpse for some time. When at last she was roused by John's plaintive cries, I carried George downstairs for her daughter and old Dame Alworth to perform the laying out. But for the pallor of his skin it was as if he slumbered in a deep restful sleep. He rests in peace now.

The parochial ministrations of the Sabbath required a swift return to the church. Mrs Grey seemed not to hear me as I left the cottage with a promise to return that night to provide counsel to John.

My flock were in need of consolation. With many fallen to the infection the congregation was diminished. The second chapter of Jonah was appropriate to strengthen them in this time of great suffering. I cried out from the pulpit verses nine to ten: 'I will pray that that I have vowed. Salvation is of the Lord. And the Lord spake unto the fish and it vomited out Jonah upon the dry land.'

After evening prayer I retired to my study with the church wardens to discuss the distribution of alms. It was my honest intention to return to the wharf but the day's cares and onerous night had taken much from me and I was awoken in my chair by Emma early Monday morning.

Urgent ministrations requiring my attention prevented me from returning for two days – there are many that seek help – the death toll increases daily: we are too busy with burials.

Only on Wednesday evening did a lull in my duties permit a visit to the cottage on Strand Wharf.

The malady had made steady progress with John. He breathed with great difficulty and had become insensible. Mrs Grey had attended to his bedside night and day. She was drawn and languid and at my request went downstairs briefly to repose while I prayed over young John.

Mrs Grey called me down. She had made tea. I was hesitant to take it as the smell of the cottage was repugnant. The stench of death and disease crept through the walls and seemed to seep into the very mortar of the building. But inspecting the stone floor I saw that, though there was little comfort, she had kept the place tidy and as clean as she could. We sat on hard wooden chairs in front of the feeble hearth. Mrs Grey placed a clay pot of hedge roses on the mantelpiece and presently their fragrance eased the sour reek of the air.

Both beyond the point of exhaustion we supped in silence. In the absence of conversation I conveyed my condolences to her once more. She turned to me and, with some ferocity, informed me it was her due. I refuted that and alluded to God's mystery and the divine plan for each soul. She meditated on this awhile. Then she asked how much sorrow a soul should take for a sin they had made when young?

I said my Lord was a God of Mercy: there was no sin that could not be forgiven if the sinner were truly repentant. She sighed, I think, with understanding. So I asked her the circumstance of the sin.

At this point it was plain to see the burden of grief that agonised the woman's senses. Her pallor was grey, her eyes, which were of a dark green, seemed to see past the walls of the cottage, flitting skyward then to the bare boards. She wrung her hands as she began to speak, rambling falteringly through the memories of her childhood. She took a locket, bejewelled with garnet, from her dress and begin to twist it fretfully, then Mrs Grey, Sarah, as she now bade me call her, described a decent home with a firm father, Alfred Sutton, who schooled her in some basic principles of education. His Christian upbringing was tempered with instruction from the mother, who was cousin to a local man of some notoriety: the sorcerer Cunning Murrell. This man alleges he can break curses, cure warts and such and seek answers from the stars. Sarah Grey's own mother was rumoured to have inherited some gifts similar to that of Murrell: the ability to locate lost objects and such.

She kept me enthralled as she described the family cure-alls that her mother brewed, formed by various concoctions of herbs

228

and plants collected along the wayside by her daughter. At this Sarah confessed she exceeded in aptitude.

The father's good standing in the community and his Christian devotion awarded the family with some appearance of respectability. Though there were regular visits from friends and kinsmen in search of things misplaced or desiring of these miracle cures, it seemed the Suttons were largely shunned by those not in want. Mrs Sutton, in her latter years, and against the warnings of her husband, had made more of her 'gifts' than the townsfolk were comfortable with.

The steady trepidation and fear that this disease spreads has wearied men of the most robust mental condition but I was in thrall to Sarah's words. I lost track of time as she wandered about the landscape of her mind. I was called back into the room on hearing her name the Lady of the Manor. Mrs Grey's face was rapt, her eyes bright and her coarsened voice lighter. She was reciting an account of her 'great disappointment' and as I focused on the narration the most extraordinary story unfolded.

Sarah first encountered her love whilst strolling about the fields of Hadleigh, in particular the ruined castle where she would collect herbs for her various brews. The man, it seemed, was a handsome fellow, with eyes green like hers, and dark skin 'the colour of wet sand', which Sarah found beautiful but which also forced an exclusion of sorts by the society of Leigh people who considered him a 'furrinner' and therefore to be treated with suspicion. They are not cosmopolitan and indeed those that hail from neighbouring towns such as Rochford, in the very same hundred, are also considered 'furriners'. This chap, it appeared, lived under the protection of the Lady of the Manor as some high-ranking servant of sorts. 'He gave me

229

this,' she hung the locket over her chest. ''Tis beautiful. I know he saved long and hard for it. Now it is all I have of him.'

Now, I cannot attest to the validity of my next statement yet Sarah swears by our Lord it is true. Her love, Tobias Fitch, she said, was the son of Brigadier General Robert Bernard Sparrow, Lady Olivia Sparrow's late husband: the issue of time spent in Barbados, an unfortunate coupling with a favoured slave. I cannot comprehend this behaviour in a noble man of such stature as the Brigadier, yet Sarah insisted that Fitch's mother, expiring in childbirth, convinced Lord Sparrow to provide for her son. That he agreed or didn't agree we will never know. For the Brigadier died on board ship from a fatal fever as he journeyed back home. The boy, it seems, was sent to Lady Olivia by members of the crew who did not wish to be saddled with another mouth to feed. Presented with the child it appeared that instead of sending Fitch away to the orphans' asylum 'the Lady of the Manor did throw her arms around him and weep'. That is how Sarah described the scene. My dealings with the Lady have not revealed such tenderness, and yet, part of me can believe it. Whatever the truth, the boy was installed in the household and shown special favours by his genial benefactor. The latter of course resulted in jealousies which effected the alienation of Tobias from the other domestic servants.

The Lady of the Manor enjoyed the hunt and Fitch often joined her on trips as a fetching-boy or steward. It was on one of these visits to her grounds in Leigh that Fitch met Mrs Grey, Miss Sutton as she was then. Accustomed to the mistrustful slurs of other servants Tobias sought the refuge of solitude in fields and woods. One late summer's day Sarah recalled falling over in one of the ploughed fields. Fitch hurried to her aid.

And that is when their friendship took root. Both were treated with caution by the communities in which they lived. They developed an immediate affinity, which over the course of the coming months, became coloured by more passionate thoughts.

It seems that the sin of which Sarah spoke was that which is common amongst women of a lower class. When she found herself with child, Fitch hastened to seek permission from Lady Olivia to make good Sarah.

Lady Olivia did not conceal her disdain. Sarah was not of the rank she desired for the wife of her protégé. Nor was the reputation of her family palatable to the Lady of the Manor. Lady Olivia foresaw a contamination of such great malevolence she not only refused Fitch's request but forbade him to see Sarah again.

Such rebuttals, of course, do little to dampen the ardour of youth. With help from a friend, unknown to Sarah, Fitch arranged an elopement. Sarah was to meet him at a local spot, Adam's Elm, a grand tree hollowed from within which, it is said, can conceal as many as thirteen men. Deferred by some trivial chore, when Sarah arrived a scene of uproar spread before her: Tobias was in the grips of a press gang. The man fought bravely, knocking one man to the floor and throwing off another. Sarah ran immediately to his help but was thrown aside, hitting the elm with such force she lost sensibility.

When she came round Doctor Hunter had been summoned to help. He had bitter news: one of the mob had been killed by Tobias and in revenge they had taken his life.

Sarah paused now, reliving the moment her heart was broken. 'The doctor said his body had been returned to lie with his mother. I had nothing. No place to mourn him. I thought I would never know such inward sorrow, such deep loss. To

231

come from the blissful joy of impending marriage to that. I knew at that moment I would never love truly again. And it has been so.'

She slumped into a reverie and fearing that she may swoon, I brought her back with a question about the child. 'Doctor Hunter conveyed my situation to his Lady. They found a man who would take me for a wife, with the promise of fifteen pounds and a sack full of ale. I wouldn't have him. I . . .' she faltered here. 'I did not want to live. I went to the Drowning Pool. But it would not take me. So they pulled me out and called me witch. They had been waiting to do that. A Sutton, witch girl like my mother and uncle. We have never been so. But,' she sighed, 'they got their way.

'Robert Billing raised his fee to twenty pounds (which he spent over time in the King's Head, and they wed me to him. My son was born shortly after. Folk knew he wasn't Robert's. He had his father's eyes and his sandy skin. But he was such a beautiful child even my husband could not but love him too. Nine short years I spent with him. Each was a wonder. My sin has haunted me through my life, claiming all those I love.'

I uttered some well-chosen words of reassurance and reminded her that the Lord would not countenance self-murder. I duly expected that she would repent for her sins and was dismayed when Sarah revealed she cared not to. 'My love with Tobias, that wasn't a wrong. 'Twas a blessing from above. No, my sin was that I killed Tobias. If I hadn't delayed at the house we would have been away before the gang got there. My actions brought about the death of the most noble, righteous man the world could ever know.'

I was stunned by her profanity and urged her to repent the sin of carnality. After discussion that threatened to linger into *the morning, Sarah agreed and together we sat down and prayed to our Lord above.*

When we had finished I took my leave and went to the door. Sarah handed me my coat and hat. As I stepped onto the wharf, she said this. 'They slaughtered Tobias that night, sir, but they took no other Leigh man. Don't you think that strange for a press gang, Reverend?'

I replied, 'Such men take flight as soon as danger looks their way.'

'But why were they there at all, Reverend? At the Elm? It's far from the town.' She reached out to touch my arm, as if to stay me. I shook her off with some words of comfort and made my way back to the rectory.

That night in my study I would think about her words until the curate called. Another soul required my ministrations and blessing before they made their journey towards God.

It was very late now but I was wide-awake. Sarah was right. Adam's Elm was a way away, up by the Elms pub. I checked a map that I had bought in the Heritage Centre. Yep, nothing up there but Elm Farm and the highway.

It was ludicrous that a press gang would just happen to pass by at exactly the same time Tobias had arranged to meet Sarah. They must have had a tip-off. Perhaps from Tobias' 'unknown friend'? Could I find out who that was? Or was there actually any point? Was the sad case of Sarah's murdered love just that? A tragic accident. I contemplated that it could have nothing to do with her death but I jotted down 'The Friend' in my own notes anyway.

The clock chimed the half hour. Half-past twelve exactly. I pulled out the final journal and turned to Andrew's

Post-its. The first was noted with a number one. The second further back read 'And finally . . .'

I flicked to the first. In the margin Andrew had drawn a line in a fluorescent marker indicating the section I was to read – December 1867. The entry began with a detailing of Eden's routines. By now he had become the Primus of Scotland and it seemed he was indeed a very busy man. There were rants about people who had written to him, a great passage that covered the demise of Olivia Sparrow and pages and pages of religious guff I didn't understand. Andrew obviously expected me to have more of an interest in Eden's regular ecclesiastical life than I actually did. Finally I came to page twenty-seven of his neatly written notes. At the foot of it was the note of interest, highlighted in the margin with a pink fluorescent line.

'I have also received a letter from my old parish of Leigh. The hand was almost illegible but with some great effort I was able to decipher some words. Dated the 4th of December it implored me to come there at once. "A great injustice has been committed, sir," it read. "I ask you to come to Leigh at once so that you may understand the grievance that must be redressed."'

A line after this was unreadable, the hand too wild and sprawling, but underneath this a signature, much like that of a young infant's, read *SARAH GREY*. Andrew must have copied it from the original letter.

'It is an unusual request but I am very busy at present. Though Emma has been saying a trip away might be a welcome tonic to the great cold here. The Leigh air was always so good for her. I shall mention it and if she is willing shall plan a trip for the New Year.'

He then returned to musings on his next sermon. There

was nothing else of interest for a good few pages till I reached the last Post-it Andrew had left for me.

The previous instalment of the journal bore the date 10th of March. The section Andrew indicated had been written on the 25th. It was three in the morning. I was tired and my eyes ached but I was too wired to sleep. I needed to know what had happened.

I peeled off the last Post-it and began to read.

It is a delight to return to Cliff Hall. Our lodgings have been restored to a glory that preceded Lady Olivia's time spent here. The previous tenant has divided up the great hall into more useful rooms befitting a residence the main service of which is to house as many short-term visitors as is comfortable in a condition of luxury as befits the exterior architecture. As such our rooms have been gaily painted in vivid colours, the likes of which no doubt would have bewildered the Lady of the Manor were she still alive. Though there were disagreements between us I am sure Leigh will miss the favours of its generous benefactor. Lady Olivia's lands have been disentailed and sold off to diverse parties. There is no longer a Lady of the Manor. I believe the manorial rights to have been purchased by some merchant type.

I was glad to see that our drawing room still housed the mantel of Spanish oak. As Emma and I sat by the fire on our first night of occupation my dear wife suggested the sounds of revelry could still be heard faintly through the corridors.

The following day Emma renewed acquaintance with her good friend, Mrs Hilton. I made a round of visits to my former parishioners. Inevitably the number has depleted yet there were still many whom it was good to see. We supped with the Hiltons and agreed to visit Southend with them the following afternoon. It wasn't until Friday that we were able to visit our former home, now the rectory of Walker King and his large family.

The day was changeable and though the morning had brought with it a clarity of sunshine one can only find on these southern shores, by the time we approached the rectory a frightful wind was whistling through the great oaks and cedars of the gardens, the gulls shrieking against it. The sound quite unsettled Emma (she is sensitive to these things, I have found). I, however, experienced no presentiment of what was to come.

Our host, Walker King, was a cordial man of middling years. The parishioners I had encountered of late spoke of him with great respect. His manner was humble and easy, his smile appearing often. I could see at once Reverend King was a like-able gentleman.

After dinner the reverend and I retired to the study. He had moved the furniture in a way which I did not wholly approve: a great chest of drawers was now removed to the window and prevented one from taking in the magnificent view of the gardens.

We conversed a little about parish affairs: the ivy on the north of the church tower, the dwindling offertory, the opportunist nature of some fishing folk. The troubles that irked me some fifteen years previously continued to vex Reverend King. I commented on this and we shared some mirth. Then I spoke of the matter that had brought me here.

King was economic in his words: Sarah Grey was dead and buried.

I have to admit to being somewhat shocked by this. A coil of unease snaked round the pit of my stomach. Dead. I had come too late, then.

236

Much alarmed I enquired as to the cause. The reverend became circumspect. He spoke of the dignified family wake, the supportive community. The death of an elder was not so unusual and yet I was taken much aback by King's description: when I left the small town, Sarah Grey was attributed a witch, after another abominable cholera outbreak. Yet King referred to the widow as 'the Good Mother Grey' almost as if the people of Leigh had made their peace with her.

'Tell me,' I pressed, thinking of the note she had sent. 'What were the circumstances of the widow's demise?'

The reverend grew agitated and took to his feet. 'It appears she had been ill and frail for some time. Doctor Hunter confided that the family had been concerned over the wanderings of her mind. But she was an aged woman and that is at times not uncommon in those approaching the night of life.'

'Ah, I see. Yes, lamentably, I have seen this many times. Grey had, I believe, an older daughter and several other children. I trust they nursed her as she had nursed them?'

The reverend had begun pacing. 'She was overtaken by an illness whilst on a walk.'

'Regrettable. With the family at least?'

The reverend stopped and watched me as he said, 'Her remains were found alongside Doom Pond.'

This caused me to take a sharp intake of breath. Could it be so? Doom Pond – the ancient place where, in unenlightened times, those accused of witchcraft were once so barbarically treated?

I paused for air. The reverend was watching my face as if forewarned of the effect his words might have on me. 'Can I ask,' he said at last, 'the reason for your personal involvement in this matter?'

I told him of the letter.

My words startled him. Alarm flashed from his eyes. 'She should have come to me. I had no idea that she might have been aware that she was in danger. I assumed it to be a quarrel or . . .' He put his hand to his beard and stroked it. 'When was this?'

I told him of the date mark, December the 5th, but that I had received it on the 9th. As justification of my delay I outlined the duties that prevented me from responding. Though, I must say, the kernel of trepidation was growing within and a shudder went through me.

The reverend promptly ministered to my ill ease. 'There was little you could have done. On the 9th of December we buried Sarah Grey.'

This was of some comfort. Yet I could see there was more he was not telling me: the news of the letter had brought about such a great change in his character.

'Reverend,' I dictated in a tone that commanded him to reply as honestly as he could. 'I must ask you to apprise me of the circumstances of her death.'

At this the reverend let out a long, pitiful sigh. The night had come in and King moved himself to shut the curtains. He rang for a servant and ordered two brandies before falling silent. Once we cradled the glasses in our hands he secured the study door with a key.

The man was by now in a state of high anxiety. Once more he checked the doors and windows. Only when he had ascertained our discussion would be completely private did he at last answer my question.

'What I tell you now must go no further. I am breaking a vow of secrecy but you, good sir, are my brethren. I must ask

you never to speak of this again. You are a bishop. I need not hear an oath but I must have your word, sir.'

I acceded to his request, though found it bordering on obsessive.

'You must understand,' he told me, his eyes fretful and grave. 'Leigh is a place caught in a delicacy of balance. We are too big for a village and too small for a town. There is poverty and death and as a consequence the best that can be done to keep prosperity within is to ensure a situation of balance for all who live here. The church's role is often to maintain this subtle equilibrium. Sometimes we must serve the Lord in protecting this for the greater good of the people, notwithstanding the tragedy of the few.'

I said that I understood. My incumbency had seen plans and conflicts that preceded the coming of the railway. I recalled hearing of one great battle between the fishermen and the navvies. The men of Leigh had won that night. It wasn't always so.

Assured of an affinity he continued. 'Many ships stop here on their way from the port of London to the continent and beyond, to stock up on food and linen. Many make a fair living in trading with these vessels and it is important that their crew continue to be welcomed in Leigh.'

I nodded. It was clear enough. The same practice had occurred in my time.

The reverend took a sip of his liqueur. 'It is also of note that there is no group of men and women as fearful and super-stitious as fishing folk.'

This too, I knew to be true.

'I noted your surprise when I spoke of Sarah Grey as "Good Mother". It was a tempering of the truth. I do not wish to speak

badly of her but Mother Grey was not well liked. She was feared in these parts. I see you knew of this too.'

'Yes. I had some knowledge of it when I lived here. But,' I stressed to him, 'I visited her home several times and found nothing of witchcraft there. The woman trifled with herbs but there seemed no other evidence of ungodliness.' I did not speak of the confession she had once made of her sin.

He leant forwards. 'I agree. What little I know of her, her reputation had little foundation. Yet as I told you she was found by the Drowning Pool. Fortunately (please forgive the use of this word but you will understand it presently) it was my curate, Henry, who made the grim discovery in the early hours of the 5th, brought to the pond by the yapping of his hounds. He hastened directly here. On informing me of what he had found I directed him to call the physician, as is the common practice. Henry was in a state of extreme disquiet and insisted I saw it for myself. When we reached the pond, he took me to a bush where he had concealed the corpse.'

The reverend paused to take a deep breath. 'She had been bound, as witches were swum: her right thumb tied fast to the left toe.'

I expressed my repugnance. 'She had been drowned then?'

The reverend paused, then nodded his head away from me as if he could not meet my eye. Slowly King turned, and looked directly at me. 'I must tell you this: she had been beheaded. We identified her by a locket that she was known to wear. The scene of the atrocity, dreadful though it was, was bloodless. A later search did not throw up the head. We have not found it yet.

'We called upon the nearest physician – Doctor Hunter. On examination of the corpse he declared it most likely she was

240

dead when the head was removed and that the body had been submerged for some hours. The tying, too, had come after death, he suggested, to suggest the woman a witch.'

I took this on board. 'Aren't they innocent then if drowned? That is what the fishing folk believe. One might say she achieved some kind of vindication at last. Though that is of little consolation to the dead.'

'Of that I cannot make comment. You must understand the implications of this for the church. We have moved on from those times but there are those within the parish who will cite "thou shall not suffer a witch to live" on a daily rote.

'Hunter's footman helped us to transport Grey's body to the doctor's house. At this he remarked that the folk by the river were all a chatter about an incident that occurred the night gone by. Sarah Grey had been seen speaking passionately with the captain of a vessel bound for Antwerp. There was some dispute. Folk supposed she had begged him for a penny to bless his passage home, not received one, so cursed him instead and run away. The captain had hastened to sea, for a storm was on its way. One that the fisher folk believed Sarah had called down on him.

'It was a difficult matter to decide upon. I have not always seen eye to eye with the doctor but the man was admirable in his loyalty to the law and insistent we call the coastguard to pursue the captain. "It was he that must have done for her", he said. "Or if not him, then some crusader from your church."

'His words struck fear into my heart. The ramifications of a churchgoer involved in this horrendous crime stirred me into a great anxiety. The unusual position in which Grey was bound, the absence of her head, suggested superstition, and a zealous antipathy to "witches". Hunter was sympathetic and suggested we then urge discretion in the matter. All those involved were soon sworn to secrecy, never to utter a word. As mayor of the town, Hunter was able to command a great respect and authority. He took it upon himself to make investigations and agreed to send men to pursue the captain of the ship, who was, according to Hunter's man, of a distinctive cast.

'It was agreed that we should not expose the family to the unfortunate circumstances of their mother's death. We sealed her in a coffin that night. Doctor Hunter agreed to insert "carcinoma" as the cause on the certification. As I said, we buried her with dignity within the walls of the churchyard.

'There has been little made of her death and yet rumours abound. I suspect the source to be one of Hunter's men but there is little one can do to silence wagging tongues and many suppose the story an invention of sorts.'

The reverend fetched more brandy as I digested this in silence. When he returned I asked what Hunter's men had found.

'Nothing,' he said. 'The captain had gone to ground. Tipped off, I presume, by someone at the port. We have agreed unless there are any further deaths of this sort that it may be concluded the captain was the culprit. And, my friend, I wish that it is so. She was an old woman and she was given a Christian burial. We can but pray for her soul in heaven.'

And with that, we sat down and did pray for poor Sarah Grey.

When we had finished I agreed I would not speak of it again. No good would come of it for the family or for the people of Leigh. We could but wait.

I was disturbed by the turn of events and did not wish to linger. Emma could see my mood was somewhat diminished and did not delay our departure. I could not speak to her of *what had occurred in the study but she detected something grave had taken place. Having made our way back to Cliff Hall she did not demur when I made plans for our return home the following day.*

Yet even in my home, my dreams are uneasy, my conscience is brought low. I pray soon this will fade and I can return to my duties with a focus that at present eludes me.

I worry for the legal ramifications of my suppression of evidence and the complicity this confers. Even as I write these words I know they may be held against me. But I need to think and to pray and the exercising of the event through my pen is coincident with some coming of clarity. I cannot destroy this paper yet. I will pray for guidance. But if you, my sons, read this and I have not concluded the matter I must ask you to swear to hold the truth. Or obliterate these words.

I was fatigued now, pierced with compassion for Eden. I could understand his guilt. Briefly I wondered why his words had not been destroyed but was thankful that they had not. They were indeed an illumination on the past.

And then suddenly I was full of anger at the injustice of it all.

I could smell the sulphuric mustiness of estuary mud: Sarah was about me, floating in the watery film that separated our worlds, waiting in the shadow pools, urging me on.

Help me, Sarah.

A pressure on the back of my neck propelled me forwards. A shudder convulsed my upper body. I needed to let her know I was with her but my voice was sticking.

The stench in the kitchen intensified.

I forced myself to speak: 'I won't let you down.' My voice was hoarse, frail and unconvincing but this time I meant it.

The fusty tang of seaweed lingered a moment more. Then a pine cone dropped onto the floor.

Sarah had heard me and she had gone.

I felt sure she would return to me in a dream that night and as a result I tossed and turned as if thrown about on an unquiet sea. At one point I thought I heard the spiteful laugh of a man on the stairs, but when I looked there was no one there. Before morning broke, I gave way to exhaustion and sank finally into a dreamless sleep.

Chapter Seventeen

I was woken at ten by a text from Martha. Alfie had got into bed with me at some point during the night and was playing with his Action Men. I was surprised he hadn't roused me earlier. For once I didn't have a feeling of pity or sadness about me. Instead I felt OK. Stronger even. I was starting to understand Sarah. Her awful tragic life. Her restless body in her grave. I was still tired and as edgy as hell, but I felt I was getting somewhere now, making progress.

Martha's text was a round robin reminding everyone of her party that night.

I, of course, had completely forgotten.

To be honest it was the last thing on my mind.

I resisted the urge to phone Andrew immediately, recalling his one hundred per cent accurate prediction that I would want to speak with him first thing. Instead I texted Giselle to see if she could babysit.

It was her night off but fortunately she said she would do it.

After another hour, in which I showered and breakfasted, I gave in and texted Andrew. He replied saying he had to wait in for a delivery but that I was welcome to come over.

My head was on fire with questions, so I coaxed Alfie from the television and within a few minutes we were sauntering down the Broadway.

A barrel of chirping Sea Scouts were heading straight for us, taking up most of the pavement, so we crossed the road to avoid the inevitable collision and found ourselves outside the church. And, you know how sometimes your feet decide to take you somewhere before your brain has made any such decision? Well, it was a bit like that. One minute we were on the pavement in the shade of the large bushes, the next we were going through the east entrance. Alfie found a large twig and started firing it and shouting, 'Cover me!'

I improvised a pistol with my mobile and we fired at each other for a while, sporadically ducking behind gravestones and rolling over on the grass until Alfie found what he thought was 'a worm eating a snail' and became instantly engrossed, poking it with his gun.

I stood up and stretched my legs, then wandered quietly round the east wall and along the hedge to the south. A lot of the headstones looked like they were sliding down the hill pointing accusingly to the sky at forty-five-degree angles.

Walker King had said Grey had been given a good Christian burial and I wondered if she might still be here, but squashed the thought when I remembered reading somewhere that many of the graves were moved to make way for the Broadway. I think they went to the cemetery just south of the old highway, London Road. She was probably there, I imagined. Even so, strolling round to the more populated west side, I stopped to inspect a few of the graves. Some went back to the 1600s. Inscriptions carved in an archaic curved hand had been rendered pretty much illegible after hundreds of years. A big, dark, black one in the corner looked quite interesting. The ground was slightly springy to the touch and as I crouched down to read the memorial my heels sank slightly into the grave.

Soon Alfie came scampering up and announced that the snail had won. Before I could stop him, he shot me (at close range too) and ran off to the north of the church.

We weren't in a hurry but I wanted to move on now. I had told Andrew I wouldn't be long.

I fished out my mobile and fired after him. As he rounded the north-east corner of the church he disappeared from my view.

Bugger. I would need to use guile to flush him out.

'Alfie. Where are you, mate? Come on. We can't be too long. Andrew's waiting for us.'

'Come and find me,' a little voice sang from the shadows.

I sighed lightly.

Alfie's giggles came from straight ahead. I stepped up from the path onto the grassy verge.

He was in the corner behind a marble slab.

I nipped behind an arch-shaped stone and saw his golden head pop over the top of the gravestone. 'I'm coming to get you, ready or not.'

Alfie squealed and ducked down.

I sprang from my hiding place, sneaked closer to his, then dipped beneath a stone lump half sunk in the ground. As I was getting up I brushed my elbow against it, dislodging a layer of yellow-green lichen that had obliterated the wording. I saw an H then GRE.

I stopped, knelt back down, rubbed the space next to the H and uncovered SARA. This had me rocking back on my

247

knees. I took a deep breath and started brushing off moss after the E.

Slowly the Y came into view, then 'BELOVED MOTHER'. The rest of the script had been eaten by earth.

Of course it was there. Of course it had to be: in the shade of a cedar tree.

'So, is this where the pine cones have been coming from, Sarah Grey?' I whispered softly. 'I know that you're not easy in your grave. I understand it now.'

I touched the grass by the headstone, aware that whatever was left of Sarah's remains lay decomposing beneath me, separated only by six feet of earth. We had never been so physically close before. A huge sense of pity came flooding over me.

'Hey!' Alfie was at my side, indignant. 'You were meant to find *me*!'

'I'm sorry, honey. I found someone's grave instead.'

'Ohhhh!' He inspected it. 'It's not very big.'

'I think it's sunk over time. It wouldn't have been like that to start with.' Or would it? Would they have wanted to conceal the witch's grave?

Alfie nodded, and then tugged my hand, visibly running out of patience. 'Can we go now? Can we go?'

'Yep.' I stood up and clapped my hands. Then I said to the grave, 'I'm getting there, Sarah. I promise to find out for you.'

I was grateful there was no response – not even the plop of a pine cone from above. But then she wasn't there, was she? She was roaming over Leigh and stopping by my house.

Alfie put his hand in mine and yanked.

We tramped out of the graveyard with a somewhat hasty gait.

Within twenty minutes we had found our way to a Leigh suburb that didn't exist when the Reverend Eden inhabited these parts.

A tired and sleepy Andrew opened the door to us in tracksuit bottoms and a stained t-shirt. He'd caught some sun up North and his arms were bronzed, sinewy and muscular. He was ruffled and messy but *louche*. Alfie pushed him aside and marched straight into the house, leaving me to apologize for my son's manners.

'It's all right,' he laughed. 'They've got no idea at that age, have they?' and led me into a large, open-plan kitchen. Well, I say large, but Andrew's house was a terraced cottage. It had that developer look to it: the walls of each room were a characterless cream: the kitchen, smart and modern, seemed ill thought out as though whoever had designed it never had any intention of living there. There was a feeling of emptiness and a slight echo in the room when I spoke.

Lack of storage space meant spices, herbs, cooking oils and condiments spread out untidily across the surfaces. 'A chef too,' I caught myself thinking with approval. I blushed and bent down to speak to Alfie so Andrew couldn't see my cheeks.

Andrew apologized for the mess and made a token effort to clean up, pushing everything into a corner and dumping unwashed crockery into the sink. Apart from that the kitchen was spick and span.

Andrew put the kettle on and made some space for Alfie to play in the middle of the room. When he'd made up a pot of proper coffee we went through to the sitting room, which was simply and blandly furnished like the rest of the house.

'Do you like jazz?' he asked, sorting through a rack of CDs.

I would rather stick needles in my eyes, I thought. 'Yes,' I said.

'Good. This is a nice Saturday afternoon mix.' He stuck it in the player. A track, which to my relief had words in it, floated out of the speakers.

Andrew picked up his mug. 'Cheers. So?'

I launched into the fray. 'So, what do you think? Who killed her? It's weird isn't it? I thought it might be something like that. And what do you think about the captain?'

Andrew was smiling as he watched me. He had a look of satisfaction on his face and seemed to get off on my enthusiasm. 'I knew it'd get you going. I re-read the journals last week. It *is* a good story.'

'Tragic though. If it's true. Both her death and her life. Losing her lover in that way.'

'Well, there's a thing – I've not found mention in the local papers of a murder at that time. Neither his nor the press ganger. Of course if Fitch had murdered a press ganger maybe the news would have been suppressed. They weren't popular, were they? And Lady Olivia had money and authority. She would have wanted to give the scandal a complete body swerve. I have no doubt those involved could have been bought off fairly easily.'

'But there were press gangs operating then?'

Andrew nodded. 'Yes. It's a credible story to a certain extent. The impressment laws didn't become obsolete until 1835. Did you see my notes underneath that bit? The last

Leigh man known to have been press-ganged was Goldspring Thompson. He died in 1875.'

'Blimey,' I said. 'You've got a good head for names and dates.'

He laughed. 'How could you forget a name like that? Press gangs targeted Leigh a lot through the centuries – young men who had good sea sense and knew about boats were always in demand. With it being on the coast and unfortified it was an easy target. One of the books I read said there used to be a secret passage in St Clements beneath the flagstones of the tower. All the eligible men would hide there while the press gang sharpened their cutlasses on the Mary Ellis grave. That's the big one outside by the cemetery gate. You can still see the marks the knives have left.'

'Aha. Yes, I know it. Came up in a quiz question once.'

Andrew gave me a lop-sided smile.

I responded lightly. 'Impressed by my local knowledge, I can tell,' I said, wondering simultaneously at the easiness of our banter – how we could move from heavy and historical to flippant and frivolous in the beat of a heart, neither of us irritated or put out of kilter by the mercurial change of tone. 'So,' I returned to the story, 'do we work on the theory Sarah's story is true?'

As he nodded a lock of hair flopped over his eye. He pushed it back. 'I'm inclined to want to believe it as much as she did. Although,' he stopped and gestured to the ceiling with his free hand, 'as a historian, one always has to consider the possibility that she could have made it up. We can't forget that she was grieving when she told Eden; she was probably extensively sleep-deprived and delirious too. We both know the effects loss can produce on a fragile mind.'

My head shook vehemently. 'No way,' I said, surprising myself with my passion. 'She didn't make it up. I know it.'

'How do you "know" it?' He drew inverted commas round the word. 'I understand that you might want to believe it, but how do you know it to be true?' It was the academic speaking.

I put my cup on the carpet and stared at him. I wasn't sure myself until now. But I did believe what Sarah had told Eden. Something had resonated with me as I had read his account of her. It *felt* true. And it fitted completely with what I'd seen in my dreams.

I paused. Was this the right moment to tell him about my ghost?

No, it was the moment that Martha decided to phone me.

I glanced at Andrew and apologized.

'Go ahead,' he said. 'Don't mind me.'

Requesting that I bring some sausage rolls, 'about fifty', and cucumbers 'cut into lengths of about two to three inches', Martha prattled on about the decorations for the house, asking if I thought she might need more blue balloons, enquired what I would be wearing and who I would be bringing, if anyone.

I thought thirty-six blue balloons was probably enough, told her I hadn't thought about my outfit yet and was just about to duck out of answering her last question when an idea popped up out of nowhere.

I covered the mouthpiece with my hand and mouthed at Andrew: 'You doing anything tonight?'

He shrugged and shook his head. 'Don't think so. Why?'

'Do you want to come to a friend's party? It's round the corner from here. I haven't got a date and she'd be really pleased if I actually turned up with a bloke for once.'

He shrugged again. 'Why not?' Then laughed, and crinkled his eyes into a wicked looking smile. 'Did you just ask me on a date? Och, the tongues that'll wag in the staff room!'

I broke off from informing Martha of this new information and whispered at him shrilly, 'Don't push it.'

'As if,' he said, and added something else in an undertone that, as Martha was in the middle of saying a long, convoluted goodbye, I didn't manage to catch. Instead I pulled the cushion from behind my back and lobbed it at his head. He ducked and made for a book at the foot of the armchair, then the doorbell rang.

Alfie swept into the room as Andrew was answering the front door. He eyed me suspiciously. 'What are you doing, Mummy?'

Arrangements sorted, I hung up and told Alfie I had been playing. He accepted that, and then announced he needed a wee. I didn't want to disturb Andrew, who was directing the movements of two deliverymen unloading a flat-screen television, so I took Alfie upstairs to find the bathroom.

It was as featureless as the kitchen. Again, dirt-free and neat but with no clue to the identity of its owner.

I couldn't help myself though and on the pretext of looking for some more toilet paper I opened the only cupboard in the room and rifled through it: razors, deodorant, paracetamol, shower gel, plasters. Pretty functional. The most luxurious item in there was some alpine air hair gel. No condoms.

If I hadn't had my son in tow I might have had a quick look at the bedrooms, but there was the possibility that Alfie might blurt something about it, so it was off the agenda. For the moment.

Downstairs Andrew had restrained himself from ripping

open the wrapping of his new TV. It was placed carefully against the recess in the wall that had once been a fireplace.

'Plasma screen?' I read the packaging.

'The old one was just about to conk out,' he said shiftily.

'Right.'

Alfie plodded over to him. 'Can I watch it?'

'Not now, darling,' I said.

'Aww.' His bottom lip went straight out.

'Listen, Alfie,' Andrew crawled over to him and tugged playfully on the toggle of his dungarees. Alfie giggled.

He looked so cute. My son didn't look bad either.

'This will take me a long time to set up. Why don't you come round again when it's all sorted out?'

Alfie put his head on one side and weighed it up. He wasn't convinced.

'And,' Andrew continued, 'I've got a television in the kitchen that's just for kids. It's very tiny. Only children can see what's on the screen. Do you want to have a look?'

Alfie perked up. 'Just for kids?'

'That's right. Wanna see it?'

My son slipped his hand into Andrew's and they disappeared into the kitchen. It was an odd little scene. I was still smiling when Andrew returned alone. The tinny sound of a children's programme wafted in with him.

'So?' he said, and took his place on the floor next to the TV. 'Where were we?'

I said, 'Tobias Fitch.'

He nodded. 'Yes, that's right.'

'So, do we think he was real?' I asked.

Andrew looked up, a half smile on his lips. 'Oh, I know he was real.'

'You do?' I looked back at him astonished. Could this be some kind of test? 'How?' Now it was my turn to use my fingers for speech marks. 'How do you "know" he was real?'

'Because I've found him. Well, actually I've located a living relative. At least that's what it looks like.'

'How on earth . . . ?' I was on the edge of my seat.

'I've had several years' head start on you. I did some research back when I was looking at Eden. There's a guy that has the same name *and* can be traced back to a man of the *same name* who lived in the 1800s. Not sure exactly how that's happened but Tobias Fitch is alive and kicking. Well perhaps not kicking. He's ninety-two.'

'Good grief!' I sat up straight. Wow. 'Well, we need to talk to him. Can we see him?'

'Well, I contacted his son six years ago on the pretext of researching my Eden biography. I think Tobias had a stroke. I'm not sure. I phoned again and was told he was too ill to see me and had no knowledge of the Primus. I left it to them to contact me and then . . .' he shrugged. 'I got distracted by my own problems. They never phoned me back. I didn't pursue it.

'Last Tuesday, when I was back at home, I found my notepad. It had all his details in so I dialled the number on the off chance he'd still be at the same address and not in a home or dead. There was an answer-phone so I left a message.' His voice went sort of sheepish. 'I said I was calling on behalf of you. Hope you don't mind. I know it was presumptuous.'

I shook my head lightly and grinned, but to be honest I was thinking: 'Oh you did, did you? Why would you do that? Why not wait and give me the number?' Was this over-enthusiasm or something darker? Perhaps it was simply that he couldn't resist taking over, like most men who got involved with a project at the beginning. I made a mental note to think about it later and shrugged.

'Anyway,' he continued, leaning forwards, oblivious to any change in his audience, 'two hours later his son phoned me back. Tobias Fitch will see us next week.'

I was silent for a minute, momentarily stunned. I leant forwards on the sofa. 'This is incredible. Where is he?'

'Antwerp,' said Andrew, watching the implication sink in.

I blinked and let my mouth fall open. That town had come up before. The last part of the journal. 'Isn't that where the captain who may have killed her fled to?'

'According to Eden's journal it is.' Andrew shrugged. 'We can't presume anything but I'd say Mr Fitch was worth talking to. Only if you want to? He might know nothing about Sarah Grey.'

'Yes, yes, I know, but I've come this far.'

'Mind if I tag along?'

'Of course not. But next week?'

'He's old and frail. We need to act swiftly.'

'Gosh, yes, I suppose we should.'

'I'll research the flights and hotel if you can sort out who's going to look after Alfie.'

I nodded. 'OK. Sure.' I reached into my bag and pulled out my phone to text Mum. She'd probably be up for having Alfie. 'How long will we be away?'

'Not sure,' he said. 'I'd say we should have at least two days there. You know what it's like with old people.'

I told him I didn't actually.

He smiled kindly. 'Yes, of course. I used to see them all

256

the time in my previous career. They have good days and bad days. Sometimes they're bouncing around but I'd hate us to go all that way and find him on a bad day and either not get to see him or not get much from it.'

I agreed. 'So I'll ask Mum if she can have Alf for three nights. If she can't I'll ask Lottie. My sister,' I added, in response to his raised eyebrows.

On my phone there was another text message from Martha: 'could u drp cucumbs round now? Also pre-cook sausies, please. x x x'

'Look, I'd better go,' I said reading it. 'Gotta sort out some stuff for Martha and I am knackered. I need to get a rest before the party.'

'Yep, that's cool,' he said, as we both stood up. 'I'll get online and check out some prices.'

We were standing in the centre of the lounge a few feet apart when Alfie wandered in. I think I must have been looking at Andrew, adrift in his gaze, as I didn't glance at my son. It was only when I heard him say, 'Look, mummy,' that I turned around.

He was standing in the doorway picking at something in his hand. 'It's like Sarah's.'

As my eyes focused the room around me receded. Alfie's fingers slowly uncurled. There, in the centre of his little white palm was a pine cone.

My stomach lurched, and before I could think rationally I flung myself at Alfie and pulled him to me with all my strength. 'Where did you get this from?' My hand latched on to his wrist. I was kneeling in front of him so our faces were level. 'Where? Tell me.'

My voice must have been shrill, inner horror exploding

out of my mouth unchecked by customary maternal reassurance, for Alfie's little mouth trembled and formed into a wail.

'It's OK, Sarah.' Andrew was beside me, hushing and gentle. 'Let him have it. I don't mind.'

'Shut up,' I spat. 'You don't understand . . .'

Andrew's voice rose over mine, firm but filled with confusion. 'I've just always liked the shape of them.'

Alfie's sobs were full on now, his body shaking with the rhythm of his breath. 'On, on the table.'

'That's right.' Andrew bent down, plucked the cone from Alfie, tossed it in the air playfully and caught it with the other hand. 'It was a habit of Imogen's that I've kept on. I have a ceramic bowl on the table. As a centrepiece. Not particularly original, I know, but . . . well, it's a sort of reminder.'

I looked up at him. 'It's yours?' My breathing abated slightly.

'I collect them now and then.' His eyes skated from Alfie to the pine cone to me. 'You OK? I don't mind him having it, honestly.'

Anger, fear and all those horrid emotions that had me in their grip a mere second before collapsed instantly into relief. Wretchedly I hugged Alfie tightly my arms. 'Oh I'm sorry, honey. I thought . . .' My son willingly surrendered to this gentler embrace and hugged me back, then he punched me lightly on my shoulder. 'Naughty Mummy. You made me upset,' he said, nuzzling back into the crook of my arm.

I squeezed him tenderly, my heart falling back into a more regular beat. 'Sorry, Alfie. Mummy's a bit tired.'

'Silly Mummy. Can I have an ice cream?'

I wiped away the stains of his brief tears. Smiling, I conceded, 'I think it's the least I can do, don't you?'

Enjoying his brief conquest, Alfie extricated himself from my arms and walked to the door. 'Get it then.' Everything has to be instant when you're four.

In spite of myself I laughed. Andrew's hand appeared before me. I took it as he pulled me to my feet. 'You all right?' Above the easy smile his forehead was furrowed.

'Sorry, yes.' I shook my head and tried to grin. This wasn't the time to explain. 'I don't want him thinking he can take whatever he wants from other people's houses, you know.' Sorry, Alfie, I thought. You can have a double ice with two flakes.

'It's all right, really. I know what they're like at that age . . .'

Now it was his turn to mask himself: his shoulders swung sharply towards the hall but I caught the shadow of desolation darkening his eyes before he could dodge my gaze.

I drifted after him, out into the hallway, still reeling but doing my damn best not to show it. 'So, we are agreed – we must go to Antwerp next week. I want this sorted out and tied up quickly.'

'Yep,' he nodded. 'My thoughts exactly.' He unlocked the latch and opened the door for us, sort of went a little red and said, 'Do you want me to pick you up tonight?'

I smiled, 'No, it's fine. I'm going to walk and you're on the way.'

The purchase of the ice creams did Alfie and I the world of good. We walked down to the Old Town and sat on the sea wall, swinging our feet as the lemon sorbet and lurid double bubblegum scoops melted down our hands and dripped onto the sand.

I was feeling better in myself, but still weighed down with a good helping of self-reproach and guilt. I should have been more restrained. I stole a sideways glance at Alfie: blue ice cream covered the entire lower half of his face. He was watching one of the fishing trawlers coming in past Bell Wharf. The tide had turned and there was a lot of activity out in the estuary: yachts and dinghies were being pulled up the side of the beach. A couple of coastguards stood outside their watch house, training binoculars at a sand bank across the water. Gulls shrieked and flapped in the trail of a fishing boat making its way back to shore.

I said to Alfie in a bright, high voice, 'Hey, Mister. Do you fancy going to Adventure Island tomorrow?' It was a fairground by Southend pier. A hallowed place for local kids.

He squinted his eyes at me and shrugged. 'Nah!'

This was unusual. 'No? Why not?'

'Let's just come here and have a chat,' he said.

It was so gorgeously put, so marvellously understated, so completely Alfie's way of telling me everything was OK, I felt tears well up and had to look away. I put my arm around his shoulders and pulled him into my side. Then I bent down and kissed his head. He looked up and smiled. I kissed his blue cheek and the tip of his nose. He squirmed away but he giggled. Then he said, 'Why do sailors walk funny?'

I laughed. 'Is this a joke?'

He ignored me and squawked, 'Pieces of eight, pieces of eight.'

'Oh,' I said. 'You mean pirates.'

'Yeah, sailors.'

'Well, some of them have wooden legs. I suppose that can't help.'

'Wooden legs!' He looked as if this was the first he'd heard of such a ridiculous notion.

We looked at each other and giggled. Then Alfie jumped off the wall and made like a robot doing a sea jig. With a final 'Ha, ha, me hearties,' he swung around and hopped dramatically down to the shoreline to have a root around in the surf.

I stared after him. When this was over I would take him to Euro Disney or somewhere he'd like. He had been so amazing lately. I almost felt grateful to him. Sometimes he seemed so much older than his years. So wise.

Unlike me, who was starting to look unstable. Andrew probably thought I was completely neurotic. Or over-protective (which I was at the moment). But then the Andrew that I had known prior to the holidays was a borderline control freak anyway. My son was my priority and rightly so.

Andrew's pine cone collection was worth thinking about though. Was that a coincidence? A clue?

Or a warning?

It was difficult to work out. Let's face it, *he* was difficult to work out.

Alfie got bored with throwing stones at jellyfish and came back to the wall, pushing his luck with a polite demand for sweets. By then I had resolved to stop jumping at the slightest thing. And I'd made a silent promise I'd sort this out once and for all. Then it would all go away. It had to.

Before we left I spent the last two minutes visualizing such vivid blue spheres that when I opened my eyes the beach looked purple, but I felt more composed.

* * *

After dropping off cucumbers and buying 50 sausage rolls I found the post had come in my absence. I sorted through a couple of bills, *Music Weekly* and a letter from the doctor requesting I attend an appointment at 3.45 p.m. on Thursday afternoon. I stuck it in my phone and busied myself with cooking, feeding Alfie and resting before the party. Things were moving on.

The party was in full swing when we arrived. Martha immediately made us feel like film stars and announced us to the twenty or so folks in the house. I went to put the sausage rolls in the kitchen whilst our host took Andrew by the arm and led him into the back garden, where most of the guests were hanging out.

We had been lucky with the weather. In the warmth of the evening, the azure glow of the garden lights and the white wooden furniture could fool you into thinking you were in the Med.

'Reminds me of being on holiday,' Andrew commented. 'It's really nice.'

I agreed. 'They've put a lot of effort into sorting the place out. It was a shell when they bought it.'

Andrew had washed his hair tonight and made an effort with his clothes. A short-sleeved, but kind of funky patterned shirt, showed his lean tanned arms. He'd put on some nice jeans and a decent pair of trainers. If I'd bumped into him in a bar I might have fancied him on sight.

My friends certainly took a shine to him. Sharon, resplendent in sequins, snuck into the kitchen when I was refilling our drinks. She was, of course, already drunk and was making pantomime innuendo. She kept winking and nudging and said in a ludicrously loud voice, 'Oooh. Don't mind yours, madam.'

'Shh, Sharon! He's not *mine*. We're just friends.'

She'd gone over to mix a jug of cocktails and kept glancing back at me with a wide grin, absurdly pleased to have hit a soft spot. 'So he's up for grabs then, is he?' The more animated she got, the louder her volume.

'Come on, Shaz. Be quiet. I don't want him to hear!' Mortification wasn't a strong enough word.

'Might realize that you're flesh and blood, after all?' Sharon put her arm round my shoulders and gave me a squeeze. 'Just joshing. Never get a chance to tease you. We're pleased, you know that.' She slipped her arm through mine. 'Come on, introduce us. I'm dying to meet him.'

I rolled my eyes to the ceiling and gave up.

Sharon pulled me through the back door and out onto the decking, then marched me over to the patio area further down the garden where Andrew was sitting on a stone bench in conversation with Corinne, her husband Pat, and Martha's Deano.

I handed him a glass of wine, while Sharon pulled a plastic chair over, scraping the decking loudly.

Pat was delivering a punch line. I could tell the joke was bad as Corinne had clenched her hands into fists. This often happened when Pat had had one too many. Deano found it hilarious, and was rocking back and forth, tears in his eyes. He was sitting on the bench next to Andrew, a telltale joint hanging from his right hand.

The musk of weed hung heavy in the smoke around us. I glanced at Andrew. We hadn't mentioned recreational drugs, and what with his former occupation, and indeed, his position as my boss, I felt a twinge of apprehension. But he either hadn't seen it or didn't care. His eyes wrinkled with gentle laughter and he nodded his head in appreciation.

A cough from the plastic chair reminded me introductions were due so I accordingly presented Sharon.

She fluttered her eyelashes and tinkled out a little greeting. 'Delighted to meet you, Andrew.' Her estuarine accent had developed consonants. 'So, how did you two meet then?' She smiled, and took a big gulp of her margarita, spilling a large part of it on her dress.

I cringed involuntarily and, without really processing what I was doing, let my hand stray onto Andrew's leg. It was more of a supportive gesture, really.

'Oh,' he said. 'We work together.'

'Ha,' laughed Corinne. 'You're not that awful boss, McBastard are you?' She cackled away to herself.

Andrew, bless him, grinned. 'One and the same.'

'Oh.' She recovered herself quickly, and shot me a look of panic laced with an eyebrow's worth of scorn.

I bounded in. 'We've made our peace though now, as you can see.'

Andrew laid his hand over mine. 'We've got to know each other better recently,' he smiled, 'while I've been helping Sarah research her family tree. We're both interested in the sea-witch, Sarah Grey.'

'Ah, that's right . . .' Corinne started. 'Hang on – family tree? You're not related are you, Sarah? I thought Grey was your married name?'

Everyone had stopped chatting. The collective gaze of the circle burnt my cheeks. Andrew's smile wrinkled into a frown.

My lie had caught me, right in the headlights.

'Yes, it is. I mean, that's to say, yes Josh was a Grey. I . . . I didn't say it was my family history. I said . . .' I flailed around mentally.

'My mistake, I must have misheard.' Andrew was graceful but his tone was contrived courtesy. Slowly he withdrew his hand.

'So how's that coming?' Corinne asked. No one noticed the change of temperature between us.

'Good. Good. Andrew's found a contact in Antwerp that we're going to visit next week. May shed a new light on the old mystery.'

'Really?' Sharon's eyebrows arched with glee.

'Actually,' said Andrew, 'I was going to say earlier, but I've found some cheap deals. If we fly out on Thursday we don't get hit by the weekend rates.'

'Oh,' I remembered my appointment with the GP. 'I don't think I can do Thursday. Got to see the doctor. Although I suppose I could cancel it.'

Sharon coughed on her drink and waggled her finger at me. 'Uh-uh. No way. You're bloody keeping that.'

My eyes darted to Andrew. He had turned to me sharply. 'What?'

'I could reschedule it,' I repeated.

'You can't reschedule a hole in the head.' Sharon looked meaningfully at Andrew, and made a circle motion round her ear. 'She's nuts. Don't let her, mate.'

Everyone stared at me again.

Deano scratched his cheek. Pat gave Corinne a shrug.

I caved in. 'OK, I won't. We'll have to go on Friday, Andrew. Is that OK? I don't mind paying a bit extra and it might be easier for Mum to have Alfie at the weekend.'

'That's fine,' he said, faintly.

'What's wrong with your head?' asked Corinne, still puzzling over the scene.

'Nothing,' I said.

Sharon objected. 'A possible tumour's not nothing.'

I fidgeted and crossed my legs. 'Look, can we not talk about this now, please? It's a party.'

Our group sat in awkward silence until Pat piped up with a really naff 'Doctor Doctor' joke.

When the punch line came we all groaned, Deano wept and Sharon spilt the rest of her drink on the floor. The tension eased out and it seemed like the party might recommence, but Andrew had shrunk away from me, a couple of inches of bench becoming a gulf.

Later he walked me home. We'd both drunk too much by then and had embarrassed ourselves by dancing in Martha's living room. It seemed the problems of the early evening had faded somewhat. My fingers were crossed, hoping he'd forgotten it all. I invited him for a drink, and once I'd paid Giselle and sent her off in a cab, I offered to open a bottle of wine.

Andrew yawned. 'Actually, I could do with a coffee.'

I put the kettle on instead, a little miffed although outwardly accommodating.

'So, what's this "hole in the head" business, if you don't mind me asking?' He hugged his mug to him.

I took a seat at my old pine table. 'I suspect it's nothing,' and pointed to my eye. 'I thought that this lid had dropped but the doctor thinks the other one might have got bigger.' And then I filled him in on what had happened, hoping to play it down. 'Mrs Falwahi, the neurologist, had no sense of urgency. In fact, she told me not to worry. So I'm taking her lead. She knows better than me.'

He processed my words. 'Well, you should definitely keep your appointment. Sure you'll be up for flying on Friday?'

'Yes, I'm sure. I want to find out about Sarah Grey.'

'Hmm.' He fixed me with a long, piercing look. Its intensity made me look away. 'So what did bring you into this area of study then? If it wasn't your family? You did tell me that, you know?'

I looked back and saw suspicion hovering behind his eyes. I didn't like the way this was going. It was time to come clean. 'I know I did, I'm sorry. It was just that I didn't think you'd believe me if I told you.'

His gaze held strong. 'Give it a go.'

I took a breath. 'OK. Well, it started happening about a month ago. Just before the school broke up for the holidays. At first I thought I was going mad.' I told him about the cockleshells, the moment on the beach, the night of the storm, the mannequin, and the dreams. 'I can feel her, Andrew, she's in the house with me. She needs me to find out what happened. Only that will let her rest in peace.'

The change in him was striking. He started off calmly enough, but drew in sharply breath when I recalled the first manifestation. Now he sat across from me with his head in his hands, holding his breath. Silent.

I waited.

At last he looked up and regarded me from under his long eyelashes. There were tears in his eyes and he reached out and grabbed my hand. 'Listen,' his voice was hoarse and

267

strained. 'I want to tell you something but I don't want you to freak out.'

I said I wouldn't and laughed. What else could possibly freak me out?

He didn't smile. 'One of my good friends in Aberdeen, best man at my wedding. Used to see him all the time. He was a teacher at the local high school but quite private out of hours. I used to go over to see him. He was a strong man, very resourceful. He spent his spare time building this magnificent house.'

Andrew released my hand and bit his lip. 'This is hard,' he said.

'Go on,' I urged him.

He looked away, out into the night garden. 'One evening I went over and he was wired. He was convinced there were Chinese girls living in his house. I tried to find them for him, but of course, they weren't there.' Now his eyes returned to me. He swallowed. 'It was the first symptom of the brain tumour. It killed him in two months. I'm sorry.'

He finished with a kind of gasp and stared at me expectantly.

I was surprised by the emotion his words had woken in me. I felt angry, defiant, annoyed. Andrew sprang to his feet and began walking to and fro.

'I don't think you should go to Antwerp,' he said flatly. 'I'll go on alone. I'll find out and report back.' He stopped pacing and stood still.

But I couldn't believe it. 'Hang on. I'm the one who has to find this out, not you.'

Andrew stared at me for what seemed like an age and then said, 'There's no need for you to come. Really.'

I jerked my chair out from under the table and made to stand. 'No way. This is my story, right?'

He took a deep breath and glanced from me to the table, then said, 'I think you'll find I started the research first.'

How typical. The man was taking over. I slapped my cup down on the table, spilling the coffee. 'I can't believe you're doing this. You're managing me, like a . . . like a bloody manager!'

He couldn't meet my eyes. 'Which I am,' he said, quietly.

I stood up. 'Not now. Not here. Not any more.' I bit my lip.

He lowered his gaze to the floor.

'So stop managing me. Please.' I took a step towards him. Despite everything I wanted to touch him. My hand reached out to his shirt. He caught hold of it and looked up quietly.

'But you read the journal. You saw what Eden said – is there any point in raking over the muck from years ago?' He was softer now.

'You just said it was you who started it . . .'

He let go of me and put his own hand up in mock surrender. 'OK, OK. I have some interest in this of course, but what if you're ill, Sarah?' There was an unsteady, fragile look to him. I think if I'd pushed him he might have broken into a thousand tiny pieces.

'We don't know for sure. And I can tell you it's *not* a tumour that's making me see things. I haven't actually been given a death sentence yet, you know. I am still here. And I have stuff to do.' A tone of desperation had crept into my voice. 'Andrew, she's real. I've seen her.'

He put his hands on his hips and shook his head.

I carried on. 'I'm not the only one. There's Marie! You

269

know John O'Connor? He has a sister in California. She's seen the ghost too.'

This got him. 'Seen her?'

'I was on Skype, Sarah appeared behind me. Marie saw her. She believes me.'

He sighed. 'Skype! It could have been an optical illusion or a break in the signal or . . . Look, there are no such things as ghosts, Sarah. There is no afterlife. There is no other world and there is no God.' He was back to pacing up and down.

I stepped towards him, pleading. 'I know what you're thinking. I used to be the same. You're thinking about Imogen and Amelia and your son. You think that if there *was* another world of existence then you'd know it. They'd somehow reach across the divide to let you know they were happy and OK. You'd feel them, right?'

He avoided my eye and leant over the table, spreading his fingers across the surface.

I took another step and placed my hand on his shoulder. 'I know because I've been there too, remember? When Josh died? I wanted it to be true. But it didn't happen because he didn't come back either. But this is real, Andrew. I swear. It's not a hallucination. I can smell her, I can hear her. Sometimes I feel her.'

He dropped into the nearest chair and tugged his hair nervously. His face was pensive but his tension seemed to have eased a fraction.

'And what about you and me?' I moved to stand in front of him. 'Why are we here now? Talking about this? Something or someone has brought us together to sort this out. You're a descendant of Robert Eden. He failed Sarah Grey the first time. But now you're here with me and my name's Sarah Grey for God's sake. It's all happening for a reason. And we're on to something, that's for sure. I know you believe that, at least. Pooling our resources has taken us further than anyone has got before. It's like Marie said – time isn't linear – it folds back on itself, it tears and loops. We've got a chance now, right now, to untangle all of these threads. What if we don't go and Tobias dies? We've got to follow this through and put it to rest. I need to know what happened to her.'

I sighed loudly. 'At the very least we can clear Sarah's name. That, if nothing else, matters to me. Even if it doesn't matter to you.'

Silence enveloped the kitchen. I could feel Sarah watching from the shadows of the garden.

Andrew pulled his head from his hands. His eyes bored into mine. I was so close I could smell the wine on his breath. 'I want full feedback from your appointment, young lady.' Then slowly he got to his feet. 'I'd better book those flights, then.'

We were not more than a foot apart.

'Thank you,' I said.

He took a deep breath and then turned away.

Just before he reached the front door, he stopped and said, 'You'd make a good teacher, you know.'

Then he left.

Chapter Eighteen

I arrived in good time for my appointment, hoping to catch Doctor Cook early. I had a lot to sort out. We were flying out early the following day. Mum wasn't a fan of early mornings so I agreed to drop Alfie at her place and have tea with her so I could help settle him down.

Sharon volunteered to look after the little man while I was seeing the doctor. I calculated that I had just enough time after my appointment to dash home, pack Alfie's bag, pick him up from Sharon's and get across town to Mum's before the clock struck tea-time (five). Of course, the best laid plans . . .

Doctor Cook and his junior partners were running late. The waiting room was packed. A solitary empty chair beckoned. No sooner had I sat down than I realized why the several patients over by the windows preferred to stand. The man next to me stank like a cross between a brewery and a cheese factory. He lolled my way, moaning, and bumped into my shoulder, introducing himself as 'Jesus Christ, our saviour'. It was the start of an excruciating five-minute conversation in which I somehow managed to offend him, after which he gestured in a

vaguely threatening but very wobbly manner. The receptionist decided to take things into her own hands and
speed him through to one of the junior doctors. No one
objected.

Ten minutes later I was in Doctor Cook's consulting room,
a tad wobbly myself by now.

The doctor asked his usual questions, which I answered
fairly honestly, took my blood pressure (normal), inspected
in my ears (clear), and my eyes (no comment) then asked
me why I'd come to see him. I reminded him of my appointment with Mrs Falwahi. He did a double-take, apologized,
took his spectacles off, put on another pair and examined
my notes.

'Goodness,' he said. 'The report isn't here. I'm sorry. Perhaps
Janice hasn't passed it through yet. Do excuse me one minute.
I'll go and check.'

Outside the open French doors the afternoon sun
descended through the topmost branches of the cedar tree.
A slight breeze brought me the rich scent of the garden,
textured and finessed with the fruity tang of flowers at the
height of their summer bloom. It was a quiet retreat from
the chaos of the waiting room and for a moment I closed
my eyes.

When I opened them I focused on the bench around the
cedar tree. It took me a minute to assimilate what I was
seeing and then a further ten seconds for my brain to catch
up: a black shape hung in the air.

I hastened to my feet and took a step towards the strange
apparition, an uncanny buzz filling my ears.

The blackness swirled and circled like a swarm of wasps.
I crept forwards to clear my view.

273

'Sarah?' I said. But something was different.

The blackness funnelled itself into a shape – the outline of a figure? I couldn't see it properly. Without conscious awareness of my movements, I felt my body compelled outside into the garden. As if in caught in a tractor-beam, the thing drew me across the lawn.

In the dark shadow of the cedar tree the cloud became corporeal.

I perceived narrow shoulders and the curve of a hip, a female form. As indistinct as it was I could tell it wasn't Sarah.

That's when the fear kicked in. I took a shaky step towards the cloudy shape then halted. The vague outline of a face formed. From what could have been an eyebrow a trickle of blood thickened and dripped. The phantom's mouth opened, not to speak but scream.

'Ms Grey!'

I spun round.

Doctor Cook was marching across the lawn. His eyebrows knitted together over his glasses. His mouth was thin and set.

'Are you all right, my dear? It's a lovely view but do come inside. Heavens.'

Then he was right beside me and so close he must have been able to see the fear etched on my face. Unthinkingly, I reached out to tug the sleeve of his linen jacket, like a child almost. 'There, there was a thing here.'

Cook followed my gaze to the cedar tree. The bench was empty. 'Nothing's there, my dear.'

His fingers gripped my elbow, guiding me back inside the surgery.

'She's gone. Not a real person, she was . . .' I gave up mid-sentence. I sounded unhinged.

Or ill. Like someone with a brain tumour.

We entered through the French doors. Doctor Cook pushed me firmly down on the chair.

He felt for my pulse. I knew it would be fast.

When he spoke his tone was patronizing, the first time I had heard him speak to me this way. 'Come, come, dearie. Now calm down. Who do you think it was, this woman? Do you know? One of the receptionists perhaps? I'm not sure if the gardener is about today . . .'

I shrugged helplessly. 'It's not Sarah Grey.' The sight had knocked the stuffing out of me.

Doctor Cook resumed his seat behind the desk and tried to obfuscate the look of consternation that had flitted briefly across his features. 'Sarah Grey? Are you talking about yourself, my dear?'

'No. The old sea-witch. She's haunting me.' It came out in a tumble. 'She's been giving me nightmares. I'm trying to find out about her past. My friend Sharon Casey has dug up quite a bit of information and another friend, Andrew . . .' I was babbling.

Doctor Cook interrupted. 'Sharon Casey?'

I nodded.

He cleared his throat and hardened his mouth. 'Sharon Casey is not the most stable person to advise you around here.'

'But I think I've seen this room in my dreams. I know something happened here, Doctor. Something bad.'

Doctor Cook stared at me, his mouth half open, eyebrows high. Then he coughed, plucked a handkerchief from his pocket and wiped his face. His right hand reached for his notes. 'Has this been going on a while?'

I paused, not sure of what to say or do.

'A few weeks.' Give or take.

He wrote something down. 'But you said that it wasn't her?'

'No,' I shuddered. 'That was someone else.'

Cook's spectacles had slipped down the bridge of his nose; he pushed them back up and wiped his brow with the hanky again. 'Are you saying it's a ghost?' It was evident from his indulgent tone he now thought I was gaga.

'It could be.' I was in a doctor's surgery. I had to be more guarded.

Cook coughed violently for a moment then took a sip from a glass of water on his desk. 'What do you mean by that?'

I shrugged. 'It's just in my head.'

Doctor Cook stopped writing. 'Do you know this ghost's name?'

'No.'

'How old is she?'

'I don't know. She's bleeding. That's what killed her – a blow to the head. Maybe this is how they show you what happened – almost like it's a clue,' I said, more to myself than him.

'I can't go through this again!' The words escaped me before I could stop them. Please God, I thought, don't tell me I need to find out how she died too?

Doctor Cook put his notes aside and fixed me with a look of total incomprehension. 'Have you thought about perhaps having a rest? I know of some very good clinics that you could have a look at . . .'

Then it dawned on me this was serious. 'Are you talking about sectioning?' He didn't react. It was all getting a bit much. I needed to regain control of myself and the situation. 'I'm not mad. At least I don't feel mad.' Oh God, that sounded mad.

With great effort, I moderated my voice into a more reasonable, and hopefully sane, tone. 'I've been getting these impressions and I just, well, I just thought I saw something under the cedar tree.'

The doctor nodded, affecting his usual calm.

'Do you think this is an illness? Have I got a tumour? It all feels real enough but . . .'

I stared back at him, waiting for him to move. He didn't. I suspect he was considering the pros and cons of carting me off in a straitjacket.

Outside in the garden a magpie called to its mate.

It brought Cook back from his reverie. He coughed and picked up what I presumed was Mrs Falwahi's report. The leaves of typed paper shook in his hand. 'Well, the results are, well . . . I'd interpret them as inconclusive. But in the light of what you've just told me I will book you in for a scan as a priority.'

Fair enough. I nodded grimly.

'Consider a rest,' he added in firmer voice. 'I will want to see you regularly now and you certainly need some medication in the meantime. No buts. I'd like to prescribe you . . .'

An urgent knock stopped him mid-sentence. The receptionist popped her head round the door. Sweaty and breathless she started speaking. 'I'm sorry to interrupt, Doctor Cook, but it's Mr McFarlane. Can you come to reception right away?'

'Goodness! Not now.' With some reluctance the doctor rose. 'Apologies, Sarah. Can you wait?'

I peeked at my watch: 4.35 p.m. 'No, I'm sorry, I can't.'

'Why not? This is important.' Even the receptionist was taken aback by his rough tone. Cook made a hissing noise with his teeth. 'Tomorrow then.'

I didn't want to make a fuss but . . . 'Sorry, I'm away until late on Sunday.'

'All right, then. Without delay. Janice, show me where he is.'

The door slammed shut.

Did he really mean he wanted me to come by late on Sunday? I ducked out into the waiting room to seek clarification. The majority of the surgery staff were attempting to restrain Jesus, but a younger man, in his late teens, possibly on work experience and clearly out of his depth, hung back by the desk.

'Excuse me,' I touched his arm to get his attention. 'I think Doctor Cook has asked to see me on Sunday. Would that be right?'

The young man barely registered my touch. Unable to take his eyes off the scene unfolding in front of him, he held the telephone receiver in one hand. The other hovered tentatively over the '9' button, should urgent assistance be required. 'If he said that, then yes.'

'On a Sunday though?'

Jesus yelped, 'You're going to hell in a handcart.'

The young man fingered the number nine button. 'He sees emergency patients at the weekend sometimes.'

'So I'll just turn up when I'm back?'

He nodded and held the receiver to his mouth. 'Police and ambulance please.'

A number of patients were fleeing out the front door now, so I joined them and legged it down the drive.

They say God moves in mysterious ways . . .

Sharon lived in an old fisherman's cottage, which stood at the foot of the hill, opposite what used to be the Old Town square but was now a car park. With her hectic single lifestyle I expected her to live in chaos but her home was always immaculate. She had good taste in interior design – the dining room was knocked through into what had been the parlour, and filled with light from the various mirrors positioned at strategic points against a cream and chocolate colour scheme.

I got there by five, narrowly avoiding a crash – my mind was on the apparition and my health, not on the road.

Of course Sharon wanted to know all about my appointment. I hesitated at first, then I took her by the arm into the kitchen, away from Alfie, who was playing inside a wigwam made of throws and brooms.

My face must still have been ashen. 'I've got to have a scan.'

She nodded thoughtfully. 'Must have been a shock.'

'Yep,' I said. 'There was a weird thing too. Thought I saw, I dunno, something in the doctor's garden. It's making me think there's definitely something unbalanced in my head. But then again . . .' I looked at her. 'Do you believe in ghosts, Sharon?' I'd broken my silence on the matter with Andrew, with the doctor, and now my thoughts gushed into the real world unchecked.

Sharon had lit a cigarette, that was now poised in her fingers on her way to her mouth. She let it dangle. 'What do you mean?' She eyed me for a moment, then took a heavy drag on the fag.

'You know Sarah Grey?' I ventured. 'I think she might have communicated with me. I've been dreaming about her since that night at the castle.'

Her tight, narrowed lips blew out smoke in a long, thin line. 'Dreams are dreams, Sarah. Not ghosts.'

'But it's not just been dreams. She's been leaving me pine cones.'

'No shit. For real?'

'I think it's for real. It's hard to tell. I mean it sounds crazy. And what with this brain stuff that's being checked out, I don't know if I'm mad or ill or, shit, clairvoyant or something.'

A change had come over Sharon. Her eyes were fixed on a point beyond me. She wasn't looking at me any more. 'Or just seeing ghosts.' She took another pull on her cigarette. 'But your eye . . .'

'I know,' I said quickly. 'My dreams have corresponded with what I've learnt about Sarah Grey. But I had the dreams *before* I found out about her life . . . I thought I'd only seen Sarah.' I remembered Andrew's words. I didn't *know* it was her. 'At least I get a strong sense that it's Sarah Grey. But now, today, at Doctor Cook's, that wasn't her.'

'Doctor Cook? He's your GP?' Sharon stubbed her cigarette out in the glass ashtray.

'Yes,' I continued. 'This apparition was female too but . . .'

Now she was watching me with an intensity that made my flesh chill. 'What was she like?'

280

I described what I'd seen, then sensing Sharon's sudden agitation I added, '. . . but it wasn't like Sarah. Though there was a feeling of violence there too.' I sighed. 'I don't know. I don't know anything any more.'

'Right.' She glanced down at her feet, her hair obscuring her face. If I'd had my wits about me I would have seen she was hiding her expression. But I didn't. I was caught up in myself. 'What are you going to do about it?' An undulating tremble had crept into her voice.

I leant back onto the countertop. 'Not much I can do about it right now. I'm going to Antwerp tomorrow. I guess I'll see what happens when I get back. I don't want to turn into some psychic investigator but I get the impression that this one isn't going away either.'

'You're not scared though?' she asked, still looking down.

'It's unsettling. And yes, I think I'm always scared of it.'

Sharon straightened her shoulders and brought her face up to mine, smiling once more, but there was a distance in her eyes. 'Well, I know you've got to hurry. Can we talk about this when you're back? Come over and have a glass of wine.'

Time was getting on. 'Sure. Sorry I've got to love, scare and leave you. Thanks so much for having Alfie.'

She was the old Sharon again. 'No problemo.' She pecked my cheek.

I went through to the living room and gathered up Alfie.

At the door Sharon waved us goodbye. 'It really would be good to see you when you get back, OK? We need a chat. Let me know if you find out anything about Sarah. I'm in it too, remember? I want to be the first to know.'

I promised her I'd be sure to do that.

Then I legged it to Mum's.

I was going to write that it was the last time I would ever see her. But of course it wasn't. The last time was far worse. Seared into my brain now, I know I'll take our last meeting with me to my own grave.

Chapter Nineteen

When I got home I was knackered but there was something I needed to do before I could get going on the packing.

Marie's face had a craggy look to it when she came on screen but she seemed pleased to see me. 'My friend,' she croaked. 'How goes it with you and your ghost?'

'Try using the plural,' I said, and filled her in on the developments with Sarah Grey. To my irritation she seemed quite thrilled by my latest episode in the good doctor's garden. 'Please don't tell me I have to find out who she is too.'

Marie, for all intents and purposes, looked like she was impressed. 'Jeez. Do you think there's a connection?'

I wasn't sure and told her that. 'Logically, you'd think so wouldn't you? But does logic have anything to do with this kind of stuff?'

She nodded. 'I think so. There is usually some design behind it. Although it may not be obvious to mere mortals.'

'Everything else has been linked. I think. To be honest, I do hope there is some kind of connection.'

Marie cocked her head and looked at me. 'I wonder if you've switched something on somehow? Maybe you've

283

become some kind of beacon for lost souls. How amazing would that be!'

'Not very. I still find this whole thing unnerving. And perhaps it is some side effect of a malignant growth. My results are inconclusive by the way.'

Marie grimaced. 'Sorry to hear that, chick. But I think you need to view this as some amazing skill that's been given to you.'

'It could be madness.'

'Could be, true. But wouldn't it be nice to feel good about it? You can't necessarily control what you're seeing or experiencing. Not yet. But you can control the way you feel about it. Wouldn't it be better to be more positive about it than negative? It is, after all, your choice.'

I thought on this some more. It was a very American, New Age opinion. And yet Marie was right. If it continued to happen and I felt the same way about it all, then it would surely become a curse. There were those out there who were desperate for insights like this. Didn't people call it a 'gift'? Could it be a blessing?

'I'll make enquiries,' Marie continued. 'What is it about this new sighting that has disturbed you?'

'That it's a new problem.'

'Is it? It could be a sub-haunting like before. A one-off like the burning girl.'

'I don't know.'

'Seriously, I think if you talk to someone who might be more skilled than me – I can only tell you what I know and, honey, your situation is going way out of my league – then you might feel better. You need to learn how to control it.'

'If it's not a tumour.'

'If it's not a tumour or madness or stress-related.'

'Not right now, though,' I said, holding my hand up. 'I'm off to Antwerp tomorrow morning. There's a link there. A descendant of someone who might have played a part in Sarah's death.'

'Wow. Things are moving quickly then?' she said. 'You never know, if you get to the bottom of it then it might all disappear.'

'I'm hoping more along the lines of "*will* disappear" than "'might"', I said, and sighed.

'I'll be thinking of you,' she said, and sent me a wink. 'Tune in when you get back. Good luck.'

Chapter Twenty

The view over the town square was awe inspiring. Andrew had done well to book one of the city's newest and most modern hotels. He'd gallantly offered me the larger of the two rooms, though there wasn't much in it. Exquisitely decorated in creams and whites, adorned with fur rugs and funky plastic chairs, the room had its own bar, CD player with a small selection of discs: mostly jazz, a couple of classical and some rock compilations. The plasma TV on the wall opposite displayed a screen-saver of an open fire. A nice touch, even in summer.

I hit the play button on the CD remote. The gentle chords of a blues guitar tinkled out of the speakers. I surveyed the bed, then launched myself at it and kicked off my shoes.

Tired, I wasn't; the journey had been pretty effortless. We'd managed to fly from City Airport, which was a boon. The plane had been on time. Customs had been obligingly dismissive of the influx of British tourists, so within half an hour we'd jumped into a taxi and whizzed through Antwerp to our central hotel.

All very easy.

I had a bit of a panic on the plane when I realized that this would be the longest I'd ever been away from Alfie. After I'd gone through the whole 'I-hope-I-don't-die' anxiety at take-off, and blocked the tumour business out of my mind, I gave myself permission to enjoy the adult nature of the trip.

The room helped: no small extra bed, no scattering of toys. It was grown up and chic, and ever so slightly sexy.

Andrew came knocking after half an hour. I was still gazing at the ceiling. The door was unlocked. I yelled for him to come in.

This led to an ever so slightly awkward moment as he clocked me on the bed, froze, fetched the chair by the balcony and brought it alongside me. It was an incongruous scene and we both knew it.

He cleared his throat. 'Um, I've spoken to Tobias' son, Laurens, the younger Mr Fitch, although he sounds like he's in his late sixties/early seventies. I'm afraid Tobias is tired today.'

Bugger. I pushed myself upright. 'What does that mean? We can't see him?'

Andrew shook his head. 'No, not today. Laurens suggested we give him a call tomorrow morning to see how he is. He's quite keen to see you in fact. Apparently he's at his best after lunch.'

'Have you got an address?'

'Yes. He's in one of the nearer districts.'

'Can I have it?'

'I can't remember it off hand. It's in my notebook.'

I propped my back against the pillows and brought my knees up. 'Let's see it then?'

He cussed. 'Damn. I've left it upstairs.'

I said, 'Oh well. Is it easy to get to?'

'Looks pretty straightforward on the map. He lives in an inner suburb to the south-east of the city. Shouldn't be a problem to find it.'

'Perhaps we should have a dry run today?'

Andrew laughed and raised his eyebrows. 'Never thought you'd be this cautious.'

'I just want to see him, that's all. We're here now. I feel like we're about to nail it.'

'If Tobias can wait one day, so must we.' He grinned. 'But that doesn't mean we need to sit around. We're in Antwerp, we should go explore.'

'That'd be great. Let me change into a dress. It's hotter here than at home.'

He pushed back the chair and stood to go. 'Sure. I'll go back to my room, you can pick me up.'

'Don't be silly,' I said. An undertone of flirtation had crept into my voice – we both noticed it. I blushed. 'I mean – I'll get changed in the bathroom. Here,' I got to my feet and chucked him the remote. 'Check out the music.'

Antwerp was at the seasonal peak for tourism and the main square, the Grote Markt, was crammed with folks equipped with videos and cameras. In the afternoon sun the gothic roofs of gabled guildhouses reflected a beautiful airy light onto the cathedral's spire.

We sat by the Brabo fountain in the centre and agreed our visit would not be worth mentioning if we didn't go to visit the Reubens museum.

But we never got there.

The streets that led off the square were far more fascinating than I'd given Antwerp credit for: winding and cobbled, full of tucked away gems and statues. We wandered past bars and mussel restaurants, tourist shops and boutiques, charmed by the sights and relaxing into the carefree holiday vibe that others around us emanated as they dawdled by.

When the evening sun's rays dropped over the Scheldt River, we stopped at a bar and had a drink. It was a warm evening, coloured by the tangerine glow of sunset. In the end we stayed for three.

It wasn't till we got to the third drink that the conversation turned to our reason for coming.

'We haven't really discussed Eden's papers,' I remarked, holding my wine to the fading sun. It smelled of fruit and the lost promise of holidays with Josh. But it was OK. I found, if I searched inside, only a smidgen of guilt. True, I still felt it nonetheless but it wasn't as stifling as it had been before. In fact, I was almost enjoying myself. 'Why did Tobias Fitch even have to mention his proposed engagement to Olivia Sparrow?'

Andrew was sitting back in his metal chair watching the river. The tension in his neck, apparent in my room, had eased out of him. 'Customary at the time. If the Help got married, where would the spouse live? Was there a space in the household? If not, what then would the married couple do?'

I found that ridiculous. The woman was loaded. 'Olivia could have made room, surely. I wonder why she said no?'

Andrew made a face. 'You're joking aren't you? a) Sarah Grey dabbled with herbs and medicines. That would have

289

been viewed with great contempt by someone of Lady Olivia's views. She was Low Church. That sort of thing was akin to heresy. b) In terms of status, Sarah would have been a huge come down for Tobias. It sounds like his mistress favoured him. She may have even believed him to be the Brigadier's son, though of course she could never admit to that. But she certainly wouldn't want him throwing his life away on some ill-thought-of daughter of a linen draper. It would have been social suicide.'

He sank his lips into the frothy head of a Belgian beer, and licked them. 'c) It would have brought an element of disgrace to Olivia's household. She was the boss: devout, upright. The Lady of the Manor. She had made a huge effort to bring morality to the people of Leigh.'

I paused to take a sip from my glass. Its alcohol content was joyously coursing through my veins. 'This anonymous friend who was going to help them elope, the go-between, who have you got in the frame for that?'

'I don't know. There's very little written about Tobias. Your guess is as good as mine. It could have been another servant or it might have been someone from within Leigh society. Although Tobias' position was fairly lowly, he wouldn't have been able to advance anyone. But his closeness to the Lady of the Manor may have been seen as an opening to that household and her circle . . .' He set his glass back on the table. 'That might have been attractive in the long run.'

'To whom?'

'I'm hoping we're going to find out tomorrow.' He turned to me, the fading light catching his eyes, bringing out their depth. Small flicks of amber swirled within them.

We were close now, physically. I could smell the faint aroma of pine combined with the base note of his own male skin. It was a heady perfume. But ogling blokes wasn't my style and might prove a bit of a turn-off for a former vicar.

'Tobias,' I said, alert to the slight slur of the 's'. Then realized I didn't know what I was going to say. As nice as this giddiness felt, if I didn't consume something solid soon I'd start swaying, which although I was feeling brazen, wasn't a good look in the trendy part of town, whether anyone knew me or not. 'Can I suggest we get something to eat? I'm about to tip over the edge of sober.'

Andrew laughed. 'We're on holiday. Enjoy it.'

He'd been on the beer while I'd downed more than a half bottle of wine. I paid up before my resolve dwindled.

We walked around for a while, unable to decide what kind of cuisine we fancied. In the end Andrew forced the issue and we took a table at an open-air fish restaurant. I couldn't tell whether the place was full of locals or tourists, but the crowd dining there seemed very stylish and laid back and soon Andrew and I had eased ourselves into our chairs, ordered our meals and bottle of wine, and were happily watching people stroll by.

We played a game as we ate, trying to decide the names and relationships of those who caught our attention.

'Gloria,' said Andrew, indicating a buxom blonde of about twenty-five arm-in-arm with a swarthy middle-aged fat guy. 'Russian. Formerly a lap dancer. Now rescued by Marco. Celebrating their anniversary.'

'Which one?'

'Six weeks,' he said, with a glint in his eye.

I giggled like a teenager. The food hadn't done much to soak up the alcohol. 'If the folks at school could hear you now.'

He smiled and leant closer. 'What would they say?'

'They'd think you were human after all.'

He honked out a bray-like laugh. The booze was getting to him, too. 'Well, I might show them that side of me. If only I could extract the management chip from my main-frame.'

Now it was my turn to snigger. He was getting funnier and funnier. 'Shall we walk on and get an after dinner liqueur?'

The vodka bar we found ourselves in had a kind of literary vintage style. Lit by large 1950s standard lamps, poems and newspaper cuttings we couldn't translate were pasted all over its walls. Comfy over-stuffed armchairs were scattered here and there, seating a distinctly bookish crowd. It was, it had to be said, a lucky find: it was romantic.

We staggered through the main bar down a narrow corridor into a smaller but less crowded salon. A couple of men in suits laughed at a joke as we passed them. One of them reeled backwards, chuckling away. Unsteady on my feet now, I was about to collide with him. Expertly Andrew slipped his hand into my fingers and pulled me closer to him. Obstacle avoided, I went to release his hand but then stopped for a second and thought about it. I liked it. And Andrew didn't seem to be in any hurry to let go of me.

Installing ourselves at a round table at the back of the

room, Andrew called the waitress over and ordered us two chilli vodkas.

I leant towards him across the table, and propped my face in my hands. His eyes were shining and a couple of drops of perspiration dotted his forehead, but aside from that he oozed confidence and charm. Only a dopiness in his smile indicated a certain level of inebriation. He stuck his elbows on the table and mirrored my pose, and for a moment we just sort of sat there, gazing at each other, not saying a single word.

'Who'd have thought?' Andrew said at last.

I sighed loudly, dislodging a lock of hair, which fell across my face.

'You and me,' he continued, and reached over and tucked the rogue strands behind my ear. 'Here,' he said, letting his hand rest at the back of my head. 'In Antwerp. After all these years.'

'What do you mean? Years?' I pulled a face.

He grinned. 'I mean months.'

I swallowed and scowled. 'You said "years".'

My brow tensed into a frown.

'Oh yes, you're doing it again, Sarah Grey.' His voice had become soft and husky. His shoulders came nearer still. With his free hand he ran his finger over the profile of my nose, down across my lips. I forgot my apprehension and surrendered to the electric touch of his skin on my face. 'Enchanting, charming. I believe you've put a spell on me.'

It was overwhelming. All those months, years without a lover's touch. I'd forgotten what it was like. Dormant desire erupted within, spreading ripples to the surface of my skin.

So I did what any woman in that situation would do. I reached for his chin and brought him closer.

Then I kissed him.

It was a long, lingering first kiss: breath-stopping, head-spinning, brimful months of longing. We tumbled into each other, his tongue finding mine, licking, probing, gasping, oblivious to the world outside of our table.

Until the waitress coughed and plonked two vodkas noisily on the table.

Andrew paid her and turned back to me. 'Oops,' he said, to the large shot glasses. 'I'd forgotten about you.'

'Me too,' I stretched my hand across the table and took his. 'Come on, let's down them and go back to the hotel.'

Neither of us mentioned what we were doing, or spoke a single word from the moment we tottered into my room until the end of our lovemaking.

There was no need. We communicated with our bodies and fingers and lips, touching, teasing. When he came inside me, the first time, he held my face and looked into my eyes. The involuntary arch of my back snatched my gaze from his briefly, but when I came back to him, I hit a feeling I couldn't describe – a sense of absolute rightness, of belonging.

The opposite of loneliness.

It was like I'd come home.

As the first light of dawn seeped between the blinds, he said, 'One of us is going to have to resign.'

The rock of his body was behind mine, tensed and meaty against my more wobbly flesh. 'I know,' I said, and kissed his forearm. It retained his tan.

And it was wrapped around me.

My stomach lurched with another spasm of desire.

'I have some money,' he said. 'I was thinking of maybe going back to finish what I started up North.'

'You mean the biography of Eden?'

'Yes. This should be chronicled. Not just his story, but Sarah's too. Don't you think?'

'I do, I do,' I said, wriggling out of his grip and turning to face him. I stroked the curve of his right cheek. 'Does that mean you'd go back to Scotland?'

His eyes sought mine. 'Would you mind?'

I exhaled loudly. 'Of course I'd bloody mind! I don't want you to run away just as I've . . .'

He stopped me with a kiss. 'I was hoping you'd say that. No, I'd have to visit a couple of times to sort through things but I can order what I need through the libraries.'

'So you don't have to move?'

'No. I don't.'

'Good.'

'I just love it when you flip out. You get this startled look in your eyes and your nose wrinkles up. It's really cute. You don't realize you're doing it but it's driven me mad a couple of times way back when I had you in my office.'

'Mmm. Now that's a thought.'

'Don't start thinking about that, you foul temptress. I'll still be your boss for the next three months.'

'That sounds like I could have a lot of fun with you then.'

'We can have a lot of fun now, don't you think?' And he kissed me again.

*   *   *

When I next woke the small hand was almost touching eleven. I rolled over and found that I was alone. The dryness in my mouth bordered on painful. I crept out of bed and stole over to the bathroom expecting to find Andrew in there. It was empty.

I guessed he must have gone back to his room. I jumped in the shower for a few minutes, towelled, threw some clothes on, grabbed my bag and went down the corridor to find him, humming some silly love song that'd been going round my head since I awoke.

The door of his room was half ajar, the sound of a vacuum cleaner coming from within. I pushed it to and found a chambermaid cleaning. She turned off the hoover when she saw me, and cocked her head enquiringly, a small questioning smile on her lips.

'Er,' I stumbled through my 'O' Level French. '*L'homme est ici?*'

She shook her head. '*Non. Il est parti.*'

'Departed?' My brow creased into an instant frown, and I looked around the room.

'*Oui.* Departed.'

I straightened up. 'Really? *Où?* Where?'

She shrugged and said, 'I don't know,' with a nonchalance that suggested I should leave the room and let her get on.

I turned back into the corridor and wandered to the stairs unsure of where to go. What had he done? Where had he gone?

A half-thought that had been growing at the back of my mind zoomed into sudden focus. *If you can trust him.*

Surely, he wouldn't leave me like this? Not after last

night. Or maybe, a little voice whispered, especially after last night.

He'd got what he'd wanted. Maybe it was all fair in a godless universe? Perhaps without God anything went.

No, I thought firmly. Andrew McWhittard was a good man. Upstanding, caring. A decent man with a tragic past.

Or was he indeed? I only had his word that the story he had told me, his connection to the investigation, was true. To all intents and purposes, he was a man without a past. I had met no friends, heard of no acquaintances since he turned up at St John's last year. No one had.

It suddenly hit me that I knew very little about the man I had slept with last night. The man in whom I had placed my trust and shared my secrets.

A ripple of fear convulsed my stomach as panic began to set in. What if he had gone to Tobias without me? I didn't have Mr Fitch's address. Andrew had been circumspect about it when I'd asked to see it.

But why would he do that?

To steal the key to the mystery for himself.

The research he'd done was solid and true. The man had been studying Sarah Grey and her confessor, for sure. The facts tallied with my own investigations. *And* he wanted to write a book.

The bastard.

I had reached the foot of the stairs now, and marched across the lobby and through the revolving doors. I had given it all away! I should have remembered my initial repugnance, my early gut reaction to him. Even Sarah had warned me but I had been seduced by the man.

Outside on the street I stopped for a moment. Where was

297

I to go? Across the road stood a bus stop. I dodged between the traffic and squeezed past a couple waiting to scour the map on the timetable.

My heart was still pounding when I heard my name. 'Sarah!'

Andrew was standing outside the hotel waving a map in his hand, a black leather satchel over his shoulder.

His eyebrows arched quizzically as he crossed to me. 'What are you doing?'

I tried to keep my face calm and my tone casual. 'I'm just checking out the buses. What are *you* doing?'

He sent me a funny look. 'The bus we need is up the street and round the corner.' Then he leant down and slipped his hand under my chin, cupping my face. 'You all right?'

I pulled his hand down and stepped away from him, still uncertain. 'Where were you? I went to your room. The maid said you'd departed.'

'I tried to wake you earlier but you were out for the count. So I showered then headed back to get changed. The maid turned up to do the room so I nipped out to a bakery and got these.' He waved two freshly wrapped baguettes at me. 'I figured we would miss breakfast. I got you cheese and salad. Sorry, couldn't remember if you're a veggie or not.' His grin had assumed a confused, sheepish quality. To be fair, he looked clueless. Or he was doing a bloody good impression of it.

Either was possible. But I was coming round to him.

I pouted a bit and wasn't going to say anything, but like I said, I blurt. 'I thought you'd checked out. Or gone ahead. Left me.'

He laughed, and then realizing I meant it, took my hand

and raised it to his lips and kissed it. 'Why on earth would you think that? I'm crazy about you. You must know that by now?'

I looked up into his face. It was shining and glossy with a thin layer of perspiration. 'You're sweating,' was all I said.

'It's hot. And I'm excited. Come on, it's time for us to go.'

I let him tug me into his stride and tried to shrug off the doubt that had wrapped me like a shroud. I didn't want it to ruin the day.

The number eight bus dropped us off, just after one o'clock, in a small suburban square. We followed Andrew's map to a nineteenth-century red-bricked building that stood five storeys high. On the journey there, he had gabbled on about the first time he had found Tobias Fitch, the thrill of it, and how he had whooped like a dog in the stern Scottish library. Privately I thought this irritating and self-indulgent and didn't say much. But in the end his excitement was contagious and I found myself squeezing his hand as we stood up for our stop and he told me he couldn't believe that we would meet Tobias at last. I noted his use of 'we' rather than 'I'. Maybe I was paranoid.

Shuttered windows were decorated with flower boxes bursting with a variety of brightly coloured plants in full bloom. The old iron outer doors to the vestibule were wide open. Andrew suggested it would be better if it was me who rang the bell. I took a breath and pressed the green rectangular button beside a neat printed label for the Fitches' residence.

After a few seconds the intercom buzzed. Without asking who we were a wheezy male voice told us to take the elevator to the fourth floor.

The lift, set into the stairwell, was a wobbly 1970s contraption, which quivered arbitrarily on its torturously slow ascent. With barely enough room for two adults, I took the opportunity to press against Andrew's chest, overcome by a flush of anxiety.

Not about Andrew, though that hadn't disappeared altogether. Another thought had bubbled up. What if Tobias Fitch had lost his wits? What if he had nothing new to tell us and we had come all this way for nothing? All this way when I should probably be spending what little time I may have left with my son.

The hangover was kicking in and bringing more hurtling, barely repressed fears.

I'd pushed the memory of Doctor Cook's last consultation into the far recesses of my brain. The events of yesterday and this morning had distracted me, but now I was tired and tremulous. I felt I could cry at any moment.

Andrew read my expression. 'You OK? It'll be fine.' He took my hand and raised it to his lips again. It was a touching gesture. 'I promise.'

'Are you sure?'

'I'm here.'

It was what I needed right then and I surrendered to his strength and buried my head in his chest. He *was* there for me. Or was that wishful thinking?

The lift came to a shuddering halt and we moved down the landing to a painted white door half ajar at the end of the corridor.

A man in his late sixties, wearing a sports shirt and jeans, stood in the doorway. He extended his hand to me. 'Sarah Grey? My father is delighted to meet you.'

I shook his hand, slightly thrown by the odd greeting, which was repeated to Andrew, and we were shown through a tiny hall into a bright, high-ceilinged room with three windows that faced onto the street. It served the purpose of both living room and diner and was elegantly furnished in old wood. A couple of sofas were arranged around an empty fireplace and an ancient looking television. Pine panels adorned the walls behind framed pastel watercolours and cheesy family photographs.

The man I presumed to be Laurens gestured to a rickety table covered in a beautiful lace tablecloth, which stood by the open windows. The subtle bouquet of geraniums filled the room. 'Please. Claudia is with my father. He is preparing for your visit.'

I nodded, wondering why the old man needed to be 'prepared' but then realized this could be a translation quirk. Perhaps Laurens meant his wife was getting him dressed.

In stilted English the old man offered us tea, which we both accepted. He told us to sit down and disappeared through a door to the left of the room.

I obeyed his instructions and took my notebook out of my handbag. I'd also, on a whim whilst packing, tossed an old Dictaphone into my case. I placed it carefully on the table and pressed play. A gaggle of Alfie-talk sounded loudly across the room followed by a brief rendition of 'Postman Pat'.

Andrew laughed.

'Just needed to test it.' I pressed record and asked him what he had for breakfast.

He leant in to the small oval microphone. 'You,' he said, just as Laurens returned with a tray filled with cups and teapot.

I rewound the tape and heard myself ask Andrew the question. It was clear, so I turned it off quickly and turned to Laurens, who had positioned himself opposite me to pour the tea. 'Thank you, that's lovely. It's very kind of you.'

'I have to say,' he said, not taking his eyes off the stream of liquid, 'I would prefer you not to see my father.'

'Oh?' Andrew took the cup and saucer and declined the milk. 'Why is that?'

Laurens offered me sugar, which I took, and answered Andrew. 'He is not a well man. He, you know, suffered a,' he searched inwardly for the right word. 'I'm sorry my English it's not good. Claudia is better. She'll be in soon.'

'I'm sorry.' I moved the sugar bowl across the table to Laurens. He directed my gaze to his chest. 'He suffered a . . .'

'Heart attack?' Andrew suggested.

Laurens stirred his tea. 'A paralysis. Here – arm and face.' He patted his cheek.

'Oh.' I stopped the firm fixed smile I'd worn since arriving in his home. 'A stroke?'

Laurens pointed in my direction with his forefinger and nodded. 'That's it. He should not be,' he paused, 'over stimulated.'

'I see.' At once guilty and intrigued, I figured Tobias must have something important to say. Why else would he see us?

Laurens continued. 'But I understand his will. I would tell you, but Father wishes for you and he to converse. My thought,' he raised the china teacup to his lips and took a small sip, 'we do not gain from it. Many years ago is gone. But that generation, they lived through much devastation, loss. The continue, continuation? Is that right?' he asked, though I was unsure if he was referring to his choice of word or the convoluted concept that he was trying to get across.

Andrew stepped in. 'Continuation? Yes that's right.'

'The continuation of *l'histoire*, of legacy. It means much to him.'

I was beginning to doubt that our interview with Tobias would yield much at all if he had the linguistic skills of his son, as nice as Laurens was.

'Ah,' Laurens broke off and glanced over my head to the doorway we had come through. A dark-haired woman of about my age came towards us, smiling widely. 'Claudia.'

Claudia was obviously not Laurens' wife as I had assumed. Fashionably dressed, wearing three-quarter-length cropped jeans, trainers and a tight-fitting green t-shirt, with a designer logo emblazoned across the left breast, which brought out her vivid green eyes circled in dark eyeliner and the olive glow of her skin. Claudia was a very attractive woman. Her black hair was platted into a loose pigtail that hung down into the small of her back.

She came straight to me. 'Sarah Grey!' Her English was practically perfect. I rose from my chair to greet her and thrust out my hand but she ignored it and threw her arms around me and kissed me. 'It's good to meet you at last.'

I darted a look at Andrew. He seemed as mesmerized as me. Claudia followed my gaze. 'Sorry,' I said, disentangling myself from her arms. 'This is Andrew McWhittard who has . . .' I was going to say accompanied me but Claudia sussed it, bent down and kissed him on both cheeks.

'The scholar of the bishop,' she said, stepping back to survey Andrew. 'He doesn't know of your Eden,' she said

303

very suddenly. 'But you,' she turned back and patted my arm. 'He has waited a long time for you. We all have.'

Laurens muttered something in French, evidently telling her to sit down at the table. She rolled her eyes at us but moved to the window and took a chair beside her father. 'He's worried I'll say too much.' She laughed. I shot another glance at Andrew. His mouth was half open, his teacup frozen mid-air. He looked from Claudia to Laurens and back again.

'I won't though.' Claudia reached across the table, earning a 'tut' from Laurens, and abruptly changed the subject. 'So where are you staying?'

We informed her of the hotel's name and location and she remarked that she knew it, and approved of our choice. Again Laurens said something in French. Claudia answered and then put down her cup.

'Are you ready to see Grandfather, then?'

We both nodded. I drained my cup and picked up my belongings. All apart from Laurens stood up.

'No,' Laurens said, wagging a finger at Andrew. 'Only the women.'

Claudia took me gently by the arm. 'Sorry, Andrew. It is only possible for Sarah Grey. He has nothing for you.'

Andrew hovered between dismay and protest, unsure whether he should object. My heart went out to him – to be denied like this at the climax. But then again, this was *my* story.

'Can he not come in and listen?' I asked Claudia.

She shook her head firmly. 'Too many strangers will tire him.'

'It's all right,' Andrew said. 'This means more to you. Can you record it on your Dictaphone?'

I looked at Claudia and pointed to the device in my hand. 'If that's OK with Tobias?'

'Oh, that will be fine,' said Claudia breezily. 'Can't be too long though. He's an old man, you know.'

She squeezed my arm as she led me into the darkness of the corridor beyond.

Chapter Twenty-One

Tobias Fitch was propped up on his bed. The stroke seemed not to have incapacitated him as much as I had expected, though it must have been a while since his skin had seen daylight. It was almost the same colour as his thick, white hair, trimmed smartly into a short back and sides. He wore an open-necked shirt and suit trousers, as if he had dressed for the occasion. Although slim, he didn't look wasted. He smiled as he saw me enter. The same green eyes as his grand-daughter flashed at me, full of intelligence, though hooded by age.

'Here she is,' said Claudia with a flourish, and pulled out a stool by the bed.

I half expected her to pull up a chair herself but she simply asked Tobias if he needed anything and, finding the answer negative, withdrew leaving the two of us alone.

'She is much like my mother, Evalina,' Tobias said, as the door closed. 'Not married yet either. Like Evalina. You?' His voice was gentle but hoarse with nearly a century of use. I was relieved his English, though not in the same league as his granddaughter's, was far superior to his son's.

'I was,' I said. 'But he died.'

Tobias beckoned me closer to the bed. I shifted the stool over. 'History repeats itself then? You and I, we are living proof of that in our names, yes? My mother named me after her grandfather. And you too have inherited the name of old Madam Grey.'

He assumed then, not illogically, I was a descendant of Sarah Grey. It was pointless explaining how I'd come to trace him, so I let him conclude what he wanted and instead flattered him on his excellent English.

'Yes.' Tobias did his best to nod amongst the overstuffed pillows. 'My first wife was English.' He wheezed out the last consonants.

'Laurens' mother?'

Tobias' green eyes squeezed shut as he spluttered out a laugh. 'No, no. Laurens' mother was Belgian. Irene was killed in the war. With my mother. We had no time to have children.' He winked then added, somewhat inappropriately I thought at the time, 'We have many wives in this family.'

Surprise must have shown on my face because he reached for my hand. I offered it to him and he gave it a pat. 'One after the other. Not together. One after the other. You have widows, am I right? And we have widowers. History repeats itself.' His eyes glittered in their sunken sockets. 'And so do I.'

The old man was growing on me. A strong sense of mischief projected from him. Although his mouth was lopsided as he spoke, sometimes obscuring his words, there was no doubt that neither the stroke nor his maturity had destroyed any brain capacity. Tobias Fitch was as sharp as a razor. It was I who needed my wits about me.

'So, Sarah. You must pass me that book and the box.'

Tobias extended a finger to the table on my right. I picked up the two objects placed in the middle: an ancient looking exercise book and a wooden box about the size of a paperback, and placed them in Tobias' hands.

He let them rest on his lap and gave them a pat. 'So, it is all here. My great grandfather's confession. It is what you have come for, yes?'

The word confession hit me. My mind raced through the connections – confession – crime.

Without realizing it I had moved to the edge of the stool. 'Can I record you, Mr Fitch? Would you mind?' I held the Dictaphone up.

'I have no objections.'

I clicked on the record button.

'So,' he repeated. 'It is not quite as he spoke it here, but you will gain an impression. My mother took down my great grandfather's words in 1896. She was only thirteen and did not realize what she was writing at the time.'

He had lived on then.

For a very long time.

Sarah was right to have had her suspicions.

'1896?' I double-checked. 'Are you sure?'

'Quite. The journal was dated. My great grandfather was becoming ill and knew he would be nearing the end. He had a wish to tell of what he had done. He was not proud of it, but he wanted to confess. Evalina was his favoured granddaughter. Bright and educated, he requested she write it down. She kept the book for many years, not understanding what my great grandfather had to say.'

Tobias tapped the exercise book. It was plainly not an antique. His keen eyes read my gaze. 'That book was destroyed by the bomb that killed her and Irene – New Year's Day 1945. The war would end that year.' He looked away, grief plain in his face. But he mastered the emotion and went on. 'She read the book to me. I don't know why. I don't think she knew either. Maybe she wanted to share the burden of the secret. Maybe it was just to amuse me. If it was, it worked. I loved it as a child and as a teenager it fascinated me. I didn't know my father. He died before my mother knew she was pregnant. He and Evalina never married. There was no time in that war. I did not have the privilege of knowing my great grandfather either. He passed away twenty-one years before I was born. But his story caught my imagination. He wasn't just a man but a hero, so it seemed in my youth. His tale was an adventure, like a romance . . .'

I held the recorder closer to the old man. He was looking straight ahead, away from me, smiling at his memories. 'Like Sinbad, he sailed the seven seas. When the book was destroyed I took some time to write down what I could remember so I could pass on the story to my sons and grandsons when they came to be born. That, Sarah Grey, is what's on the pages in here.'

Tobias fingered the exercise book. It trembled and yawned open as he held it for me.

Beneath my fingertips the fine leaves of the script were fragile, delicate, browning. With trepidation I opened the first page.

My heart sank.

It was in French.

Of course it was. Why wouldn't it be? Nethertheless I was crestfallen. 'What does it say?' I asked, too taken aback to remember my manners.

Tobias coughed. 'You must get it translated. Claudia perhaps. It will have more to tell you than I can.' He raised a shaky hand to his head and pretended he was knocking on his skull. 'But I will try.'

He reached a shaky finger at the Dictaphone. 'It is on?'

I showed him the glowing red button and he began.

'Tobias Fitch, my great grandfather, was of disputed lineage. He never said who his mother was but Evalina suspected that she was a slave. After her death he was taken aboard a ship bound for England by General Sparrow, a well-known Brigadier and a Lord. It was Tobias' early assumption that the Brigadier General was his father, but he had no clear idea. I think as he grew older, he wondered if the Brigadier had perhaps merely shown Christian compassion or was helping a friend or a faithful servant. We don't know. Nor will we. It is of little significance to you.

'The Brigadier did not survive the journey home. A fever took him. His men buried him on the island of Tortolo. But Tobias did survive and on his return was given to the Brigadier's widow, a woman who treated him with some affection. She often made trips to the town where he was to meet your ancestor, Sarah. Is that right?'

I spoke urgently, impatient now. 'That's right, Sarah Grey. Do go on.'

'He described your Madam Grey with fondness. Blackest hair of the raven, eyes afire like an angry sea. She was a beauty. He loved her very much and intended to marry her. He told his employer, Lady Sparrow. I understand there was a disagreement between them. Lady Sparrow did not want him to marry Sarah. She was suspicious of her intentions.'

'Of Sarah's?'

'Your forebear was not well thought of. There were rumours of witchcraft. Of course Tobias knew Sarah was not a witch and tried to appease Lady Olivia but to no avail. She forbade him to see Sarah again.

'But Tobias had a friend in whom Lady Olivia had confided also. And so, this man offered to help them to elope. Tobias was overjoyed. His friend had promised him a wedding gift – money enough to set up the couple with a shop in a neighbouring town. It seemed there was nothing to stop the two now.

'The night of the elopement was stormy and wild. As he waited for Sarah, taking shelter in a huge elm tree, he was seized by a mob of men. He was a strong man, my great grandfather, and fought hard with his attackers, redoubling his efforts as he saw Sarah approach. She too tried to help him but was thrown off by one of the gang. Enraged by this Tobias struck down one of the men who had touched her. Then he was struck down himself.

'When he regained consciousness his friend was there at his side. He announced the dreadful news that Sarah had been killed by the fall and that the man he himself beat down had not survived. Tobias Fitch was without his betrothed and now a murderer too. It was his aim to stand trial and face justice, but his friend urged him to flee with the money he had given him. In the dark hours of the next morning, before the sun had risen, he was conveyed in a Leigh boat to a waiting ship that brought him via many different routes eventually to Antwerp.

'A quick learner, whilst on board he had made himself useful, and got friendly with the captain and the crew. They taught him the skills of the open seas and he put them to use. Fearful that he was still hunted by the mob for the death of their man, he did not disembark when the ship put in at the first port of Calais, but remained aboard, not as a passenger but one of the crew.

'For the next six years he traversed the globe. That was until he caught a fever in the South Americas which left him washed up in the docks of Antwerp.

'He made money from his time at sea and had also not touched that of his friend, meaning to repay him one day. Tobias found lodgings in the city and convalesced.

'It was during this time that he met my great grandmother, Alice. She was the landlord's daughter and very pretty. He would never forget the tragedy of his first love, but he and Alice were happy together. They had two sons, Jools and my grandfather, also called Tobias, then Greta. I remember her.

'When Alice's father died, Tobias used his savings to buy the property and for a while they were content. But once a man has gone to sea it stays in his blood and it called to him to return. Alice did not like him to be away for such lengthy periods so after two years he gave it up.

'The property business went well and over the next decade Tobias acquired more lodging houses by the docks. The family became affluent, but my great grandfather never forgot his humble background nor the friend who had helped him to escape the punishment that he felt sure would catch up with him one day. He was a good man and with his wealth he built a home for aged seamen. He insisted his stewards rent half of his properties to poor families at a fraction of the cost that they could command.'

'In 1865 he was made a burgher. I think it was that, combined with the gradual onset of rheumatism in his legs, which spurred him to return to England one last time while he was still able. He told Evalina he was to repay the debt to his friend. Alice consented. He chartered a boat, disguising himself as the captain, still fearful of being recognized and caught.

'In 1867 he travelled to England, and docked one last time at the town of Leigh. Tobias planned only to stay to find his friend, if indeed he were still alive, then intended to go on to London to buy items the family had requested.

'He dined in an inn by the waterside with his men. There was great unease amongst them for the weather. The sea was tempestuous and the sky black – a storm was drawing close. Tobias resolved to find his friend and leave as soon as possible.

'That afternoon, as the clouds rolled in above the town, he saw a hunched figure shuffling along the high street. He would never have known her, she had changed so, but she saw him and called out his name. At first he panicked, thinking he'd been recognized as the murderer, but when he looked beyond the lines of age, he found himself gazing into the beautiful eyes of his former lover, Sarah Grey.

'For several moments he could not speak. Sarah took him by the arm to a small tavern across the railway away from the main town.

'I cannot imagine what their reunion was like: two lovers battered by age, circumstance and tragedy, together again, risen from the dead. I do know she told him she had borne him a son and that later she showed him the grave.

'I also know Tobias raged and moaned and protested that he had been told she had perished. They both understood that they had been duped. Yet Sarah remained silent, asking only one question when Tobias had worn himself quiet. "Who was your friend?"

'It was an answer he wished he never had given. For she may have lived longer. She lived in terrible poverty and he had money he could give Sarah to improve her lot. "Who was your friend?" she asked again and again. So he told her the truth, "The man I thought had helped me, who posed as my confidant, was Doctor Hunter."

'It was then that Sarah went into her own rage and swore she would speak with him. Tobias begged her not to go. The doctor would know that he had returned and could alert the authorities to his presence in the town. But Sarah scoffed. There were none, she said, who had thought him a murderer. No death was reported but his. But, she cried to him and to those around, she must see her own justice served. And despite his protests she left the wharf.

'He never saw her again.' Tobias was silent for a moment.

'His intention was to return and to bring her some money and goods or to settle her in some way that might make amends. But two days after he arrived back in Antwerp he heard Englishmen were attempting to track him down. On the pretence of looking for contraband, the ship that he chartered was searched. But Tobias had a good name now and fine friends in the port. Soon he learnt the men were reporting he attacked and killed a woman of Leigh: the old widow, Sarah Grey.

'The doctor had succeeded in finally silencing the woman who could reveal what he had done.'

The old man continued, urgent now. As if justifying his great grandfather's actions he emphasized the words. 'Tobias would have returned to settle the score, to confront the doctor, but Alice would not let him go, urging him to caution. He and his wife had three children, eleven grandchildren and a reputation to protect. And so Tobias did not pursue it. He did what he unwittingly had done many years before – he abandoned Sarah Grey once again.'

The younger Tobias sighed loudly, dislodging some phlegm and setting off a dry cough. He paused to rest and to inspect my face for signs of emotion.

I said nothing, too absorbed in thought, though the logic of it was dawning on me. According to Eden's journals it was Hunter who had sent the men after Fitch. There was no other investigation.

The big picture was coming into view.

Another bout of coughing came and went. Tobias eased back on his pillows, exhausted now. 'What happened to her? Madam Grey?'

There was no easy way of telling him. 'Someone . . . no, not someone, it was Doctor Hunter . . . he cut her head off and tied her up like a witch.'

He winced and shuddered. 'I'm sorry. Still,' he grasped the box on his lap and lifted the lid, 'I have for this for you, too. Mother's neighbour came across it in the rubble of her building. It had her jewellery in it, and this.' He picked out a small gold band and gestured for my hand.

'What is it?' I asked, nerves alert.

Without speaking he slipped it onto the index finger of my left hand. 'It fits. It would have been Sarah's wedding ring. He kept it, all that time. It was the only thing he had to remind him. It is yours now. You are the rightful owner.'

It shone on my finger. 'I can't . . . no, you don't understand.'

315

'I, we, insist. A great wrong was done to your family. To give this to you . . . it is the least we can do. It is what Tobias intended. You must take it back to Leigh.'

That was assured, but my easy deception troubled me. 'I'm not her direct line.' I was reeling. The new shock of the treachery was giving way to a different emotion. Salty water pooled in my eyes.

Tobias raised his hand gently and hushed me. 'Then take it to her, wherever she is. And tell her he loved her.'

I nodded and jogged the tears out of my eyes. One splashed over my cheek. I turned away to hide from Tobias but he was wise to it. 'It's sad, yes.'

'I feel so sorry for Sarah. And Tobias.' I was weeping at the unfairness of it all. 'It was so wrong. They should have been together. They were in love.'

'If they had married, I wouldn't be here today, my dear. And neither would my family. Nor the descendants of the families Tobias gave shelter to. Certain things aren't meant to be.'

Suppressed anger at the travesty of it all bubbled close to the surface. 'I don't think Sarah was *meant* to be murdered. She didn't deserve it and she doesn't warrant the reputation she has even today.'

'Well, you can do something about that, can't you, Sarah?' He smiled, then rasped into a second bluster of coughing.

I rose to assist him but he waved me back. 'If you don't mind I would like to rest now. Talking so much does wear me out. But I wanted to see you. Very much. Now Claudia and Laurens will see you out.'

I understood. And I was obliged to him. 'Thank you, Tobias. I really am very grateful, you know, for everything. For these.' I held the book in my ringed hand.

'No,' he said, though it was clearly becoming some effort to speak. 'It is I who must thank you for coming. The family wanted it. And now at last Tobias can rest in peace.'

'For my sanity let's hope Sarah can, too.' I bent over and kissed him, then I left the room.

Chapter Twenty-Two

We said our thank yous to Claudia and Laurens, refusing the offer of more tea. I reached the outer landing, handed Claudia the old exercise book and asked her if there was any possibility she could translate it. 'It would be a pleasure,' she said. 'If you give me your address I will send it to you.' I scribbled it onto a piece of paper and within five minutes was through the vestibule and on the street outside with Andrew.

I felt too shaky to consider public transport and he was eager to find out what the old man had to say. We ducked into the first café that we came to.

Over steaming coffee I relayed Tobias' story. My own response was still muddled and chaotic, so to see him process the new information with a logical mind was a comfort of sorts.

'Christ! This is astounding. We've cracked the mystery.' He leant over and rubbed my hand.

I withdrew it and ran it through my slightly sweaty hair. 'Have we?'

'It's got to be Hunter, hasn't it? Is there anyone else in the frame? What do you make of Tobias Fitch – do you think he was telling the truth?'

A queasiness was growing inside, but I managed to answer him. 'It had to be authentic. Why would he fabricate it this way? I mean, it was an age ago. Why bother?'

'To clear his name? His family's name?'

'But then why would he hang on to the ring?'

'Don't murderers take trophies from their victims? Souvenirs?'

We sat for a moment mulling things through. My stomach was curdling. 'I don't buy it,' I said at last. 'He was sincere. The old Tobias' story makes sense when you think about it. It ties up with everything else we've found out. It has to be Hunter.'

'I agree. It can't be the Primus, or Canon King. There's no motive.'

I opened my notebook and read out my list of suspects. 'She was murdered fifteen years after the child Jane Tulley was burnt to death, and seventeen years after the second cholera epidemic. Way too long after the events for the parents to exact revenge. Elizabeth Little was another name I had written down. She was a smuggler. But I'm not convinced she had anything to do with it. Not now. Not after listening to what Tobias had to say.

'It has to be Hunter,' I said firmly. 'Sarah sees Tobias again. They both think the other one is dead. Can you imagine? Then the realization that they've both been had. Hunter ruined their lives.'

Andrew picked up the thread. 'She goes to confront him. Tells him she knows what he's done and threatens to blow the whole thing open. But he can't have that . . .' A sickness was coming up from my stomach. I swallowed and strained to hear him.

319

'So, maybe she goes to his house and it's not intentional but ...' Andrew's words were growing fainter, distant, echoing into the vaulted ceiling of the room.

The nausea lurched within me just as the café dimmed and receded.

Light vanished.

Then suddenly a new landscape surrounds me. I drag my skirts through the bushes, limping, forcing my body to the cliff top.

Rain pelts against my face and drenches the rags of my robe. The wind howls its warning through the trees but I don't stop till I see the house come into view. The thorny undergrowth tears at my hair as I enter the garden and cross the lawn. The house is in darkness but for a lamp at the French doors.

Through the glass I see him hunched over the hearth fire. Older now, a pair of spectacles on the end of his nose. I put my hand on the wet handle and push.

The sound makes him turn. When he recognizes me he grimaces, then a half-amused smile plays on his lips. 'Sarah, I am not at home to visitors ...' Then he stops. Something in my eyes tells him to take care.

I am on him in an instant, as close as I can get. 'You lied, Festus Hunter. You told me he was dead.' I am pleased to see I have taken him off guard. He staggers to the fire and grabs a poker from the grate. 'You are mad, woman. Sit down.'

But my fury is more potent than his staying words. 'You will command me no more. Why did you do it?'

Hunter backs away, then suddenly thrusts the poker forwards, brandishing it at me, a warning. I am beyond caution now, wanting only the truth, and I push it aside with my hand. 'Tobias. You told me he was killed.'

A glimmer of recognition seems to light in his eyes. 'You were never going to marry him. Do you think Lady Sparrow would have welcomed you? My actions back then were rewarded lavishly.' He laughs in my face.

I spit on the floor. 'You could have left us alone. Instead you ripped out my heart. You . . .' The doctor has raised the poker above his head. There is danger in the room. I step back falteringly. 'Evil be as evil does and all will know. All.'

He takes another step towards me, his cheeks now pale, eyes dark with a black fire.

'Ha,' I say, seeing what he fears now. 'I will tell of your sin. So all will know. And God will force you to atone.'

The doctor makes to catch my arm, but tired as I am, I dart to one side and turn, fleeing through the doors onto the open lawn. My fury spurs me on, giving me strength to fly. With new resolution I grip the locket in my hand. The truth will out.

The wind roars over the fields, lightning flashes across the sky, illuminating the grand cedar tree. I head for its protection, not able to think of any other escape. I have almost reached its dark shadow when I feel a blow to the back of my head. As I fall, I hear my voice cry out. 'I will tell the world, Hunter . . . Evil be . . .' Then blackness and life no more.

I jolted up, back into the café, breathing hard and fast.

Andrew was up beside me, a hand on my shoulder. 'Are you OK? You completely zoned out.'

I buried my face in my hands. The room was spinning.

'I'll get you some water. It's probably the heat.' And he left the table.

I put my head on the table's cool surface and gripped its edges to make sure I was back in the room.

It was the last piece of the jigsaw. The final revelation. She had given me the key to it all.

Poor Sarah. Her tragic life, so blasted by meanness, so ravaged and tattered, was cruelly snuffed out.

As I sat there in that foreign café, sweating and shaking, I was washed away by a colossal wave of grief and found myself weeping for her, then for Tobias, the children. Then, as my heart sank into it I cried for Josh, and Alfie, for Imogen and Amelia and Andrew. Then finally, when I was almost dry of tears, I wept at last for me.

Chapter Twenty-Three

It was only later, when we sat back at the hotel, barely eating the meals that Room Service had delivered, were we able to start speaking of it again.

After what Andrew called 'my attack' in the café, he had ferried me back in a cab. I can't really remember much about what happened when we reached the hotel, but Andrew informs me I slept for hours while he held me.

When I woke the light in my room was clearer. The air smelt fresh and cleansed as if by a storm. My environment had become different. As if some skin or layer had been rolled back, revealing a new world.

Although my head ached I felt relief throughout my body, and calm. Almost relaxed.

But I had merely entered the eye of the hurricane.

As we picked at the platter we'd ordered I felt able to return to the conversation where we had left off.

This time I felt no overwhelming emotion. I examined the new information in a more precise manner, as though I was detached, an observer, only needing to get the facts straight in my head. 'I still don't understand,' I said to Andrew at last. 'Why did she end up in the Drowning Pool?'

We were holding hands across the small, chrome table on the balcony. The evening's rays were bouncing off the terracotta roof tiles of the houses beyond. In the distance the river sparkled. Leigh was a million miles away, thankfully.

'I think,' he said softly, and rubbed his thumb on my palm, 'it would have been to throw people off the scent. Sarah was the only person left in Leigh who knew what he'd done. There's Tobias of course, but he left with the storm. Sarah's first husband, Robert Billing, who could have testified to the truth of her story, was long dead. She may have even confided in her second husband, John Grey. But she probably didn't. I imagine it would have been too shameful. Mother Grey already had a reputation as a witch, so Hunter took his opportunity and capitalized on that, tying her up like they used to when they swam witches. And Doom Pond was close to his house.'

'The Drowning Pool,' I murmured. 'It took her at last. Though she was never guilty of anything.'

Andrew sighed and caressed my hand. 'It was pretty typical of the time, I'm afraid. A woman speaks out, crosses the lines of gender and class and ends up dead as a result.'

'Like the witches did.'

Andrew tutted. 'They didn't even need to step out of line. They just needed to be different.'

I pulled out a cigarette and lit it. 'Anyhow, Sarah wasn't a witch.' I blew out and watched the smoke drift to Andrew. 'Thing is, thinking back, you have to wonder in the first place why Hunter betrayed Tobias at all?'

'It's obvious – Olivia Sparrow. Remember Eden's journal? Most people had wised up to Hunter's ambitions. The Lady of the Manor was the most powerful woman in the area.

One who could help him. And don't forget, he did succeed in becoming mayor. First one ever. He must have been clever, an arch manipulator. That would have taken quite some manoeuvring.'

I considered this for a while. In my vision he had said he'd been rewarded. 'Do you reckon Olivia Sparrow was in on it?'

'I doubt that she was briefed on the exact details, but Hunter would have indicated that his actions had averted a scandal. He succeeded in neutralizing the threat, Sarah, and spiriting away Tobias. Olivia would have felt indebted to him. Hey presto – he's suddenly the mayor.'

I shook my head. 'But if Tobias was Olivia's favourite she wouldn't want any harm coming to him.'

Andrew released my hand and fished out a cigarette from my packet. 'You have to understand what society was like back then. The Victorians feared disgrace so much more than damnation.' He blew out a plume of smoke. 'With Lady Sparrow's Low Church views, she would have taken the view that Tobias' immortal soul had been saved. She would have seen it as a sacrifice that was well worth making.'

'Even so, murder. That's a cardinal sin.'

Andrew hunched over and tapped the ashtray with his fag. 'That's the point, isn't it? There wasn't a murder. Not in 1823 at least. There was no mention of it in any newspaper at the time. I assumed that Olivia Sparrow had bought everyone off. But maybe there wasn't one at all? Tobias struck someone down, yes, but that person could have easily recovered while Tobias was out cold. Sarah was only told Tobias was dead by Hunter, right?'

It was true. 'Yes. And the doctor told Tobias Sarah was dead and the press ganger too. And now we know that Hunter was the "unknown friend" you have to realize the whole thing was a set-up. He was never going to let them elope. I doubt that there was a press gang at all. I bet they were Hunter's men, dressed up to look the part. When she heard what Tobias had to say Sarah would have worked things out for herself. Do you think she meant to kill Doctor Hunter?'

He shook his head. 'She wouldn't have had it in her. She was too old. And she wasn't a bad person. That's the misinformation put about by the legend.'

Andrew put out his cigarette and picked up his espresso. 'He silenced her.'

'Yep,' I said. 'That's what I'd seen.'

'Though who would have believed what she had to say? Her reputation was tarnished.'

'Clearly the man was mean and a control freak. No way would he allow any slur on his character. He was the mayor. And Tobias wasn't dead. He could vouch for what Sarah had to say. Hunter must have realized that. Kill Sarah and frame the foreign captain – perfect. If I didn't feel so much hatred towards the man, I'd probably find myself grudgingly admiring his plan. What a clever bastard.'

'Quite.' Andrew nodded, and looked out over the balcony to the apricot sunset. 'But we've found him out.'

I was feeling more human now. 'Shall we have a glass of wine? I think it'd steady my nerves.'

Andrew nodded. 'Here or in the brasserie?'

'I think I can manage the brasserie. Don't fancy going outside of the hotel though.'

As I stood up and fetched my bag, a thought hit me. 'But why should he cut off her head?'

Andrew drew back the doors onto the balcony. 'Probably

to delay her identification as long as possible. Or to obfuscate cause of death. The beheading and the tying up of her body hint at some kind of warped ritual in keeping with her reputation as a witch. And you can see from Eden's journals, it worked. No one suspected Hunter.'

'But she had the locket in her hand according to Walker King. That's how they knew who she was straight away.'

'Hunter can't have seen it.'

My bag was heavy. I removed some of the contents to lighten it. 'So, we've solved the mystery. Almost.'

'It's got to be Hunter,' Andrew demurred.

'Has to be,' I agreed. 'But we need more proof.'

'How are we going to get that?'

'Hunter killed her and took her head. It was never found. He might have hidden it somewhere in his house.'

'Well, we don't know where his house is, or was, do we? It's probably been demolished and built over.'

As he said it, I realized that though I hadn't announced it out loud, I knew exactly where it was. 'It's Doctor Cook's,' I said simply. 'He might have a different name but it's the same surgery, I mean the same room, the same house, that I've seen in my dreams.'

Andrew shrugged his shoulders. 'You've done all right so far. But,' he lowered his voice, 'dreaming about the surgery could be purely symbolic: it's the place you're getting treated for your eye. According to you it also happens to be where Sarah's life changed and ended. But think about it – you're living through a traumatic time – you see yourself as having a parallel story: a widow with a son, a single mum whose status puts her on the outside of society. You're empathizing so much with her . . .'

I interrupted, my voice sounding firm and strong. 'Andrew, you have to trust me on this. Call it intuition.'

My tone brooked no argument.

'OK,' he squeezed my hand again. 'Let's say the skull is there. How do you propose we go about finding it?'

I grinned and blew my cheeks out. Sometimes he was so obtuse. 'We ask him. He might know. Perhaps he's heard rumours about the place. Every house has a skeleton in its closet. And that place has at least one. I've seen it. It's hanging up in his consulting room.' I laughed. Andrew didn't. 'Look, he must have bones and skulls all over the place. And I doubt he'd mind if we asked to look at them. I've got to go and see him when we come back tomorrow. I'll ask him if he knows anything about it.'

Andrew looked unsure. 'This doesn't feel right.'

'Why would he mind?'

'Well, it's a bit of an odd request, isn't it?'

'But it was 150 years ago. We're not accusing him of anything.'

But Andrew wasn't convinced. 'I don't know.'

'Doctor Cook's nice and really caring. I doubt that he'd give a toss to be honest.'

'All right,' he said, shaking off his unease. 'I do feel like a drink now. Let's go down.'

'Hang on.' I pulled my phone out and checked it for messages. One from Mum saying she and Alfie were fine.

The phone bleeped. I hadn't brought my charger and it was just about out of juice.

'Bring it downstairs.' Andrew was not good at hiding irritation.

'No point,' I said, running my fingers over the buttons.

'Battery's going. I've just got to text Sharon. I promised her I'd tell her first.'

He opened the door and shifted from foot to foot as I typed in the text message.

'OK, I've sent it. I just wanted her to know as soon as I did. She's done an awful lot of research for me.'

I popped my phone on the side table and we ambled to the brasserie.

I'd written: 'It was the doctor!'

Chapter Twenty-Four

I suppose the first thing that alerted me to the fact that things weren't as they should have been was the call I received from Corinne that Sunday at Duerne Airport.

We had gone through security and were waiting in the bar before we boarded. It was only by chance that I had my phone on at all. I was about to turn it off to save what little there was of the battery; I'd just phoned Mum to speak to Alfie. He had offended yet reassured me with a total lack of concern for my absence, curious only to know if I was bringing him a present. An affirmative answer roused a certain amount of enthusiasm for my return but not enough to sustain his interest in a very short description of my trip. 'When you coming to get me?'

'Well,' I put my best motherly voice on, 'I've got to go to the doctor's then I'll be back.'

'No,' he said sharply. 'Don't go there. Do not!' Alfie's voice was insistent.

'Honey, what's up? What's the matter?'

'You mustn't, Mummy.'

This was strange. 'Come on, Alfie, it won't take long. I'm going to get on an aeroplane now and fly, in the sky, to London then I'll . . .' I gave up speaking when I heard him

330

squeak an abrupt 'Goodbye' followed by the clanking of the receiver and then a 'hello' from my mum. Kids have no subtlety when they're bored.

Alfie had apparently been in good spirits all weekend, enjoying his outing to Sunday School (I squirmed) and a visit to his cousin, Thomas. I informed Mum I'd be back early evening. She said her grandson was being an angel and she would be more than happy to hang on to him another night. Apparently Alfie was up for that too so I eagerly accepted – it would leave me free to hang on to Andrew one more night. 'Oh yes, Sarah, I spoke to Aunty Brenda about the Leigh connection. She's digging out some old document she thinks she's got.'

My phone did its irritating 'nearly out of battery' bleep so I spent twenty seconds thanking Mum for everything profusely then hung up.

I suggested Andrew come over to my place for the evening as soon as I terminated the call.

He did a kind of 'um-let-me-see-if-I've-got-anything-on' thing which lasted a millisecond then nodded, on the proviso he could nip back home, freshen up and then come round later. I had no objections. He wanted to make himself nice for me. Sweet.

So when the phoned beeped again I assumed it was my battery. But it was Corinne, a tad out of sorts.

She was phoning from a farm in Danbury on the off chance I was in the Old Town and could pop into Sharon's to see if she was home.

She'd forgotten that I was in Antwerp with Andrew and cracked a rather un-Corinne-like joke about dirty weekends when I told her. We chuckled over that and she requested to know if we'd consummated the relationship. I wasn't prepared to go into details while Andrew sat by my side, so I changed the subject and asked her what was up.

'It's Aunty May and Uncle Tom's ruby wedding, yawn, yawn. Me and Shazza went halves on a red vase. She's got it at her house and she's not here yet. The party started over an hour ago. I can understand her cutting it fine, it's no rave, if you know what I mean, but we were meant to meet for Sunday lunch at the King's Head, up the road. She was definitely up for it when I spoke to her on Friday: she's got no one on the go at the moment and a couple of Pat's friends were joining us too. You know how she is. Loves a bit of attention. But she didn't show and I can't get through to her on her mobile.' My phone beeped a warning.

'She might be in her kitchen,' I offered hopefully. 'You know what the signal's like in the Old Town.' Privately I imagined Sharon had a big one the night before and was probably still sleeping it off.

'Mmm,' Corinne concurred, though she sounded as unconvinced as I was. 'What time are you back?'

The phone beeped again. Twice this time. 'Evening-ish. I'll pop round to her place if you want?'

There was a slight pause at the end of the line. 'No, don't worry. Fingers crossed she'll be here by then.'

'Well, I've got something I want to talk to her about anyway.'

'Ooh, what's that? Length and girth?'

'Stop it, Corinne! No, Sarah Grey stuff. I think I know who did it.'

'Amazing. Well done. Gonna tell me?' she asked.

My phone did a triple bleep and turned itself off.

* * *

Six hours later the sun sank behind Hadleigh Downs as Andrew's silver Citroën swept us from the station towards the Old Town.

The slopes of Leigh Hill cantered down to the sea, twinkling in the sunset, as the last fading rays caught the open windows of the villas and cottages that populated its contours. Out in the estuary the sailing boats sailed, the jet-skis whizzed and the faint buzz of the day-trippers sitting outside the pubs drifted up to us through the open car windows.

I directed him to Sharon's as best I could. When we pulled up by the kerb he asked whether he should hold on to my case.

It would have been a hassle lugging it back home up the hill so I said that would be fab, and gave him a nice, protracted goodbye kiss.

'I shouldn't be too long,' I said, when he broke off for air. 'I'll just check in on her then nip to the doctor's for the prescription. I'll ask him about Sarah Grey too. See what he has to say or maybe arrange a time when we can both get to talk to him. I know you want to be there too. Anyway I won't be long. Hopefully, an hour max.'

Andrew glanced at his watch. 'I'll give you sixty-five minutes,' he grinned and blew me a kiss, then drove off.

I was staring at her door as I walked to it without really seeing it. In my head I was going over the sweet nothings Andrew and I had shared on the flight. I didn't think I could call him 'boyfriend'. It was too young. Lover sounded too old-fashioned and what we'd started was neither of those things. 'Bloke' would have to do for now. On the plane his every touch, no matter how slight or mundane, trailed sparks over my skin. I could still feel the tingles now. It had only been seconds since I left his side yet already I felt a yearning in my stomach for more.

I pressed the bell and must have stood there for a few minutes, lost in my own erotic musings, till it dawned on me nobody was at home.

The front door opened onto the living room and although it was locked, I peeped up at the little window, which had a view into the house. As I peered through the pane my hand froze in mid-air: the place had been completely trashed. Drawers had been pulled out and chucked aside; papers spilt over the floor. The cottage had been ransacked.

Worried now, I crouched down and hollered through the letterbox. 'Sharon? You there?'

No answer. I remembered she had a back door that opened into the kitchen and raced round to try it.

It was unlocked. Though I was relieved to gain entry, once inside my anxiety escalated.

A pile of broken crockery was spread all over the floor and surfaces. 'Sharon?'

An eerie silence filled the house. Frowning, I leapt up the stairs, two at a time, and inspected the bedrooms. Though not as bad as downstairs they had a rifled-through look about them.

There was no sign of Sharon.

What the hell was going on?

I went back downstairs and examined the dining area of the living room. On the table were several glasses, bottles of spirits and wine and a couple of overfilled ashtrays. Perhaps she'd had a party that had got out of hand?

That wasn't out of character. But somehow I think I knew.

I slumped down at the table and tried to concentrate, lit a fag, took a moment to think what to do.

Call her.

I reached into my pocket and pulled out my phone.

Dead.

I pulled on my cigarette hard and glanced from side to side, checking the mess, trying to figure out what was going on.

As I leant to flick ash in the ashtray, the edge of a golden picture frame caught my eye, poking from beneath a pile of old photos. I pulled it out and studied it. The photograph was of three women in their thirties, arms draped round each other's shoulders, caught mid-laugh.

There was a likeness in the redhead on the left of the group: it had to be Sharon's mum. The one in the middle had Corinne's nose and easy grace. Probably *her* mum, Joy. As my eyes rested on the woman on the left, my heart stopped and missed a beat. The slim build was familiar.

There was a resemblance to the vision of the dead woman I had seen in Cook's garden.

A vibrating ring-tone came from beneath a pile of papers on the carpet beside me. I reached beneath and brought out Sharon's iPhone. 'Corinne calling' were the words on the screen. Underneath the screen was opened into a text message. With an increasing agitation I saw the text. 'It was the doctor!'

Sent by me.

I scrambled to my feet and hit the answer button.

'Sharon! For fuck's sake I've been . . .'

'It's me. It's Sarah,' I bellowed down the line, frantic now. 'Corinne, I think I might have messed up . . .' I quickly

335

explained the scene that I had found. She was calm at first but when I described the picture and my text, she shouted for Pat.

I was adding things up, leaping to conclusions and getting more alarmed by the second. 'I was referring to Sarah Greys,' I told her, 'when I sent that text. But now I'm wondering if . . . well, you know what you said about her mum and the accusations . . .'

A crack on the window stopped my high-speed ramble mid-sentence. As I looked up a pine cone rolled across the living-room floor.

For a moment the world stopped.

I staggered back and dropped the phone.

The next thing I remember is running up the hill.

Night had sucked the dying rays of day behind the hills. The moon was full and wide sailing through the clear sky. Myriad stars shone their ancient light upon the sea. It seemed the very earth of Leigh stirred beneath my feet as I raced to Cook's home.

A terrible feeling was growing in the pit of my stomach.

History repeats itself, Tobias Fitch said. I crushed a thought that was forming in my head. What if Hunter and Cook were from the same line? Could some weird looping behaviour be surfacing through time?

No, it was crazy.

Sharon was in a pub somewhere. I was being silly. But I was breathless and panting with more than just exertion as I reached the surgery.

The house was cast in darkness now. As I tried the front door I was somewhat relieved to see there were no lights on. Maybe he was out?

I took a few steps back and assessed the situation: the curtains on the upper two floors were closed. No signs of life here. Not in the attic, nor in the ground floor of the surgery.

I hesitated for a moment, unsure what to do, then I found myself dodging round the gravel drive at the side of the house, coming out from the shadows into the back garden.

It was as beautiful at night as it was by day. The cedar tree stood proud in the moonlight, at its roots a shadow moved about. I jogged towards it, hearing the grate of a shovel.

Adjusting to the darkness, I could just make out a figure under the tree, standing up. It was barely discernible in the moonlight but I recognized that familiar bow tie.

'Hi,' I said awkwardly. 'It's me, Sarah.'

Doctor Cook didn't make a move immediately, just eyed me and leant on what looked like a spade. Then he threw it down behind him.

'You said to drop round for a prescription.' My voice was uncertain.

'It's a Sunday, Sarah.' He took a step towards me.

'I thought you'd indicated that would be all right.'

'It's not strictly the hours I like to keep but as you're here.' He picked up his pace.

A moan threaded through the night air. It had come from the glasshouse, its door ajar.

The doctor stopped, then sighed and continued on his path towards me.

'What was that?' I asked, starting to edge to my right away from him.

'Nothing. A fox rutting no doubt or some badger.'

The moan came again. It was human, even I could tell

that. I edged further towards the cedar so I could get a view of the greenhouse and the source of the sound. I stumbled over a mound of what looked like earth to the side of the bench. 'What are you doing, Doctor Cook?'

'Some late night gardening.' He continued on his path to the house. 'Clearing up some weeds. I hadn't reckoned on being disturbed.'

I took a step towards the greenhouse and saw a deep rectangular shadow in the lawn. 'What are you doing to the tree?'

For a moment Cook paused and put his hands on his hips, hesitating or calculating in the darkness, I couldn't tell which. 'The bench needed attention,' he growled in a tone I'd not heard before. Then, with a heavy dose of contempt he snarled, 'Even someone with your somewhat impaired cranial capacity can surely see that.'

Quite unexpectedly he turned to the house. 'Come in to the consulting room and I'll write you that script.' Then he disappeared into the shadows.

Paralysed for a moment, I stared into the opening. The atmosphere was pregnant with violence and fear.

In the dimness the white of an arm flopped out the greenhouse door.

I brought myself together and hurried to the figure on the floor.

It was Sharon, her face white and drained. Around the wrist of her arm, I felt the damp ends of rope. One of her silk scarves had been tied round her mouth as a gag. I slipped my hand under her head and undid the knot. Her hair was caked in dried mud and dark blood that poured from a deep gash above her ear. She flitted in and out of consciousness, her eyes half open. 'He killed her. Tell them,' she wheezed, her voice barely more than a sigh.

I knelt down and whispered in her ear. 'It's Sarah. Hang on in there. I'm going to get you out of here.'

Sharon tried to move, groaned, and murmured something I couldn't understand.

'Honey, it's OK. I'm phoning the police.'

I took her hand to pull her into the recovery position but her cries, faint as they were, stopped me: she was too broken to move. I reached for my phone. Shit! No battery. I'd have to run next door and get help. It would mean leaving Sharon alone but there was no choice.

I scrambled to my feet and turned towards the house. A black shape loomed in front of me. I don't know how he crept up on me like that but there was no time to think. Cook's eyes were black holes in his skull, burning with demonic fury. Devoid of humanity, something dark possessed them now. His mouth contorted into a cold snarl. He raised his arms out towards me.

As he lunged forward I ducked to my right. He had something in his hand, which in the half-light I couldn't make out.

'What are you doing?' It was my voice but it came from nowhere. I wasn't even sure my lips had moved.

The mask had fully slipped away now, revealing the terrifying malice of the monster beneath. He spat out his words. 'I suppose she put you up to it, did she? Those episodes, that fake tumour, all part of some fishing trip then? You must have known that drooping lid was down to overtiredness. I imagine Casey suggested you make more of it than you needed to . . .'

I was edging backwards, away, conscious of Sharon's whimpering, trying really hard to think on my feet. 'You mean I'm clear?' I stalled, trying to engage him so I could get a handle on what was happening. 'I don't have a tumour?'

He staggered towards me, raising his right hand. I saw what was in it now – a syringe. On reflex I reached out and tried to knock it out of his grip.

A spiteful laugh rose up from Cook. 'Don't even try it. You know you never had a growth. You made it up. I don't know how you two put it together but it didn't cut with me. At first I wasn't sure, then last week I worked out exactly what you were after.' With one hand he grabbed my wrist. I pulled back but he was surprisingly strong. There was a sudden sting in my shoulder. My yelp of pain pierced the night air. I staggered back.

Cook withdrew the syringe and threw it carelessly on the ground. 'I never thought anyone would believe her. Not against me, the fine upright pillar of the community. The word of a wild child, dabbling in drugs. It was ridiculous. But she got you going, didn't she?'

I was backed up against the trunk of the cedar tree now. Cook, or whatever had been Cook was staring at the glass-house. My left foot slipped on something wet. Glancing down I saw the hole he had dug. At the bottom a human ribcage poked out from the soil.

I inhaled audibly but tried to cover it by saying, 'We were looking into Sarah Grey, that's all.' I needed to raise the alarm. Maybe someone next door had heard the commotion? 'I told you. I thought something had happened here. Sharon was probably just coming to ask you about it.'

Something large and hard prodded into my back. I slipped my fingers behind and felt a wooden arm of the bench. It was loose. He must have dismantled it to dig the hole.

He laughed coldly. 'Old Mother Grey? That was my great, great uncle's business not mine.'

Ignoring the scalding pain in my shoulder, and now also fighting an oppressive sensation of drowsiness, I sent a silent prayer to the heavens and I closed my fingers around the end of the wood.

'You mean, Doctor Hunter is your ancestor? I had no idea. I wouldn't have made the connection. Your name . . .'

'Silly women, meddling in things that don't concern your kind,' Cook was saying. 'There is an order to things which must be maintained. Veronica could not see that either. Reputation, standing. These are the tools that consolidate power. Sacrifices have to be made.' He clucked his tongue in disdain. 'It was so tidy before. It was . . .' A caw from the magpies above us in the tree momentarily drew his attention.

With all my might I seized the piece of wood and swung it at his head.

It caught his neck with a loud crack. He toppled backwards, stunned, then dropped to his knees. His image fractured into a million spinning pieces. Everything was beginning to recede into the distance. With gargantuan effort I managed to kick him in the stomach. Instantly he fell sideways, missing the grave by inches.

Picking up the piece of wood and mustering the remainder of my strength, I stepped over Cook's body and headed for the house.

The last thing I remember is losing the horizon, seeing grass then passing through it into darkness.

'You've got to get up now.' The voice was shrill, slightly choked, familiar. 'Sarah! For fuck's sake, *now.*'

A tugging at my wrists brought me sharply into consciousness. And pain. A lot of it. Across my jaw and round my back. My mouth was full. The bitter tang of blood and gritty mud made me instantly gag. Wetness was coursing into my eyes making it hard to see, but I could make out movements underneath the cedar.

Cook was by the grave, shovelling earth.

I was on the grass a few feet from him. My hands were crushed, fastened together behind my back. Alien fingers slipped between the ties that bound them. 'I've got your back.'

Sharon!

I craned my neck to glimpse her but I could hardly move. My shoulder was throbbing.

'Thank God, you're OK,' I whispered to her. 'What the fuck's happening?'

'No time to explain. You've got to get up, Sarah. *Now.*' I heard her shuffle to my ankles and untie the ropes there.

Ignoring the pain I wrenched my arms in front of me. 'You get help,' I whispered to her. 'Go next door.'

'Play dead.' I heard her hobble away across the lawn.

My head throbbed and my eyesight was coming and going but I could see that a few inches to my right, lay the wooden arm of the bench I had used to deck Cook.

The monster by the grave rested for a moment to grumble to himself, and arched his back. I clamped my eyes shut and froze.

'Good girl.' He must have been looking at me. 'You can sleep well now, after all.'

How he didn't hear my heart thumping, I'll never know. But seconds passed and soon the soft thud of earth came once more from the grave.

I opened one eye and nudged my shoulder closer to the block of wood. It was a real effort not to make any noise. I stifled a cry as a stabbing pain kicked in hard then became motionless once more as I heard him pause.

Another inch and I could reach it.

I heard the dull thud as Cook tossed the spade down and brushed his hands off.

It was now or never. I threw my hand at the wood and grabbed it. In an instant it was under my body. Trembling, I shut my eyes tight and did my best to still my breathing.

Cook staggered away from the grave.

'Goodbye, girls,' he said.

Footsteps came towards me.

I held my breath.

Two heavy footfalls either side of my prone body.

He stood right over me now.

'Curiosity, curiosity . . . Do none of you pussy cats get it?' I could hear his breathing come heavy as he bent low over me.

A globule of saliva trailed down onto my cheek.

Thick fingers closed round my t-shirt for leverage.

I opened my eyes and shrieked, 'Fuck you!'

There was a dull splintering sound as the wood collided with his skull. His head snapped to the right. Put off balance he rocked back, then forwards, and collapsed on top of me.

I groped around to find a hold, and prise myself from

343

under him, but his weight was too much, pinning me down on the muddy lawn.

With only my hands free I thrashed at his chest. He grunted in my ear and pressed himself up. Then he spat and slapped my face. His hands fastened round my neck.

I clutched at his chest ineffectually, then changed tack and forced my fingers into a fist. It connected with his jaw but did nothing to halt him.

His venomous smile swam above me, bopping up and down like a grotesque kite.

The pressure on my windpipe was indescribable. This is it, I thought, and tried to scream but all the air had leaked from my lungs.

I was weakening, losing focus.

Slowly he spoke, 'You stupid little girls.'

My head pounded like a beating drum, heart convulsing like it would burst. The huge weight of Cook on my chest was crushing. I found the soft flesh of his neck and dug my fingernails in, drawing blood. He yelped and relaxed his fingers. For a millisecond I drew in a smidgen of air, then he was squeezing and squeezing.

I knew my death had come.

The blackness that had been so swift before faded in gently from the edges of my vision. A whirl of dark fog swirled around Cook. His form blurred, then doubled, tripled, dimmed. Within the darkness a light appeared. Small at first like a candle flame then growing, expanding until three figures morphed from the luminous air. And there was Sarah before me. Smiling, beautiful and young.

'I've got your ring,' I whispered to her, and slipped it from my finger. 'It's yours. He always kept it.'

Her eyes were brimming with pleasure. I'd never seen that before. She slipped it on her finger. 'It'll be right.' Her voice was relaxed, light, tinged with an accent that was more North Essex than South, almost rural. 'You've got to get up.'

But it was much calmer there. Peaceful. 'He always loved you,' I said.

Her lips were disappearing into the nothingness, like the Cheshire Cat, leaving only her sea green eyes floating before me. 'I know that.' The words echoed in my head. 'You'll forget this.'

'Yes, forget, forget . . .' It was another female voice, low and soft but urgent.

A woman with short cropped hair smiled into view. Veronica. Cook's wife.

I was beginning to make sense of it. 'Did he kill you? Doctor Cook?' She didn't answer, as another woman had come into being to my right. The redhead from the picture reassembled herself and bit her lip. 'Before she forgets it she has to wake up.' Her voice had a bassy tone like Sharon's. It was Cheryl, her mum. 'Go back and tell them. Get outta here.'

She seemed angry that I wasn't listening to her and started shouting. It was far too noisy for me. I put my hands over my ears. I was free. Relaxed. It had been a hard day. The softness of my surroundings was tempting. 'I'll be all right,' I said. But the women were getting brighter now, urging me to fight the peace. Shimmers of white light radiated from their triple form.

For a brief second I perceived the face of Cook through their wafting outlines. He had eased off now and was wiping sweat from his face. But behind him an intense amber light was gathering, beaming up into the sky.

The form which was Sarah seemed to hover for a moment before it sank itself into Cook's body, Cheryl and Veronica following her.

A shriek came from Cook's lips. His face took on a stricken, terrified look. Suddenly his body spasmed. He tottered faintly above me, his hand clutching at his chest.

He looked as though he was about to say something, but then withdrew his hand and tried to hit out at something indiscernible in the gloom.

The light behind him built into an intensity that was almost blinding.

Evil be as evil does.

Cook swatted at something invisible by his head.

There was a brilliant flash.

And that's when I saw him.

Above Cook, bathed in a dazzling sunshine, Josh's figure stood proud.

He gave me that dopey smile of his then, raising his own hands above Cook's head, I heard him whisper, 'Everything's going to be all right.' Then he hurled himself at the doctor, pushing him hard.

A whooshing sound swept past my ears. I smelt honey and saw, for a split second, nothing but the clear pure light. Then the doctor buckled, folding in on himself and then out onto my shoulder, obscuring the view of my dead husband's face.

'Josh,' I managed, as air rushed inside my throat.

Then there was nothing but grateful black.

I came round into hazy artificial brightness. Green-suited paramedics stood about me. I was being jogged to and fro.

346

Andrew's face swam into view.

'Sarah, you're OK. I'm so sorry.' He was crying.

It was extraordinarily painful to speak but with some effort I managed, 'Cook?'

'He's got the medics with him. But the police are there too.'

The blackness was approaching. 'And Sharon?'

A female paramedic came into view. 'She's all right.' Gently she brushed Andrew aside and reached down for my wrist. 'You need to be calm, Ms Grey.'

So I was.

I'm not stupid. I've always been a good girl.

Chapter Twenty-Five

Puzzles have never been my strong point. Even when I was little, jigsaws left me hopelessly floored. This one came in odd, jagged pieces that belonged to two separate sets. The only common factor was me, Sarah Grey.

The more pressing, of course, was the scene in the garden. Believe me, it took a while to get the whole picture of that. But it did come, and when it did it was devastating, but I had help and support and in the end I got through it.

Andrew was brilliant. Both a support and a protector. He was as concerned and remorseful for his lack of action, as I was about dragging him into all of this. I feel bad that I ever doubted him but you know what I was going through.

It was he who broke the news that Sharon was dead. It wasn't easy and I had trouble believing him at first. But then there's a lot I have trouble believing in now.

She hadn't made it out of the greenhouse alive. So he said.

When I saw Cook scooping earth into the grave, he was burying her fresh corpse.

Of course, I ranted and raved – no, Sharon had helped me, she'd untied my bonds and woken me up. But the coroner confirmed she was dead before the doctor buried her. The official version is that I was concussed by my fall.

Andrew says the mind has a funny way of dealing with things, and that's his explanation for what happened, the things I saw in the garden that night. I told him about Sarah and returning the ring but he was reluctant to accept it as gospel, as it were.

No ring was found. His reasoning – it had fallen off en route to the hospital.

But I know what I saw and there's no point people trying to convince me otherwise. The dead women were there when I needed them: Sarah, Veronica, Sharon's mother, Cheryl.

And my friend Sharon, herself.

There was justice to be had and of course, justice *will* be served. Cook's looking at a double life sentence, and possibly a third. They're exhuming Cheryl next week to see if he was responsible for silencing her doubts over his wife's where-abouts. That was what their argument was about. Sharon had been right to suspect the doctor.

And it's cut and dried with Veronica. She'd been under the cedar tree for decades. The only one who hadn't fallen for Cook's story that she'd left to find herself was Cheryl. And her daughter.

One can only imagine what horrors Veronica endured when she told Cook she was going to leave him for good. He says it was an accident, that she flew at him wildly with the strength of the insane. His blow to her skull kept her with him in the garden forever. He built the bench so he could watch over her. Making sure she'd never escape.

When they excavated the garden, they found something

else, just below poor Veronica's grave: a female skull with a gaping hole in it. And on that I had a lot to say.

Of course the police weren't interested in what I told them. I'd already proved unreliable with my version of events. But the evidence that Andrew presented made quite a splash in the local papers and was picked up by several nationals too. It was time to fulfil Sarah's last words – *all will know*.

'Missing Head Horror – 144-year-old murder solved' was the subtle headline in one broadsheet. The paper did a trace themselves and clarified the direct lineage between the doctors: Cook indeed was Hunter's great great nephew who'd inherited the surgery from his mother. It was another symmetry. There were lots and lots of them surging up.

I got a name check in the report and a few of the tabloids came sniffing. I wasn't out of hospital at that point but Lottie and Andrew did a good job of fielding reporters and enabling me to heal in peace.

In fact all my friends and family came to see me. Martha was a love and Lottie a real tonic, sorting out the practicalities of childcare between her and Mum. She brought me the news that the Sarah Grey pub had commissioned an artist to paint a more positive picture of her on their sign: early sketches show a young, black-haired woman in a bonnet, with a strong chin and rosebud lips. She looks directly at the viewer as if challenging you, a glimmer of triumph in her sea green eyes.

Mum's visit was a bit of a revelation. She came with Aunty Brenda and a copy of their family tree. It was a large and sprawling map, covering over three hundred names. And there in the right-hand corner was Sarah Grey. Our route descended from her son, Alfred Grey, or Alfie as he was fondly known. It was a wild, watered down connection that had travelled across the country from Leigh to Maldon, then to Rochford, Hockley then to Thorpe Bay for the last generation. And it came down, after Alfie, through the female line. Without good reason to trace it we would never have known of the lineage at all. But there we were at the end of the line, Sarah and Alfie Grey. Again. It was an incredible coincidence and yet another symmetry which made sense of everything: the connection, the bloodline, the choice she made in me. I just wish I hadn't feared her so. I don't now.

However, there was one person I was dreading seeing. Corinne. The responsibility of her best friend's death was a heavy burden on me. I may have been given the all-clear but the guilt that had grown within me felt like a tumour: deadly and wretched but deserved.

As it turned out, I didn't have a monopoly on it. Corinne didn't blame me – she'd put herself in the frame. Her refusal to countenance Sharon's accusations over Cheryl's fatal heart attack and Veronica's disappearance ate her up from the inside. She kept going over events, wondering if she could have stopped the bloody crescendo I had witnessed in Cook's back yard.

But I reckoned that I had sent Sharon to her end. My description of the phantom apparition in the doctor's garden must have got poor Shazza thinking, going over his involvement, adding things up. She must have had too much to drink, got emotional, then my text must have got her concluding things that no one else had put together. Of course I wasn't referring to Doctor Cook but as Marie once told me – 'You start going down certain paths and you start

351

waking ghosts. Sometimes you set in motion things you have no idea about.' And I woke ghosts all right.

I can picture Sharon now, rummaging through drawers, pulling out chests, searching for who knows what evidence. The coroner's report? A local newspaper cutting? We'll never know. But the conclusion she came to had her practically destroying her house with anger and frustration. Then when she was done she set off on her last fatal journey to confront Cook.

I should never have sent that text.

It was my fault.

Although, on that, Corinne and I disagreed.

Whatever, both of us could see that we going to be haunted for the rest of our lives. 'But we've got to make sure we remember her well,' I told her, and on that we both agreed.

Sometimes there's nothing else you can do.

The Fitches must have got wind of the dramatic finale. I received two letters, a card from Tobias and a package from Claudia. Inside it was a translation of the journal. At the end of the document she had scribbled a note: 'Let us hope we can *all* rest in peace now.'

We're burying Sarah's head with her body next week, in a ceremony as quiet as we can keep it. It's an odd feeling knowing and not 'knowing' as I do. And I'm not sure how I'll react. I know she's at peace as I've not felt her since.

I've not felt Sharon either. Nor have I felt Josh.

They've both flown away into the ever-after. And I reckon that's OK. See, Andrew says it was he who felled Cook as the bastard was strangling the life out of me. That Corinne was arriving in her car up the sideway, that the headlights caught the scene as she turned into the garden, bathing him in their dazzling light. But I know what I saw and it was Josh.

He came back.

They do that, you know.

He wanted me to live and he brought me back to life on so many levels that I can't list them all here.

You see, the dead are all around us: in names, places and sometimes in person. But it's just not healthy to live in the past.

And my new love has been doting: attentive if not overly so. Helping round the house, running errands and keeping me warm in my bed at night. Lately he's been paving my way to return to college. The old crowd, of course, are a bit baffled but oozing with sympathy and, I think, genuine concern. John and his wife, Glenda, came to see me in hospital when I was still swollen and bruised. She was lovely and demure. Not what I expected at all. He, of course, bounded in and jumped on my bed. 'So what did you do over the holidays then?'

It hurt too much to smile.

He brought in his laptop with a message from Marie, and also his digital camera so I could send a message to her. I told her I'd be in touch, that things were resolved and I thanked her for her guidance. I said she'd done a good job.

John's been good in taking Alfie out a couple of times or so. He's enjoyed that a lot, my son. The only one completely oblivious to the whole strange end of the affair.

When they finally discharged me Sue came to visit. She'd given birth to a gorgeous baby girl.

We sat in the garden while the little one slept and Andrew played with Alfie as she had a word with me.

'Sarah,' she said. 'I know what's happened and I don't want

you to take this the wrong way. But we'd planned to call her "Sharon". It was Steve's mum's name.'

She sat back and blew a satisfied plume of smoke from her mouth. 'Would you be all right with that? I know you've lost your friend and I know I didn't know her myself but I thought it could be sort of commemorative.'

'It would be brilliant. Sharon would like that,' I told her.

'Bloody good Essex name,' she said.

'She was a bloody good Essex girl,' I answered back.

'This one will be too. Just wanted to check you were all right with it. I don't want no histrionics at the christening,' she said and winked.

Sharon's christening is tomorrow.

Life goes on.

We're edging into autumn now. I don't mind the season at all. Though the leaves fall and rot they speak more to me of cycles: death, birth, rebirth, tradition, legacy. The only end I feel coming is the last part of my story.

I'm not sure of what conclusions I can make. Andrew keeps telling me 'Life is for living,' and that's what I'm focusing on doing.

I'm moving on in lots of ways and I tell him that too. Allowing myself to get intimate. Allowing myself to be reassured that what I saw will fade with time. That ghosts don't exist and my experience is just the result of an overactive imagination, combined with some chemical hallucinogens courtesy of Doctor Cook and his syringe.

'You're right, I know,' I assure Andrew, as we lock up the house tonight.

But I leave the French doors open, should my dead friends wander by.

354

A Note to the Reader

While Sarah Grey is a fictionalized character she has been based on Sarah Moore, the sea-witch of Leigh, who lived in the nineteenth century and who died in 1867. The legends surrounding her have been replicated here as they are spoken of in the town and indeed Sarah Moore does have a pub named after her. Although much of Sarah Grey's biographical data has been drawn from my research into the real sea-witch, of course a great deal has been fictionalized: Leigh-on-Sea has never had a mayor; Doctor Cook, his line of ancestors and house were plucked from my imagination; as are many of the Leigh society figures that feature in the Reverend Robert Eden's letters and journals including the effervescent Mr John Snewin and, sadly, the wronged but noble Tobias Fitch. Whilst the Reverend himself once lived here and did go on to become Primus of the Church of Scotland, leaving behind a wealth of published sermons and pamphlets, the words within these pages are mine not his.

Although Lady Olivia Bernard Sparrow's Leigh Hall did at one time sit just north of Leigh Broadway, it was demolished, like so many elegant buildings of the town, sacrificed by the greed of the few to the detriment of the thousands who live amongst the landscape. It now lies under the new houses on the road to which it gave its name.

Disregard for the past will never do us any good. Without it we cannot know truly who we are.

Read on for an exclusive extract of Syd Moore's new book,
to be published by Avon in Autumn 2012.

Chapter One

I used to think nothing of significance could ever happen on a Wednesday. It's too mediocre: neither at the beginning of the week's uphill climb, nor over the hump, looking to the weekend. Not like Thursdays, which loosen you up for the weekend, nor Tuesday, with its blues.

Wednesday, well, my Wednesdays had always seemed rather bland.

But I bet you don't know that Wednesday is dedicated to Woden (Wodensday) – the ancient god of the Anglo-Saxons, ruler of the Wild Hunt and Wind and, allegedly, conductor of the dead leading souls through to the afterlife? Well, me neither. But it is. So with that in mind, I guess it was fitting that The Powers That Be chose the Wind God's day to put in motion the chain of events which would, in a relatively short space of time, terminate my life.

That particular Wednesday seemed nothing out of the ordinary.

Or so I thought.

The weather was, perhaps, a little gloomier than one might expect of a March afternoon.

Someone more sensitive to these things might have sniffed

out foreboding in the shrill north-easterly wind that had everybody buttoned up, faces down, slanting diagonally into its oncoming draughts.

Or maybe they would have sussed that the very same wind that was screeching through the bare branches of the sycamores could be trying, with all its might, to halt my progress through the wide Georgian avenues of Southend's conservation area.

But me? Well, as ever, I was clueless to the warnings. And anyway, somehow I know I would have made it to West Street where the offices of *Mercurial*, a quarterly arts magazine, nestled between an ancient accountancy firm and a design agency. You try harder to get somewhere that you really want to go, don't you? If it had been a visit to the doctor's or an appointment at the bank, I might have pulled back the curtains and thought, 'Bugger that.' But that Wednesday afternoon, five months ago, I knew Maggie Haines was waiting for me with a large mug of fresh coffee and the possibility of a commissioned article.

To be honest, I don't think a hurricane would have stopped me getting there: it'd been a while since I'd managed to net a commission from anyone and Maggie was hinting that there might be a healthy fee involved. Besides, I liked working for *Mercurial*: as a freelance writer who specialised in Essex affairs, kudos was rather thin on the ground. The magazine's cachet rubbed off on me.

In the couple of years that I'd been living in Southend I had grown very fond of the staff at the office. For a bunch of artistic individuals they were all pretty down to earth.

I'd known Maggie, the editor, for nigh on twenty-five years, as we'd attended the same high school. Though far more rebellious than me, Maggie and I had shared a couple of boyfriends and cigarettes at the bottom of the sports field, promptly losing touch when we left school and went on to different universities. Bumping into each other a year ago, she invited me for lunch and we soon ping-ponged into regular friends again.

I think it was on our third or fourth lunch date, as we knocked back a few bottles of plonk, that Maggie suggested I wrote a small piece for her mag. I leapt at the chance and once she had worked out that I was as good as I said I was she began feeding me more assignments. Though our friendship developed a more professional edge and lost a smidgen of its social intimacy, the deal proved both lucrative and enjoyable, catapulting me into a frighteningly dynamic arts scene. I saw Maggie from time to time at launches and events, but the demands on both our lives meant that I hadn't seen her privately for quite a while.

She was sucking on the end of a biro, squinting at a document in the small box room she called her office. The Victorian sash window was a couple of inches open but the air was thick with the stink of cigarettes.

'You'll have to get an air freshener,' I said as I cantered in and threw my satchel on the floor. 'It's against the law now, you know.'

Maggie's wild tangle of pillarbox red hair jerked up. She dropped the pen on the mound of paper. 'Shit, Mercedes! Can't you knock before you come in?'

Blessed with piercing green, intensely beguiling, almond-shaped eyes and a cute button nose Maggie's face had a distinctly kittenish look to it – which was thoroughly misleading. The pretty feline exterior concealed a steely determination and unsettling intelligence that had notched up two degrees, an MA and a doctorate, and which had far more in common with panthers than domestic cats.

'Everyone else has to go outside for a fag,' I laughed.

She shrugged, relaxing now and held her hands up in mock surrender. 'Fair point. I know I shouldn't. Just got really into this submission – new writer. Very good. Looking at the Internet: facebook, myspace, blah blah, as Generation Z's youthful rebellion.'

I sauntered over to a filing cabinet that stood by the window. It was sprayed gold and decorated in what was probably radical art works but to my uninformed eye looked like bog-standard graffiti. It was very *Mercurial*. The gurgles from the coffee maker on top indicated it was ready to pour.

'Interesting spin,' I said and took two mugs from the shelf above. 'I'm presuming this is for me? Mags, would you like one too?'

She grunted an affirmation and grudgingly gathered up the sheaf of paper, stapling the top right-hand corner and dumping it on an in-tray already several centimetres high. 'Might as well close that window too,' she shivered and pulled her fluffy purple cardigan tight over her shoulders. 'I thought it'd be warmer this week.'

I placed the mugs on her desk, and brought the window down with more force than I intended, resulting in a loud bang. 'No such luck. They reckon we've got at least another three weeks of this before it turns.'

Maggie cast her eyes through the windowpane at the fluttering leaves of the sycamores. A plastic bag whipped up from the street and caught a branch directly outside. 'If only the wind would drop.' She grimaced and turned back to me. 'Right,' she said. 'Fire.'

I took a sip of my coffee and removed my notebook from my bag. 'You mentioned another Essex Girls piece?'

I'd been fascinated with our regional stereotype for a long time. Firstly because, as a raven-haired, olive-skinned Essex chick, I adored the leggy, booby, blonde ideal. Surrounded by Barbies and Pippas from an early age, I'd cottoned on to the fact that this was the generally accepted notion of beauty. I couldn't believe it when, as I made more excursions beyond the county's limits, I started to discover that this was considered vulgar and stupid – and a lot lot worse.

Later, as I left the borough I'd lived in all my life to venture North for Uni, I realised that far from being a joke, mentioning my home county often resulted in humiliation and embarrassment. My surname, Asquith, did little to temper the constant barrage of wisecracks that I faced, as an Essex Girl called Mercedes. It was both frustrating and extremely formative: as a consequence of this constant battle I went on into journalism 'to get my voice heard without shouting' as my mum used to put it. Although I didn't relate my pieces to my county or my gender, there was always an edgy, working-class feel to my tirades. Luckily, people liked them and I was able to make a living from my rants.

Returning to my roots, the good Maggie indulged me and published a series of articles in which I challenged the bullshit. 'Essex isn't like other counties. Its daughter isn't like those of Hertfordshire, Herefordshire or Surrey,' I wrote. 'She isn't demure, self-effacing or seeking a husband. She's audacious, loud, drops her vowels and has fun. Like Essex itself, the Girl is unique. It's about time we showed some filial pride.' Got a good reception, that one. Circulation went up. Maggie commissioned another one, and another, then another.

In an attempt to trace the etymology of the Essex Girl, my last feature looked back across the centuries to the dark days of the Witch Hunts and examined whether there was a link between Essex's reputation as 'Witch County' and the genesis of the Essex Girl. I concluded that there was – and readers and commentators alike had not stopped filling up the web forum ever since. Many comments spilt over into other sites, forums, newspapers and magazines.

Positive or intensely outraged, Maggie didn't care how they reacted, just that they did. 'This is the kind of thing the *Mercurial* needs. It's getting our name out there into a broader market. We need more, and I'll up your rate. Just give me something good and meaty,' she'd said on the phone last night.

So here I was, with something I thought if not *meaty* as such, certainly spicy.

Maggie took a tentative sip of her coffee then blew on it. 'Go on then – spill it. What you got for Mama?'

'Okay,' I flicked open my notepad and traced my notes to the relevant entry. 'I'm delving deeper into the Witch Hunts.' I glanced up to catch a reaction. Maggie was nodding, so I ploughed on.

'Something is pulling me back to it. I mean, why did Essex lose so many women to the Witch Hunts?'

Maggie snorted. 'Did we? So what?'

I leant in to her. 'No seriously, Maggie. The combined total of indictments for witchcraft in Hereford, Kent, Surrey and Sussex put together was 222. In Essex alone over the same amount of time it was 492. More than any other county in the UK by a long stretch. You've got to wonder why.'

Maggie let out a low whistle. 'Okay, now you've got me. You didn't go into that in your last article did you?'

I shook my head. 'No, it was more about the witches themselves and the qualities they shared with the contemporary Essex Girl . . .'

Maggie cut in. 'Yep, yep. They "were poor, dumb and 'loose' as in not controlled by, or protected by men".' She was quoting my article. 'So *why* exactly did it happen to the extent it did here? I assumed that Essex and its inhabitants already had a reputation for being thick, flat and uninteresting?'

I coughed. 'No, not at all. Up until the Witch Hunts, Essex was seen as the "English Goshen".'

'I last heard that word in Sunday School. Something to do with fertile land the Israelites had in Egypt or something? Now don't go all religious on me. It doesn't sell, Mercedes.'

'I'm not. Goshen also means place of plenty. Essex has an interesting geology. Sits at the southernmost point of the ice sheet that covered the rest of the island. Soil's full of rich mineral deposits brought down from up north via the glacier.'

Maggie pulled a face.

'I'll get to the point. It's perfect for farming, for cattle, for livestock. It's surrounded by rivers and the North Sea for fishing. Until the 1600s it was seen as a pretty cool place to be. After that point it changed.'

'Because?'

'Well, this is where I come in. I think a) because it was quite the revolutionary county in the civil war. Backed parliament. Wanted reform. And b) because of the extent of the Witch Hunts.'

'Which were because?' She cocked her head to one side and sat back in her chair.

'Lots of things really but mainly it was to do with class aggression – you look at the European witch hunts and they had

365

it in for all different types of people: aristocrats got burnt at the stake and their lands neatly confiscated by the Church. But in the Essex Witch Hunts the victims are mostly poor, mostly operating outside of society and mostly women deemed "loose", as in not under the control or protection of a man. Then into this, insert a little guy called Matthew Hopkins whose dick must have fallen off or something.'

Maggie coughed and sent me a what-are-you-on-about look.

I shrugged. 'Well, he's got serious issues with women. He decided to call himself the Witchfinder General and managed to get rid of whole families of,' I lifted my fingers to draw imaginary quotation marks, '"witches" in his brief career from 1644 to 1647. Some sources suggest that he was from Lancashire, others from Essex or Suffolk. That he worked in shipping as a clerk and spent some time in Amsterdam learning his official trade where he witnessed several witch trials. Controversy also exists over whether or not he died in 1647. No one is sure, if he did actually cark it, what the cause was. He would have only been in his mid-to-late twenties, though that was middle-aged back then. Lots of theories about what happened to him.'

I looked up to catch her expression. 'And?' she said, eyebrows furrowed, not giving anything away.

I jerked my chair closer to the desk. 'Well, I'd like to find out more about him. There's something there which doesn't add up.'

Maggie nodded. 'And your suspicions are?'

'I'm wondering how he died or where he went. I think he might have ducked out of the country and spread his poison elsewhere.'

'Angle?' Maggie drummed her fingers on the desk.

'I don't want to say yet. He had female collaborators. Could be part of a bigger series – The Essex Girls' History of the World.'

'Now you're talking. What you thinking – six, twelve?'

'I don't know yet. Let me see what I can come up with.'

'I like it. I *really* like it. Oh yes,' she reached into her handbag. 'Remind me to tell you about something when you've finished.' She brought out a small rectangular card and laid it on the desk. 'Go on. I've stopped you mid-flow.'

'Well, that's about it really. I'm going to get something good out of it – I've got a tingle that's telling me I've hit something hidden which could be eminently controversial.'

Now she came to life. 'That's what we need. Do you reckon we could get some coverage in the nationals with it?'

I nodded. 'Deffo. This is far more than an "And Finally" on *Look East*.'

Maggie's eyes were fixed on my face. 'Good, good. God knows we need to boost circulation.' She heaved herself forward and picked up the mug.

I mirrored her and took a sip of coffee. It was still hot but delicious so I gulped it greedily, feeling it heat my throat, then said, 'I thought you were doing great.'

Maggie sighed. 'We are, in terms of readership and profile. Best it's ever been. But our landlord's putting the rent up; the price of paper is going through the roof right now, and what with the recession or whatever this dire slump we're passing through is called, a lot of our regular advertisers have had to pull. A fair few have gone bust, owing us. Marketing is always the first thing to go when times are hard.'

I stared up. 'I had no idea.'

Maggie reached for a fag and projected her chair to the sash window. Lighting it, she pushed the bottom half of the window up and craned her neck to the opening.

'Please don't tell anyone, Mercedes. I'm confiding in you as a friend not an employee. I don't want it to get out to the others.' She blew a long sigh of smoke out through the gap. 'We'll be lucky if we're still trading this time next year.'

'Shit,' I said.

She turned to face me. The kitten face had disappeared. There was more of a hungry alley cat look going on there. 'Pull this article off and I'll triple your fee and throw in expenses.'

I sat back and looked her squarely in the face. 'That's a generous offer. Considering . . .'

She laughed, and the kitten returned. 'Let's call it a calculated risk. I have faith in you.'

A strong blast of cold air came in through the crack, scattering several loose papers across the desk and blowing my notebook shut. I gathered them up and returned them to the desk, feeling a little less excited than I had been just moments before.

'Thank you for the vote of confidence. I'm not sure that I deserve it. Not yet. You said there was something else you wanted to tell me.'

'Oh yes,' Maggie flicked her half-smoked ciggy butt out of the window and pulled it shut. 'I had an intriguing encounter on Saturday. Creative Industries networking night up in London.'

'Sounds interesting,' I giggled. 'Does Jules approve?'

'Shut up,' she said but softened it with a smile. 'Nothing like that, you foul-minded harlot. Some posh bloke. Full on Man-From-Del-Monte linen suit, cut glass accent.' She plucked a card from her rolodex and read it. 'William Roben, of Portillo Publishing. He'd heard of the magazine. Loved it. Or more to the point, he loved you.'

'Me?' I was gobsmacked. Although I was developing a reputation locally I had no idea that anyone outside of the area might have read my work.

'Yep. Very intrigued. He's looking for authors to develop their historical list. History being the new black and all that. I hope you don't mind but I gave him your home number. He said he'd give you a call.'

'A book! Is that what you mean?' I couldn't quite believe it. Though I was happy as a hack, every journo secretly yearned to write a book. Even as a child I had been drawn more to the idea of books than journalism, but making a living as an author seemed far more of a Herculean effort than writing short sassy pieces that were published quickly. And, more importantly, paid promptly. But to publish a book. Wow.

'I think that was the suggestion, given that he's a book publisher. But wait and see. He might just want you to come up with some ideas, then commission them to other established authors. I dunno. I'm not big on that area of the industry. But,' she leant forwards and waggled her right index finger at me, 'if you get anything going with him, I want to be able to say "you read it here first", right?'

'Of course.' I promised to be true to my word. After all, Maggie had been great to me.

'Okay,' her tone changed: she was finishing with me now. 'Can't stay here chatting about books and whatnot. You get going. Crack on with your witches. When do you think you can give me an idea of where you're going with these leads?'

I told her about two weeks should do it and stood up, dismissed.

'Great,' she said as I made for the door. 'Oh and Mercedes. How's your mum?'

I paused and turned, glancing out the window at the waving branches of the sycamores, unable to meet her eye. 'Just going there now. Not good I'm afraid.'

She nodded slowly. 'Well, give her my love. You know where I am if you need anything.'

I told her she'd be the first on my list and said goodbye.

She was third actually but I appreciated the gesture.

Contrary to popular belief, in my experience hospices are bright places full of chit-chat and laughter. People tend to think of them as dark and depressing but they're set up to send folks off in the most life-affirming way. If you get what I mean.

Mum had been moved to Green Acres two weeks ago after her last stroke. The consensus was that this would give Joe, her boyfriend, a little respite, but looking back now I think I knew she didn't have much time left. I just didn't want to admit it. To me the stay was all about rest and recreation.

It had been a gradual deterioration. I assumed that her first bout of depression came on after Dad left us, when I was fifteen. But later conversations with my father when I was adult enough revealed Mum had been in and out of hospital all my life. At the time, I couldn't quite believe him but afterwards, reflecting on my childhood I started to remember the absences, when Mum, a relatively successful landscape artist, had travelled off for 'commissions' around the country.

It turned out two-thirds of her sojourns were spent in

private hospitals. She wasn't too bad for most of my twenties, then as I entered my thirties, she had a couple of wobbles and ended up inside for a month after I divorced my husband, Christopher. I always wondered if that had something to do with it. She hated me living alone and had objected to me reverting to Asquith, which I thought was mad. But there you go. I did it anyway and moved back here, for a change of scene and because I wanted to be nearer Mum. Good job too, as three months after the move, she had her first stroke. Then another. The third one left her permanently cared for in the home round the corner. This, the fourth, had left her paralysed down the right side of her face.

I tried to get in on most days, but I'd had stuff to sort out and that Wednesday was the first time I'd seen her since the weekend.

Don't get me wrong – it wasn't that I didn't want to see her. To me she was still as fresh and fragrant as she had been in my teens – a wonderfully charismatic woman with dark lustrous hair and an hourglass figure, reminiscent of Gina Lollobrigida. I adored her. Though I had more of an inclination for books and sailing, like Dad, than I did for sketching and oils, I'd often accompany her on trips around the East coast, where we'd set up easels and stare out over the North Sea trying to capture the day in a picture. She of course did it wonderfully. More often than not, I'd get bored and go for a walk or a swim returning home with just a thin strip of horizon which my dad would scoff at but which Mum would fuss over and hang on the wall.

Best of all, I liked watching her paint in her studio when she had her hair tucked back into a scarf, one of Dad's old paint-spattered shirts on. She would screw her dark brown eyes into little nuts of concentration and paint for hours and hours, tiny little brushstrokes that came out of nowhere and massed into landscapes from her imagination: steep craggy mountains, high sun, storms and pines would emerge on her canvas. Alien, undulating landscapes in ambers and reds and violets and greens that were rarely seen in our flat Essex world. They were the pictures that came into my head before I slipped into dreams at night and more often than not, they'd form the background to some of my more exciting adventures.

I'd brought some of them with me on my last visit to Green Acres. I think Mum had been appreciative, though it was hard to tell. Her speech had been greatly impaired by the last stroke and we communicated mostly with our eyes and gestures.

I was relieved to find her sitting up in bed.

'Cedes.' Beneath the twisted features I could see a half smile forming. She held out her good arm to me.

I took it and kissed her forehead. 'How you doing, Mum?'

She did a sort of nod using the upper left half of her body.

I smiled and perched on the bed by her good side. 'I've just seen Maggie Haines. She sends her love.'

Mum squeezed my hand in approval. She had always liked Maggie. Even when the teen vixen was leading me astray Mum actively encouraged the friendship, calling Mags 'a woman of character'. That's how she spoke, my mum: in impeccable received pronunciation, articulating every consonant, nuancing each spoken vowel like the Queen. A lot of our neighbours thought it was affected, 'put on', 'all airs and graces'. After all we lived in a modest terraced house with a reasonable but not overly comfortable income. But Dad loved it and encouraged me to adopt Mum's fashion. Despite their efforts I ended up with an Essex accent that dropped its consonants and cut short on the vowels. 'People will think you're stupid,' Dad said.

'I'll just 'ave to prove 'em wrong then, won't I?'

Anyway. So there I was in hospital, rabbiting on about my meeting with Mags, when Mum squeezed my hand and mouthed as well as she could – 'JOE.'

I'm ashamed to say I felt a little indignant, even as she was lying there virtually at death's door, but in all honesty I did. I hadn't even got on to the publisher yet but she'd cut me off mid-flow.

'What about him?' I asked, knowing my face was screwed into a frown but not bothering to hide my displeasure.

It clearly took her a lot of effort but with the grunts and a pen in her left hand I learnt her boyfriend had not been in to see her for a while. They had met fifteen years ago when they were both 'inside'. Joe had been an undiagnosed bi-polar, but since then had medicated himself into a relatively regular existence returning to the occupation that had 'set him off' several years before – teaching. In terms of success stories, he was up there in the hospital's top three. He'd done so well, he'd even climbed a few of rungs of the hierarchy in his school and was now a Head of Department. Although he lived in a flat round the corner, Mum and he had never moved in with each other. They needed to keep separate, he once told me, so that they didn't become dependent. I understood that. He loved Mum dearly and it was clear from early in their relationship that the feeling was mutual. He visited her as often as his work schedule permitted, usually twice a day, and at weekends he spent whole days at Green Acres.

The frown lingered on my forehead. 'Perhaps he's busy. You know what his job's like. Marking? Parents' evenings? How long since you last saw him?'

Mum's elegant fingers groped round the pencil I had placed onto the pad of paper that never left her side. It took her a while but soon a sketchy figure three emerged.

I looked at my watch: 16.34 pm. 'Three hours? He hasn't been here today?'

Mum's lips suckered in. She was disagreeing.

'Not three hours. You can't mean three days?'

Back in her bed Mum's eyes widened.

'Three days? Really? Do you know what's going on?'

Mum did the best she could at shrugging but I got the drift. She was worried about him. Her hand went to the pad again. I tore off the three and left her a clean sheet.

With effort she wrote. 'Go Joe flat. Key my bag.'

It was awful to see her brought so low. So imperfectly unable to express her thoughts or articulate herself as she had once done. Poor Mum.

'Of course.'

She threw the pen at her bag. It hit the leather handle and fell into the dark silk interior. 'Good shot, Mum.'

She grunted with irritation. 'Nah.'

I took in the creases across her forehead. 'Now?' She clenched her good hand.

'Okay, okay.' I pulled her bag onto my lap and rummaged through it until my fingers closed round a jumble of keys. Two had been placed on a football key ring. They had to be Joe's. I jangled them in front of Mum's face. 'These?'

She nodded and moved her left hand over mine. 'Hank you.'

I leant in and pushed a couple of black strands of hair from her eyes. Despite everything, she still had only a light dusting of grey. 'Stop worrying about everyone else and take some time to get better yourself.'

In response she squeezed my hand again.

I asked if she wanted me to turn on the TV or fetch a drink but she didn't. She just wanted me to check Joe's place out. So, I promised her I'd let her know and return asap, insisting as I left, that there was nothing to worry about.

Like I said, I've always been clueless to warning signs.

LUCIFER'S TEARS

James Thompson

A brutal murder.

A country's darkest secret.

A detective pushed to the edge . . .

His previous case left Kari Vaara with a scarred face, chronic insomnia and a full body count's worth of ghosts. A year later, in Helsinki, and Kari is working the graveyard shift in the homicide unit.

Kari is drawn into the murder-by-torture case of Isa Filippov, the philandering wife of a Russian businessman. Her lover is clearly being framed and while Ivan Filippov's arrogance is highly suspicious, he's got friends in high places. Kari is sucked ever deeper and soon the past and present collide in ways no one could have anticipated . . .

Discover the hottest new voice in Nordic crime-writing, perfect for fans of Jo Nesbo and Stieg Larsson.

ISBN: 978-0-00-733231-9
£6.99
Winter 2011